GLORY DAYS

"...I found Glory and Rafael, and I liked them a lot. Unfortunately they were, as my grandmother so delicately pointed out, not a matched set."

Showandah S. Terrill

GLORY DAYS

Book One of the Peter Aarons Novels

SHORT
HORSE
PRESS

This book is a work of fiction, and any references to historical events, real people or real locales are used fictitiously. Other names, places, characters and incidents are products of the author's imagination, and any resemblance to actual events or locales or persons, living or dead, is purely coincidental.

Despite the fictional nature of this novel, the portion of this book that deals with Johnathan and Marie Berry--and their work with the Navajo Nation--is based on a true story.

The text for this book is set in Times New Roman
Manufactured in the United States of America
Library of Congress Control Number: 2019936619
Published April 1, 2019; 2nd Publication: July 13, 2021

ISBN: 978-1-7328052-7-9 (hardcover)
ISBN: 978-1-7342194-7-0 (eBook)

In Loving Memory of God's Servant

Ken Morphet-Brown

"The Buffalo Soldier"

CHAPTER ONE

It was barely dawn in the foothills of the Santa Monica Mountains when I waved the taxi on and punched in the code that would open the tall wrought iron gates leading to my grandmother's home. I shouldered my duffle and trudged the hundred or so yards to the kitchen door, breathing in the fragrance of wild spring grasses from the hillside and freshly mowed lawn. God, it was good to be home. It was so good to be home.

I half expected to see Gram out on the balcony, watching the birds as they awoke for the day in the great oaks which overhung the house. It was nesting season, and she was an avid birder.

I opened the kitchen door quietly, and Mrs. Gustafson, the housekeeper, looked up in surprise. I put my finger to my lips and eased the duffle off my shoulder before creeping up on my grandmother, who was sitting in the morning room with her back to me, watching the birds in the native lilacs which bordered the patio. I dropped my hands lightly onto her shoulders and said, "You women let just anybody in here, don't you?"

She jumped a rewarding distance and even as she was throwing her strong arms around me she was exclaiming, "Peter Aloysha Aarons, scare an old woman half to death why don't you!"

"Nothing on this earth could scare you to death and you know it," I laughed, wrapping her in my arms. "Happy birthday, Gram."

"What a wonderful, wonderful present! I didn't think you were getting out for another two weeks. Let me look at you!" She held me at arm's length, and her smile faded as she studied me. "Aloysha, Sweetheart... you're out because you're sick."

"I just had a touch of some kind of jungle crud," I shrugged. "They figured I wouldn't be fit for duty until my tour was up, so they went ahead and cut me loose."

Her hand was instantly on my forehead. "You should be in bed. You have a fever, and your hands are shaking, and they're so cold! You're going straight up to bed, young man!"

"Can I have a little chicken soup first?" I teased. "Gram, I'm fine. I didn't get much sleep last night, that's all, and in case you haven't been outside yet, it's chilly out there."

"What do you mean, 'jungle crud'? I thought you weren't anywhere near Viet Nam. I thought you were in the embassy in Rome, using your fluency in Italian to translate for a bunch of stuffy, safe diplomats." Her black DiPirelli eyes bored into me, and it made me squirm uncomfortably. "Peter Aloysha Aarons, where have you been and what have you been doing?"

"That's kind of classified," I grimaced. "Please, Grandmother, I'm fine, really I am. I just need to rest up a bit and get a few good meals in me. Mrs. Gustafson, how are you these days?"

"I'm fine," she nodded. "May I fix you some breakfast, Mister Aarons?"

Mister Aarons. She'd known me since I was five years old, and always it had been either Master Aarons, or Mister Aarons, never Aloysha, or Bud, or even Peter. She was a typical, stiff servant – Swedish, efficient, no nonsense sort of a woman. What had kept her with my free-wheeling grandmother for forty-odd years was a mystery to me.

"Mister Aarons?"

"Breakfast. Yes, please. That would be very nice. Grandmother, sit down and tell me what you have planned for your day."

She was still drilling me with her eyes, seeing if she could open up a hole from which would pour information about where I'd been and what I'd been doing. I'd been in a far corner of the Annan Highlands, where Cambodia, Laos and Viet Nam all intersect, using my fluency in Russian to spy on the comings and goings of the Red Menace. It was miserable, boring, occasionally dangerous work – but mostly, miserable and boring. I wasn't sure what I'd done to piss off the health gods – drunk the water, eaten the food, gotten bit by some damned bug or other, but I'd awakened one morning burning with fever, too sick to get out of bed. By the time they'd gotten medical help to me, I'd been delirious and half dead of dysentery and dehydration. The medic, a beautiful lady some years older than I – pleasingly plump, red haired, kind faced – had sat up nights with me, pumping fluids into my body and speaking softly and cheerfully to keep me from despair. Her name was Bobbi Bates, and she said when she got out in a few months, she'd look me up, being star-struck and all, and I had invited her to make my home hers until she could get settled in sunny southern California and find work as an up and coming starlet.

"You're not going to tell me, are you?" my grandmother sniffed, breaking into my thoughts. "As if a little old lady could possibly use whatever information it is you gather in that...*job* you have." Little old lady my ass. She skied the black diamond slopes from Sun Valley to St. Moritz. Every unattached man over fifty on three continents wanted her, and not just for her money, which was considerable.

"Had. I'm out. Through. Done. Served my time. I'm home to pick up my plans to form a production company with Tommy and Kit, make a movie or two with my dad, pound my Steinway until I'm the best in the world, and aggravate you as much as possible without getting myself hurt."

"And get married?" my grandmother twinkled. It was her favorite subject. "I'm old, Aloysha. Old women want great-grandchildren, you know. Think of how wonderful this house would be with children in it."

"When I find the right girl I'll marry her, I promise," I grinned. "But," I sang softly, "I want a girl, just like the girl, that married dear old Dad. So it could take a while."

"You're an aggravating child, all right," she chuckled. "I'm glad you're home, Sweetheart. When did you shave and shower last, may I ask?"

"I'm not sure," I sighed, "what's today?"

"My sixty-ninth birthday!" Grandmother laughed. "Aloysha, eat your breakfast, have a nice hot shower, and sleep for a bit. Your father is sending Max for us, for me, at one O'clock. Does he know you're home?"

"Nobody knows but you," I said, thanking Mrs. Gustafson as she put my breakfast down in front of me. "This looks very good."

It looked good, and it tasted good. The eggs were real, the toast was fresh, the coffee had been dripped, not boiled. We visited a bit while I ate, but I realized I was fading fast and excused myself before I fell on the floor and further alarmed my grandmother. I cast a longing look at my Steinway, went up the floating staircase, and walked into the dimness of my bedroom. It was just as I had left it; dusted, of course, but in no way disarranged. I took off my uniform, and in a moment of abandon, I kicked it into the closet, where it landed with an unceremonious clack of buttons against the back wall. Mrs. Gustavson had preceded me up the stairs, and my bed was turned back. There were fresh towels in the bathroom. My bathroom. My private bathroom. The soap did not smell like latex paint. The shampoo did not smell like kerosene. The water was soft and did not smell like purifier tablets. I was home. Thank God! I was home. I lathered myself all over, pretending like I was a big, fluffy sheep, then stood a bit, letting the hot water beat on me before toweling off and crawling into a bed that was long enough, and wide enough to be comfortable in. I would have been content to lie there and think about things, but even before the sheets were warm, I was asleep.

I awoke to Gram's cool hand on my cheek, and as I smiled she said, "You really are feverish, child. Maybe you should just stay home in bed." "Tomorrow," I said. "Promise. But today is your birthday, and I want to see Dad and Mother and the girls."

"As you wish, but I have every intention of making you a doctor's appointment. I hope you know that."

"I do know that," I said, trying not to laugh. I was a buff twenty-six year old. I was immortal. Didn't she know that, too?

"As long as we understand each other," she said. "Max will be here in twenty minutes."

"I'll be ready," I smiled, and went off to comb my hair and put in my contacts.

After I was dressed in slacks and a sweater I still had a couple minutes to light a cigarette, pick up the phone, and call my best friend. When he heard my voice he was delighted, and I was no less so. It had been Kit and me since kindergarten. It had been Kit who taught me English, who had befriended me when I was a skinny kid whose hands and feet were too big, eyes too large in my thin face, who called me his buddy when the other kids were calling me a freak. "Mom will be glad you're home," he said in a somewhat different tone. "She really wants to see you again."

My heart sank. "Is she that bad?"

"The doctor says another couple of weeks. Maybe a month at the most. He's just keeping her comfortable."

"There's nothing they can do?" I whispered, tears starting in my eyes. "Kit, there has to be something they can do."

"The cancer's all through her, Bud. It's in her liver, and her lymph glands. "As soon as you can get away from your family, please come over and we'll go see her, okay?"

"Tomorrow morning first thing," I said, forgetting I'd told my grandmother I'd be a good little guy and stay in bed tomorrow. "How's that boy of yours, and his beautiful mother?"

"Both fine," Kit said, and I could hear the smile in his voice. "We're kind of thinking we'd like to have another one here pretty soon. A girl this time."

"And you know how to arrange that?" I chuckled. "Kit, I hear Gram calling me. Will you be home this evening? I'll phone you."

"I'll be here," he smiled. "Tell Gram happy birthday for me. Tell you what, I'll pick you up tomorrow morning and bring over her birthday present."

"Great," I said. "I'll see you then. Give Billie and Travis my love."

I parked one hip on the banister and slid down into the living room, taking a hop to catch myself, and then looked up to see my grandmother watching me. "See?" I said, trying not to look embarrassed, "I'm fine. Are you ready to go, Birthday Girl?"

"Max is waiting for us," she smiled, with a flash of straight white teeth that were all hers, and I dropped my arm around her shoulder, picked up my leather jacket off the back of the big chair in the corner by the fireplace, and escorted her out the door to where my father's limo waited.

"Bud, you're home!" Max exclaimed, extending his hand and a smile. "Are you out for good at this point?" He shot my grandmother a look, because some members of the Aarons clan weren't big on associating with the servants, but Gram just smiled and nodded. She was not a snob. I was not a snob. Dad, was the snob in our family. I guess my grandfather had been just like him, but I hadn't really known Gramps. He'd died in a plane crash when I was eight, and I scarcely remembered him.

I took the hand Max offered me, gave him a one armed hug in greeting, and got into the car with my grandmother. The sun was high overhead, and it was a warm day – not too breezy – not smoggy. Too early in the year for much smog. The ride to our ancestral home in Bel Air was pleasant. The traffic was light, and I got Gram going on the subject of which birds were nesting in the yard this year, and off the subject of how I was feeling, and what I'd been doing during my tour of duty overseas.

Rolling up to the Bel Air house after an absence was always a little awe inspiring. Gram's house was a comfortable size at nine thousand three hundred and sixty square feet, but it had been built as a weekend get-away spot back in the twenties, and was neither formal nor imposing. This house, was both. It was also huge. It resembled a Moorish palace, and had been built by my great grandfather shortly after the turn of the century. It sat on three acres of immaculately groomed landscape, and was obviously the abode of someone rich and famous. This generation, it was Dad.

Dad was an executive producer, a movie maker in the upper echelon sense of the word. He was a financier, and rapidly gaining a reputation as the best in the business. He played hunches and played them well. He could spot a successful production from the time it was a gleam in a screenwriter's eye. He played the stock market and won big, because he was careful, and cunning, and brilliant. He played people, and he could be ruthless. He rarely smiled, except at my mother, and I adored him. He was my hero. Bigger than life. I would have walked over hot coals to please him.

I was an actor, because that's what he wanted me to be. Given my druthers, I'd have spent all my time at the piano, seeking through playing and composition to dominate the latter half of the twentieth century as my idol, Sergei Rachmaninoff, had dominated the first.

I was good. I was very good. No brag, just fact. I had huge hands and the soul of a poet. I could reach a thirteenth on the keyboard, and into the depths of the artistic wellspring. Mostly, I was good because I practiced like hell, hour after hour, day after day. When I wasn't playing some character role in a movie or a television show, or fiddling with my stock portfolio, I was practicing at my Steinway.

The car door opened, and I realized I was wool gathering; probably jet lag. I thanked Max for the lift, gave Gram my hand, and walked in the direction of the massive front door, which opened to reveal my father's tall form and handsome countenance, my stunningly beautiful mother beside him. It was kind of funny when I thought about it. At forty-four my mother was one of the most beautiful women in Hollywood, though she was not an actress and had resisted my father's efforts to make her into one. She was nearly six feet tall, with cider brown eyes and a creamy Russian complexion. Her dark hair was swept back in thick waves, her figure could strike a man dumb. My father, at almost forty-seven, was as handsome as she was beautiful. He was six foot three, with jet black hair just beginning to turn shock white, and rugged features marred only by the haughty look which occasionally rested upon them. My lovely grandmother, his mother, was still five foot ten and straight as a rod, with snow white hair and snapping black eyes just like her son's. Then, there was me.

I was the same height as my father, broad in the shoulders and chest, long legged – not bad, really, but that's where the resemblance ended. Except for the big, black, beautiful DiPirelli eyes and jet black hair, I was an oddly unattractive combination of features that worked well for everybody else. I had sharp, craggy features that were far more Russian than Jewish, a Greco-Roman nose that was a little too flared at the nostrils to be classic, a bottom lip that was too full – and dimples – of all things. At thirteen, I had looked eighteen. At twenty-six, I still looked eighteen, which was of considerable annoyance to me at the time. Worst of all, I had this voice, and where it came from I don't know, but it was a true Russian bass, deeper and more ominous than any voice on the entire planet, and it had made me sound old and austere since its catastrophic plummet at age fourteen. Junior Keiger, who had been the bane of my existence from kindergarten on, said I sounded like a bullfrog in heat. I just shook my head and chuckled.

"Peterkin!" my mother called, and ran to embrace me. I swung her around in my arms and she laughed like springtime. "You're home early, and you look...thin, or tired, or both. Are you all right?"

"What kind of a greeting is that?" I snorted. By that time Dad was beside me, and I left one arm around my mother and stuck out my hand to him. "Dad, it's good to see you!"

"And you," he nodded, taking my hand. "And you, Bud. Welcome home."

"Thanks," I said, though in actuality, this had never been home. Since my arrival in the United States with my mother at age five, I'd always lived with my gram, as had Dad and Mother for some years. Then, Dad had recouped enough of the family fortune, depleted in the stock market crash, to repurchase this place, and he and Mother had moved down out of the hills to take their rightful place amid Hollywood society, and begin having babies again.

One of those babies appeared and came running to greet me – Racheal – long brown hair flying behind her, her laugh reaching me before she did. She launched herself into my arms and I swung her as I had my mother and kissed her on each cheek. At almost fourteen she was a beauty, haughty like my father, but with moments of utter charm that gave me hope for her. "Where's your big sis?" I asked, putting her down, and she gave me a deprecating look which foreshadowed a truly evil temper.

"Probably someplace with her nose in a book, or asleep," she snorted.

"Your sister's not well," my mother admonished, and Racheal slewed her eyes in Mother's direction, the set of her mouth registering annoyance, though she said nothing.

My father put one arm around his mother, one around me, and escorted us into the house. Once inside the women headed in the direction of my mother's rooms, and Dad and I settled ourselves in the den to talk. He took a cigarette, offered me one, and lit both of them. I inhaled through my nose, then exhaled sharply. I knew I shouldn't smoke, but I'd started in the service. I was such a fidgety, nervous, high strung kid in those days, wanting to be and do so much, and not having any real idea where to start. Smoking gave me something to do with my hands when I wasn't playing the piano.

Dad talked to me for a bit about the family business, and what the stock market was doing, but it didn't take him long to figure out that I wasn't focusing very well, and he reached over and laid his hand on my thigh. "Bud? You look very tired. Do you need to lie down for a bit before dinner?"

"No, Dad. I'm fine. I'm just thinking, you know."

"I don't know. I don't read minds. I do read bodies, and yours has dropped weight. Your color isn't good, and I assume you're home early because of that fever I can see burning in your eyes. I trust you're going to see a civilian specialist, soon."

It was disconcerting to have him do that. My wife does it to me all the time these days, but back then I considered myself inscrutable, counting heavily on my dark, unreadable eyes to keep my thoughts concealed. Apparently, I was hiding nothing from Dad. "I got some kind of a bug," I chanted methodically. "I'm fine. I'm just...it's...Geneva Miller. She's dying of cancer, Dad."

"I know," he said, his expression giving me no hint as to his thoughts on the subject. For twenty-one years Kit Miller and I had been best friends, and our parents hadn't gotten together half a dozen times. But then, they came from different worlds. My parents were very wealthy and Jewish by faith. Kit's father was a Methodist minister, and his mother had worked at a car dealership to keep Kit in the private school we'd both attended. The member of my family who associated with the Millers, was Gram, and that wasn't often. They just had so little in common. I don't think it ever really bothered us kids. I was always welcome in Kit's home. He was always welcome in mine. That was enough. "I am sorry."

"Me too. I just wish there was something I could do for her."

"Aloysha, sometimes there just isn't a damned thing you can do," he sighed, and I knew he was thinking more about my sister, Esther, than he was about Geneva.

If money, power, influence, desire could have cured her, she'd have been well in a heartbeat – no pun intended. That's what was wrong. Esther had a weak heart, and no surgery, no European spa, no therapy of any kind seemed to help it. My parents had taken her literally all over the world in hopes of finding a cure, but so far there had been none. She spent her time pretty much as Racheal said she did, with her nose in a book, reading of far off enchanted places and people who were well and energetic and dynamic...like me, she always said. It made me feel guilty in an odd sort of way. I worshipped and adored my sister, who seemed older than I, though she was only sixteen. I knew, we all knew, Esther was living on borrowed time. Racheal resented her. My mother fretted openly, my father brooded, I hovered helplessly, and Esther pretty much ignored the situation.

Now that I was home we would begin spending time together again. I would give her piano lessons, and we would swim together, and sit and read or talk quietly, or go for walks in the country. Occasionally we would go out to the club where we kept the family horse collection and ride, as we always had, and Racheal would avoid us pointedly and scoffingly, which suited us just fine.

Esther had been napping, it turned out, and didn't realize I was even home. She hurried downstairs just before dinner, full of hugs and kisses, and sat on the piano bench beside me, and laid her dark head on my shoulder while I played for her. I was very rusty, and a little shaky with fever and jet lag, but she didn't seem to notice. If the rest of my family noticed, they were too polite to say anything. As we were leaving, my father did admonish me to go see a doctor, and I promised I would do so.

My grandmother was not thrilled to discover the next morning that I was up and dressed. She reminded me of what I'd promised, and I said that, yes, I remembered, but Kit was coming over, and we were going to see Geneva Miller, who was back in the hospital. Gram didn't say anything. She just kissed the top of my head where I sat at the piano, and went on into the morning room.

When Kit came to the door it was Gram who answered it and gathered him into her arms. She was as tall as he was, and I watched him bury his head against her shoulder, just for a minute, gathering strength from this beloved mother figure. When he turned to me, there were tears in his hazel green eyes, and Kristoffer Miller was not a bawlbag like me. He was not a large man, but he was strikingly handsome, and already a sought-after leading man in Hollywood.

I put my arms around him, kissing his temple, and we just stood and held each other. No words needed, which was a good thing, because I had none. I'd rehearsed some possible lines last night in the shower. *So,*

Kit, how's the weather been since I've been gone? So, Kit, sorry about your mother, but at least you still have Billie and Travis. So, Kit, made any good movies lately? So, Kit, what should I say to your mom? So, Kit, what should I expect to see when we get there, and am I going to be sick?

He stayed to have a late second breakfast with us, and gave Gram her present, a beautiful crystal quail, and then looked at me and said, "Let's do it, Bud." As we were going out the door he told Gram he was going to take me to his house for lunch so I could drool over his beautiful son, and he'd return me primed for marriage and an immediately pregnant wife.

"Thank you!" my grandmother laughed, and said quietly to me, "Tell Geneva I'm thinking about her and I'll be in to see her in a day or so."

Cancer in the sixties was not a condition, it was a disease. It was a horrifying, mindless, mysterious entity that sucked the life from its victims and their families. A great number of people still believed it was contagious, and, like AIDS victims a few years ago, cancer patients were often pariahs. That particular ward of the hospital was darker, and quieter. It smelled different, and the halls were oddly deserted. Without really meaning to, Kit and I put our arms around each other as we walked, like we had when we were little and something was scaring us.

Because Kit was making good money in the flickers, his mother was in a semi-private room. She didn't want to be absolutely alone, she said. The drapes were partially opened, and a broad shaft of light was coming in to rest as a benediction on the foot of her bed. I sat down beside her, and took her hand and kissed it, and began to cry, because I really couldn't think of anything else to do, and she was obviously slipping away.

"At last," she smiled, "an honest man. How are you, Bud?"

"Glad to be home," I said quietly, sniffing and drying my eyes. "Geneva, I'm so sorry this is happening to you. Is there anything I can do to make this easier?"

"Take care of Kit for me."

"Well, no. Anything other than that?"

She laughed and gave my hand a failing squeeze. "Your smile does my heart good, young man. I'm glad you made it back safe."

We visited, and I told her where I'd been and what I'd been doing, because she asked me to, and there was nothing I'd have refused her. I told her about some of the places I'd seen, and the people I'd met, and some of the attitudes I'd changed and opinions I'd formed. She told me again to take care of Kit, and to keep plugging away at repairing that old boat Kit and I had bought together after high school, because plugging away was what got things done. She told me to be happy, and to find a good woman, and not to be too sad when she was gone. She was ready to be rid of the pain; ready to go home to the Lord and His many mansions. As I was leaving I gave her a kiss and told her I'd be back with Gram tomorrow. It was like kissing a corpse.

We didn't talk on the way to Kit's house. There was nothing to say after that. We didn't talk until we had Billie and Travis to talk to, and about. Billie met us at the door with Travis in her arms, and gave both of us a kiss as we went inside. Already Kit lived in a nicer house than his parents ever had, and although Billie had put her acting career on hold for a few years to take care of the baby, it was obvious she was used to having money. She was a beautiful young woman, glamorous even in blue jeans and a man's white dress shirt. She had long dark hair which I found to be her most attractive feature, and she had a slightly high voice that always seemed to be concealing a giggle in it somewhere. She was a typical starlet in many ways, but she seemed to have a level head on her shoulders, and after three years of marriage she and Kit still seemed happy and in love.

Travis was just about perfect. He was the spitting image of his doting daddy as far as features went, and he had rusty blond hair and his mother's brown eyes. He was two, and a bit stand-offish for a few minutes, until his dad sat in my lap and said, "See, Travis? Your uncle Bud's an okay kind of a guy." Then he laughed, and came over, and joined his dad and me while Billie put lunch on the table. I watched Travis in his high chair, just learning to feed himself and making a mess, and I wondered when I'd have a little boy or girl of my own.

Before having a son it seemed somehow appropriate to have a wife, and therein lay the problem. At twenty-three, Kit had been married with a pregnant wife. Just out of college, still struggling to get his career on track, but he and Billie had taken one look at each other, and they just knew.

Three months later, they were husband and wife. Me? At twenty-three I'd been focused on my Steinway and a double Master's, still having the kind of frantic, sweaty, self-centered sex that satisfied the loins only, not the mind or the heart.

I knew it was out there. I could see it in the way my father held my mother, and that's what I wanted – something enduring and tender and passionate – and I had no clue how to go about finding it. That, was one thing Dad couldn't teach me. He taught me about stocks, and investments, and multi-national trading, and how to evaluate all the points of a deal before making it, and at twenty-six I was becoming wealthy in my own right. Dad had sat me down and told me under no uncertain circumstances to keep Old One Eye in my pants, or in a condom if he was out for exercise, and to never, ever pay a bit of attention to what the female of the species said about her level of protection. That was my responsibility. But he couldn't tell me how to recognize love of the kind he shared with my mother. He could only say that it would strike like lightning, and the flash would never fade. If it faded, it wasn't worth having.

I had that double Master's under my belt, my military service was behind me, and my Steinway sang her siren's song to me. But love's old sweet song, eluded me and I didn't much care. I watched Kit going in a dozen directions at once, and although he seemed happy enough, I wanted one thing and one thing only, to be the best in the world at the keyboard of a piano. I knew I was sexually immature, but nothing really told me I needed to change that. I didn't need to be a good lover, I needed to be a great pianist.

It occasionally passed through my mind that I was a twenty-six year old man who lived with his grandmother. That I was a twenty-six year old man who had absolutely no meaningful relationship with a woman his own age...whatever that meant. What remained in my mind after the doubts had flown through, was that I could sit at my Steinway twelve hours a day if I wanted to, and nobody was going to tell me I couldn't. I could take two or three years to get some business deals rolling that I'd been putting off, and then go to Juilliard and do a doctorate in Piano, and nobody who mattered was going to criticize me for it. Nobody was going to ask me to pay the rent, or change the baby, or go to the store for toilet paper and bread.

I had responsibilities, but they ran to managing my portfolio and sitting at my father's knee learning the family business. Gram taught me to oversee the household staff, both on-site and off, and in general prepared me to be the scion I was. I didn't consider myself coddled or spoiled, and I'd never been one to do bratty, self-indulgent shit. I was learning what I needed and was expected to learn. The only thing I wasn't doing that I was expected to do, was marry and produce the next generation of little movie moguls. Dad and Mother never said a word about it, but it was becoming a litany with my grandmother.

When I walked in the house after my visit with Kit and his family, her first words were, "Isn't that the most adorable baby you've ever seen? And Billie is such a lovely woman. Did Kit tell you she has a sister who's in the process of moving to Los Angeles?"

"He did," I smiled. "When she gets here the four of us are going to do something together to kind of introduce her to the city."

"And how is Geneva?"

"She's dying," I said quietly, lowering myself into one of the big easy chairs in the living room. Somewhere in the course of the day I'd picked up a bitch of a headache, and aspirin wasn't touching it. "Her skin is really tight against her body, and she...her eyes are sunken into her head. She's always been such a pretty woman, so full of life, and to see her like this, just makes me sick inside."

"Science is doing some wonderful things, Aloysha. Sooner or later they'll cure cancer."

"Not in time to help Geneva," I muttered, and let my head rest against the back of the chair. Closing my eyes didn't help. The pain continued drilling in tight circles around my eye sockets, and I was thoroughly annoyed. It had completely slipped my youthful mind that I'd been sent home because I was too ill to finish out my tour of duty, and Uncle Sam wasn't one to cut just anybody loose. I'd been sent home to rest – to convalesce at somebody else's expense – and I'd forgotten. Only when I could barely drag myself up the stairs did I remember. By then I was cold, and even standing in the shower letting hot water beat on me didn't warm me up. When I did warm up it was all in a rush, and my lunch came up, and my guts twisted and wrung themselves out into the toilet, and I just barely got myself into bed without falling on my face.

My gram, who even at her age was pretty nearly as impetuous as I was, didn't jump me or say I told you so. She did tattle on me to my parents, who were not pleased, and the next morning she had our family G.P., Jack Boyd, come around to see me, and he gave me something that pretty well knocked the starch out of me for a few days. That was Thursday.

I drowsed in relative comfort and oblivion until Sunday morning, when Kit called to tell me that Geneva had passed away. It was Easter, and although Kit wasn't one given to saying religious things, he did say she'd risen with her savior and gone home. Then, he cried, and I cried with him, and it made my head pound, and I felt useless and helpless and weak – all of which I was at that moment. By sheer tenacity I made it to the funeral, and served as a pall bearer, and collapsed back into bed for another few days.

In that time Mrs. Gustavson was in and out of my room for different reasons, but she didn't stop to visit, or ask me how I was feeling. She'd ask me if I needed anything, but I always said no, because I sensed her reluctance to get close to me, not because I was sick, but because she was distant by nature. It always left me musing about why she had stayed with my grandmother for so many years. They had no kind of a relationship at all that I could see, and that seemed rather a waste of forty years. Even Dad the snob had a real friend in Max, his chauffeur. Not that they were buddies, they definitely were not. But they were friends of the sort who trusted one another implicitly with information or pain either physical or emotional. Max had left Gram's employ to move to Bel Air with my parents, and was raising his own family under my Dad's roof. Max had married late, and while he was my Dad's age, his son Britt was only five. It was assumed Britt would take Max's place, as Max had taken his father's place, and my father valued that, if nothing else.

Gram usually drove herself, or had an off-site driver, though she borrowed Max on special occasions. As a matter of fact, most of Gram's staff lived off-site these days. Gram kept saying she was going to change that, but talk was as far as it ever got. The only one here was Mrs. Gustavson, who occupied the maid's quarters on the ground floor, having abandoned the Chauffeur's quarters over the garage after her husband unceremoniously abandoned her one summer's afternoon.

Gram wasn't one to want a lot of servants under foot, and had little need of them. She was a capable woman, and enjoyed her autonomy. There was a good bit of bustle in the house, but those people were friends, and Gram was often gone visiting them, as well, or off on a cruise someplace to watch penguins nesting, or off in some remote corner of the globe skiing or soaking up the sun or spying on some new species with wings.

Lying there getting my strength back I had time to hope Bobbi Bates really would look me up and come stay a while. It would be nice to live with somebody who was actually home most of the time, and who shared my interest in acting. The fact that she was beautiful and intelligent and had a wonderful spicy laugh wouldn't hurt, either.

I did my level best to stay in touch with Kit and to help him grieve. He'd come and sit with me and we'd talk, or just sit. He had to be strong for Billie – the husband, the daddy – he didn't have to be strong for me. With me he could cry and rage and curse and pound his fists against the wall, and I'd take him in my arms and let him cry, or I'd play the piano for him, or tell him all the dirty jokes I'd learned in the Army, but I never told him to buck up, or be brave, or get over it. Sometimes all I could do was help him cry. I did a lot of that. I gritted my teeth, forced myself to take it slow, and in a couple of weeks I was pretty much back on my feet.

One bright morning in April when Kit wasn't filming and Billie and Travis were off visiting Billie's mother for the weekend, I stuffed Kit into my old red Benz and we headed for the marina to visit another beloved relic, *Tiger Lily.* She was a thirty foot wooden cabin cruiser, and we were determined that one day she'd be the classiest boat between Seattle and San Diego. We'd made a pact that we were going to be the only ones who ever worked on her. We'd do the sanding, the refinishing, the outfitting. We were even brash enough to think we could overhaul the engine, which is where we were at that point. Had been for some time.

"Well, shit," Kit snapped, putting his bleeding knuckles in his mouth, and I picked up the wrench he'd dropped to the bottom of the engine compartment and handed it back to him.

"Wearing gloves might be a good idea," I observed, wiping the sleeve of my sweatshirt across my forehead. "It's downright hot in here, have you noticed?"

"And have you noticed, Rachmaninoff, we have parts left over? What is this thing, anyway?" He held up something that looked rather like an octopus. It was pretty big, and we both knew it did something important.

I began thumbing through the repair manual, looking for a picture of whatever it was. "Do you remember from whence you removed it by any chance?"

"Shit no. I don't even think it goes with this engine."

"What makes you say that?"

"Because I think it's a distributor cap, and this is a diesel."

"Kit," I said patiently, "why would it be here if it wasn't something we took off in the first place?"

"Because somebody had a rotten sense of humor, that's why," Kit snarled, and the offending object made a long, clean arc to land in the deep water off our port bow.

"Oh, nice going, Sunshine!" I exclaimed, hauling myself the rest of the way out of the engine compartment and tossing the repair manual aside. "Now we'll never know what the hell it was!"

"I don't care what it was," Kit sulked. He slitted his eyes at me, got another beer out of the ice chest, and we sat staring glumly at the ruins of the big engine. After a bit, he began to snicker, and I began to snicker, and pretty soon we were laughing like loons.

"Which solves nothing," I reminded him, wiping my eyes and fishing a Coke out of the ice chest.

"Bud, maybe we should rethink this whole do-it-yourself approach, you know?"

"I thought the object was to learn how to do all this stuff before we ever put out to sea, so that if something went wrong we'd know how to fix it and get ourselves back to port."

"That's why God invented radios. When's the last time you got laid?"

I lost about three ounces of Coke out my nose, and spent a minute sputtering and cursing before the pain ebbed enough for me to speak. "That, is none of your business!" I laughed.

"My God, has it been that long? Bud, you're going to atrophy from disuse."

"Where are you going with this, Kristoffer?"

"I was thinkin'...Tijuana, maybe? I need to relax."

"Or not!" I exclaimed.

"Give me one good reason. Nothing relieves stress like a little gratuitous sex."

"I'll give you about three good reasons. Billie, and Travis, and the films they showed us in the Army. Kit, you can get diseases that defy description from gratuitous sexual encounters. I, for one, don't want my dick reamed out with a red hot poker."

"They don't do that anymore," he said placidly. "Now you just get shots."

"What about the other two reasons?"

"Oh, them. I wasn't going to take them along." He paused and looked at me. "Maybe I wasn't going to have sex myself, maybe I was just going to watch you."

"Damn, you're an icky bastard, Miller." I hated to admit it, but the idea had some real appeal for me about then. Not the part where Kit got to watch, but the rest of it, definitely. I wasn't crazy about prostitutes, but neither was I into calling up girls of my acquaintance and asking them if they wanted to get together for a little sex. Going it alone was a momentary relief – it let you get back to sleep – but it wasn't in any way satisfying.

"You're quiet all of a sudden, Aarons," Kit chuckled. "Penny for your thoughts."

"What I'm thinking isn't worth even that," I sighed, and began picking up spare engine parts.

We ended up in Tijuana. I spent a couple of hours naked with a large breasted young woman with hard eyes, who grunted convincingly, and cried out passionately in Spanish at all the right times, and left me feeling like I needed a bath and my mouth washed out with soap. Where Kit went I didn't ask, and didn't want to know, and if it hadn't been for the lingering smell of cheap perfume, I could have convinced myself he'd been off drinking someplace.

I suppose it was to our credit that we didn't laugh all the way home about where we'd been and what we'd done. It took Kit awhile to get around to asking me how it had been, and I said it had been great in a steamy, strange sort of way. I was glad I spoke Spanish, so we could have a conversation while we … you know.

"You're too much of a romantic," Kit laughed. "You're more sensitive to what you're doing against custom than what you're doing against nature. You're a man. Men have needs."

"If you're trying to paraphrase Plutarch, you're doing a lousy job," I muttered, lit another cigarette and focused on the white line disappearing into the darkness ahead of us.

"You're not thinking about you," Kit said quietly, "You're thinking about me, aren't you?"

I shrugged with my eyebrows. "Thinking about things in general, I guess. What time are Billie and Travis supposed to be home?"

"You are thinking about me."

"Because you smell like a woman, Kristoffer. Yes, I'm thinking about you, and about your wife. How can you expect your marriage to last if you cheat on your spouse?"

Kit gave me a look of genuine puzzlement, and lit a cigarette of his own. "It's not like we've never done this before."

"It's not like you've ever been married before. Hell, Kit, we haven't done this kind of thing since college."

"I guess I just don't see what the big deal is."

"How would you feel if Billie went down to Mexico and picked up some well hung guy and had sex with him for a couple of hours and then came home and pretended like nothing ever happened?"

"It wouldn't exactly be the same thing, now would it, Bud?"

"And why wouldn't it, Kit?"

"Because men are different. If I went out with some white, middle class girl with nice tits that I found attractive, and we had dinner and then shacked up in a motel room somewhere, now that would be cheating. This isn't. These women provide sex as a service. Did you feel any love for that girl? She was very pretty."

"No, of course not, but..."

"I didn't either. I rented a service, just like you did. Now if Billie did that, she'd feel guilty, and dirty, and she'd cry and be upset and hate herself..."

"And you'd hate her, too."

"Probably. Because women and men are different. Billie's a lucky girl. She gets what she wants and needs at home. She has a nice house, plenty of money, plenty of sex. She's had one baby and I think she's pregnant with another. What else does a woman want? Face it, Bud, nice girls don't go to Tijuana and get laid. Nice guys do, and that's okay."

"Why?" I asked. "Why do nice guys go to Tijuana and get laid, especially nice married guys with beautiful wives?" and he had no answer, though he spent the rest of the drive trying to give me one.

I was sitting in Grandfather's smoker, swilling Sidecars straight up and getting drunk on my ass when my grandmother found me. She waved her way through the smoke and sat down on the small sofa close to the chair I was sprawled in. "It's three O'clock in the morning, Aloysha."

"Am I keeping you awake?" I growled. "I've always thought of myself as a quiet and considerate drunk."

"I heard you come in a while ago, and when I didn't hear the piano I thought you might like some company."

"What if I'd been in here having sex with some woman?"

"I assume you'd have locked the door. I'll leave if I'm intruding."

"No. Stay. I just...I guess I do need some company. Well, I don't need company, I need advice. Female advice. Got any of that?"

"Some, maybe. What do you need to know?"

"Can I fix you a drink?"

"No, Dear. It's nearly time for my first cup of coffee. Tell me what's on your mind."

"Well," I said, staring into my drink, "I guess you should know first that Kit and I have been a'whoring in Mexico these past few hours."

"So I gathered from the smell of you."

"I smell like cheap perfume, don't I?"

"That's not all you smell like," she chuckled, "but I'll spare you the graphic descriptors and hope you had brains enough to wear a rubber."

I just cringed. "Am I as pathetic as I feel?"

"I don't know. Give me some more information and I'll tell you."

"Kit says nice guys have sex with all kinds of women because it gives them experience and keeps them fresh and interesting, but nice girls have sex only with their husbands, and if they don't, they're whores. I mean, me having sex with some woman I don't know is one thing, but Kit? Gram, he has a beautiful wife and a sweet little boy, and to me that's just downright damn cheating, but he says it's not because it's a service. He brought it up, and I was weak enough to go along with it, and now I'm not only disappointed in me, I'm disappointed in him, and I can't ever remember being disappointed in Kit Miller, and I don't know how to handle it."

"And your question is?"

I gave her a puzzled look. "Didn't I just ask you?"

"You rattled off the usual penis-encumbered claptrap about the validity of the double standard for sexual behavior, and then you said something equally male about being disappointed in Kit and yourself, but you didn't ask me a question."

"Am I wrong? Is Kit wrong?"

"Yes. Anything else?"

"You're not going to make this easy, are you, Grandmother?"

"What do you remember about learning to ride a bicycle?"

I blinked stupidly. "Uh...not much, I guess."

"What do you remember about learning to be a champion diver?"

"Oh, God. Falling on my back, on my face, on my belly. Learning to keep my arms straight and my legs straight and my toes pointed and my eyes focused and my mind working all at the same time."

"You learned to ride a bike in an afternoon. It took you two years to win your first diving competition, and three years to get to state the first time. That's why you remember diving better than you remember learning to ride a bike."

I sat there contemplating her for a bit. "I don't have a clue what you're trying to tell me, I'm sorry to say."

"Your diving coaches told you to keep your arms and legs straight, your body in control, your eyes fixed on a certain point, and landing on your back and your belly and your face taught you why. I've told you all I can about what you just asked me. I've told you it's bullshit, and it is. Now, you have to figure out why it is, and you can only do that by experiencing it for yourself."

"I'm not married..."

"Has nothing to do with it, Aloysha, and what do you mean, you having sex with someone you don't know is one thing, etcetera? Do you think that because it's what she does to earn enough money to feed herself, and you paid her, that you have the right, morally, to inflict yourself on another human being in such a manner? What's the difference between your attitude and Kit's?"

"I'm not married," I said through my teeth. "If I learned to repair stoves for a living, and nobody wanted their stove repaired, I'd starve, wouldn't I?"

"Would you repair stoves naked, so that you could titillate your customers? Would you allow them to say insulting things to you, and sweat all over you, and hurt you and be abrupt with you, and look upon your work with distain, and maybe give you some terrible disease? But you repair stoves, because that's all you know how to do, and your father found it more economically feasible to educate his daughters than you."

"But..."

"I'm not worried about Kit's attitudes, Aloysha. I'm worried about yours. They stink, and so do you. Take a shower before you go to bed, and try not to puke on the carpets." She got up and left, closing the door just a little too hard behind her, and I sat there like the idiot I was, wondering what had pissed her off.

My next stop was my father's office. He'd know about such things. By this time I was shaven and showered and looked like the little gentleman I was purported to be. I parked the Benz Gram had given me for my sixteenth birthday in a space marked Aarons, and went through the tall glass doors, nodded to the guard, and hopped an elevator going up to the penthouse offices of Aarador LA.

Dad's secretary smiled and waved me through. "He's expecting you," she said, and I smiled back.

My father looked up from whatever it was he was doing and gestured toward the comfortable chair across from him. "What's on your mind?" he asked, unsmiling as usual. He offered me a cigarette and sat back to contemplate me, his eyes twinkling with something akin to good humor. "My mother seems a tad disenchanted with you at the moment. What's up?"

"She didn't tell you?"

"No. Her exact words were, 'JR, that boy is too much like you, sometimes.'"

"That's it?" I frowned, staring out the windows toward building after building stretching to infinity against the hills and sky. Why was this bothering me so deeply? I couldn't fathom why this was bothering me so deeply.

"That's it. I have a part in mind I want you to read, by the way, and there's one Kit should read for as well."

"Dad...thanks. I will read, sure. But I need to talk to you about something first, if that's okay?" He nodded, and I told him about Kit and me, and where we'd gone and what we'd done and how I'd felt about it, and he just sat there, listening and smoking and staring at the Renoir on the wall over my left shoulder.

When I was through he shrugged and said, "Boys will be boys, Bud. A little indiscriminate screwing around is a part of growing up."

"When you were my age, Dad, you'd already found out you had a son by the woman you loved, and you'd spent no end of time and money and taken all kinds of risks to shake them free of the Third Reich and bring them to America."

"So?"

"That's hardly indiscriminate screwing around."

"Sure it is. That's how you got here, Bud. Not that it's something I brag about. I rescued you and your mother because it was the right thing to do." He saw me jump a little and added, "I adored your mother. I'd planned to go back for her when the war was over. Finding out I was a father..."

"Was horrifying," I chuckled, trying to sound amused.

"Finding out the damned Germans had you and your mother and her whole family...that was horrifying. Seeing what they'd done to you...that was horrifying. Finding out about you? That really wasn't so bad. Aloysha, what's bothering you, anyway?"

"I just tried to tell you what's bothering me," I grimaced, scrubbing fitfully at my face. "I tried to tell Gram, and she just about went into orbit. I thought maybe you...I mean, you and Mother are so happy together. Have you ever..." I lost my nerve and just kind of grinned painfully at him, like a cowering puppy.

The shape of his eyes told me I was over the line, which was a dangerous place to be with my father, but his voice stayed even. "I would suggest you stop pursuing this before you get yourself hurt," he said. "Kit's under a lot of strain right now, having just lost his mother. He's still trying to break in the domestic harness, and quite possibly feeling a slight pinch. I think you'd better stop trying to figure out whether to praise or blame him, and concentrate on keeping your friendship intact. That, after all, is the most important thing. Your Grandmother is upset because she's spending entirely too much time listening to these damned women's libbers who are running around burning their bras and trying to act like men. It's unpleasant, it's ungraceful, unfeminine, and unwise. Take this script," he said, tossing a red folder across the desk at me, "and be at the Burbank studio tomorrow morning at nine O'clock for an initial read-through before casting. Oh, and bring your best friend, too." It was an order, not a request, and I didn't miss the implication.

"Thanks," I said quietly, and took my leave, no more enlightened than when I'd arrived.

I drove to one of the tree lined parks near Dad's offices, and stopped the car in the shade, and read that script he'd given me. I knew which part he had in mind for me and my dark, craggy features and deep voice. The great Chief Cochise of the Apache. Lots of riding, war paint, and angst. A great part, lots of location shooting. A much bigger part than I wanted to tackle just now, but Dad wanted me to, so of course I would. I was guessing Dad wanted Kit to read for the part of Thomas Jeffords, whom the movie was about.

I sat smoking and staring off into space, wondering if maybe I was wrong and Dad wanted me to read for the part of Jeffords. Somehow, I knew he didn't. He knew I'd hate the part. I wasn't a leading man, and didn't want to be. I preferred to hide behind a character, Dad respected that, and I loved him for it. He had a discerning eye for films, and this one looked like a winner. A good way to get back in the traces and used to working long hours again. I dropped the script off at Kit's house, visited a bit with Billie and Travis, and went home to face my grandmother, though God knows what I was going to say to her.

There was a strange car in the drive this warm April day, and I found Gram sitting on the sheltered patio, having lunch with our old friend, Steven Effendi. He'd been my counselor when I was a little boy trying to forget the horrors I'd been through, and Steven had been kind and gentle, nonjudgmental, and a good basketball player. He'd always brought his ball when he came to see me, and as I stuck my hand out to him I asked, laughing, if he had it with him. He laughed in return and said no, his knees were going on him these days.

Steven was probably in his early fifties and recently remarried, having lost his first wife several years before. He was telling my grandmother about the new baby he and his wife, Rosmy, had adopted, and I remember distinctly standing there thinking what a burden it would be to be an elderly man in my fifties saddled with a baby who wasn't even my own flesh and blood. If someone had told me I would be a first time father at fifty-three, or a busy fifty-eight year old leading man with six adopted kids including a set of rambunctious six-year-old twins and a wild-eyed twelve-year-old to boot, I'd have fallen on the floor in hysterics.

He produced a family picture and showed it to us. Very interesting family for the racially uptight sixties. Steven was an Anglo, but Rosmy was Panamanian, and little Efram was African. I figured restaurant seating wasn't going to be a given anymore, but from the look on Steven's face, he didn't really care. He was Baha'i, and such things were of no concern to him anyway. His faith commanded him to be a compassionate, well educated, well informed, gainfully employed world citizen, intermarrying freely regardless of color, and the rest of it was detail.

My grandmother went into the house to have lunch prepared for me, and Steven gestured at the chair to his right. "Sit," he said, "tell me what you're doing these days. You look good. Esther tells me you're out of the service now, and ready to get your civilian life back in order."

"I hope to," I smiled, seating myself.

"What are your plans?"

"Tommy Sinclair and Kit Miller and I have been talking for the last four years about forming our own production company, and that's at the top of my list of things to do. Well, no. It's not at the top of my list." I shrugged a little and gave my head a shake. "What I really, honestly want to do is what I've always wanted to do, be a world class concert pianist. And that's going to involve lessons, and some more study time in Europe, and, if I can get in, a trip to Juilliard for a doctorate. Around that, I want to get involved with Tommy and Kit in the movie-making business."

"Carrying on the family tradition?" Steven smiled.

"On a very, very small scale," I said, resisting the urge to light a cigarette. "But then when your father is *the* Peter Aarons, everything you do is small by comparison."

"Does that bother you?"

I studied him a moment and began to smile. "You're not here by coincidence, are you? Gram called you to come and shrink me a little."

Steven shook his silvering head and laughed, "Intuitive as ever, I see. Esther said you might want to talk to an uninvolved party regarding some issues that concern you, that's all. I always love seeing her, and I love seeing you. It wasn't a very hard sell. What's up?"

"I went to Tijuana with Kit a day or two ago, but I suppose Gram told you that."

"No. She told me exactly what I just told you she did, no more."

"Oh boy. I have to hear this pathetic tale come out of my mouth yet again?"

"Maybe it'll be like learning lines for Shakespeare or Ionesco. If you say them often enough they'll begin to make sense."

"God, I hope so," I sighed. "I don't even know why this is bothering me so much, and when I try to talk about it, the part that bothers me, doesn't bother Gram, and the part that bothers her, doesn't bother Dad. The longer I think about it, the more confused I become."

"Try me," he said, and so I did. Gram did not reappear, but Mrs. Gustavson came out of the house with lunch, saying that Mrs. Aarons was on the telephone and would return to us shortly, and that left Steven and me free to talk while we ate.

I related the whole incident to him as best I could, trying to be straightforward and unbiased in the telling of it. He just sat there nodding a bit from time to time, indicating that he was listening. He interrupted me only once, to ask if this was my first time with a female of the species, and I said it was not. I'd been sexually active for about ten years, since my sixteenth birthday, to be exact, and though I didn't mention it to Steven, that had been Kit's doing, too.

"I think, Aloysha, you're struggling with more than one issue here. The more you reflect upon this, the more they're ganging up on you. Initially, you felt bad because Kit, who is married, had intercourse with a prostitute, and you viewed that as cheating, correct?"

"Um hm."

"But he didn't?"

"No."

"And then he gave you this whole nine yards about men and women being different, and you're not sure whether that's valid, or just rationalization, right?"

"No. I'm not sure I understand the attitude enough to be able to evaluate it as valid or rationalization. It's a completely foreign concept to me."

"Why?"

"I dunno. I don't have a clue, which isn't helping. It just doesn't make sense."

"What do you suppose upset Gramma Esther?"

"Well, I think it was this poor young girl having to sell her body, and me taking advantage of it, like the rutting pig I am."

"Of it, the situation, or of her, the person?"

"I just don't know, Steven. I hadn't thought about it in that much detail."

"What would have made the experience with that girl more pleasurable?"

I sat and thought about that for a minute or so, concentrating on my lunch while I considered the question. "You know, it was pretty darned good just the way it was. No dinner to buy, no strings attached. I really enjoyed it, and I felt like I really needed it. I think I treated her respectfully. I didn't ask her to do anything really perverted. I spoke her language, and she seemed to enjoy my company. I think what would have made it better, was if I'd known her, and if...Kit hadn't been next door with another prostitute."

"Because he was cheating on his wife. And you can't shake that feeling, even though he doesn't feel like he was cheating."

"Right."

"What did your dad have to say about it, since you said you asked him for his opinion?"

"He said Gram was spending too much time listening to the women's libbers and that making too much of this could irreparably damage my friendship with Kit, and that my friendship with Kit is the most important thing of all."

"And what does Kit, who seems to be at the center of this, say?"

"He says, and I quote, 'It's not like we haven't done this before.' And he's right, of course. Kit and I have always tended to share our sexual adventures. But, he's married now, and to me, when you get married, that's it. You're committed to one person, period. Kit sees it as a service, and he's the son of a minister, so maybe I'm the one with the prudish and repressed attitude."

"Why does he need such a service, did he say?"

"Because men and women are different, whatever the hell that means. He also says there are things Billie won't do for him...with him, I guess, and he enjoys those things, and since he doesn't want to inflict them on his wife, he goes elsewhere to get them. Not to a middle class white female to whom he is attracted, because that would be cheating. He goes to a hooker to whom he is not attracted except in the carnal sense, and performs these acts, like anal intercourse and whatever else it is, and then goes home all ready to accept his wife for who she is and what she likes." I paused and took a deep breath. "Is this making any sense?"

"Um hm. I'm just trying to figure out exactly which bogey man is chewing on you. Esther is right, you know. Taking advantage of someone in a disadvantaged situation is beneath you. No pun intended."

"I don't see it..."

"Sure you do, Aloysha. You just won't admit it. You were little, but you remember what it was like to be treated as garbage. You remember the fear and humiliation. You may not remember the details of it at this age, but believe me, when you were five, you remembered it all too well. I'm not sure trying to make you forget was such a good idea, now that I think about it. Maybe this girl is you in another reality. Maybe Kit is you in another reality, and never the twain shall meet."

My fork slipped out of my fingers before I really put it down, and Steven's hand was quick on my forearm. "I didn't mean to shock you, or bring up terrible memories, Bud, but you're trying to figure this out, and to do that you need information about why it's really eating you at the molecular level. Esther is right, but so is your dad. Kit's friendship is precious, and to lose it would hurt your very soul for the rest of your life. People aren't going to behave in a prescribed manner for your sake. You have to accept their behavior as best you can, if you need to have them in your life. If you can't say something loving and constructive to Kit about how his behavior made you feel and why, it will fester between you. You need to work through this for your sake, not his, because he's all right with the behavior. Maybe we should revisit some of the issues you brought with you from Russia..."

"Stop!" I said sharply. In retrospect, it was a terrible mistake. I should have let him be my guide dog, but I was terrified, and the very last thing I wanted was to remember details. Just the remembrance of the fear – the sound of my mother screaming – was almost more than I could tolerate. "Just stop, Steven. You're over-analyzing this whole thing. I'm not traumatized, for Godssake, I'm just pissed off. Can't a guy be pissed off without getting his head shrunk?"

"I'm sorry," he said contritely, and took a sip of coffee, his eyes studying me over the rim of his cup. "Consider this, then. You were once a disenfranchised person. You don't really remember it as an experience, at least I hope you don't, or your gram wasted her money. But there's that lingering discomfort with the whole concept. Kit is trying to convince you that men and women are different. Your dad agrees with him. Your grandmother, with whom you have always lived, disagrees with them, and taught you better than to believe it. She knows the truth. To soar, a bird must have wings of equal strength. The loss of so much as a feather can mean the difference between life and death. All of a sudden we are seeing in this country the stirrings of that realization. Men and women should be equal. The races should be equal. Marriages should be equal partnerships. You are disturbed because you are a man of conscience, and inequality and the ill treatment of the disadvantaged bothers you. You've been sick. You're tired. You don't want to think about anything but your piano. Closer?"

"Maybe," I said, and allowed myself a slow smile, but his words had penetrated deeper than I wanted them to go, and my lunch and the rest of the conversation held little interest for me. As soon as I politely could I excused myself and went inside to pound my Steinway and think about things in general. God, how annoying. I just wanted to get on with my life, not analyze every aspect of it. I sure as hell didn't want to revisit parts of it. Those were the vaguest kinds of memories, neither conscious nor painful unless stirred, and I wanted to keep them that way. How could something so simple and straightforward have become so convoluted and intrusive? Kit enjoyed the company of prostitutes now and then, big deal. How did that translate itself into the disenfranchisement of women and minorities? How did I get from Kit Miller to Martin Luther King and Gloria Steinem? I didn't want to think about this shit. I didn't need to think about this shit. I wasn't competing for a job or a seat on the damned bus. I was through. What Billie didn't know wouldn't hurt her. Let the world have its causes. I had my own.

CHAPTER TWO

L ike Doctor King, I had a dream, a recurring dream, but it was definitely not a good one. I'd had it off and on for as long as I could
remember. It was a disjointed dream, and terrifying, having neither
beginning nor end, but seeming to be always in progress. This man-snake
thing with huge bulbous eyes and protruding, misshapen genitals came slith-
ering for me, his hands cold prelude to the pain he was going to inflict, and
nothing I could say, no crying, no begging, nothing, could deter him from in-
flicting himself on me. He penetrated and pushed until my flesh tore, groaning and gasping and making animal noises, adding his semen to the blood he
was causing me to shed. Sometimes he ejaculated in my mouth, gagging me
until I could no longer scream with the fear and indignity of it.

They say men do not dream in color, but this man-thing, was red. I
could see it, or sense it. He was red. He extracted himself from this red aura
to mount me, and even though he hurt me, and horrified me, I never told my
mother, but I didn't know why for a long time. I only knew that I couldn't
tell, or he would hurt her, too. It was so real when it was happening, and so
vague when it was gone, and it would be another twenty-six years before I
fully remembered and understood what the dream meant.

Over the next week and a half, I had that dream twice. Both times I
woke myself up screaming and begging for mercy. Once my grandmother
woke up with me and came hurrying in to put her arms around me as she had
since I was five. She didn't ask me what was wrong. She knew, even though
I'd never described that dream to her, Dad, anybody, even Steven Effendi.
I couldn't. I didn't know what it was once it was over; I only knew it was
something of which to be deeply ashamed. She held me close and let me sob

and shake until the dream was gone and I was awake again. Then she kissed me and went back to bed, and I went and took a warm shower and tried to go back to sleep.

The second time, Gram was gone for the weekend with friends and I was alone in the house except for Mrs. Gustavson. It happened like it always did. He was just suddenly there, at the foot of my bed, or behind me or on top of me, crushing my chest until I couldn't breathe. I woke up gasping and choking and gagging and sobbing – the usual sorry mess. Until I was fully awake I was five again, wondering desperately where Gram was and why she didn't rescue me. When I finally got my breath back and realized where I was, and that I was alone, I lit a cigarette and went and stood on the balcony and looked east, out over the trees in the direction of the city, smoking and pacing back and forth to get the shaking stopped. I had Steven Effendi to thank for this. I hadn't had this dream for over a year, and now it was back to haunt me. Leave it to a psychologist to over-analyze things back to their deepest, darkest roots.

Dammit all anyway. I'd been annoyed with Kit because of what I viewed as him cheating on Billie. Now, suddenly, I was wrestling with my past. What, who, was this creature? Why did he come upon me? I knew I'd been through a lot of trauma before my dad got to us. I knew Mother had been through just as much. I really didn't want to ask her if she could make anything of the fragments of this dream. It was so shocking and horrible I couldn't bear to repeat even the fragments of it out loud – never could. Gram knew it was a nightmare. If she knew the nature of it she never said, and I never asked, because I was afraid to know. Was I some kind of pervert that I would dream such a thing? Had I actually been through such an ordeal? Probably not, or I surely would have been dead. No five-year-old could sustain punishment like that. Why did I dream this, and get an erection in the process? God help me, why did I dream this? Was I a homosexual? Was I a pedophile?

For the second time in two weeks I presented myself to my father and asked for an audience. He was sitting in his study in slacks and a polo shirt, and a camel tan cashmere sweater, smoking a pipe, and he looked like the poster boy for puissant Omni-competence. I felt like the sniveling, ragtag, bastard son, come to beg yet another boon of him. I was exhausted and confused and it showed in my eyes and my carriage, and I very nearly couldn't face him with the question weighing on my mind.

"You look like hell," he said without preamble, pretty much validating my self-assessment. But...he was the only one I felt I could ask, so I sat down across from him and just took a deep breath and dove in.

"Dad, I need to know what happened to me during the time Mother and I were held prisoner by the Germans. Please. I need to know."

He studied me in silence for a minute that lasted an eternity, then said, "Your grandmother says you haven't been sleeping well. It's a big adjustment, going back to civilian life, and you need to give it some time, that's all. Have you decided on that part, yet? I'd like to start the rest of the casting in another week or two."

I could feel my shoulders sag. He wasn't going to discuss this with me. I pulled a card from the bottom of the deck. "I could ask Mother, I guess," I said, rising from the chair.

"Sit down," Dad said, not loudly, but with absolute authority. "You will not discuss this with your mother under any circumstances, young man."

"She's not my first choice, that's for sure," I sighed, "but, Dad, I keep having this nightmare, over and over for the last twenty damned years and it's always the same. This thing, with buggy blue eyes that look like ice daggers...comes crawling toward me...I think...and he...breathes on me, and he...puts his hands on me, and then he..."

"Stop!" my father said, and when I looked up from the floor where I'd been staring, he was white as a sheet.

"I'm sorry!" I exclaimed, springing out of my chair to his side. "I'm sorry. I just... I'm sorry!" I made a soft sound of utter confusion and discomfort, and he reached over and gave my arm a pat.

"I'm sorry too, Bud. I've spent so many years, trying to forget, you know? I know your mother has. Sit down. When you were six, remember being in the hospital?"

"I'm not really sure I remember it so much as I remember the story. Complications from circumcision?"

"And a story it was, for the benefit of the masses. You were doing a lot of bleeding that led the doctors to think you might have been... inappropriately used. I...please, could we discuss this another time? I'm expecting a call from Toronto, and I do need to prepare myself." He caught his breath, and when he opened his eyes again, he was inscrutable. "Have you decided on that part? I think it's a good one. Give you a chance to spend some quality time in the great outdoors this summer. Location shooting is going to be in southern Utah, by the way, not Arizona."

"Sure," I said quietly, "count me in." I got out of my chair, and went around the desk to give him a kiss on the temple as I left. "I didn't mean to upset you."

"The only thing that upsets me, is that you have any memories of that time at all, Bud. Try to put it out of your mind. It's past. It's over. Consider it fixed and forgotten, like I do, and let's just get on with today's business, hm?"

"Sure," I said, "Thanks, Dad," and let myself out.

So...so. I didn't have a clue what to think. I felt like I was stalled on the train tracks with the car doors locked and me inside. Should I feel better? Should I feel worse? I was still such a tender kid, capable of such shock, and such emotion. It's almost funny, now, but it sure as hell wasn't funny then. That was a much less accepting time. They were still stamping "Illegitimate" on birth certificates some places. People were still riding at the back of the bus because of the color of their skin. Hungry people with money to spend were being denied service because there was no place for them to sit on the black side of the cafeteria. Homosexuality was a crime, literally a crime. And by association, I was a homosexual, or so I felt.

I could feel myself pulling back inside myself as I had in the old days when my English failed me, and I went the same place I'd gone then, to my piano. Twenty years of lessons, and I still felt like a beginner. I had so much to learn. So much to accomplish. I focused on that which centered me best. Gram went on about her life, the staff worked around me as if I was an animated piece of clockwork, and I thought about the music. Only the music. I played eight, ten, twelve hours a day, day after day.

Kit called to check on me, and to tell me he'd been cast as Thomas Jeffords so we'd be working together, and he said he'd heard through the grapevine that the Greater Los Angeles Symphony needed a pianist to fill in for a musician who was taking a leave of absence for six weeks.

On a whim I asked for and received an audition. I was so excited, and so nervous. I made it a point to tell them I was Aloysha Aarons, which was strictly a family name, not Peter Aarons. I'd done quite a bit of acting around town, but nothing that would peg me by face as "an actor", or worse, as Peter Aarons' kid, and that was important to me. I wanted to be just another anonymous musician, on equal footing with everybody else. That way if I won the part, I'd have won on merit alone, and that would mean a lot.

I needed to select a piece to play that was more than three and a half minutes, less than five, and I wracked my brain. Schumann's *Toccata in C major Op. 7* was a flashy piece, but everybody knew it, and everybody played it. I was not a fan of Mozart. I loved Ernesto Lecuona, but nobody took Lecuona seriously these days, and I wasn't yet in a position to change that. I needed to play Rachmaninoff. He was my hero. If I was going to ride to success I wanted to do it on his coattails. I settled on his *Prelude in G Minor Op.23 number 5*. It ran a scant three minutes and forty seconds, but I'd have to take that chance.

On the appointed day I went to the Hollywood Bowl, because that's where they were holding auditions, and I presented myself to the woman who was seated at one end of the first row, checking off names. There were three. Mine was last.

The first woman, who was about forty, played the Schumann piece I'd decided against, and played it well; bit heavy on the pedals. The next gentleman was older yet, fifty or so, and he played Mozart. His touch seemed too light to me, his Mozart a little too wispy, more Bach-like. Both of them were elegantly dressed, which hadn't occurred to me. This was an audition. They were interested in my music, not my wardrobe. I was wearing a nice pair of black slacks and a maroon button up shirt, and I felt suddenly like I was giving the impression I took this whole thing casually, which I didn't.

When I was called upon, I introduced myself, sat at the keyboard, and contemplated the piano. Neither of the other two had checked it out first, and I wondered if I should. I'd already warmed up at home. I didn't need to run any scales to get my fingers limbered up. Still, having thought a few seconds, I began at the bass end of the keyboard and ran every key, checking it for touch and rebound as I checked the pedals. I dropped my hands into my lap and waited for the sound to fade. When it had died away completely, I took a deep breath, asked the ghost of Rachmaninoff to keep me company, and began to play.

For the next three minutes and forty seconds there was nothing but the intricacies of the music – the dynamics, the complexity of Rachmaninoff. God, that man composed like an angel – a possessed angel, mind you, but an angel. Again I dropped my hands until the sound faded, and as I stood up the man in the front row said, "Play something else for us, will you?"

I sat back down again. "Certainly," I smiled. "What would you like to hear, Mister Saucedo?"

"Something a little lighter, maybe a bit more familiar," he said, and the twinkle in his eyes caused me to suggest something that, ordinarily, I wouldn't have.

"How about something by that most excellent gentleman, James P. Johnson? One of the great composers of the twentieth century, and a hero of mine."

He nodded. "Excellent. One of his stride pieces, perhaps? *Carolina Shout* would be perfect to see what you're made of."

"The test piece of the twenties," I chuckled, and turned back to the piano. I knew the piece very well. I played it for fun, and to challenge myself when I was in a mood for ragtime. I saw the older gentleman who had auditioned ahead of me get up and walk out in a huff, but I didn't let it bother me at the time. If he didn't like ragtime, or James P. Johnson, that was his loss, not mine. I just relaxed, and let my fingers fly. Again I turned on the bench to get up, and the two gentlemen gestured for me to stay seated.

"You have a nice touch," Saucedo said. "Are you still in school?"

"No," I smiled. "I've been out about three years."

"I meant college."

He was serious, and I shook my head and tried not to laugh. "So did I. I'm twenty-six."

"And you've been taking lessons for...?"

"Twenty-six years."

"Dad's lap?" he chuckled.

"My grandfather's."

"Been in any competitions?"

"A few."

"Here, or abroad?"

"Both," I said. I really didn't want to go into what had been won and where. This, right now was what was important.

"Win any of them?"

"A few." I'd won most of them, as a matter of fact, and I could see by the look on his face he knew it. Did he know who I was? Who I really was? Did I care? Maybe not. I really wasn't sure. I was not embarrassed by my family's prestige, but I was certainly not going to use it to get my foot in the door.

"Where have you studied piano?"

"Mostly right here in Los Angeles. Some in New York. I had private instructors, and great profs my six years at UCLA. I spent eight summers studying in Europe; one in England, two in France, two in Germany, one in Austria, two in Italy."

"You smile when you say it, but you also sound like you think you've been robbed. Where would you most like to study?"

"Here, Juilliard. Definitely. Worldwide, Russia," I said without hesitation. "The greatest pianists in history, and many of the great piano composers, have come from Russia. Unfortunately, one does not go to Russia for any reason these days."

"What do you want to be when you grow up?" he smiled, and his tone and his beautiful, dancing eyes told me I had nothing to fear from his questions.

"Sergei Rachmaninoff," I grinned.

"We'd best get you started, then," he laughed. "Can you begin rehearsals tomorrow morning?"

"Absolutely," I said. "I thank you, Mister Saucedo."

"You may not be anxious to do that after you've worked under me for a bit," he said soberly. "Mrs. Dexter will give you the address of the rehearsal hall. Be there at eight O'clock."

I sailed home on cloud nine. I opened the kitchen door, bursting with good news, called for Gram, and she answered from the morning room. I found her in her favorite chair, crying softly. Grandmother rarely cried sad tears. Happy tears, emotional tears, often, like I did, but she was a great one for keeping a stiff upper lip. I think it was that 'living through the depression and a world war' thing. I sat down on the ottoman facing her and took her hands in mine. "What's the matter?" I asked, reading her face for a clue.

"Edythe...is retiring. She's given her notice," Gram said. It was half squeak, half sigh, and I knew she was devastated. Edythe Gustavson had been a part of this place nearly from the time it was built. When Gram was a bride, Mrs. Gustavson had been here. When Dad had been born, and Uncle Nate, Mrs. Gustavson had been here. When Uncle Nate had been killed, and then my grandfather, Mrs. Gustavson had been here. After my parents' departure, after Mister Gustavson's departure, Mrs. Gustavson had been here. Even I, who had always found her cold lutefisk, was shocked that she was actually leaving. I'd always imagined finding her dead in the kitchen one day in her stiff grey uniform, and we'd have her stuffed and mounted and put in the dining room next to the china cabinets with a feather duster in her eternally raised hand. Apparently, that was not to be. She was joining her sister in Hawaii. We had four weeks to find a replacement.

Gram was first in shock, then in a blue funk of the worst kind. She smiled mechanically. She ate mechanically. She lost interest in what was going on around the house, or outside it, for that matter. I endured a week of torment, wondering every time I went to work if I was going to come home and find Gram in her favorite chair, clutching her chest. Every day I scooted out of rehearsal with apologies to one and all. No time to socialize. I put off Kit and Tommy as far as the production company went. They were annoyed until I told them what was going on. Then they pitched in and tried to help.

There is nothing quite like three guys in their twenties trying to help, to make a situation like Gram's completely intolerable. We encouraged her to begin interviewing before she was left alone with just me in the house, and she went down to the agency. She returned more depressed than she'd left, and after that, she would have none of it. She was too broken hearted.

I suggested that Mrs. Gustavson do some interviewing for a replacement, and Gram gave that some consideration. Mrs. Gustavson said she would offer an opinion on a new couple, but she would not do any interviewing. She had too much to do to get ready to hand over the reins of this house, and prepare herself to go to Hawaii. The tanning sessions alone were eating up any spare time she might have.

The seventh evening I came home after four hours of rehearsal, a meeting with Tommy and Kit, a read-through for the new film, and a fitting to have shoes made, because in those days finding comfortable size sixteen shoes was absolutely unheard of, and Gram announced that we had company coming for dinner.

"That's great!" I enthused. She was finally coming out of her funk. "Who is it?"

"The Schwartz's, remember them? They have that lovely daughter, what was her name now...?"

"Isabelle," I sighed. It was starting. Isabelle was a nice enough girl, but she was not my type – not my type at all. She was very Jewish, very upper class, very finished. She walked with her severely Anglicized nose in the air as she had been taught, and she laughed like Woody Woodpecker.

Dinner was something to be endured rather than enjoyed. Mister Schwartz was a wealthy plastic surgeon. Mrs. Schwartz was about an inch deep, and Isabelle chatted about all the wrong things. All of them wanted to know what I'd been doing in the military, and I said it was classified. If I told them, I'd have to kill them afterward. They found that highly amusing. They wanted to know what I was doing these days, and I told them I was playing with the symphony for the next few weeks, and forming a production company with Kit Miller and Tommy Sinclair, and Isabelle said she thought Kit Miller was just the most adorable thing. What a lucky girl his wife was. And when was I planning on getting married? *Wink wink.*

"Not for a long, long, time," I said, sipping my wine and eyeing my grandmother. "I want to go back to school, and I still have a lot of wild oats to sow. I don't want to be doing those things and trying to look after a wife and family. Too complicated and risky."

Boy, did I get my butt chewed after they left. "We are never going to get another woman in this house if you're going to take that attitude with them!" my grandmother exclaimed.

"Gram, I don't need a wife, you need a housekeeper! Let's not confuse the two, shall we? Isabelle, for all her shiny caps and her expensive nose job, is not my type. I want a girl..."

"I know, I know," Gram sighed, "like the one who married your father. I suppose you think she's a prize every moment of every day? No. That woman has a temper. That woman is stubborn and self-willed, and when she gets tired of telling you what's what in English, she switches to Russian. What you need, is a sweet girl. Let me check my little black book."

Two nights later, it was the Rosallini's, and their daughter, Melanie. She was shy and pleasingly plump, with big dark eyes and a sweet smile. When I asked her if perhaps she'd enjoy taking in the revival of *Porgy and Bess* downtown, she said, and I quote, "There's so much music in it, it makes it hard to follow, don't you think? Besides, who wants to see a play about a bunch of smelly old niggers and cripples. You don't really like that kind of thing, do you?"

"It's one of my favorites," I said. "But if you don't want to go, perhaps you'd rather go hear Coretta Scott King speak?"

Needless to say, my grandmother had things to say about that evening, too. One of the things she said, was that she'd go hear Mrs. King with me, and we dismissed Melanie Rosallini by mutual agreement.

Sunday night, it was the Goldmans. They had a ten year old son who was every bit as charming as an anaconda, and they also had Nina, who was lithe and lovely and who carried on a very nice conversation about things in general. With her, I got as far as an honest-to-God first date. We went to dinner, and to a play, and afterward we went for a moonlight drive to the beach. I stopped the car on a bluff overlooking the water, and she put one languid arm around me, and as she kissed me just a little too deeply for an introductory kiss and her hand slid down my side into my lap, she said, and again I quote, "I have a friend who was on the UCLA women's dive team. She says you have the biggest dick she's ever seen in a set of speedos, and that's the only reason I'm here." I jumped high enough that there was air between me and the car seat, and when I came down Nina's hand was firmly on her prize. "Oh, my God," she groaned, "fuck me." So I did, but I didn't ask her out again.

That was Tuesday. Wednesday after rehearsal, I was in the employment agency my gram had visited earlier, the one best known for handling all the right domestics for all the right families, and I was serious about finding a couple. The woman I sat down to work with was Mrs. Bartos. She was haughty and vaguely insincere, and so condescending she did everything but pat me on the head and ask how Gramma's little boy was today, but I did not care. One more dinner with Isabelle Melanie Nina Gotcha, and I was going to be in the mental ward.

"Mrs. Bartos, as you may know, my grandmother's housekeeper, Mrs. Gustavson is retiring in a couple of weeks. I need to find a replacement for her, and I would like to find a gardener and general handyman as well. A married couple. Do you have some resumes I can look at, some recommendations you can make? I'd like to get this ball rolling as quickly as possible."

She gave me a dainty porcelain cup of coffee, a handful of file folders, and a few minutes to look them over. None of them read particularly well from my standpoint, but then again, I wasn't the only one in the house. I tried to put myself in my gram's position, and read them again. "Have you found any you like?" she asked upon returning.

"Since these are the ones you handed me first, I'm assuming they're your top candidates. Which ones would you recommend?"

"Mister and Mrs. Osbourne are a fine couple," she said immediately. "They're in their forties, so they are stable and have plenty of experience, yet they are young enough to have many good years of service left."

I resisted the urge to chuckle. I wasn't buying a used car, here. "They look as good on paper as any," I agreed, "Please set up a time when they can come out to the house and meet with us."

They arrived the next day promptly at one O'clock. She was in a severe navy blue suit. He was in a severe navy blue suit. I was in jeans and a sweater, Gram was in her gardening togs. We'd both been out messing around in the roses, and we were busy dabbing hydrogen peroxide on each other when Mrs. Gustavson showed them in. "Welcome," Gram smiled, and they both nodded graciously, but did not smile in return. Their eyes roamed around our plain, boxy house. What they sought, eluded them.

It was a long, long hour and a half. We talked, and we showed them the house and the grounds, but the thinly veiled look of distain with which they'd arrived remained glued to their faces the whole time. They made it clear that they were very impressed with the Aarons name – very. But neither we nor our house were up to their expectations. The main house in Bel Air would have been fine, but this? Well, we did very little formal entertaining. We had no formal gardens. There was obviously wealth here, but no...elegance. They were accustomed to elegance. We thanked them for their time, and the next day I was back at the agency.

I told Mrs. Bartos that the Osburnes were probably wonderful given the right set of circumstances, but for us, they weren't a good match. She got out another handful of resumes, I got another cup of coffee to go with them. This time when she came back and I asked for a recommendation she pulled a file from the stack and dropped it under my nose. "The Lagervahls," she said, "definitely. A most efficient couple, and more rugged than the Osburnes."

He was big and red faced, with piercing blue eyes that made me immediately uncomfortable for some reason. She...if she'd whipped out a Viking helmet and a brass brassiere, it wouldn't have surprised me a bit.

"You have been a long time without a man's hands on this place," he said as we showed him the grounds. "These gardens need a thorough cleaning out. So many brambles. Such an unkempt look."

"Many of those vines are the kinds of things birds love," my grandmother smiled. "They provide shelter and food."

"And places for vermin to hide," he said. "This oak tree nearest the house should come out before it falls over and kills someone."

"I built this house next to that tree," Gram said, still smiling an inscrutable smile that reminded me of Dad. "It was here first. Actually, I'm hoping it does fall over some night about twenty years from now and that it crushes me in my sleep. It would be so nice to die in the arms of an old friend."

Lagervahl made an odd sound through his nose. "And you," he said, turning those eyes on me, "what is your function here?"

"I am Mrs. Aarons' grandson," I began.

"I know who you are," he responded, "I asked you what it is you do."

"I spend most of my time tethered to that piano in the living room."

"I see," he said. "I assume you do not pound that thing when people are trying to sleep."

By the time we got back in the house Mrs. Lagervahl had every single cupboard and drawer in the kitchen open and was evaluating what we ate, even as she was beginning to prepare the meal that was part of the interview process. It looked white, and heavy, and German – like Mrs. Lagervahl. "No wonder you are thin," she said to me. "You don't eat enough starch." She smiled and gave my forearm a pinch. "I'll fatten you up."

I did not tell her I was one of those people who had a hard time keeping my weight up. I just smiled a little and shook my head. "Thanks, but I have no desire to be fat," I said. "I jump rope, I swim, I lift weights, I run, to stay trim. My grandmother is very active as well. We value foods packed with nutrition, not calories."

"I see," she said with grim disapproval, and we began the death march through the house. "These floors are a nightmare to take care of. We should carpet over them. What are they, anyway?"

"Teak," I said. "Hand rubbed teakwood. Sawn especially for this house."

"I don't do teak, hand rubbed or otherwise," she said firmly. "I don't do windows, and if those bird feeders stay on the porch, I don't clean up what's under them, either. Who takes care of this monstrosity?" She was looking at my beloved Steinway.

"Mrs. Gustavson keeps it polished. Other than that, nobody touches it but me, or my grandmother, or maybe Kit Miller once in a while."

"I see," she said. "Good. I trust you don't pound it at all hours of the night when people are trying to sleep."

I pointed to the antique Persian carpet under the piano and asked, "How would you clean that?"

"I would not," she sniffed. "I don't do area rugs."

She didn't do windows, or teak, or bird leavings, or general shopping except for the groceries she needed to cook. If the list she'd given us in preparation for today had been any indication, just the shopping would be a full time job for her. She would manage the off-site staff, but reserved the right to hire and fire at will.

He didn't do pools, or wash cars. He would oversee the landscape, but he expected to have underlings come in and do most of the work. He would need a new pickup every two years. His wife would need a new station wagon every two years. Their quarters were marginally acceptable on a temporary basis, as long as nobody pounded that piano at odd hours of the night when people were trying to sleep, but they did expect the chauffeur's quarters over the garage would be expanded into the adjoining space and refurbished to their specifications in a relatively short time. They were religious people and required every Sunday off. They knew we were Jewish, and would tolerate it. They assumed I didn't have loud parties with my hoodlum friends. I said no, but my grandmother had a lot of them – both loud parties and hoodlum friends, and I never played the piano after two or before four in the morning, except on special occasions. Was that going to be a problem? The meal, which Gram and I laughingly referred to as 'death by white sauce', didn't make me fat, though it did make me a little sick, and Gram stayed pretty close to the bathroom for a whole day afterward.

The next time I walked into that employment agency, I was pissed. "Please," I smiled through my teeth, which I was rapidly grinding to nubs, "Let me have all the files. All but the ones you've shown me in the last two visits. *All* the files."

Mrs. Bartos produced the rest of the files, yet another cup of coffee, this time in an earthenware mug which she banged unceremoniously down in front of me, and left me alone for about forty-five minutes.

There was one file that absolutely glowed, and when she returned I dropped it under *her* nose for a change, and asked her why in the world she hadn't shown me these people in the first place.

"They may look fine on paper," she said, "but in the flesh, they do not. Let me show you some others."

"You have shown me others. There were the Osbournes, who would prefer something with a moat, thank you, and the Teutonic terrorists. I want to see this couple."

"They're not suitable."

This was the oddest attitude I'd ever encountered, and I think it was beginning to register on my face and in my voice. "He has an AA degree in Landscape Management. She's an excellent cook with a strong background in nutrition..."

"Mister Aarons," she said with some exasperation, "this is not a suitable couple for a prominent household. To be blunt, she is a southern Negro, which I suppose is acceptable enough in itself, but she...does not seem to know..." she groped for the politically correct phrase..."exactly what her place should be. He, is a Mexican. They have these two very young mulatto boys who are going to be an embarrassment to the household in which they grow up. As a couple they are an embarrassment. She has this terrible accent that makes her sound like that ignorant pickaninny in *Gone with the Wind*. They both have this...attitude that seems to say that they think the world owes them something, and they are not suitable to be employed anywhere, much less in an aristocratic old household like yours."

"Is it that they're not suitable for employment, or just that they don't suit you?" I asked with equal annoyance. These were the best resumes I'd seen, and they were being dismissed out of hand because of how they sounded and what color they were? The comment Nina had made about my...endowments...came back to me with a rush of blood to my face. It had stung – it really had. I didn't like being labeled, judged, dismissed, used...there had to be a word for this feeling of impotent outrage...and I was guessing others didn't like it, either. Admittedly, the kids would probably be the kicker, but I was going to interview them anyway, just to piss this arrogant woman off. "They're young, their educations look good. I'd at least like to meet them."

"Not them," she said. "If you wish a colored staff, we have such people. Ones who know their place in a prominent home. Ones who are not so...." She trailed off.

"Uppity?"

"This is not something to be joked about, Mister Aarons. They have absolutely no experience!" Mrs. Bartos exclaimed, and her voice was loud enough to turn heads.

"With you for an agent I can see why," I smiled sweetly, batting my lashes at her. That signaled the breakdown of civilities.

"She's washing dishes and he's picking oranges and that's as it should be. I know you think you're helping your grandmother, Mister Aarons, but do let older and wiser and cooler heads prevail here."

"Mrs. Bartos," I said firmly, "I am a grown man, and a reasonably successful one in my own right. You need not look out for me, nor for my poor little old grandmother. These people are being discriminated against, pure and simple, and I am not about to dismiss them out of hand. I am going to interview them at a time that is convenient for them, when she is not washing dishes and he is not picking oranges. Do not ask either of them to take time off from work...oh, never mind," I sighed, reading her face, "give me their phone number and I'll call them myself. Don't worry, I'll see that your agency gets its damned cut if I hire them."

"They have no phone," Mrs. Bartos said with obvious satisfaction. "They check in with me. From the way they look and the way they smell, I think they live in a tent somewhere, or in their car, like gypsies or migrant trash. Since you're bound and determined to embarrass yourself, be my guest. Here's the address of the greasy spoon where she works. You can catch her after five. Just ask for Gloriosa Daisy Ruiz. For Godssake, who would name a child such a thing?"

"Probably the same kind of person who would give a kid a middle name like Aloysha," I chuckled, by this time thoroughly amused. "Tell me, why do you have these people listed with your agency if you find them so undesirable?"

"We pride ourselves on being open minded about such things," she said, and, hysterical as it seems, she was dead serious.

"Oh," I said, totally bemused. I took the address she ripped off and thrust at me, and let myself out the door into the afternoon sunshine.

I didn't go home. The restaurant was half an hour from me in the opposite direction, and it was nearly four O'clock. I figured if I could catch her just before she went on shift I wouldn't have to interrupt her work and

possibly get her in trouble with her boss. That much, I knew from the Army.
I drove until I was fairly close to where I needed to be, and then I parked
and got out and walked around, giving this some real thought. Why was I
setting up this interview? Was it because I was serious about the possibility
of hiring these people, or because I was being defiant? Where would we
house a couple with two children? What would my grandmother say? Was it
worth the hassle of getting these people's hopes up only to dash them again,
and if I liked them enough, was I willing to go the distance to see them hired?

Admittedly, I wasn't particularly impressed with my forthrightness
of late. I had let the thing with Kit gnaw me nearly to the bone before
confronting...no, approaching him with my concern. When I explained to
him how deeply I felt about what I viewed as infidelity, and how much his
friendship meant to me, he took me in his arms, and kissed me on each
cheek, Russian style, and said he'd never, ever do it again. He was sorry.
Then, we'd gone out for a couple of drinks, and in an hour we'd been as close
as ever, if not closer. I'd done it with Kit. I'd stated my concerns and gone
to the mat for what I believed. If I had to do it again, at least I'd had recent
practice. Really, I just wanted this over with so I could go back to playing
the piano in peace. I was loving every second of playing with GLAS, and
when I was invited to stay for jam sessions, or to go out for coffee and I had
to refuse because I had to be about my grandmother's business, it galled me.
But I did want the very best for Gram, and I was determined to find them, no
matter where they might be hiding. Maybe they were hiding in the guise of
people with children; people who lived in their car.

About twenty minutes before she was supposed to go on duty I went
into the restaurant, a dark place with a bar at one end and too much smoke
even for me, and told the bartender I'd like to meet briefly with Mrs. Ruiz
before she started work. He blinked at me momentarily, placing the name,
and then jerked his thumb toward a set of swinging doors at one side of the
bar.

"Oh, you mean Glory. She's already here. Pulling a double shift this
week for a guy who's out." He looked at me more closely and added, "She's
not in any kind of trouble, is she?"

"Not that I know of. Why do you ask?"

He shrugged. "She's a nice lady, that's all. She's in back there if you want to talk to her."

"Is that okay?" I asked.

"Sure. Make it quick." He glanced at his watch. "She's due for a break in a half hour or so, but she may have plans. Better touch base with her, just in case."

I nodded, and eased myself through the swinging doors into the kitchen. I'd seen enough Marx Brothers movies to know one could get walloped with those things. It must have been ninety degrees back there, and as I approached the big sinks, the humidity increased to a nearly unbearable level. I walked up beside a very tall, very black girl swathed in a big white apron, and asked if she was Mrs. Ruiz. She turned her head to flash an absolutely dazzling white smile at me without turning from the sink, and nodded, "I am Glory Ruiz. Can I help you?"

Her voice was like cream in coffee – very soothing, very southern – nearly as beautiful as she was. She was sweating like a horse, but by then I was beginning to do likewise, and I wasn't standing with my hands in hot water. "I'm Bud Aarons. I was wondering if you and your husband were still interested in maybe finding a position in a household."

"And give up all this?" she laughed, and I liked her instantly. "Yes, we are."

"Would you be interested in interviewing for..." about that time a busboy came roaring up with another tray of dishes that threatened to tumble into the sink, and she was quick to steady them. "You're due for a break soon, or so says the bartender. Could you spare me a few minutes at that point?"

"I surely could, Mister Aarons. They make a good cup of coffee here. Not as good as mine," she winked, "but passing fair. You get you one of those, and I be out as quick as ever I can."

I took her advice and sat at a table in the corner near the kitchen, sipping coffee and mopping my face. In about twenty minutes she appeared, taking off her apron to reveal a house dress that was faded, wrinkled, and scrubbed nearly through to keep it clean. I stood up as she approached, and she held out her hand to me. Her grip was firm, and very warm. "Thank you for waiting," she smiled. "Where would you like to talk?"

"Here is fine," I said. "Would you like something to drink?"

She looked uncomfortable and shook her head. "I...no. Thank you. Would you mind if we went outside? I do so enjoy a little air between shifts."

"Whatever," I smiled. "We can go out front and walk a bit if you'd like."

"Best we go out back," she said, and gestured toward the kitchen doors. "I can't afford no talk to my boss, and goin' out front with a nicely dressed white gentleman could just bring some on, I'm sorry to say."

"And I'm sorry to hear it," I said, embarrassed not to have been worldly wise enough to realize the situation. I just smiled, and followed her out into the alley.

She was carrying a paper bag, and when we were outside she gestured at it apologetically and said, "I do need to have a bite while we talk. I don't get but fifteen minutes, and..."

"Please," I said.

"We have preferred seating right over here," she said, gesturing toward a couple of trash cans, and so I parked on one, she parked on the other, and then she opened the bag. It contained table scraps which at first I assumed she'd gleaned from the plates coming back, but she saw the look on my face and shook her head. "This ain't what you think it is. The cooks, they make mistakes, and I get 'em sometimes. Tell me who it is you represent?"

I decided she was probably as comfortable as she was because she didn't know I was a potential employer. If I asked her any questions at this point, I was going to maybe embarrass her. I'd never been in a situation like this before, and I wasn't sure what to do. "There's a family up in the Santa Monica Mountains. A grandmother, grandson team. They have a nice place, nothing fancy, but lots of work, nonetheless. The grandson thinks he's a musician. The grandmother is an avid birder, loves a yard that looks like a jungle."

"My Rafael, he loves birds. Loves all the little critters that come around, squirrels and such. He knows which plants each of 'em likes. He'd enjoy workin' with your grandma."

I could feel my face flush. "I didn't mean to deceive you, I just..."

"I was settin' on a garbage can eatin' scraps, and you was afraid of makin' me feel bad about what I was doin'. That be right considerate, Mister Aarons, but let me tell you somethin', just so's you know. I ain't ashamed of what I'm doin'. It be honest work, and when I can eat discarded bits, that's just a little more food that I can take to my babies and my husband. Right about now Rafael's eatin' oranges to the point he ain't never gonna have scurvy, but it be somethin' to fill his belly. He bring home fruit and vegetables when he honestly can, and we get by that way. Ain't no shame in bein' poor. There's shame in bein' dirty, or indolent, and we ain't neither one of those things."

"No, you're not," I smiled. "And both of you have a dynamite resume'. I'm amazed somebody hasn't snapped you up."

"Are you really?" she twinkled. "Funny, you don't look all that naive."

I just burst out laughing and shook my head. We chatted a bit more, I set up a time for her to bring her husband and come out to the house, drew her a map on her paper bag, and when I walked out of that alley, I was determined that, one way or another, Glory Ruiz was going to be my housekeeper. Maybe not Gram's, unfortunately – but mine.

When I walked in the door Mrs. Gustavson was all over me in a hot second. "You are not bringing a colored mammy and her pickaninnies into this house!" she said in a voice so angry it rocked me back on my heels. "How dare you even consider the possibility! You young people and your equal rights trash. People who are not equals should not be treated as such! I told your grandmother that very thing when she decided to take *you* in, and this just proves my point! She was ill, literally physically ill when she found out about your mother and you. But because she is a charitable woman she did her duty and took you in and let you use the family name. Put up with all your screaming and hiding in corners like a little animal! She tried to raise you properly and give you an education, gave up her own life to make a home for you after your parents chose to leave you behind, and this is how you repay the humiliation she went through because of you, by bringing even more humiliation on this house? For shame!"

I stood there, trying to swallow my heart, gather my scattered thoughts, get over the feeling she'd punched me in the stomach, find my voice again. Finally, with a rather too obvious gulp I managed, "I assume Mrs. Bartos called?"

"Of course she did. She knew your grandmother would not stand one second for such foolishness. Now you go find her and you apologize to her."

I stood there a moment more, then I drew myself up, looked her straight in the eye and said, "And when I come back, you may apologize to me, Mrs. Gustavson. What you said was unwelcome, and unwarranted. You judged me twenty years ago like you are judging Mister and Mrs. Ruiz now. They don't deserve it, and neither do I."

"You didn't get half what you deserve, you arrogant little bastard," she said, and marched off in the direction of her quarters.

I stood there blinking angrily at the tears in my eyes. Why should I care what she thought of me? I knew good and well who I was, and that I was my father's flesh and blood, didn't I? The fact that I was a bastard was certainly no surprise. I'd been born six years before Mother and Dad married, and everybody knew it. But all those years when Edythe Gustavson had put a plate down in front of me, when she'd changed my sheets or ironed my shirts or put clean towels in the bathroom for me, she'd begrudged me the effort. It wasn't that she was distant, after all. It was that she disliked me and thought I was a usurper and a user. I looked at my hands and realized that they were shaking, betraying my emotion when my eyes and my voice did not.

I looked for Gram for a bit, and found her upstairs on the balcony, reclining on a slatted mahogany chaise, peering with binoculars up into the huge oak under which she lay. "Who's doing what in the neighborhood today?" I asked, folding onto the cool concrete beside her.

"Mother Robin is feeding her brood, as usual. She and her mate feed them an average of a hundred times a day. Did you know that?"

"Yes, but only because you taught me long ago. Gram, I met the most wonderful woman today. I think she and her husband are going to be just perfect for this place. She's honest and straightforward and strong willed. Her husband loves plants and birds and timid woodland creatures in general. I'm really, really impressed."

"These are the people who have the two little boys, right?"

"Right. But I'm sure I can work that out. I've been thinking about it. It would take some quick cleaning and refurbishing, but we can put them in the old chauffeur's quarters, at least temporarily. We could put up a fence that wouldn't even be seen from the main house, so the boys can't escape and roam freely off into the pool or wherever. We wouldn't even know they were here."

"What a good plan, Aloysha. I see you've given this some thought. Are these the same two people who are colored – and not the same color?"

I was careful to keep my voice light and level. "Right again."

"And what plan do you have for that particular contingency?" She hadn't moved the binoculars from her eyes, and without being able to see them, I couldn't really know what she was thinking. Her voice was calm enough, but then it usually was, even when she was contemplating mayhem.

"I didn't think I needed a plan to cover something like that. They are what they are. I wasn't thinking about dyeing them to match, if that's what you mean."

"Aloysha, they have two small children, that's strike one. They're unfortunately matched, color-wise. That's strike two. They have absolutely not one shred of experience in California, and that's strike three. I'm sorry. I won't consider them."

"I'm sorry too," I said quietly. "Glory is a lovely person and I think you'd like her a lot. I have no way of contacting them to let them know not to come tomorrow afternoon, so you'll have to indulge me at least that far. If Mrs. Gustavson wants to be gone, I will understand. Even if you want to be gone, I'll understand. I'll interview them for the sake of courtesy. And I did ask her to prepare a meal because she's supposed to be a gourmet cook. And that will be the end of it."

"Thank you for being so reasonable," Gram said, and put down the binoculars to give me a kiss on the cheek. She looked into my eyes, I into hers, and we both knew – this was war.

We opted for dinner in the morning room, as we often did, and when Mrs. Gustavson banged my plate down in front of me, Gram looked up in surprise. I gave her the slightest shake of my head, and when Mrs. Gustavson was safely out of earshot I said, "She feels like I've put you through enough in the years I've been here, without bringing a troop of colored people into the house. She really does think she has your best interests at heart. I can't fault her for that."

My grandmother scowled. "She told you that?"

I just shook my head. "What's done is done. I know Mrs. Gustavson is under a lot of pressure because of retiring and getting ready to move after almost fifty years. It's all right, Gram. Really it is."

We ate for a bit in silence, and I could feel the food sticking in my throat. The silence was awkward, and I wasn't sure why. Was it the Ruiz family, or was it Edythe? I probably shouldn't have mentioned anything at all about her speaking to me. In trying to smooth things over, and sort things out, I'd made them worse.

"What did you ask this woman to prepare?" Gram asked rather abruptly. "Whatever it is, Edythe is going to have a conniption."

I stopped playing in my green beans and mushrooms and said, "I asked her to do her best with whatever she could find in the fridge."

"That's quite a challenge for someone who doesn't even know her way around that old kitchen."

"I know, but...I get the feeling this girl is used to thinking on her feet. Besides, she only had fifteen minutes between the two shifts she was working, and I didn't want to ask her to come up with a menu and give me a shopping list and eat her own supper all at the same time. She was hot and tired, and she still had a hell of a lot of dishes left to go."

"How old are these boys they have?"

"Two, and four I think. When she talks about them, she just lights up, you know?"

"I wonder what she does with them during the day. Your father and your uncle Nate were two years apart. Pass the butter, please. What does she look like, the red bandanna, the big chest, the..."

"...stereotypical black housekeeper?" I teased. "No. She's very tall for a woman – about Mother's height, I'd say, and she's big, but she's not fat. She's...well, she's an Amazon is what she is. Pretty, though, with really jet black skin and hair."

"Not that I care, mind you. I'm not in a mood to consider a couple with so many strikes against them."

"I understand perfectly," I intoned, and realized I was cutting my Beef Wellington into tinier and tinier bites rather than putting any of it in my mouth.

Gram realized it about the same time. "Aloysha, the object is to eat that, not worry it into oblivion," she said, pointing casually with her fork. "I talked to your father today about our dilemma. I thought maybe he'd have a solution, or a suggestion, or maybe he'd pull a couple out of his hat, like rabbits. After all, he stole Max and Coco. He owes me."

"Did you tell him that?"

"Of course I did," she snorted. "Surely you don't think I'd keep so high a card hidden in my hand. By the way, when's the last time you played bridge?"

"Serious, go for the jugular bridge? Not since you and I played partners against Mother and Dad that night...when, last year just before Thanksgiving? Can it be that long ago?"

"I may be lining us up some patsies," she grinned, and about then Mrs. Gustavson reappeared from the kitchen.

"Mrs. Aarons, would you like anything else?"

"Yes," Gram said, "I'd like you to tell me what passed between you and my grandson. He is upset, but hardly forthcoming. Is there a problem I can help with?"

"Gram, please," I said, flushing uncomfortably. "It was just a few words between acquaintances of long standing. I don't even remember what was said, and I'm sure she doesn't either. I think we're all a little upset by the changes about to take place."

Mrs. Gustavson had been watching me out of her cold blue eyes, and when I was finished she folded her arms and said, "I do remember what was said, and I'll say it again, since I'm leaving, and if it will make more of an impression on you this time, Master Aarons. Your attempt to bring racially inferior people in here, thinking they could possibly do my job, is demeaning to me, and to your grandmother, who has been through entirely too much on your behalf as it is, and who knows better than to think a colored person, can reason like a white person. You put Mrs. Aarons through hell when your alleged father brought you into this house, and I do believe, given the opportunity, you will do it again, which reflects very clearly the sort of..." she paused, groping for just the right adjective. It eluded her. She shook her silver bunned head and snapped, "...the sort of person I have always considered you to be."

Grandmother had dropped her fork and was sitting there like Edythe had fired a shot across her bow, and I hastened to say, "Perhaps the charity my grandmother showed me, despite questions about my bloodlines, impressed me enough that I want to pass it on to others who might also benefit. I can't think of a lovelier person to work for than Gram, can you? Or a more beautiful spot to raise a family than right here in this old bird house of ours. You're not being replaced, Mrs. Gustavson. Nobody could ever do that. But you are leaving, and I'm trying my level best to keep my grandmother happy during this difficult transition. I hope you understand."

"I understand better than you think I do," she said quietly. "I just understand more than servants are supposed to. That's probably why you want a nigger in here."

I squeezed one eye shut and thought about that one, but it made no sense. As she turned on her heel to leave, I said, "As part of her interview tomorrow, Mrs. Ruiz will be cooking a dinner from whatever is available in the refrigerator, so if anything is off limits, please label it as such and group it on a shelf."

Mrs. Gustavson looked right through me to my grandmother, who was still sitting bolt upright and dumb at the head of the table. "Are you going to allow him to do this?" she demanded.

Gram blinked a couple of times and reentered her body from wherever she'd been. "Allow? Of course I'm going to allow it. We had Mrs. Lagervahl cook. We'd have had Mrs. Osbourne cook if the interview had gotten that far. Mrs. Ruiz is being interviewed as a cook, it only makes sense that we have her cook. What on earth is the matter with you, Edythe?"

"I have served you for forty-eight years," she said through her teeth. "I helped you shape this household and raise your sons, I gave my life to this house and the people in it, even that *boy* there, and now he's bringing in some ignorant female with big, dirty black hands..." she turned abruptly and walked out, eyes brimming with tears.

"I didn't mean to hurt her," I murmured. "I honestly didn't mean to hurt her, Gram. I just want to find someone really nice, and really competent. Maybe even somebody who cracks a smile every now and then. I know you don't want these people interviewed, and I appreciate you backing me anyway. I'm so sorry if this is causing you pain. I never meant to cause you pain, even when I was little and cried and screamed and hid in corners all the time. Did I really do that?"

"Hush, heedless one. I'm going for a walk," Gram said. "Try to stay out of Edyth's hair while I'm gone, will you?"

Hush, probably meant, yes, and I was embarrassed. I nodded, and after I'd helped her with her chair and she'd taken her leave to prowl the nature trails around the house, I went into the living room and sat down at my Steinway, losing myself and my troubles in the music I needed to know for tomorrow's rehearsal. What a beautiful piano it was – a full concert grand – top of the line. My gram and my parents had given it to me when I'd received my master's degree. This piano, my piano – had been played by Sergei Rachmaninoff. He had used it extensively during his years in New York, and it had been shipped to California...for me. Surely I was the luckiest of all men in the world to have people who loved me so much. I played, and as I played in that expansive living room in my beautiful home at my million dollar piano with an antique Persian carpet under my custom shod feet, I wondered about Glory and Rafael Ruiz, and where they were sleeping, and what they'd had for dinner, and what hope they were holding out for tomorrow as they lay together talking in the darkness.

For the first time in the weeks I'd been playing with the symphony, the conductor yelled at me for not concentrating. We had a concert in three days, and I was off wool gathering. I'd missed my cue to solo by half a beat. I was chagrined, and I said so. He accepted my apology, and when we had a break he asked me what was bothering me. I gave him a brief sketch of the problem, and when he gave me an odd look I remembered – nobody knew who I was. Probably not many of these people had problems with their staff.

I could have kicked myself. Well, I sighed silently, the damage was done now. Perhaps it was to my credit that I wasn't into deceiving people.

I focused extra hard for the next couple of hours, had lunch and did paperwork with Kit and Tommy, went home, and collapsed for a nap before my interview with the Ruiz family. Mrs. Gustavson was conspicuously absent, and, to my disappointment, so was my grandmother. The fever was flaring up again. I could feel it in the ache of my bones, the dryness of my eyes, and the distant roar in my head. It made me think of Bobbi Bates. I wondered where she was, and how close she was to mustering out, and if she'd really come see me in Los Angeles.

I awoke with twenty minutes to spare, and after a quick shower I went downstairs for something cold to drink. When I opened the refrigerator, it was empty, and I do mean empty. There was a partial half-gallon of milk, a package of flour tortillas and some eggs, a block of cheese and some butter, some cold drinks...half a jicama that had definitely seen better days, a cabbage...and three apples. Period. No meat, no fresh vegetables, no salad greens, no nothing. I was vaguely amused, but I was also outraged. It was all too obvious that Mrs. Gustavson wanted Glory to fail, and that she wasn't one bit afraid of crossing me to make her point. I wondered if Gram had checked the fridge before leaving for parts unknown.

I had little time to brood. Promptly at two O'clock there was the sound of an engine, and an old Chevy pickup with an ancient, rusty camper on the back came laboring through the opened gates and up the drive. I stepped out and gestured them into a parking spot, and I could see they had the children with them, riding up front with Mom and Dad, and all eyes. The man who bounced out of the driver's side was lithe and handsome, and half a head shorter than Glory. He opened the door for her, then turned to me and extended his hand, saying, "I'm Rafael Ruiz."

"I'm Bud Aarons," I smiled, appreciating the firm grip, noticing the clean, work-roughened hands. "Welcome to our home. My grandmother is off someplace this afternoon, but I'm more than capable of doing the honors. Glory, welcome. I see you brought the boys."

"We have no choice," she said. "We don't know a single soul here, and we not leavin' our children with strangers."

"I don't mind a bit having them here," I said quickly. "Bring them in if you'd like."

"They go to work with me every day, so they're used to sitting," Rafael said, "but thank you." He looked around, and his arms spread with his smile. "What a beautiful spot. The gardens are lovely. Like a big park to be enjoyed by all who enter."

"Including the deer," I chuckled. "They've been doing an excellent job of keeping the shrubs clipped this year. As a matter of fact, they've been doing too good a job, and none of the sprays the off-site staff uses seem to help."

"You need to try something a little more low-tech," Rafael laughed, and I liked him.

"Such as?"

"Pee on them."

I burst out laughing. "You mean just..."

"...hose 'em. Yup. Drink lots of water, or cerveza, or coke, and go around and urinate on the shrubs. The deer hate it. Another thing that works is to get human hair clippings from your barber and spread those around. Adds new meaning to the term, organic, doesn't it?" His healthy white teeth flashed in his good natured face, and I could picture us working in the roses together, and telling jokes. "But you know, it doesn't pollute the water table, it doesn't kill the bees, or the birds. We're just now figuring out that all this stuff we've been spraying is rising up to bite us. Simple ways are best for all concerned." He turned to the bigger boy, who was sitting on the front seat next to his sleepy brother. "Royal," he said, "You take good care of Titus, and if anything goes wrong, you give us a toot on the car horn, okay?"

"Okay," Royal smiled, and his father shut the door gently, so as not to disturb the baby.

"Come in," I said, and it felt much more like I was inviting friends than getting ready to interview strangers. "Are you really sure you don't want to bring them along?"

"If we let them come along, they'll get used to it, and they'll want to come along all the time," Rafael sighed. "Our hope, dream, goal, is to get settled out here with a house and permanent employment before Royal starts school. My parents followed the crops with us kids, and we were sent to school, but it was tough – so many schools in a year. My mother's whole kitchen was a cast iron cooking pot with a hand whittled wooden spoon, and my whole life was in a castoff suitcase we salvaged from a dumpster behind the Goodwill. They loved us a lot, but I don't want that kind of life for our boys."

"Mister Aarons don't care about that," Glory said very quietly to her husband, and he flushed slightly and glanced over at me as we walked.

"Sorry. I didn't mean to rattle on. I just don't want you to think we abuse our children."

"Never crossed my mind," I said firmly, and opened the kitchen door, gesturing them through. I watched Glory's face as she surveyed the room with its high ceilings and antiquated cupboards – cramped in spots, expansive in others – like many very old kitchens whose function had changed over the decades. She ran her hands lovingly over the wood, and the marble counter tops, and I prickled all over with annoyance at the remembrance of Edythe's comment about dirty black hands. She didn't sniff disdainfully as Mrs. Osbourne had done, or lay everything bare as Mrs. Lagervahl had done. She just...made friends with it, a bit at a time.

Rafael and I watched her unselfconscious movements, and he whispered, "It's a woman thing, Senor Aarons. She'll snap out of it in a few minutes."

I just nodded and smiled. "Would you like some coffee? I can make a fresh pot, or there's soda in the fridge." I remembered my earlier pilgrimage and said to Glory, "You really don't need to cook for us this afternoon. Someone got a little over-zealous about cleaning out the refrigerator, and to tell the truth, there's not a thing in there."

Glory turned from what she was doing and smiled her straight smile. "May I?" she said. She reached for the refrigerator door, looked inside, top to bottom, then opened the freezer compartment and moved things around a bit. "There's plenty here," she said. "Won't be real fancy, but it'll give you some idea 'bout whether or not I can burn water. Unless you don't want me to cook for some reason."

"Absolutely not!" I laughed. "Pull off a miracle for us. I'd love to see it."

"Jesus done it with some little loaves of bread and a couple tiny fish. I can surely do it with what's here. I'll just set a thing or two out to defrost if that's okay with you."

"For today, it's your kitchen," I smiled. "Oh, sorry. I offered you coffee and then didn't move to make any, did I? I'm not thinking clearly."

"You runnin' a fever," Glory said casually, opening the cupboard which contained the coffee. How did she do that? Find the coffee and see the fever? "Fever make you feel dull. You let me do this. What you takin' for that, anything?"

"No," I sighed. "I picked it up a few months ago overseas, and now it just comes and goes at will. The doctor said it would for a while."

"Got some suggestions for an herb tea that'll make you more comfortable while it's flaring up like this. I'll put a note on the fridge. How strong you like your coffee?"

"Just to where you can stir it before it eats the spoon handle," I chuckled, "but you make it however you folks like it."

"Sounds perfect," Rafael laughed, and pointed out the window. "The robins love that shrub, it's *Myrica Californica*, isn't it? Pacific Wax Myrtle? And what a beautiful specimen. Great choice for that spot, being on the resistant side of Oak Root Fungus."

"Right you are," I said. "Gram tried for a long time to get *Myrica Pensylvanica* to grow there – just a regular old Bayberry, but I guess it's too warm here for it, or not humid enough, or something. She settled for its California cousin instead."

We talked for nearly an hour before we ever left the kitchen, and in that time Glory went through the cupboards and found the things she'd need for dinner, set them aside, took the cabbage, the apples, and the Jicama – did some chopping and some grating and some slicing and added something out of a little can in the cupboard, then herbs or spices from the rack, and set the salad, or so I assumed it was, back into the refrigerator. I took them on a tour of the house, and when we got to the living room I pointed to the Persian carpet and said to Glory, "How would you clean that?"

She put one knee down beside it, and ran her hand across the surface.

"This is in excellent condition! I believe, I'd use the vacuum hose with a soft brush on the end, and go over it in all directions real gentle like and then smooth it back down. Carpet sweeper might be all right, too. Wheels might leave tracks. I do believe...I'd ask an expert first." Her eyes twinkled up at me, and I was in love for life with these people, their youth, and their enthusiasm. As she stood up she ran her hand over the ebony finish of the piano and said, "You play this." It wasn't a question, but I nodded anyway. "You are a fortunate child," she said. We were children, all of us, but too young to know it at the time.

We went on walking and I took them upstairs, explaining as we went about the house and when it had been built, and what the various materials were, and I asked them questions, and their answers told me that they knew how to care for these things, and valued them for what they were. We stood on the balcony and looked out toward where their pickup was parked, and I could see that both little boys were asleep on the seat. I pointed out the boundaries of the property, and the network of nature trails my gram had had put in forty years before. "She's a good steward," Rafael said quietly. "I'm sorry I won't get to meet her."

My heart just sank. He knew, didn't he? "She'll be home," I said firmly. "She's probably out doing some more stuff to get Mrs. Gustavson on her way to Hawaii next week. I left for rehearsal early this morning and she was out watching the birds, I guess, and I didn't get a chance to talk to her about our schedules. I am sorry."

"It's a lovely day," Glory said. "It's a lovely day, no matter what comes of it."

Just then, as if in answer to an unspoken prayer, either theirs or mine, Gram's Mercedes sedan came purring up Sweet Sage Trail and turned into our drive. "Told you so," I grinned, and we went downstairs to greet her.

She had packages in the car, and some bags of groceries, but no Mrs. Gustavson, and even as I was introducing Glory and Rafael to her, they were just automatically, gracefully helping her with the bags and making their way back into the kitchen. "There," Rafael said abruptly, stopping in his walk and jerking his chin in the direction of the swimming pool, "that shrub just coming into bloom, what is that, Mrs. Aarons?"

"That's a native lilac," she said.

"It's beautiful. What does it attract, butterflies, hummingbirds?"

"Both. The real hummingbird magnet is this *Lonicera Sempervirens* right over there around the corner, but it's wanting to die back on me, and I'm not sure why. Put those down and come with me, I'll show you."

They began this animated conversation, dumped the bags unheeded on the kitchen counter and charged back outside like kids in a candy store, leaving Glory and me looking at each other and laughing.

"She bein' very gracious," Glory smiled. "It was kind of her to bring these here groceries."

I sat at the table which occupied one corner of the kitchen at that point in time, and contemplated this young woman who was laughing and confident, yet quiet and intuitive at the same time. I realize now, of course, that when I first met Philippa, it was like meeting Glory all over again, and that was quite probably part of her attraction for me. I was never actually in love with Glory, but I certainly loved her deeply and sincerely – like a sister or best friend I guess – right from the beginning, which at that point, seemed dubious indeed. "You...pretty much have this figured out, don't you?" I said, watching her make a fresh pot of coffee.

"I have lived with the color of my skin all my life, Mister Aarons. It don't rub off, nor wash off, nor wear off. It belong to me, and all the complications, and the determination that have to go with it, they belong to me, too. I been lucky. I had lovin' parents, and a solid bringin' up. I found me a man who love me...Lord, he love me so much...that he don't see the color no more, and that's how it should be for all of us. But I got eyes. I see how the world looks at us all slant-eyed and judgmental. That Mizz Bartos, she does everything but hold her nose when we walk in, and we ain't dirty. I got no way to iron right now, and we a little wrinkled, maybe, but we clean. We don't stink."

"No, of course you don't. I know what you mean about Mrs. Bartos, though. She looks at me basically the same way," I chuckled. "Only she looks at me like I need my diaper changed. Like I'm a snot nosed kid."

"You are a snot nosed kid."

"I'm older than you are," I sniffed.

"Uh huh," she grunted.

Even then, that was Glory's expression. By turns it means you're right, you're wrong, I'll think about it, I won't even consider it, or bullshit, depending on the context of the conversation and her position in it.

"Still, you just a young one, like me and Rafael. Takin' chances come easy for you, 'cause you got a lot of 'em left to spend, just like me and Rafael do. But you grandma, she don't have so many left no more. She gotta think about what others gonna say, and maybe do to her, or to you. Takin' us under your wing could just get you hurt, you know. And whose nose gonna turn up all disdainful when they find out who workin' here? She gotta think about havin' children on this place again, and runnin' all over underfoot. Lots of things to think about. Like eyeballin' stones for a wall. You gotta decide, they gonna be right for makin' a wall, or are they just gonna make a heap and be somethin' you gotta get rid of again? That kinda thinkin' take time. Especially when somebody you got a long history with, fightin' you hard."

"How are you figuring all this out, are you psychic, or what? And if you are, where do I keep losing the contact lens for my left eye?"

"Full refrigerators tell a tale," she chuckled, "so do empty ones. No poverty here, so it ain't that. You asked me to come and cook, and I didn't figure you for the kind to play mean jokes. Mrs. Aarons brought the groceries, so it ain't her doin'. That leave your housekeeper, who I'm visualizin' as whiter'n Sunday's linen and older'n proverbial Methuselah? That's a hard place to be comin' from, and lookin' down the pike my direction, seein' me and my ilk as maybe the future for this house."

"She's the proverbial dog in the manger, is what she is," I muttered. "She wants to be replaced by somebody just like her, only not quite as good."

"You don't like her much. How long she been here?"

"She was here when I got here twenty-one years ago. If she's ever smiled at me, I don't remember it. As you well know, all this talk about tolerance is fine, but being tolerated isn't comfortable."

She just nodded. "You got folks?"

"Sure. They live down in Bel Air with my baby sisters. I opted to stay with Gram, and she was gracious enough to keep me."

She gave me an appraising eyeball and asked, "Got here from where, exactly, may I ask? You English is real clipped, like it ain't you first language."

"It isn't. My native language is Russian. Now *your* version of the English language is unlike anything I've ever heard. Where are you from, exactly, may I ask?"

She knew I was teasing her. "I, am Gullah," she said with a most formal nod. "You ever heard of the Gullah people? Some calls us Geechee, but nobody knows just why. They's a couple hundred thousand of us yet, livin' mostly on the little sea islands 'round Georgia and South Carolina. It be real pretty there," she sighed. "Anyway, Gullah language is the blendin' of twenty-eight African languages. We got no gender in Gullah, and no plurals, and so sometimes I got 'em when I talk English, and sometimes I don't, dependin' on where I am in my mind some days. I'm not ignorant, though, and I'm not uneducated. In fact..." her speech changed dramatically, and she went on with, "...if I slow down a great deal, like this, and do a studied impression of Eliza Doolittle, I can sound like most any mainstream American. But it is extremely difficult to maintain, much like speaking a foreign language in which you cannot yet think, and it makes me feel as though my body has been taken over by aliens." She let out a whoosh, and set both of us laughing.

"I am more impressed by the minute," I said.

"Thank you kindly, sir. Now, I'm gonna take them two some coffee, since they gonna be out there until sometime in July. What does you Gramma take in hers?"

"Two teaspoons of half and half in a mug, one teaspoon in a cup."

I let Glory out the door, and she followed the voices around the corner and out into the gardens while I went back to pour two more cups of coffee for us. I'd just turned around with them in my hand when there was a timorous knock at the kitchen door, and I opened it to find a young man about thirty inches tall standing there. I squatted on my heels so he didn't have to look skyward, and said, "Hi. What's your name?"

"My name is Royal Rafael Ruiz and I'm going to be four years old in July," he said, extending his hand to me. "I didn't want to blow the horn and wake up the baby, and I need the bathroom real bad."

"I'm Bud Aarons," I said shaking his hand and trying not to laugh aloud at how damned cute he was, "and the bathroom is right this way." I walked him quickly down the hall and gestured toward a door. "There you go."

"Thank you," he said, beginning to dance just a little. "Could you please unfasten the straps on my overalls, because I'm running out of time here."

"You betcha," I chuckled, doing as he asked, and he scurried into the bathroom and closed the door.

I walked into the kitchen, and found that Glory was back with Rafael and Gram, and those two were rolling out one of the garden charts while Glory began working on dinner. "I poured us some coffee," I said, gesturing toward the cups on the counter, "but I was distracted by the arrival of a young man who needed the bathroom."

"He was supposed to blow the horn," Rafael grimaced. "I'm sorry he bothered you."

"He didn't want to wake his baby brother," I smiled. "It's not a problem. My best friend has a two-year-old," I added, not wanting him to think me completely ignorant, "so I'm more or less familiar with the species."

Royal reappeared about that time, little red and white striped shirt, little blue overalls with one strap fastened, tiny tennis shoes peeking out from underneath, big, sober brown eyes taking everything in. "Thank you for the use of your bathroom," he said to me. "I used some of your soap to wash my hands, I hope you don't mind."

"You're always welcome to soap in this house," I smiled, crouching to look him in the eye. "Is there something else you would like, a glass of water or a little snack of some kind?"

"A drink, please," he said, "then I need to go back to the car."

"Introduce yourself to this nice lady," Rafael said, indicating my grandmother, who had turned from the garden charts to study him in the late afternoon sunlight which streamed in the kitchen window.

He looked surprised to see yet another stranger. Then he smiled, walked over to her, extended his hand and said, "I'm Royal Rafael Ruiz, and

I'm going to be four years old in July."

"I'm Esther Cyprienne DiPirelli Aarons, and I was sixty-nine in March. I'm pleased to meet you," she smiled, and shook his hand. "Have you been in the pick-up all this time?"

"I'm used to it," he said. "We live in there. It's nice. I feel safe there."

"Did you say your brother is in there asleep?"

"He's in there," Royal shrugged, "I hope he's asleep."

"You're a very bright young man for only three years old," Gram said, patting the chair next to her. He climbed up into it and sat looking intently into her face. "How did you get to be so smart?"

"I'm almost four, and I pay attention," he said, "and someday when I can read better, I'm going to read all the books in the whole world. I have to go now, thank you." He climbed back down out of the chair, drank his glass of water, and, politely refusing my assistance, let himself back out the door and ran toward the truck.

"I should check on Titus," Glory said apologetically. "This will cook itself for a few minutes. Will you excuse me?"

"Absolutely," I smiled, and my grandmother nodded.

"Glory," she said, "bring the boys in here for a bit, will you, please? I think between all of us we can keep them corralled."

"Certainly, Ma'am," Glory smiled, and followed after Royal.

Gram shot me a look of pure annoyance. She was slipping, and these folks were politely stomping her fingers. I asked Rafael to excuse us for one second, and beckoned Gram to one side. "Where is your ray of Scandinavian sunshine?" I asked.

"Gone," Gram sighed. "It's just you, me and the temp service, kid."

"Aw, Gram, I'm sorry," I whispered. I was both stricken, and tickled to death. "I didn't mean to push her over the edge or anything, I truly didn't. I know you wanted a chance to say a real goodbye...."

"Oh, we said a real goodbye, all right. Aloysha, this isn't your fault. I thought it was, but now that I've met these people, I can see that it's not. You really do have an eye for quality. Not that I'm planning to let you hire them. I'm not. They're not a matched set, and the neighbors would just have a fit. My bridge club would have a fit. The gang from the Audubon Society would have a fit. Your father would have a fit. In short, everybody we know, and some we don't know, would have a fit. I'd never hear the end of it. The society pages would have a field day at our expense, and you know how your father hates that kind of publicity."

"I understand," I murmured, "and I've been thinking. I'm twenty-six years old. It's time I was out on my own, and I don't give a rip what people think. I know I should, but the fact is, I don't. So...I'm thinking I could get a place of my own, and hire Glory and Rafael, and then you could borrow them one at a time so nobody would know they were a couple."

"See there? I just don't understand why people say you're an *idiot*," Gram snarled, and went back to where Rafael was pouring over the list of shrubs and perennials.

Glory returned with a milk chocolate confection of a baby in her arms. Titus waved himself into his father's lap, and from that vantage point smiled shyly at my grandmother, who played coy games with him as she was going over the high points of the landscaping with Rafael.

In another half hour Glory was getting nervous, and after she'd set the table for two she said, "I am real sorry, but we need to be gettin' on. It's near dark, and the headlights on the pick-up don't work none too good sometimes. Now, what's in the oven'll be ready when the timer goes off. There's a salad on the table to go with it, vegetables steamed and set aside here, and a dessert in the fridge. I am sorry not to be here to clean up, but maybe Mrs. Gustavson'll be kind enough to do that for me."

"I'm sure she will," my gram smiled. "Glory, Rafael, this has been a real pleasure. And I've enjoyed meeting you, too," she smiled, indicating the boys.

Royal walked over to her, looked up with his big, serious eyes, and said, "Thank you. I liked it here. I felt safe."

At that point I got a lump in my throat, and pretty nearly didn't get it cleared out before we got to the aging truck. "You know," I said, "there's not a bit of harm in going just up that hill right there and parking in the trees. We're the last house on the road. You wouldn't be disturbing anybody."

"Thanks," Rafael said, shaking his head, "but we need to be on about our business."

"Well, don't despair," I smiled, opening the door for Glory. "Gram and I are a little way apart on this yet, but she likes you very much, and all we have to do is..." I slowly brought the palms of my hands together, and the two of them nodded.

I wanted to offer them the simple luxury of a hot shower, or a bath for the boys, or the washing machine, or the ironing board. I wanted to ask them to stay for dinner with us, but I knew...any of those things would be inappropriate. They would be viewed as charity, so with rare good grace I kept my mouth shut, and watched them go down the drive and off into the gathering dusk.

CHAPTER THREE

That really was a fabulous dinner," I said, looking over the morning paper at Gram, who was just coming through the kitchen door from her morning birdwatching expedition. "Artichoke and spinach quesadillas, jicama salad..."

"Don't start," Gram warned. "I feel bad enough as it is. Yes, it was a wonderful dinner. No, I'm not hiring them. Just having that truck come up the road got us half a dozen inquiring phone calls."

"We could buy them a new truck if they came to work for us," I said, sticking my nose back in the business section. I wanted to ask her why in the hell she would care about such things. Why would she go with me to hear Mrs. King speak, and then not hire a black woman of obvious quality? Who were all those people she'd rattled off the other day as being outraged if the Ruizs were hired? The neighbors? I knew how much regard she paid the neighbors. Most of them had built on land she'd sold them in the first place. We didn't have to keep up with the Joneses – we were the Joneses.

The bridge club? The Audubon Society? I knew Gram better than that, too. People we didn't even know? What ramifications could be bad enough to dissuade my iron-willed grandmother from doing what she wanted? Of course she'd also named my dad, and in that, I could see some possible merit. Maybe she just didn't want to name him outright as the fly in the ointment. I'd wondered when she was going to give in and tell my dad what was going on, and now I could guess why she hadn't. Still, when things got serious, my father could be counted on to do what was right. In that I had full confidence.

Gram had been right with my dad at the forefront of efforts to get us out of the hands of the Germans. While my grandfather was trying to hush things up and get some of the dirt swept under the rug, Gram had been employing a master forger to create documents for us. I wanted to ask her more about that time, but Mrs. Gustavson's words haunted me. Maybe Gram had burned herself out on that particular front. Maybe she thought the children would be too much to contend with. Whatever her reasoning, it was beyond my comprehension, but it was her home, and it was therefore her decision.

"Never crossed my mind to nag," I said as placidly as I could. "I mention it only because I ate the last of the quesadillas for breakfast, and now we are officially without sustenance. Actually, I think getting two dinners and a breakfast out of one cooking is pretty good, don't you?"

"I said, don't start, Aloysha, and I meant it. Have you exercised yet this morning?"

"I ran right by you going up the hill this morning," I said, forcing a smile. "You were staring up into one of the pine trees over near the bluff. I didn't want to holler and scare away your subject. Why do you ask?"

She shrugged. "I don't usually find you reading the paper first thing, that's all. Did you make this coffee?" She sniffed it, poured herself a cup, and sat down at the table with me.

"Um hm." I put out the cigarette I was smoking and picked up my coffee cup. I'd made yesterday's coffee, too. I wondered with some amusement if it had even registered with her that someone had to do such things.

"That was a silly question, wasn't it," she said, as if reading my thoughts. "We're the only ones here." Her tone was wistful, and I knew that despite their rough parting, Gram missed Edythe very much. "It's really quite good. I didn't know you could make coffee. Did Mrs. Gustavson teach you?"

I raised an eyebrow and shook my head. "Geneva Miller taught me. She also taught me how to use a washing machine and a dryer, and how to peel a cucumber so it isn't bitter, and other such impressive stuff."

Grandmother just sighed. All things domestic escaped her, and not just because she'd never been exposed to them. Household duties both fascinated and terrified her in a way that the rest of us, including my father, found amusing. If Grandfather had suddenly found himself penniless, he'd have had a beautiful wife to comfort him, but a messy house and an empty table to come home to.

"Speaking of which, you were very impressive in concert last night, and I'm not the only one who thought so. You need to defy your father a little more than you do and concentrate on your music, Aloysha. Don't let him make an actor out of you if you do not want to be one."

"I'll take it under advisement," I said, resisting the urge to burst out laughing. I could defy Dad, but I'd better not defy her. Dad felt just the opposite. I, for one, had no real desire to cross either of them, but, much as I dreaded it, I was about to. "I have to go out for a bit this morning. Should I stop and get some groceries, and what do I get? Have you ever eaten one of those TV dinners? Maybe they'd be something..."

"Just...stop," she said firmly. "The temp service is sending someone over at eleven O'clock. Let her deal with it. Are you going down to the studios?"

"No. We meet with our lawyers tomorrow. Today I'm going on over to Malibu."

"Meeting with Tommy?"

"Not exactly," I said uncomfortably. "He told me about a place that's for sale out there – it's near the water, quite a bit of acreage – nice sized ranch house and some outbuildings, a barn and corrals, a foreman's house. I've arranged with the realtor to take a look at it. It's really not too far from here."

I heard her coffee cup hit the table a little harder than usual, and the paper began to smoke from the heat of her gaze. "Peter Aloysha Aarons..."

"Gram, listen," I said reasonably. "I've given this a lot of thought. I'm a grown man. I can well afford a place of my own. You're still a very active woman. You'd probably like to have company in without having to arrange with me to stop beating on my piano so you can hear each other talk. You could throw wild parties and have loose men hanging around. It would be nice for me to have a place of my own where I could play my piano all night, and have wild parties and loose women..."

"And hire Glory and Rafael?" she interrupted. "That's what this is all about, isn't it?"

"Not true … exactly. I've thought about this for the past four or five years. I should be making my own way in the world, not living off my grandmother."

"Did Edythe Gustavson have something to do with this? Because I can assure you that I loved you from the day I heard about you, Aloysha. The fact that you had some problems was to be expected, and I never thought anything about them. I loved having you here."

"And I have loved being here."

"But?"

"But..." I sighed, "I think perhaps the time has come when we are on a collision course, and I don't want that. You are far too precious to me, Gram. I'd rather move out and get a place of my own than stay here and drive a wedge between us. I won't be that far away. You can come see me, I'll come see you, I promise. Did I tell you, the symphony has asked me back to help with the young people's concert series? I'm really excited."

I'd been focused primarily on the paper while we talked, and when she didn't respond I looked up again. She had tears in her eyes. I dropped the paper and reached for her hand, which she pulled back beyond my fingertips. "I truly don't understand," she said quietly. "I guess...of all the things in my life I thought were immutable..." she turned her face toward the high windows and studied something outside rather than looking at me. "I guess I've taken you for granted, haven't I? I've assumed you'd always be here. I've always assumed that even if you married, you'd live here. This is your house, you know. Has always been, will be when I'm gone. The bird house will always belong to you and your children. I suppose even that is foolish. I've always assumed you felt the same way about it that I do." She made a soft, deprecating sound. "Well, you know what they say about assumptions making an ass out of you and me. I am sorry, Aloysha. I didn't mean to chain you here against your will."

She was overreacting, of course. I needed to tell her that, but I wasn't sure how without sounding condescending. "Why don't you come with me to look at this ranch property?" I said. "Maybe getting out of the house would do you some good. It's a beautiful day. We could have lunch at the beach before meeting the realtor. Come with me, please."

Much to my surprise, she did. It was a nice drive, and we had time to chat. Because she was hurt and I was male we judiciously avoided anything we really needed to talk about, but the physical proximity was comforting.

The house sprawled effortlessly across high ground overlooking the pacific, framed by wind-tossed trees and fragrant sagebrush. It was beautiful inside. It had been designed by a master architect, and, truth be told, it was much more livable than Gram's house. There was an eight stall barn with hay storage and tack rooms and a big arena. The foreman's house was a nice little three bedroom job just up the hill from the barns. I could have my big, bald-faced buckskin here instead of stabled someplace out in the valley. Here, I would have a private music room, rather than sharing the living room with Gram and her guests. This house was built for living rather than entertaining. The gardens were a delightful blend of the wild and the domesticated. I could open the window in the master bedroom and let in the sea breeze, and listen to the roar of the waves below. I could ride my horse down to the beach. To this day I kick myself for not buying that place on the spot, but...I didn't.

I thanked the realtor and told him I'd be in touch later in the day, put Gram in the car, and headed for home.

"You should buy it," Gram said rather abruptly. "It suits you, and Buck would love it."

"I know," I replied. And that's the only thing I said the whole way back.

When we got home there was a big van parked partway up the drive near the tennis court, and a crew of three men in coveralls was busy in the wild meadow. Two of them were grubbing out the tender young plants, and one was spraying the wild blackberries and the native shrubs. "Oh, my God!" my grandmother cried, and before I could get the Benz completely stopped she had stumbled out and was running over to them. "What are you doing?" she demanded. "Stop that! What are you spraying everywhere?"

The man with the nozzle shrugged and gave the end of it a little sniff. "Dunno, lady. But it's sure as hell guaranteed to kill all this brush and shit you got all over the place." He turned the thing on again, and my grandmother began to cry hysterically.

"Stop!" she sobbed. "Oh, please stop! My birds will die! Oh God, who told you to do this terrible thing to my home?"

He turned just a little too slowly, waited just a second too long to shut the thing off again. "The crew that regularly comes out here? They said you had some things needed removing, but see now, they heard you got a greaser giving orders out here, and they wasn't gonna take orders from no greaser, so they sent us."

He gave her a look that was almost a sneer, but by then I'd gotten the other two guys stopped and spun back around to where he was confronting Gram. He looked at me, and his stance softened just a little. I was bigger than he was, and I was obviously furious.

"And just who would *they* be, exactly?" I growled, and my voice was deep enough to startle both of us. "There is going to be hell to pay for this, and a great deal of money. Our gardening orders have stood for years with your company. No herbicides, no pesticides. Who put you up to this?"

"Nobody put us up to anything," he said sullenly, "and I don't like your accusations. We was just doing what the other guys said needed doing. This place is a stinkin' mess with all these weeds. It made sense to poison them. Nice house like that, and a yard full of weeds and crap."

My grandmother was sobbing hopelessly against my shoulder and I forced myself – physically forced myself – not to reach for that guy's throat with my ham sized hands and just squeeze until his eyes bugged out. "Where in the hell have you sprayed this shit?" I grated. "Is there anything we can put on it at this point to reverse the damage? This place is a haven for songbirds. They'll..." I stopped and chewed my lower lip. "Where in the hell have you sprayed?"

"I'll show you," one of the other men said quickly, and Gram and I walked with him over nearly three acres of precious meadowland – so carefully cultivated to encourage birds to feed there and sing their songs of love – sprayed irreparably to death. "That's it," he said at last, and I could see that my grandmother was physically ill.

"Go." I said. "Just...go." and they went. Quickly.

I took Gram up to the house, eased her into her favorite chair, grabbed the phone, and called the number on the side of the van. Arthur Antrim's secretary answered, and I told her I needed to speak to Art, pronto. He answered, smiling, and I proceeded to tell him what had happened, and what had been said.

"I just don't understand what happened," he groaned for the fifth or sixth time, but by then, I was beginning to. Edythe Gustavson, is what had happened. Who else would have called the regular gardeners and told them about Glory and Rafael? Art said he'd be right over to see what he could do in the way of damage control, and that he'd be having some words with a few people, and I thanked him and hung up.

"Gram?" I said softly, and she turned listlessly from staring out the window.

"So," she said. "All of the curse and none of the blessing."

"Hm?" I put on the tea kettle and then sat on the ottoman at her feet.

"All of the curse and none of the blessing," she said again. "I turned those lovely people away because of what inconveniences might come of having them here, and this is my punishment. This was done because someone vindictive thought they were here, and yet if they had been here, none of this would have happened."

I just took her hands and kissed them. She was quite probably right, but I wasn't going to say so. "Maybe Art will have some suggestions as to how to fix this," I said soothingly. "Let me make you a nice cup of tea, hm?"

She just shook her head and went back to staring out the morning room window toward the patio. "Our summer will be full of death," she said. "My beautiful, innocent friends, who count on me for food and hospitality will die. Oh, Aloysha, I think my heart is going to break!"

She began to cry again and I sat on the arm of her chair and took her in my arms and wondered why, at times like these, there was so damned little to be done. "I suppose we should think about supper," I said at last, and reluctantly, but I knew I had to get her mind off her gardens and her birds, or her broken heart might become a terrifying reality.

"There was supposed to be somebody here from the temp service to help us," Gram sobbed angrily. "There should have been someone here."

I got up and walked into the kitchen to call them, pretty much convinced of what they were going to say.

"Nobody would go, Mister Aarons. We heard such horror stories about that Negro woman you supposedly hired, and in a supervisory position! I'm glad to hear that didn't materialize. I'm sure I can convince someone to come and help you tomorrow, now that the scare is over."

"And who told you these stories?" I asked evenly, already knowing.

"Let's just say your former housekeeper had some serious concerns. After all, it was her household for many years."

"It was, and is, my grandmother's household," I said quietly. "You owed her the courtesy of showing up as you said you would."

"Believe me, Mister Aarons, it was not my wish to leave your grandmother without domestic help, but the stories..."

"Vicious stories spread by a disgruntled and racist employee should never have been given one moment's consideration. In light of that, don't bother sending anybody tomorrow."

"What do you mean?"

"I mean," I growled, "you're fired. All of you."

"Mister Aarons," said the very reasonable voice, "Our service has provided domestic help for your family for the last twenty-five years."

"And someone else will do it for the next twenty-five," I snapped, and hung up the receiver. I turned to where Gram was sitting and said, "I'll find another temp service in the morning. I promise."

"It doesn't matter," she said quietly. "Nothing matters."

I stood in the kitchen and looked at her sitting there, rigid and distant, and I began to understand that she had been the victim of a rape. Suddenly, I was frightened for her, and would have called my dad, or our doctor, or Steven, but she read my mind and told me to leave the telephone alone – she was fine. Then she got up and wandered outside, and before long Art's truck came up the drive, and she walked slowly to meet him and with his arm around her they walked as people do through a cemetery – sadly, respectfully, purposefully – and I joined them in their silent march.

That evening lasted a hundred years. We found a meadow lark, dead on her nest. The darkness came and stayed. Art had dashed any hope of a quick fix for Gram's beloved meadow, and she sat mourning and staring into the darkness beyond the casements.

I was playing the piano, of course, because it's what I did when I was sad, or happy, or energetic or tired. It was what I did. It spoke, and spared us the trouble. "I wonder," I said at long last. "I...Rafael talked about so many low-tech things to do to make the yard a safer haven. I wonder if he'd have any weird, low-tech solutions for this."

Gram just shrugged, enervated beyond speaking. A few minutes later she kissed my temple and wandered upstairs to bed, looking frighteningly old and frail.

I got up at the crack of dawn and made a pot of coffee, and went out to the big freezer and rummaged around and found some bagels that looked pretty good, and brought them in and warmed them up and tried to arrange them attractively with some butter and jam, hoping to give my grandmother a ray of hope this chill and drizzly morning.

She came downstairs in her robe, which wasn't like her, and when she was seated at the table with a cup of coffee in her hand she said without looking at me, "You win."

"Hm?"

"You win," she said with some annoyance. "This sort of thing is what I was worried about if we hired the Ruizs, and we already have it. We may as well have them, too. You win."

I rested my elbow on the table, lips against my knuckles, and contemplated her for a while in silence, trying to think of something to say that wouldn't make things worse, or more hopeless, or drive a wedge further between us. "Gram, do you...blame me for what happened yesterday? I'll understand if you do, but..."

"Actually, I hadn't thought of that," she said, "but now that you mention it, you are a handy scapegoat. You are the one who brought those people into our home in the first place, aren't you?"

I just nodded, feeling a little sick inside. The fever was squeezing me again, which wasn't helping things any. I closed my eyes for a moment and took a deep, steadying breath. "If you do not absolutely want and desire the Ruizs to come here and take care of this household, I will not ask them. The only reason I asked them here in the first place is because I thought they could make you feel happy and secure. I thought we could go anywhere, do anything, and not worry about this house or these grounds. I still feel that way."

"What about the house in Malibu?"

I just shook my head. "When we drove in here yesterday afternoon and I saw what those men were doing...I knew...this was the most precious place in the world to me. I think it always will be. And you will always be precious to me. We're a team, Gram. This thing with the Ruizs wasn't meant to be a contest with a winner and a loser. It was meant to be a situation where everybody won. We had the couple of our dreams, and they had a beautiful place to raise their family. There wasn't supposed to be a loser and now there is. God," I said with sudden frustration, "how did this happen? Did I cause this?"

"No, Sweetheart," Gram said, and got up from the table to come and hug my shoulders. When she put her cheek against my forehead she pulled back and gave me a searching look. "I don't think that stuff they were spraying yesterday did you any good. Have you taken anything for that fever?"

I just shook my head a little and smiled. "Nothing I take does any good. Glory said she'd leave a note on the fridge – how to make an herb tea for this – but I don't see it."

"Better go ask her, then," Gram smiled. "And while you're at it, offer her a job, will you?"

"You sure?"

"I'm sure. What time does she start work?"

"Around five," I smiled. "Gram, thanks."

"You're welcome," she replied. "When the employment agency opens we'll call them and let them know we're officially offering the Ruizs a position here. Until then, I want you to go lie down."

"I should go outside and help you..."

"No. End of conversation. At least stretch out in your easy chair."

"As you wish," I said, tossed down a couple of aspirin and took my coffee into the living room. I'd gotten my way. God, that sounded so petty even in my head, but still, I wanted to spray-paint it on a wall someplace. I'd gotten my way. I knew, I really did, that this was a decision that would affect us the rest of our lives. Had I known then just how deeply it would affect us, I would have been dumbstruck. As it was, I was delighted, and between catnaps I counted the hours until I could tell Mrs. Bartos that the unsuitables were coming to live with the unconventionals.

When I called her, promptly at nine O'clock and told her we were hiring the Ruizs, she sniffed and said they were no longer available through her agency.

"What?" I gasped.

"I said, they're no longer available."

"Why is that, exactly?" I asked, amazed and appalled. Gram looked up from her garden charts, and I gave her a puzzled look and shook my head her direction.

"They are no longer listed with this agency. They had a little accident, or so I hear."

"What do you mean a little accident?" I snapped. "Are they all right? What kind of an accident?"

"That...*thing*..." I could see her gesture and her delicate shudder, "they drove around in caught fire, or so I understand."

"Oh, my God," I murmured. All I could think about was those little boys in that rusting deathtrap. "What about their children, are they all right – according to what *you* hear and what *you* understand?" Why did I have this sudden urge to start killing people who annoyed me?

"Mister Aarons, I really don't know, and to be brutally frank, I don't care. In order to be listed with this agency one must have transportation. They do not have transportation. They are no longer listed here. Is there anything else I can do for you this morning?"

"Yes! You can..." I thought of whom I was representing, and what I'd been taught about *noblesse oblige*, and bit off my words. "No, thank you," I said, and hung up.

"Aloysha, what is it?" Gram asked, eyes big over her reading glasses.

I told her, and she collapsed limply into her chair at the kitchen table. "All of the curse and none of the blessing," she said yet again. "If we'd hired them right off the bat..."

"Don't go second guessing yourself," I said firmly. "We'll find them. If it had been a real tragedy of any kind like losing one or both of the boys, it would have made the paper someplace near the front page. I didn't see anything like that, did you?" Gram shook her head. "Still, there has to be a police report. Maybe it will tell us something." I picked up the telephone again and dialed the Highway Patrol office closest to us. There was absolutely nothing. Not in a half dozen more tries did I find anything. One of the people I talked to suggested that perhaps the vehicle was parked, not moving, in which case there would be no report. If they had no insurance, either...

I hung up and sat rubbing my face in frustration. "I'm going down to the place she worked," I said rather abruptly. "Glory's work was really important to her. She'd be there, or she'd call if she could." If she could. It drummed in my feverish, uncomfortable, worried head. How had Mrs. Bartos known? Glory or Rafael had called her. Had to be. They'd probably told her where and how they were, but I knew she wasn't about to tell me, bitch that she was. I gave Gram a kiss, said I'd be back, grabbed my jacket, and headed out the door.

"I have things to do," she called after me, "so if I'm not here when you get back, don't worry."

"Well, don't do anything stupid," I hollered over my shoulder, and it still echoes in my mind as one of the dumbest things I've ever said to anyone my whole life.

It took me over an hour to get to the place where Glory worked, and by then it was nearly noon. Lunch crowd was settling in. My eyes grew accustomed to the dimness, and I spotted the man I'd talked to the first time I'd been in there. I caught his attention and motioned him to the end of the bar. "I don't know if you remember me," I said. "I was in here the other day to talk to Glory Ruiz."

"I remember you," he said.

"I...have you heard anything about them being in an accident? I called the agency..."

He nodded. "Glory called me to say she wouldn't be in, that she'd have to give up her job without giving notice. She felt really bad, but she said they had no transportation. That old truck burned to the wheels, I guess."

"Was anybody hurt?"

"I guess her husband burned his hands pretty bad trying to get some of their stuff out. She said otherwise she'd find a way to get in to work, but she had to take care of the boys because of his hands."

"Did she say where they were?"

He shrugged. "Not really. She said they were staying with friends out near one of the orange groves, but that could just be pride talking. Didn't want sympathy. You going to try to find them?"

"No," I said firmly. "I'm not going to try. I'm going to find them, and offer them the job I should have offered them a week ago. When did she call?"

"Yesterday morning," he said.

"Do you know for whom he worked, by any chance?"

"Bluebird, maybe? Bluebell? Blue something, I think." Someone hailed him from down the bar, and as he turned away he added, "Good luck. I hope you find those folks."

I thanked him and went back to my car. What to do next? There were a lot of orange groves around LA in the nineteen sixties. A lot of orange groves. Where did one begin to look for migrant workers? They were everywhere and nowhere. I sat a bit in the car, and smoked a cigarette and racked my brain, which kept announcing its intention to go to sleep on me. I needed to know who Rafael worked for, and I knew Mrs. Bartos knew. It had to be in their paperwork, didn't it? I could find a pay phone and call her. And then she'd most likely hang up on me. Going over her head was not an option, unfortunately. I could drive over there and confront her, and she'd say she'd already thrown away their information, and I'd be out forty-five minutes I could have used more productively. Driving around blindly wasn't a good option. Dad probably had some insight, but then I might, when I told him what I was up to, get a lecture instead, and I didn't need that in my state. Kit was working. I called Gram, but she wasn't home, and I wondered where she was. Stocking up on TV dinners, maybe. Or counting dead robins.

I'd had an early breakfast, and not a big one. I should probably stop for lunch, but something was pushing me – not urgently, but steadily. It was raining and chill, and those people with those tiny boys, were homeless. I put another coin in the phone and called Tommy. When I told him what was up, he suggested that I call one of the big produce distributers, or drive down to the market section of town and ask some questions. He asked me if I needed some company, and when I said no, he wished me luck and told me to call him back if I changed my mind or got hung up one way or another.

I wasn't that far away, so I took his advice and went down into the market, weaving the Benz in and out through the lug nuts of the big rigs, dodging fork lifts and dollies in the narrow streets. It was kind of a colorful place, really, moving with an entirely different pace and purpose than the rest of the city. I glimpsed a bright orange and blue sign mostly hidden behind an eighteen wheeler, and found myself, quite by God's mercy, at the citrus exchange. I parked my car and went inside. It was a rabbit warren of little offices and narrow hallways and people scurrying around, and I began to feel a little silly. If I could actually flag one of these souls to a halt, what was I going to ask?

I got my opportunity when a small man in shirtsleeves with a balding head and half steamed glasses looked up from his desk and blinked a smile at me. "Need to be loaded?" he asked.

"Uh..." I had to think about it a moment to realize what he was asking me. I looked like a truck driver? I wondered for a moment what a truck driver, a stereotypical truck driver looked like, and realized I was definitely not at my best mentally. "No. I'm trying to locate a farm, I think. Bluebell, or Bluebird, or somesuch. They raise oranges."

"Ummm," he said, looking absently around his desk. "Blue Duck?"

"I honestly don't know, but I'm trying to locate somebody, and I think he works there."

"You with immigration?"

"No. God, no. I don't want to make life hard for anybody. I have a job for this guy, and I'm having a helluva time finding him. But I know he was working in the oranges a week ago, and I think it was for someplace with blue in its name."

"I hope you got a lot of patience," the man chuckled. He gave me directions to Blue Duck Farms, told me who to ask for, wished me luck, and sent me on my way.

By now the drizzle had turned to a cold, steady rain, and I was glad of both the heater in the car and my warm leather jacket. I got off the highway at the appointed place twenty miles or so out of town, and was almost instantly in a maze of orange trees, shining in rain-washed brilliance. I drove a few more miles in winding sameness, then saw the sign for Blue Duck Farms and turned left onto a gravel road. That road took me up and behind a hill to a complex of packing sheds, and a building that had the look of an office about it.

I walked in, and smiled at the woman behind the desk. "My name is Bud Aarons," I said. "I'm trying to locate Rafael Ruiz. I believe he works for you."

She just looked at me, and I wondered for a minute if she spoke English. She looked American in a WASP sort of way. She had gum in her mouth, and I noticed that she chewed side to side in comic little ellipses like a sheep or a goat. "Herb!" she bawled suddenly, "Herb, get outtheah!"

A corpulent gentleman in a white, outdated suit wedged himself through the doorway and gave me a look that was not particularly welcoming. "Whaddya want?" he demanded.

"Just a moment of your time," I said quickly, wondering at the hostility. A thought struck me. "I'm not with immigration or anything. I'm looking for someone I believe works for you, Rafael Ruiz? His wife applied for a housekeeper's job with us..."

He snorted. "You sure you're not looking for Jesus Lopez, or Pancho Ramirez, or Speedy Gonzalez?"

"No," I frowned. "His name is Rafael Ruiz. His wife's name is Glory. They have two little boys..." I made a vague, thigh-high gesture, but I'd already lost him.

"Never heard of him," the man said, gave me a wave of dismissal, and waddled back the way he'd come.

"Sorry," the woman shrugged, cracked her gum and busied herself with some paperwork.

I stood for a few seconds, realizing I'd been brushed off and wondering why. I went back outside, leaned against the car, and lit a cigarette, trying to collect my thoughts. The rain had let up, and the smell of the orange groves was pleasant. I let my eyes wander over the place, and from around the corner of the building I'd just been in, a lanky, blond haired man appeared. He caught my eye, pointed further up the road, and then disappeared again. I was intrigued, so I got in the car and drove up the hill until I was out of sight of the sheds and the office, pulled over, got out, and waited.

In a few minutes he appeared behind me in a middle-aged Ford pickup with the farm's logo on it. He motioned me over to the open window and said, "I hear you're looking for Rafael and Glory?"

"I am."

"Why?"

He had kind eyes, so I said, "They interviewed for a job with my Grandmother and me. When I called the agency to offer them the job, there was some story about them losing their truck in a fire. Nobody knows where they are, and I want them to come to work for me."

He looked me up and down for a long minute in silence and then said, "Put your big fancy car in those trees over there and get in with me. You won't find anybody driving that thing. People see that, they think you're a government man looking for illegals. INS, you know."

I nodded, got back into my car and parked it under some willows along a small stream, noisy with the recent rains. When I got into the truck beside him the man said, "I'm Francis. Francis Monroe. Herb's an asshole. He's got so many wetbacks on his payroll, he's not going to talk to anybody about anything for fear of getting busted. He's got people camped all over in these hills back here." He squinted through the muddy windshield and waved a hand over the sagebrush and scrub oak in front of us. "No showers, no toilets, no housing, just tents and bushes. Washing themselves and their kids and their clothes in the damned cold crick. Then they gotta use that water for drinking and cooking. It's just not right."

I didn't know what to say, so I said nothing, and in a minute or two Francis picked up the conversation. "Rafael and Glory were luckier than most. They had a camper. You better be serious about not meaning those people any harm. They're real nice folks. They burned out night before last, slept all night with practically no shelter, and nothing to tend Rafael's hands with. But you know the first thing Glory wanted yesterday morning? Right after asking for bandages, she asked me, please, to take her to a telephone so she could call her work. Tried to pay me for the gas to drive her to a phone. I know even dimes are precious to those people, and yet she used them to call her work, and the employment agency. They're real nice folks."

"All I want to do is offer them a job, I swear," I said. "I'm Bud Aarons." For some reason I added, "My dad is Peter Aarons." And I offered him my hand as he drove.

"You have the look of an honest man," he chuckled, taking my hand in his firm grip, and as we drove slowly up the brush-lined road he told me a little about how the fruit business worked, and how necessary it was to keep labor costs to a minimum, and how that led, however unfortunately, to the use and abuse of those who were most vulnerable. It was Steinbeckian, and disturbing. "But that Rafael, he's different," Francis said. "I never got any sense from him that he was here because he had to be. Every morning he'd take his wife to catch a bus for town, then he'd get those little boys all set comfortable in the truck, and he'd go to picking oranges with the best of them – always watching the little guys while he worked. Good father, he is. I was real sorry when he got burned like that."

"I assume he has no insurance?"

"You are a sheltered one, aren't you?" Francis snorted. "They have no nothing. Not a thing. They're wrapped in the two blankets they managed to borrow, sitting under a borrowed tarp, because, for all his efforts, Rafael saved not one thing from that truck but his family. All day yesterday, they had oranges and a couple of potatoes that Glory bought from somebody in camp. This morning, they had oranges. Didn't want to take food or drink out of the mouths of others. I was going to bring them a cooking pot and a sack of potatoes later this afternoon. I wasn't sure how they'd react to that, but those kids gotta eat, you know?"

I nodded. Francis' comment had alerted me to the fact that my hunting them down at this juncture might be construed as charity, and they might just tell me to take a hike. I worked on a bright line of patter to allay their reservations.

"When Herb hears they've been burned out, he's gonna send them on their way for sure. Glory says she'll go out and work the trees tomorrow, because Rafael can't, but still, somebody's bound to tell the boss. Nobody stays here who doesn't earn his keep."

"Hopefully that won't apply to them after today," I smiled. I grabbed onto the roof of the truck through the open window and listened to the stones rattling away beneath our tires as we wallowed down a steep little embankment, across the shallow stream, and up the other side.

Just at the edge of the embankment was the carcass of Rafael's truck, burned clear to the tires. It was still smoldering in spots, and the smell made me a little queasy. A few feet later we were in an encampment of tarps, and tents, soggy cardboard and sagging plywood, with bits of cast off furniture and seats from old cars. It was utterly dismal, and I was appalled, though I tried manfully not to show it.

Francis looked at me and read my mind. "They do the best they can," he said reprovingly, and I felt myself flush uncomfortably under his scrutiny.

"I'm sorry," I said, and I was. We got out of the truck and wound around through a few of the tarps and tents. There were children laughing and playing, but I didn't see Royal or Titus among them at first. Then, as we cut through some willows, Royal and three other little boys came running our direction, laughing and shouting back and forth in Spanish. When they saw us they skidded to a stop and immediately became shy. Three of them ran away, but Royal stood his ground, studying us, and after a moment, I smiled at him and said, "Hello, Royal Rafael Ruiz, going to be four years old in July. How are you today?"

His smile broke and he said, "Hello, Mister Aarons. You let me use your soap. I liked it at your house. How is your abuela?"

With those words, Francis relaxed, and from the corner of my eye I could see him smiling. I was who I said I was. "Thank you for asking. Gram is a little sad today, and I'm hoping your daddy can help make her feel better. Can you tell me where he is?"

He came and took me by the hand. "Let me walk you there," he said formally, and led us over to where a brown canvas tarp was stretched into a tent, using a couple of the willows for support. Rafael was sitting with a blanket over his shoulders. His knees were drawn up and his bandaged hands were wrapped around them, his head resting against his legs. Glory, wrapped in a rag of a second blanket, had her back to us, tending to Titus as best she could. "Mama," Royal said quietly, "remember you said last night God was gonna send us an angel?"

"Yes, Baby," Glory said, intent on her task, "and he will."

"Well, I think this is him," Royal said, and Glory turned around.

"Lordy!" she gasped, and Rafael raised his weary head. He was bewhiskered, and he had burns and smudges on his handsome face.

"Aw, hell..." he grimaced, and began shaking his head. "Who told you to come out here?"

"Sorry to pop in unannounced," I said with an apologetic smile. He was openly hostile, and I didn't have a clue how to deal with it. Luckily, I was an actor. I acted. "When I called the agency this morning they said you were incognito, and I really needed to find you. Rafael..."

"I don't want your charity, and I'm in no shape to take a job right now," he growled. He put his head back down against his knees, and when I glanced over at Glory, her eyes were filled with despair.

"Please, listen to me," I said. "Three guys came yesterday and they sprayed herbicide all over that beautiful, wild meadow of Gram's. We don't know what to do, and I thought maybe you would. Gram thought you would. Rafael, the birds are already dying, and we need help."

Rafael winced visibly. "I might be able to give you some advice," he said, nodding slowly. "I'd offer you a chair..."

"Let me offer you a position instead," I said quickly. "Glory, Rafael... would the two of you please come and run our household for the two of us? I know you're in a bad spot right now, and that you wish the circumstances were better, but we really need you. Gram cried most of the night last night. Please don't turn me down, I'm a desperate man."

Rafael growled something under his breath, and slowly raised his head. "I told you, we are in no position to accept employment. We have no appropriate clothing, we have no transportation, I have no hands to work with. It would be charity for us to go with you."

"I don't need your damned hands, Rafael, I need your brains," I said tersely, which did nothing for the look on his face. Glory's eyes widened, and I realized I was losing ground.

"Okay," I sighed after a moment's thought. "I admit it. It is charity, if that's what you choose to call it. Gram and I are desperate. Mrs. Gustavson blackballed us before she left, and even the temp service won't come to our house. Gram's meadow was sprayed out of spite. I honest to God thought her tender heart was going to break last night, weeping for her little innocent birds who will die. I need your help, your understanding, and your expertise, and I'm willing to pay you well for it, house you for it, and provide transportation for it. I'll beg for it if you make me, but I'd rather not. It's charity, all right. We need yours, and we need it now."

"You..." Rafael began, then shook his head, and ever so slowly, he smiled at me. "I'm sorry," he said. "I just...I've never had to accept a job...I'm so dirty, and I have nothing to change into. I feel so inadequate."

"About like I felt yesterday afternoon," I muttered. "A good salary plus your housing, your utilities, medical insurance, and two vehicles replaced as needed. Oh, and a fence to keep the kids out of the pool. What say you?"

The two of them looked into each other, much as my mother and father did, and I was suddenly uncomfortable. "I can go someplace else for a few minutes if you need to talk. I've got about half an hour of life left in me before the fact that I only had bagels for..." I realized what I was about to say, and got myself stopped. I'd had all the bagels and coffee I wanted while sitting in a warm kitchen, for Godssake. Where was my head? "Sorry. I skipped lunch, and it makes me stupid when I do that." Oh, God, that was an even worse thing to say, and I gave myself a good, swift mental kick in the pants. "I'll just...walk around a bit, hm?"

I turned to leave and Rafael said, "That won't be necessary. I do think...my wife and children would very much enjoy becoming a part of your household."

"And you?" I asked.

Our eyes met, and there was no flinching. He allowed me access to his thoughts for a moment, then veiled his black eyes again and said, "I want what is best for my family...and for your grandmother's beloved birds."

"Then, you are hired. Both of you," I smiled, and took the hand Glory extended to me. "Do you need to stay to say goodbye to anyone? Is there anything you need to...gather up? I'm sorry. I really don't mean to be insensitive. I don't want to rush you, but neither do I want to stay longer than we need to."

"Not comfortable here?" Rafael smiled, half accusing.

"He be worried about Mrs. Aarons, his head aches and he burnin' up with fever," Glory said calmly. "All we got's these two babies and my purse. The blankets is borrowed."

"Those two babies, are all the precious stuff," I said firmly. "We'll dig up the rest of what you need. I was so afraid you'd been hurt or..." I stopped myself again. "Never mind. My car's up the road a little way."

Francis, who had been quiet up until then, said, "I'll give all of you a ride, of course. Rafael, Glory, I'll return the blankets, and when it comes time to cut the checks, I'll see you get what's coming to you." He looked at me. "Can I have an address to mail it to?"

"Of course," I said, reaching for my wallet. I took out one of my cards, and handed it to him. "This is my home address, and theirs from now on."

"Are we coming to live with you?" Royal asked, looking up at me. I couldn't tell whether he was concerned, or merely curious.

"Yes," I said. "Hopefully for a very long time."

"Will we be a part of your family?"

"Absolutely," I nodded before Rafael could open his mouth, and sealed that commitment in my heart.

"I better ride in the back," Glory said, and her eyes didn't quite meet mine. "You ain't gonna like the smell of this baby one bit. I done the best I could, but after a while, it wasn't near enough."

"Hang in there just a bit longer," I said gently, only to her. "It's almost over."

"Thank you," she replied, almost in a whisper, and stepped gracefully onto the running board and up into the back of the pickup using my hand for support.

Rafael got in beside her, and I asked Royal what his druthers were –

up front with Francis and me, or in back with his parents. "With my parents, thank you," he said, and I put my jacket around his shoulders and swung him up beside his father.

By the time we got to the Benz, I was cold, and I could only imagine how uncomfortable the Ruizes were in the back of that pickup. We all thanked Francis, and after he had driven away, Glory turned to me and muttered, "I do so hate to ask, but do you have anything at all, clean rags, anything that I could use to change this child? He was pretty well potty trained, but with the shock and all...anyway, by the time we get where we're going we'll have to burn this car, too."

"I wondered what had happened," I chuckled. "Now I know." Glory smiled. Rafael didn't. I hastened on. "Rafael, Royal, get in before you freeze. Glory, let's check the trunk." I remembered that Rafael's hands didn't work just so, and opened the door for them, got them inside, and went around to the back and popped the trunk.

In marked contrast to the orange groves so close below us, we were in a steep, dusty valley, full of grey rock, and we'd lost the watery afternoon sun that provided our only warmth. I dearly missed my jacket, and I was trying not to shiver. I pushed a couple of things around in the trunk and came up with my golf bag, which contained a good sized towel, and my gym bag, which contained another towel, a white tee shirt and some toiletries, among other things.

Glory gratefully took the towels and the soap from the gym bag and excused herself to take the baby down to the creek for a minute. She was going to put cold water on that poor child? Just the thought of it made my teeth chatter. "You get in, too," she said firmly. "That fever got you freezin' and fryin' by turns. Just leave the trunk open and I be back in a flash."

"As you wish," I smiled. I watched her walk the few steps to the creek bank, then I got into the driver's seat and started the car. There was still some warmth in the engine, and it felt wonderful blowing across my legs. "Are you two warm enough?" I asked.

"I'm fine," Rafael said quietly. He was sitting in the passenger's seat, Royal between us, still wrapped in my leather bomber jacket.

"How about you, young man?"

"I'm starved," he sighed, and Rafael jerked up straight in a heartbeat.

"He asked you if you were warm enough, not if you were hungry, Royal."

"It's all right," I said quickly.

"It's not all right," Rafael said. "He's my son. The person he needs to listen to, is me."

"Of course," I murmured.

The time until Glory returned lasted about half a millennium, maybe more, and I had ample time to wonder just how big a mistake this was going to be. Rafael admitted later he'd sat there thinking the exact same thing. When Glory opened the door and got into the back seat with the much improved Titus, both of us breathed a sigh of relief. "What?" she said, but neither of us answered her.

We were out on the blacktop and headed toward the city when I said, "I hate to bring up the subject of food, but I did skip lunch, and I need to hit a store or a McDonald's or something, so everybody keep their eyes peeled." No drive-throughs to speak of back then, believe it or not. I knew better than to suggest a restaurant, and I could hear poor little Royal's stomach growling even with the engine running and the windshield wipers going.

When the golden arches were spotted I lost no time in pulling in, asking if burgers were all right with everybody, and sprinting inside before Glory could offer me money or Rafael could chew on me about anything. I could feel another lecture brewing. His hands were wrapped in gauze that was by now dirty and ragged, and I knew he was probably hurting all over – inside and out. I didn't want to run afoul of him, but I didn't want to let him run over me, either. Most of all, I didn't want to argue in front of the kids.

I ordered burgers, fries, coffee, milk, and while I was waiting for the order I went and called Gram. By now it was nearly dark, and I knew she was probably worried. To my relief she was home. I gave her a quick sketch of what was happening and told her we'd be home in a bit. I thought maybe I needed to offer Glory the chance to stop and do some shopping for the babies. Diapers, underwear...things babies needed.

"Come straight home," Gram advised. "We'll improvise tonight and shop tomorrow when everyone is more rested and on an even keel. I'll get

Mrs. Gustavson's old room ready for them until we can get the chauffeur's quarters cleaned out." There was a pause, then she said, "Good work, Sherlock. Drive carefully."

I promised I would, the girl called my order number, and I went back to the car. Glory went inside to wash her hands, taking Royal with her, and through the window I could see her stiffen, aware of the eyes that followed them to the restroom and back. When they got in, Royal fell on his sandwich like he was starving. "Thank you," he said between bites. "Thank you."

"Thank you for letting me stop," I said, taking a sip of coffee. "I was really hungry, too."

Rafael was visibly forcing himself to eat nonchalantly, but I could tell that he was truly hungry, as was his wife, and I realized how long two whole days and nights can be when you have no hope. "Does anybody need anything else?" I asked. "Gram says this is dinner, so don't be shy about speaking up. Until my new housekeeper goes shopping..."

"Which she can do on the way home tonight if you'd like," she said quickly.

I looked in the rearview mirror and made a face at her. "Holy Toledo, you're nuts. I knew you were too good to be true."

"Then don't complain about breakfast," she grinned, and Rafael chuckled softly, love for his wife shining from every frazzled inch of him.

"Do not worry, Senor. The woman has a recipe for stone soup."

"Well, if it's anything like those quesadillas you made the other night, I'll be wanting it for breakfast," I said, and lined the Benz out into traffic.

"I need to stop and buy some things for the baby," Glory said, right on cue. "I have money to pay for them."

"Gram says she has everything you need for tonight," I said, meeting her eyes in the mirror. "She knows to the second when we should pull in that driveway, and I'd really like to make that happen for her. Two people you don't cross in my family, are Gram, and my father. Can you make do until tomorrow?"

"I can make do for as long as I need to," Glory replied, and I could see that she was relieved we didn't have to stop.

Royal and Titus promptly went to sleep, and we spoke but little the rest of the way home. It was dark, and raining, and the lights from oncoming cars were hurting my eyes. I didn't want to rub them for fear of getting a contact lens out of position and rendering myself instantly blind. My head still ached despite having eaten and I was overjoyed when the bucolic meander of Sweet Sage Trail culminated in the wrought iron gates of my driveway. "Home," I said quietly, and I meant it with all my heart.

The patio lights came on to greet us with Gram close behind, and she hurried us into the warmth of the kitchen. "Let me show you right to your room," she said. "You can all have a nice hot bath and just turn in, if you'd like. You must be exhausted." She was talking to them, but she was looking at me, and I realized I was ready to fall over and not get up. "Billie and Kit brought over some baby things for Titus a bit ago, so he's all set. Rafael, there must be something around here for those hands...."

There were bags of groceries still on the counter, and Glory exclaimed, "Have you eaten, Ma'am? It won't take a minute to fix you..."

"Tonight, I'm the one fixing you," Gram said firmly, and when Glory's mouth came open again, Gram shut it for her with a look.

I knew she had things under control, so I excused myself and staggered upstairs. My dinner was threatening upheaval, and I was so cold I was shaking. I stood in a hot shower until I stopped shivering, took out my contacts, put on some sweats, and crawled into bed. I felt bad abandoning Gram and the Ruizs, and when I was comfortable enough, and had rested a few minutes, I actually thought about changing that. I could at least have offered Rafael a clean tee shirt and some shorts, though he was more Kit's size than mine. I made myself sit back up, and after a minute I crawled out of bed, put on my glasses, gathered up some clothes, a robe, a razor, and went back downstairs.

In the downstairs hall I met a freshly scrubbed Royal, scurrying toward the kitchen in one of Esther's tee shirts to kiss his father goodnight. I walked the rest of the way with him, and again, he thanked me for the soap he'd just used. I told him he was more than welcome. To this day his eyes twinkle and he thanks me for soap, and I give him soap for Christmas and his birthday, and whenever we want to laugh together and remember our past. I gave him soap for his college graduation, and as a wedding present, and he gave me soap when I married Meg – and then to celebrate when my divorce was final – and when I married Phipps, and to herald the arrival of our children. Each time I have gotten an Academy award, an Emmy, or a Grammie I have gotten soap from Royal Rafael Ruiz, who is going to be... thirty-something...in July.

"Forgive my momentary lapse in manners," I said, walking back into the kitchen where Gram and Rafael were still talking. His hands were unwrapped and soaking, and they looked so bad I hurt for him. "I brought you some stuff you'll need to get comfortable for tonight."

"Thank you," Rafael said, forcing himself to smile. "For everything."

"Likewise, I'm sure," I grinned. "You've done me the favor. If you'll excuse me..."

"Go to bed," my grandmother smiled. "We're fine here."

"Goodnight, then," I nodded, gave her a kiss on the cheek, and went back upstairs, considering it a day's work well done. I fell on my face in the bed, noticing only momentarily that it was nine-thirty in the evening, not midnight.

At ten O'clock there was a rap on my door that I assumed was Gram, coming to check on me. "Come," I croaked, blinking at the blur of clock next to me. I turned on the lamp and Glory walked in with a steaming mug in her hands.

"Got my family all tucked in nice," she said quietly, "so now it's time to tend you and that fever." She put the cup on the nightstand and reached across me for another pillow. "I want you to sit up and drink this while it's hot," she said, and as I sat up she arranged the pillows behind me.

"Glory," I said, "you do not need to be doing this tonight. I know you must be exhausted." She did look better. She, too, was freshly scrubbed, and wearing one of Gram's soft chenille robes.

"Already done," she said, handing me the cup. "Here, drink this, it should help some, though Mrs. G. didn't keep no fresh herb supply on hand. Come mornin' I'll go stock up, and I can't very well do that if I got nobody to drive me, now, can I?"

"I don't know. Do you have a driver's license?"

"I do," she smiled. "You need to drink that while it's hot."

I sipped obediently, trying not to grimace. "Thanks. It's really...ah... What is this?"

"It got some ginger, and I found plenty of fresh yarrow in an unsprayed part of the meadow," she grinned. "Awful, ain't it?"

"Yes, it is. Anyway, if you have a license, you have a car. There's a cream colored Volvo station wagon in the garage. Keys are on the peg in the kitchen. It was Mrs. Gustavson's service car, so it's yours, now. It's only a year old, so it should be okay for a while."

Her eyes widened a little. "I can just take it and use it anytime?"

"Glory, it's your car. You'll need it, and yes...you can use it anytime for any purpose, personal or otherwise. It's your family car, too. It's part of our deal, remember? I'll put you and Rafael on the insurance tomorrow." I mentally held my nose and drained the cup, and Glory took it back from me.

"You a good man," she said quietly, gave me a pat on the hand, and turned out the light.

CHAPTER FOUR

The next time somebody rapped on my bedroom door the sun was well up, and while I was awake, I was not up with it. I had slept well, the fever seemed to be relenting a little, and I was content to lie in bed watching the sun cast patterns through the big oak onto my wall and writing music in my head. I was anxious to begin work on the young people's concerts. How exciting that would be for me! I hoped my shooting schedule didn't interfere with those concert dates, because I knew...Dad had first dibs.

When the door opened, it was Glory. Her bedraggled house dress had been washed, dried, ironed, mended, starched...amazing. She looked as fresh as the morning outside, and she was carrying a mug in her hands. When she saw the look that crossed my face she said, "Drink this like a good boy and I'll make you a right nice breakfast and a pot of good coffee."

"Deal," I sighed, and again she arranged the pillows behind me so I could sit up comfortably. "How did you sleep, Lady?"

"Wonderful!" she exclaimed. "That nice big bed and that bathroom right there...and the boys, they slept real good too, and so did Rafael. He be in a little better mood this mornin', you bet. He get around to apologizin' to you for himself sooner or later. He be proud, you know. Always one to be thinkin' he don't need no help takin' care of his family. Oh, he sent me up to tell you he gettin' ready to set a fire, and they gonna' be some smoke so don't you worry none."

I scowled. "What's he burning?"

"The meadow," she murmured, looking away from me. "He so hates to do it, but the only way to stop that poison workin' is to get rid of it. He and Mrs. Aarons, they talked for hours last night 'bout what to do, and just at dawn they was up walkin' all of that meadow lookin' for nests and burrows and things what might get hurt in the fire. He does know what he's about, Mister Aarons..."

"Bud," I said firmly, "or Aloysha, but not Mister Aarons, please. Mrs. Gustavson called me *Master* Aarons until I started high school, and then it was Young Mister Aarons until I graduated from college, and then it was Mister Aarons until the day she walked out the door. I would like this to be a relationship, not an arrangement, if that's all right with you." She looked a little startled, and I wondered if I'd offended her. Did she think I was making a pass at her? I wasn't sure what to say, so I went on as if I hadn't seen the look she gave me. "What do you mean, he knows what he's about?"

"He knows what he be doin'. He knows to the fraction of an inch how much rain fell on this very spot yesterday, and he takin' that and figurin' out just how deep that poison went, and he burnin' this off and bringin' in a dozer to dig down just that far...just that far." She used her fingers for emphasis. "Then, they bring in fresh topsoil, and...Bud, you supposed to be drinkin' that, not warmin' you hands with it."

I sipped manfully at the nasty stuff. She'd put some honey in it, and that helped a little, but not much. "Major surgery," I muttered. "That's going to cost us a pretty penny."

"Well," Glory said matter-of-factly, "Rafael, he told Mister Antrim just this mornin', he can pay the expense of havin' this done out of his insurance, or he can go to court and pay this and then some. He said it real nice, but it got said, and so the right person's payin' for it. How you feel? You look some better."

"I feel better, thanks to you," I smiled. So, Rafael was already about my grandmother's business, hm? And apparently had no qualms about confronting the established hierarchy. That was going to be good...and bad... and amusing and annoying. I downed the last of the concoction, shivered graphically and involuntarily all over, and leaned back against the pillows. I could already feel the stuff heating up in my body. "Sorry. I know that's probably premium Carolina snake oil in there, and I should appreciate it."

"You brain may not have sense enough to 'preciate it, but I guarantee you body does," Glory said sternly. "I got housework to do. Whenever you feel like comin' on down I fix you somethin' to eat, or would you like a tray up here?"

I blinked at her. "You … would do that for me?" I asked, half kidding, half in awe.

"I would do that for you," she said firmly, and her eyes began to twinkle in her pretty face. "You done told Royal we was gonna be family, remember? And though I'm teasin' you 'bout it, it was a very kind thing to say, 'cause he was real scared, and he really does believe you our angel. You and your gram be my responsibility. I gotta take care of you. You want you breakfast up here so's you can rest a little more? Probably wouldn't hurt you none."

"Glory," I smiled, "I feel one hundred percent better. I have a lot to do today, and none of it can be accomplished from this bed. I will be downstairs in precisely fifteen minutes, and whenever you have time to make me some breakfast, I will gratefully eat it. Now scoot, so I can take a shower."

She left, and I stripped out of my sweats and went into the bathroom, pointedly avoiding the plume of smoke I could see reflected against my bedroom wall. Rafael must have convinced Gram he knew what he was doing, or she would never have allowed him to do so drastic a thing as this, but the thought of these grounds, even part of them, going up in smoke, made me physically ill. I really was bound to this place, after all. I'd only just realized it, but with that realization had come another – it was most likely a permanent condition.

For good or ill, this was home, and I was content with that notion, would be for years, until my first wife started in on me about moving someplace more, as she put it, fashionable. What she meant was, someplace that would trumpet wealth and power, and make people ooh and ahh and huddle together while speaking in hushed voices and looking around in awe over their cocktail glasses. Her second husband, Richard Stein, would give her that. She'd also get the side of her beautiful head blown off.

Anyway, not being much into glamor in a domestic setting, I'd never cared a bit that our old adobe wasn't ostentatious. It didn't shriek of Hollywood, but then, neither did I. My only real complaint was that it wasn't particularly livable in a private, get-off-by-yourself sort of way. It had been built in the roaring twenties as a gift to my grandmother from her new husband, my dad's stern, distant and very Jewish father. It was meant only as a weekend retreat for them and a few intimate friends.

Gram had pretty much designed it herself, and while she had impeccable taste, she was neither architect nor mathematician, so it was a box, with everything proportioned in multiples of three. She'd joked a few times that she'd designed it using only the bottom of her coffee cup and the side of a business card, and I believed her. It had a huge pool, which my gram had had deepened at one end to accommodate my diving and I later remodeled to look more like a natural setting. It had a huge patio, a huge cabana, a kitchen more vertical than horizontal, a very gracious dining room with a living room to match, and then this warren of severely rectangular bedrooms that reminded me of shoe boxes all lined up in a closet – tons of bathrooms – a six car garage that was completely on the wrong side of the house and necessitated sprinting through the rain across the whole back of the building to get in the kitchen door. It probably never crossed Gram's mind that anybody would come in any way but through the main entrance, which was beautiful and inviting. All in all, it was a house that promoted togetherness, whether you wanted to be together, or not.

Still, it was elegant. It was done hacienda style, and the red roof tiles gleamed after a rain. There was a wide and graceful balcony which circumscribed the entire house, and the huge arched windows looked with lifted and slightly amused brows out over the beautiful ten acres surrounding it. Actually, when I was twenty-six, Gram still had considerably more than that, if I remember correctly. Most of it went to the Nature Conservancy in the eighties. On the immediate acreage there were huge oaks and pines, and myriad paths through lush growth opening up to serene and distant vistas. The sweet smell of sage and meadow grasses permeated the senses. It had been a great place to be a kid with an imagination, and it was a great place to be a young man with ambition. I knew the house would be mine – Gram had said as much. This was home. This was my home. Meg could never understand why, but she – and that unfortunate time with her – was fifteen years down the road yet.

I stepped out of the bathroom and the acrid smell of charred brush greeted me and followed me down the stairs and into the kitchen, where I stood by the window, watching years of loving care go up in flames and trying not to cry.

"Eat," Glory said gently, putting a plate of French toast down at the kitchen table, "Make you feel better. That'll look good as new before you know it."

"Thanks," I sighed, turning to my breakfast. "The thing is, will it look good as old? This smells wonderful."

She just patted my shoulder and turned back to the stove. "We'll sit some and talk about what-all you like to eat different times of the day, but for now I'm just wingin' it, so you gotta tell me if I don't get somethin' right, hear?"

"Yes, Ma'am," I said absently. It was a delicious meal, and she was right, it did make me feel better. I leaned back with a cigarette and a cup of coffee, and watched her going through the cupboards. She really was tall, which was a good thing considering the cupboards went clear to the top of the ten foot kitchen ceiling.

"You Gram, Mrs. Aarons, she not a cook, is she?" Glory asked, and when I caught her profile, I could see the hint of a rather tender smile.

"No," I said. "I've seen her make tea with a tea bag. She can open boxes, or so I assume. What makes you ask?"

"It's just that...well, it was so sweet of her to go out and buy groceries – so very kind – must've been hard, not knowin' what all goes together, bless her heart."

"Did you get an eclectic collection of foodstuffs in those bags?" I chuckled, and Glory nodded, trying not to laugh.

"The whole wheat bread and the gallon of milk – she done real good there, and she got some eggs, bless her. Then she got some pimentos, some matzo meal, olive oil, big ol' jar of peanut butter, some pickled pig's feet, capers, whipping cream, a bag of butterscotch balls and some frosted animal crackers."

"And you thought I was kidding when I said we needed charity, didn't you?" I looked for an ashtray, and realized they were conspicuously absent this morning. "Ashtray?" I asked, looking up at her.

"In the livin' room," she said pointedly. "Now, I can't rightly tell you not to smoke in my kitchen, but nothin' says I have to make it easy for you, either. I don't care what they say, them things'll kill you, and I'm already right fond of you, Boy, so please commit suicide where I don't have to watch you do it. Aw no, big old car comin' in the drive, and me with no proper uniform. You expectin' company?"

I rose to her vantage point and looked. "Dad," I grimaced, and took a deep breath. "I'll bet you even money the second that smoke plume went up, Mrs. Mayhak next door called my father. Where are the boys?"

"In our room," she said, and I could see real alarm in her eyes. "Ain't that all right?"

"It's fine," I said quickly. "Really, it's fine. I just...I just don't want them to be my father's introduction to you. Please, please don't be offended by that, Glory. Your boys are adorable, and Gram and I are both smitten, and Dad has a little boy of five in his household...his chauffeur's little boy...I just...." I shook my head in irritation. "I'm just a pansy when it comes to my father, is what it boils down to, and I'm dreading a confrontation. I'm sorry to concern you. It's me, not you. It's certainly not Royal or Titus. God, forgive me for even opening my mouth. Sometimes I don't think worth shit."

The car stopped down near the smoke and dying flames, and I could see Max letting my father out. Two others got out – smaller people. One stayed with my father, and the other headed our way, materializing with proximity into Esther.

I opened the screen door and hollered, "Hey, Sis!" and she smiled and waved and stepped up her pace a little, her hair bobbing in its fashionable cut just at her shoulders. "Hello, there. You're a little early for your piano lesson, aren't you?" I laughed, catching her in a hug, and she put her arms around my neck and gave me a kiss, laying her head against my chest for a few seconds to catch her breath.

"Glory," I said, turning Esther in her direction, "This is my kid sister,

Esther. Esther, this is our new housekeeper, Glory Ruiz. Her husband, Rafael, is out there with Gram working on the meadow."

"It's a pleasure to meet you, Miss Esther," Glory said.

Esther immediately held out her hand. "It's nice to meet you, too," she said. "Our house has been full of the talk of you this last week or so. I'm a little disappointed to see that you seem to be rather a normal human being, though a tall one. I suppose that's something."

"Sorry to disappoint you," Glory chuckled. "I could put a wart on my nose, or paint a third eye on my forehead if you think that'd help any."

"The third eye would be a nice touch," said Esther, who was deeply into science fiction and fantasy. "Red would be ideal."

"I be gettin' right on it," Glory laughed. "You need anything to eat, child?"

"Now that you mention it, I am hungry. Must be the country air, and it smells wonderful in here – like cinnamon. What did Peter have for breakfast?"

Glory looked perplexed, and I said, "I'm Peter. Gram calls me by my middle name, Aloysha, because when I came to live here, there were already two Peters – Gramps, and Dad. Dad is also called J.R., and Gramps...is dead. Mother, calls me Peter, or Peterkin. Esther usually calls me Peter. Most everybody else, calls me Bud."

"Whoosh!" Glory laughed. "Like one of them Russian novels. Now that we got that all worked out, big brother had French toast for breakfast. Would you like some? Won't take but a second for me to whip it up."

"That would be ever so nice," Esther smiled, and sat at the kitchen table, swinging her long legs against mine and looking around.

We had inherited the same coloring, except that my hair, like Dad's, was relentlessly blue-black, while Esther's was a deep sable brown, like my mother's. We shared many of the same features, and it was obvious to even the most casual observer that we were brother and sister. She had my mother's complexion and the beautiful black DiPirelli eyes which graced my father's side of the family. On a bad day she was sallow and frail looking, but today her skin glowed like peaches and cream, and she looked more delicate than infirm. Her conversation was unaffected and sprightly, and her eyes sparkled with good humor. She had a genuine smile that flashed often, and a rich laugh, and I adored her as only a much older brother can.

She held my hand until Glory put her breakfast down in front of her, then she said thank you, and applied herself to her meal, which pleased me, because very often Esther didn't have much of an appetite. As she ate she asked Glory questions about herself, and when Glory mentioned that she had two little boys, Esther was immediately enchanted.

"Where are you going to live with them?" she asked Glory, then turned to me for an answer.

"Well," I said, "We're going to have to start out upstairs in the old chauffeur's quarters. It's cramped, and it'll be hotter than blazes this summer, but it'll have to do for now."

"Won't the boys fall down those awful, steep stairs?" she asked, and Glory and I looked at each other.

"You could well be right," I said. "Glory, we need to get a fencing contractor in here to build a couple of gates across the tops of the stairways and reinforce the deck railings."

Glory just chuckled and shook her head. "You just hired a handyman, Bud. Why spend you money twice? Rafael, he can do that. We take the station wagon and get some wood here after a bit."

"What I need to do is take him out and get him a pickup," I said, "but he can't very well test drive anything with his hands all burned. I hope he's not overdoing it out there right now. This afternoon, he goes to the clinic and gets them properly taken care of."

"Ohh," Esther said with deep sympathy, "how did he hurt himself?" and Glory told her the story of how the stove had caught fire while she was cooking supper, and they'd each grabbed a child and jumped to safety, and Glory had managed to grab her purse out of the front seat, but when Rafael had tried to get back in for clothes, or blankets, or important papers...he'd burned his hands on the metal doorjambs, and had to let all of it go up in smoke.

"We need to be getting you folks restocked with some of the things you lost," I said, smiling at Glory. "Do you think Rafael would stand for letting me cut you a check in advance?"

"Only if you take it a bit out of each check followin' until it be paid back. Even so, he won't like it."

"He's noble, isn't he?" Esther said, eyes glowing with some rising romantic notion, and again Glory and I exchanged amused glances over her head.

"He be a true Latino gentleman," Glory said seriously. "He noble, and brave, and gallant, and romantic. You like him a lot, you will, and he like you, too. Bud, I need to look in on them little ones, and then, if you got a minute or two, could you show me that place upstairs so's I can be workin' on it when there's time?"

"Ohh," Esther breathed again, "Could I please go with you to see the babies? Please? I'll be very quiet, I promise I will."

I was about to give Glory an affirmative nod, but she was already saying, "Of course you can come, Child. Bud, you come along, too, and we go from there?"

"At last, a plan!" I laughed, and the three of us went down the long hall and into the small, bright room that had belonged to Mrs. Gustavson.

Royal was sitting on the floor drawing with a pencil on some scraps of paper, and Titus was lying on the bed looking out the window. How quiet they were. The day was sunny and turning warm, and yet neither of them begged to go outside. They both looked up and then scurried to their mother, and when Titus had a little trouble getting his short legs off the bed, Esther was quick to help him. He smiled at her and said something that passed for a thank you, and Esther literally glowed with delight.

"All right now, boys," Glory said, "You two just go on playin' real nice, and maybe here in a bit we'll go out on the back lawn and have a snack."

"I could take them," Esther said quickly, then her shyness set in, and she blushed deeply and gave Glory a pleading look. "Really I could. I promise I'd take really good care of them. I'm not a kid. I'll be seventeen in just a couple weeks. We could go out onto the lawn right under the big oak between the house and the garage, so you could look down and see us."

Glory didn't even glance my way. "That would be right kind of you," she smiled. "You make a proper babysitter, I know. Let me go back to the kitchen and get some cookies, and then we all go outside."

We all went back to the kitchen, with Esther carrying Titus in her arms. He was two, and should have been people-shy, but he put his arms around my sister's neck and beamed at her with his big, chocolate brown eyes, and she was in seventh heaven. It was an instant bond that lasted until the day she died, and his oldest daughter's name, is Esther.

We put them on the lawn along with cookies and milk, and Glory and I went up the long flight of stairs to an eight by eight deck, which had two doors side by side. "For good or ill, this is it," I muttered and opened the door closest to the house. With the first belch of dank air, I deeply regretted not coming up here sooner to open things up. I was embarrassed by my thoughtlessness, and I said so, but Glory waved both me and my apology aside and patted my arm.

I snapped on some lights and we entered a relatively cramped space about twelve feet wide and twenty-four feet long, which contained the living room, the eating area, and the kitchen. Under old sheets we found a tweed sectional couch that was ugly, but in good repair, a coffee table, and a big console containing a television set, a radio, and a record player, all of which worked when we tested them. The kitchen table was standing there uncovered, and the part that wasn't an inch thick with dust was covered with junk. But it, too, was usable, and there were two plastic covered chairs. "The other two are probably behind here in the attic," I said.

The counters were so filthy we couldn't tell what color they were, and there was stuff stacked all over the range, but when we turned on one of the burners we got heat and the smell of accumulated dust, and when we plugged in the refrigerator it began to hum, so we knew it worked. We went through a narrow door to one side of the living space, and found a bedroom with a double bed, a long dresser, and a closet which ran the entire width of the room. There was a full bath, with a toilet, a sink and a tub-shower combination. It was dusty, and musty, and everything was out of date and smelled of disuse and disregard.

"I really am sorry..." I began, and then I looked at Glory's face. She was crying tears of pure joy.

"A real home," she said quietly, beginning to roll up the dusty sheets.

"We can divide off a space for the boys in this big bedroom. Oh, this...oh!"
She was opening shades and throwing open windows, and I was sneezing
from the dust, and it was getting under my contact lenses, and I opened the
door to get away from it...and there was my sister, laughing on the lawn with
those two little boys. Their heads were together and they were playing some
kind of a game with acorns and some early marigolds that they'd picked...
and just for a second, just a second, I did feel like an angel.

"There are dishes, and pots and pans, and all that kind of stuff for
this place," I said, coughing and wiping my eyes. "I'm not sure where,
of course, but I know it exists, and you'll want to paint, and change the
drapes and the linens and have that couch replaced or reupholstered. I'll put
you on the household credit card and the checking account, which you are
responsible for, by the way. You pay the household bills. Did Gram tell you
that? We really haven't told you much about what your job is, have we?"

Glory was breezing around looking in cupboards and closets, and I
wasn't at all sure she heard me until she turned with a smile and said, "We
got a long time to get this all figured out. Don't you fret none, Bud."

She had dust on her arms, and her nose, and the dress she'd worked
so hard to salvage, and I began to laugh in spite of myself. She put her hands
on her hips, and I pointed to the mirror and said, "Just look, and tell me what
you see." When she had her back to me I interjected, "Glory, I don't mean
to be deceitful, but I don't want to fight with Rafael about getting you guys
some money to get started. Can't I just slip it to you, and you and I can figure
it out on our own?"

"Let me think on it," she said, chuckling at my obvious discomfort.
She was so comfortable – so at ease here. Why was that? It seemed already
that she'd always been here, and I felt like the stranger.

She was contemplating herself in the mirror which hung in the
little living room and I was laughing at her expression when the sepulchral
growl of my father's voice hushed me. It was like being up in a blind with
a lion stalking below. I looked over the edge of the railing and saw him
approaching Esther, with my grandmother and Racheal some paces behind.
"Esther June," he began sternly, "What in..."

"Look at me, Papa, I'm babysitting!" she breathed, looking up at him, and her face held such joy that he was instantly disarmed. "I've never, ever gotten to babysit, not even Britt, and Glory let me take care of her boys. It's okay. Peter said I could. Aren't they beautiful? This is Titus, and this is Royal."

Clearly my father wasn't expecting any response from the children, so when Royal marched over, pointed to his own chest, then stuck out his hand and announced, "I'm pleased to meet you. I'm Royal Rafael Ruiz, and I'm gonna be four years old in July," Dad was caught completely off guard.

"Are you now?" he said, taking the proffered hand and staring down at the child. He realized how huge he was by comparison, and lowered himself until he was sitting on his heels just above eye level with Royal. "My name is Mister Aarons."

"There sure are a lot of Mister Aarons's around here," Royal stated with a shake of his head. He slid his thumbs into his overall straps and contemplated my father. "Are you Grandmother Aarons's husband?"

I saw him wince a little at the use of the familiar, but my father was always a wise man. He knew small children only repeated what they heard. "No. I'm her son."

"Then..." Royal looked up the stairs at me, then back at my unsmiling father, then up at me again. "I don't get it," he said at last.

"You are looking at three generations of us," I said, trying to be helpful, and Dad became aware of my presence. "Gram first, then the man you're talking to, and then me. That man is my dad."

"Where's Gram Aarons's husband, then?"

"He's passed away. He's dead," I said.

"People supposed to come in pairs, like mommas and daddys," Royal mused. "That's what's so confusing about this. This family got no pairs at all."

"I'm part of a pair," my father said, cracking one of his rare and charming smiles. "I have a very nice wife who is your mother's employer's mother..."

"Daddy!" Esther, giggled, and from the look which crossed his face he saw the humor in what he'd said to this tiny person.

"Well, never mind," Dad said. "She's not here right now, but I'm sure you'll meet her someday." The interview being over, he stood up, and I breathed a sigh of relief. Thank God for Esther's presence. I noticed that Glory had stayed in the apartment, and I was glad for it, coward that I was. "Bud, have you given your sister her piano lesson yet?" my father asked, looking up at me.

"No. She decided to have breakfast instead," I smiled, knowing it would please him. "Glory made her French toast. Just leave her. I can give her a lesson here in a bit and then bring her home, if you'd like."

"Yes, Daddy, please! May I stay with Peter for the whole day?" Esther pleaded, and even as she spoke, she was reaching for Titus.

"If it's all right with your big brother, it's all right with me," Dad sighed, and turned my direction looking ever so slightly annoyed with the situation.

"Aw, man, do I have to keep her all day?" I whined, cocking an eyebrow as I came down the stairs, and she stood up and put her hands on her hips and glared with mock ferocity. "Oh, well, all right. I guess I can put up with her for a little longer than just a piano lesson."

At that point Racheal turned away with a flip of her long hair and a deprecating snort. "Well, if you get sick from eating too much watermelon or playing with the porch monkeys, don't come home and expect sympathy," she said, and my grandmother's hand was clamping down on her shoulder even before the last word was out of her snippy little mouth.

"What an ill-mannered child," my father muttered. "I wonder who she belongs to. And you two," he continued, turning to where Esther and I were standing arm in arm, "take care of each other, lest Racheal be all I have left." He shuddered a little for effect, and after a few steps toward his car he suddenly turned back and said, "I enjoyed meeting you, Master Ruiz. I loved it here when I was a child, and so did my son. I hope you will be very happy here, too."

"Thank you," Royal said, and made a slight bow in my father's direction. My father chuckled aloud, and turned with an amused little salute and a shake of his head to be about the business of running Hollywood.

Esther played the piano well. Her touch was feather-light and sensitive to the nuances of the music, and I enjoyed teaching her. We sat for an hour while she played for me and I critiqued her. The boys sat close by on the carpet and listened quietly, their eyes fixed on the keyboard and Esther's moving hands. When her lesson was over I nudged her over on the bench with my right hip and we sat laughing and playing four-handed music. When there was a pause I realized Royal was standing right beside me, Titus beside Esther. "May I...please make that sound, just once?" he asked quietly, and his eyes were huge with anticipation.

"You mean, can you touch the keys?" I asked, and he nodded. "Sure you can," I said, scooping him into my lap. He sat there rigidly, as if the piano were a living entity, so I said, "Here, I'll touch a key, and you touch the one next to it, how's that?"

"That'd be good," he said soberly. I touched a key, and he obediently touched the next one, then he looked up at me with a scowl on his face and said, "That's not what it said a minute ago. Why is that?"

"Esther and I were using twenty fingers, Royal. You and I are only using two. Each key that you strike makes a single sound, so the more you can strike at the same time, the more music you get."

He laid his little hand down flat on the piano, and got the usual unpleasant sound that comes with it. "That wasn't pretty, either," he sighed. "It's not ticklish for me. It won't laugh."

I did, though, and left him sitting on my lap while I played some songs for him that I thought he might know. After a tune or two, Esther, with Titus in her lap, began adding single notes using his little fingers, and Royal was enchanted, so we switched off, and Esther played while Royal and I added notes. We had just finished a rousing version of, *You Are My Sunshine*, when I heard Glory's horrified gasp behind us.

"Oh, Lordy!" she exclaimed, hurrying forward into the room, "I am so very sorry, Mister Aarons...Bud. I didn't realize they were botherin' youall, I..."

"They're not bothering us," I said firmly. "You gave Esther the privilege of babysitting while you got some things done, and that's what she's doing. They've been good as gold for more than an hour, and Royal just asked how the piano worked, that's all. There's absolutely no harm done, and no apologies to be made."

Glory stood and thought a minute or so, and I could see her struggling – torn between what she thought she should say, and what she really wanted to say. I was wondering what Rafael would have said had he caught us messing with his boys, and I was assuming part of Glory was wondering that, as well. "Lunch in ten minutes," she said finally, and walked away, patting at the skirt on her threadbare dress.

The boys joined us for lunch, of course, because Esther refused to be parted from them, and Gram and I denied her absolutely nothing. Glory protested, but my grandmother simply shook her head, and that was that. Glory would argue with me, I decided, but not with Gram. Over the years which followed I was proven correct in my thinking.

The day was turning into a real scorcher, and when our lunch had settled a bit Esther and I put on our swim suits and robes, and headed for the pool. "Glory," I said, "take a break. Come out and sit in the shade and have some of that good iced tea you made us for lunch, and let the boys paddle a bit."

"They got no suits," she said, and Gram shrugged it away.

"The suit police won't be around today. They were here yesterday. Let them paddle in their underwear, or their birthday suits."

"That don't seem right," Glory began, and Gram just took her firmly by the arm and propelled her outside and into one of the Adirondack chairs.

"Sit," Gram commanded. "I've spent the whole morning with your husband. Let's you and I spend some time talking about your responsibilities while the children swim."

Glory hadn't been outside much on this side of the house, and she pointed upward and asked, "What is that?"

"A three meter diving platform," I said.

"Peter's just the best," Esther said. "Show her, Peter."

I could feel myself blushing under my tan. "I certainly will not show off, Sis. I may just grab you up and chuck you in the pool, though."

I was reaching to do so when she said, "Stop it. I'm babysitting. I have responsibilities. Go. Shoo. Practice your diving. I'll be right here with Royal and Titus."

I turned quickly away, barely able to contain my laughter. She sounded like a little mommy. God, how much I wanted for her to be a wife and mother. It was what she desired more than anything else in the world – to be married with babies of her own. "As you wish, Miss Aarons," I chuckled, dropped my robe, and dove off the edge into the pool.

I swam some laps, vaguely aware that Gram and Glory were talking under the cabana, and that Esther was with the boys. I could see shapes that told me who they were. I couldn't swim with my contacts or my glasses, and I was blind as a bat without them. Had been for as long as I could remember. Made it nice for diving competitions, though. I hadn't been able to see the audience in any real detail, so I hadn't been quite so nervous. It had taken me a little longer to learn to dive, because it was hard to focus on a single spot. I'd learned to do it mentally after a while, and just fixed my eyes on a given piece of lint in the great fuzzy world of life without corrective lenses.

I did spend some time practicing my diving, because I didn't want to lose my edge. I never knew when it might serve me well in some movie or another. I nailed my second attempt at a half gainer with a twist, entering the pool with barely a splash, and surfaced to my grandmother's applause. "Not bad for an old man," she hollered, and I waved her away as I hauled out onto the warm, concrete deck.

Esther and the boys came over to visit, and most of the way there Royal stopped stock-still and pointed. "What's that?" he asked quietly.

"What?" Esther and I asked together.

"That," he breathed. "What you're wearing."

I didn't have a clue, but Esther suddenly began to laugh like a loon, and I gave her a puzzled, somewhat annoyed look. "What am I wearing?" I asked, examining my hands. "Please tell me I don't have something with lots of legs on me."

"I think," she giggled, "he's looking at..." she gave the thick black mat of hair on my chest a pat and asked, "Is this what you're looking at, Sweetheart?"

He nodded, and Esther collapsed in helpless laughter. "My brother is part bear," she gasped, wiping her eyes. "Some guys have a bare chest, b-a-r-e, but my brother Peter has a bear chest, b-e-a-r." She held her hands like paws and made growly noises at the boys.

"You're plainly jealous," I sniffed, and held out my hands to Royal. "Come here, kiddo," I said, and when he took my hands I seated him in my lap. "All your curly black hair is on your head, but some of mine, is on my chest. See?" I gave myself a pat and a slight tug. "It's attached."

I could see him studying it for a bit, then he extended a tentative hand and patted my chest, beginning to chuckle at the springy feel. "This just has been a day of discoveries for you, hasn't it?" I asked him, and he nodded and smiled up at me.

He patted the top of his own head, then my chest, then the top of his head again. "I like this," he said finally. "I want a bear skin just like yours when I grow up."

I don't know how long it might have taken me to get to know the boys if not for Esther, but by the end of that first day, we were fast friends. Esther nearly cried when I took her away from them and back to Bel Air, so I went in with her and asked Dad – Mother was in Paris – if she could come tomorrow to spend a few days with Gram and me.

Dad sat back and eyed me through a cloud of smoke. "I thought you had a movie to make, young man."

"I do," I said. "I have lines to learn and music to practice, and paperwork to do for Bellwether productions...thanks for coming in on it with us, by the way...and all the other things I usually do, but Esther can stay busy. Gram will be home most of next week, and..."

"And Mrs. Ruiz and her mud babies will be home most of next week," Racheal drawled, sprawling on one of the white leather sofas.

I was in the process of lighting a cigarette, and I nearly choked on her comment. "What the hell's eating you?" I said with some heat. "You've been a complete pain in the butt all day."

"You're what's eating me!" she exclaimed. "Do you know what it's like to be your sister?"

"No," I smirked, "but I do know, *I'm My Own Grampa*. Maybe if you hummed a few bars I could pick it up."

"And you think I'm a pain! Look at you, Bud. There you stand with your arm around Esther like you're married to her. I half expect you two to turn up in Georgia as husband and wife with five or six idiot kids, for

Godssake."

My father had said long ago that he never wore black and white striped shirts, and therefore could not and would not serve as referee, but he was certainly an interested observer at this point. I firmly curbed my rising temper, and as I was about to open my mouth, Esther said, "I'd like to marry a man exactly like Peter. He's kind and good. He's very handsome, and he was just wonderful with the boys today." She turned to me with a smile and a wide-eyed wink. "We could get married, Peter, and when our idiot kids were being really horrid we could threaten them with a visit to their Auntie Racheal."

"You're a fine one to laugh!" Racheal said, her voice rising unpleasantly. "You walk around in a fog all the time anyway. You don't have a clue what's going on at school. Half the girls in our high school want to have sex with your brother, and half the guys swear he's a flaming fag. They all think you're a nut case, Esther. And you don't see any of it, don't hear any of it, do you?"

"Gee," I chuckled, shaking off the sting, "which do I like better, being thought of as homosexual, or being lusted after by jail bait. Let me think about it and get back to you, okay?"

"And you," Racheal said through her perfect white teeth, "You go ahead and laugh, too. But you make my life a living hell. I get teased about my brother the faggoty piano player. My girlfriends drool over you, and want to meet you because they've seen you in some movie or another, and I have to tell them you don't date girls! All you do is play the piano and hang around with your little sister, which makes me think the guys are right. My brother is a queer and my sister's in love with him! Won't that look great in the school newspaper?"

The exaggeration struck all of us a little funny, but Dad was the one who chuckled. "Watch your mouth, Racheal Sophia," he said quietly, and she just lost her mind.

"*Me*? *Me*? Why is it always me who's to blame for everything?" she sobbed. "I get teased about my sister the gimp, and then Peter the queer goes and stirs up a big old pot of shit by hiring a damned nigger woman with a spick husband..."

About that time my father came up out of his chair, and his hand came across Racheal's mouth about half as hard as it should have, enraging her to screaming flight through the house. We could hear her shrieks of anger growing steadily farther away and then ceasing all together, either because she had gotten out of range, or because she'd grown tired of screaming.

"She's just having a bad day," Dad said, looking at me for understanding. "You do spend so much time with Esther, and so little time with her, Bud."

"Dad," I sighed, blowing smoke toward the ceiling and trying to stop my hands from shaking, "I try to spend time with her. I've tried sailing, I've tried riding with her, taking her to horse shows, showing with her in horse shows – no luck. We've been to the zoo, the museum, concerts, and movies. I have taken that child shopping, which was a stretch for me. Again, no luck. Basically, all she wants to do is hang out with her friends and shop...with them. I think she summed it up pretty well when she said I'm an embarrassment to her." I paused for an awkward breath or two, and then muttered, feeling nine years old, "But I am not a homosexual, Dad. I just don't...I have things I want to do besides date a lot of women right now. But I'm not a homosexual."

"I never thought you were," he said gently, and caught my face in his hands to kiss my forehead. "And neither does Racheal, I guarantee it. You go on home and try to get your new staff settled, and I'll have Max bring Esther over to you in the morning, how's that?"

"Thanks," I smiled, returned the kiss, pulled my sister's hair, and went out the door without a backward glance. God, I was hurt. I was so hurt. What Racheal said had cut me to the quick, and added to my fears that I might be a latent homosexual.

That night he came for me – buggy eyes, drooling mouth. I could feel him and smell him and taste him, and I woke up sobbing with fear and disgust. I went out and paced the balcony barefooted, smoking and trying to get rid of the shakes. What a beautiful night it was, full of moonlight and the fragrance of incoming summer. The balcony went all the way around the house, and when I glanced toward the garage, I noticed that there was a light on in the chauffeur's quarters. I stood quietly for a few moments, allowing my eyes and ears to become accustomed to my surroundings. I could hear music playing softly, and when I acclimated to the dimness I realized that Glory and Rafael were dancing – slowly, romantically – on the tiny deck. There were dust rags, and throw rugs and curtains draped over the railing, and a mop standing next to the door in a bucket and they were dancing a world away. She laughed softly. I went downstairs, and swam until I was too exhausted to think, and then went back to bed.

Esther arrived the next morning with Max in tow. He put her luggage down in the kitchen and extended his hand to Glory where she stood at the counter making coffee. "I'm Max," he said in his faintly British accent. "Welcome to the Aarons household."

"Thank you!" Glory smiled, and she was dazzling. She must have been up most of the night cleaning...and dancing...and yet she looked fresh as a daisy, which was her middle name. Gloriosa Daisy Ruiz. I loved it. Still do. Makes me chuckle and fall in love with life and growing things.

Max nodded my direction. "Good morning, young sir. How are you this fine day?"

"I'm well," I smiled, "and more than capable of carrying those the rest of the way upstairs for my sister."

"I'd be remiss in my duties if I failed to see her settled," he said, "but thank you," and proceeded up to the sunny southeast corner bedroom that used to belong to the nanny when Dad and Uncle Nathaniel were little kids.

The room was next to mine, as I occupied the old nursery. I'd occupied it since the day I arrived in America. There were five bedrooms on that floor besides Gram's, and I suppose I could have had any of them, but I liked my room, old nursery or not. I was next to Gram, where I could help her if she needed me, and vice versa. My room had a pair of arching and graceful French doors which led out onto the balcony – every bedroom on the second floor had that – and, like Gram's room and Esther's room, mine got the morning sun. I liked my room. Kit used to razz me once in a while about sleeping next to my grandmother in order to keep myself on the straight and narrow, but he knew very well that when it came to liaisons, I preferred hotels. He should. He was usually with me.

Max went out to the car, saying he'd be right back, and when he returned, he was carrying two big grocery bags which he put down on the kitchen counter. "When Coco...that's my dearest wife...when Coco heard that you had small boys, she insisted that I bring these over. Britt is five now, and he's outgrown these things before he could wear them out. I hope you don't find this offensive. My wife, you know..." he shrugged and smiled apologetically.

"Bless her heart," Glory crooned, looking in the bags. "You tell her we got plenty of use for these things, and you thank her for her kindness, Max."

"She'll be very pleased," he smiled. "Best of luck getting settled in. If there's anything we can do to help you get acclimated, you just let us know." He leaned a little closer to her and said, *sotto voce*, "You have taken up residence with two of the world's loveliest people, you have. Not an affected bone in their collective bodies. No airs put on here, nor even tolerated, for that matter. Never have been. Despite what you might hear, they were lovely to Mrs. Gustavson. Her ingratitude was shocking and unwarranted. I tell you this only because when you begin to mingle with the servants from other households, these things will come up."

"They won't be stayin' up long," Glory said with a curt nod, and Max reached over to pat her hand.

"You tell them, Little Missy. Don't let them get your goat. Young Mister Aarons and his grandmother will back you to the hilt, I know, and so will we. Again, welcome to you and your family."

"Again, thank you," Glory said quietly, and with a quick nod, Max was on his way.

"Sis, go get unpacked," I said, and when she was out of earshot I turned to Glory. "I...somehow, yesterday got away from me, and tomorrow I have to be back in the traces, and so today you and I need to get some business taken care of, Mrs. Ruiz. We need to go to the bank and get you on some accounts – checking and credit card..."

"Bud," she said quietly, "I don't mean to dig my heels in right off, but I can't be goin' in no fancy bank with this poor old dress on."

"Well, going naked is out of the question," I chuckled, and she just smiled and shook her head.

"You are a sassy one. I need to be goin' shoppin' this mornin', and so if we could go to the bank this afternoon..."

"Sure. Let me give you some money."

She shook her head again, this time in disapproval. "I don't need no money. I got some yet, and..."

"Silence, Woman. I said, I'm giving you some money. Uniform allowance. It's all part of the deal. One of the things I need to do is get a contract drawn up for you so you know where you stand. Rafael also gets a uniform allowance. I'm guessing he'll choose to wear jeans and tee shirts or button-ups, but for him, it's a uniform. He will need a black suit eventually, just in case Gram decides to put on the dog, dust off that limo in the back garage, and be chauffeured someplace, which happens about once or twice a year. When are you leaving?"

"Right after I see whether or not Miss Esther wants breakfast." Glory paused a minute, choosing her words. "Miss Esther...God love her, don't seem real strong. Is she..."

"She has a heart condition. She spends a lot of time asleep, or reading. At least until your boys came along," I twinkled. "Thanks so much for allowing her to take care of them. She really feels special because of it, and I know that's why she's back here."

While I spoke I'd been looking out the window toward where Gram and Rafael were directing the dozer operator, and when there was silence from Glory, I looked back around at her. She was giving me the oddest look. "What?" I said.

"Do you know what you just said?"

I suddenly felt a little uncomfortable. "I know what I *think* I just said. Why, did something weird or unpleasant come out of my mouth?"

"Unpleasant, no. Weird, definitely," she said. "You just thanked me for..."

"Letting my sister babysit. Yes. That's weird?"

She chuckled softly. "You have no idea. I be hollerin' up Miss Esther to see if she wants breakfast."

"You do that," I said. "Walk up with me and I'll show you where her room is. I'll be in my study." At the top of the stairs, I turned the opposite direction and pointed down the long, wide hall which followed the stairwell north and south. "That door straight across from us goes into a short private hall. Esther's closet is to your right, and her room is to your left. I have work I need to do, so please look me up before you leave. I'd like you to run an errand or two for me while you're down the hill." She nodded before striding away on her long legs, and I watched her go, enjoying the grace with which she moved. Truth be told, I didn't need any errands run, but I'd come up with a couple just so she didn't slip out without stopping for money. I knew what little they had must be precious indeed. I was pretty sure she and Gram hadn't discussed money in any way; not a salary, or a salary advance, or anything of the kind. That was my forte. I enjoyed handling money, and I'd always been good at managing it, even as a kid with an allowance. Gram, on the other hand, wasn't particularly interested in money. She enjoyed having it, and spending it, but she didn't manage it. Dad managed the bulk of her investments, and I managed the rest, along with our communal slush fund and the money needed to finance the household.

I did wonder, though idly, if Gram and Glory had discussed uniforms at all, since I was using them as an excuse to get her some decent clothes, and I was certainly no expert on the matter. Uniforms were irrelevant as far as I was concerned. If Glory used the money to buy herself jeans, or housedresses, or uniforms, she'd still have something clean and new to put on, and that was what mattered to me. She had said yesterday that she didn't have a proper dress on to receive company, which indicated to me that she had pride in her professional appearance. She was the one who had to wear whatever was chosen, so let her decide, was my attitude.

Even as I thought it, I could hear my father's disapproving comment. His servants were all liveried at all times. I was uncomfortable with even thinking of Glory as a servant, much less putting her in a fancy little outfit like a baby off to church. Edythe Gustavson had been a servant in the more traditional sense of the word, but she had been Gram's, not mine. I didn't want servants. The thought of having servants embarrassed me and made me feel self-conscious. What I wanted, was help – people I could depend on, and trust, and...admittedly, be friends with. It was a weakness on my part, and it still is.

Dad had told me with palpable disgust on more than one occasion that I must have been a peasant in a former life. I was the scion of a wealthy and powerful family, and I didn't have a clue how to act like one. I knew it wasn't a compliment, but I took it as one. If acting like the scion of a wealthy and powerful family involved behaving like Racheal or, God love him, my father did, I wanted no part of it. I knew which fork to use, I knew what black tie meant, I could tango. That was plenty. I opened the safe, put cash for groceries and uniforms and incidentals in an envelope, scrawled on it roughly how much was for what, added a bit of a list of things I needed, and set it aside for Glory.

When she breezed in a bit later I patted it, and after she'd picked it up and glanced at the notes on the envelope, she smiled, and asked me to name five of my favorite foods. "Breakfast, lunch, or dinner?" I asked.

"No category in particular. Whatever make you stomach smile."

"I'm...you know, I'm drawing a blank," I said. "Mrs. Gustavson was a good cook, but nothing was ever..." I shrugged, "nothing was ever special, I guess. She catered to my grandmother's tastes. I just lived here. I mean, she knew how I liked my eggs, and that I like blackberry jam, and my steaks medium rare and my coffee strong, but..." I shrugged again. Oddly enough, the question embarrassed me a little, and I realized Glory thought of herself as my housekeeper, not Gram's. I knew she'd be my housekeeper someday, but I guess I wasn't prepared to have it start immediately. I felt like a little kid playing at being the daddy and telling the mommy what to do.

"You like soups and stews and casseroles?" Glory asked.

"I love soups, if they actually have stuff in them. Mrs. Gustavson never made stews or casseroles, too proletariat, I suppose. She did make the occasional soufflé. Nasty things they were, too." I thought a minute. "I like Chinese food, and Mexican, and fish if it's cooked right."

"See," Glory smiled, "You doin' just fine. I do believe I'll just start cookin' and you tell me what you like as we go along."

"Wonderful," I said. "Have a nice morning. Oh, do I need to tell you where things are – the grocery store and so on?"

"No, thank you. I believe I just gonna wander a bit. That be the best way to learn about a new place." She turned at the door to my study and said, "Miss Esther, she wants me to leave the boys here with her...real bad."

"You're not comfortable doing that?"

"Bud, I am a servant. Leavin' my children to be cared for by..."

"She won't let them get into any trouble, I promise. I'll be here, and I'm fast on my feet. Besides, Rafael is here, isn't he? I still hear that infernal Caterpillar running out there."

"Esther is the daughter of somebody I for sure don't want to run afoul of for both our sakes. What if he were to come here and find me gone and his beautiful daughter workin' for me settin' my kids?"

"He didn't ask where you were yesterday, did he?" I stubbed out my cigarette and smiled up at her, trying to gauge how deep the concern was running. "Look, Esther is at our house, Glory. Our house, our rules. Dad knows that, and he accepts it, or he'd have dragged Esther out of here by the hair of her head yesterday, and she sure as hell wouldn't be back today. If I hadn't gotten a case of the yips yesterday morning and asked you where the boys were, you wouldn't even be thinking about this, would you?"

"Yes, Sir, I would. You see, I envision my place in this immediate and extended household much different than you do, or I miss my guess."

"Go to the store so you can be back to fix lunch for those hard working people out there," I said. "We'll talk about this when we go downtown this afternoon."

We did talk about it. Glory sat on the passenger's side of my Benz in one of her new uniform dresses – this one was a sunny yellow – and her attractive new shoes, and we talked about how we envisioned our roles in this household, and I think that's why to this day our home runs like a well-oiled machine. We set expectations for one another, and goals, and we talked just a bit about dreams and desires, and we set the cornerstone of a lifelong working relationship.

I did mention that the carton of cigarettes I'd asked her to pick up for me seemed not to have made it, and she just arched one eyebrow a bit and said, "Uh huh." I knew at that moment that while she might well crawl on hands and knees across broken glass to see that I was fed and clothed, I could be dying for a cigarette, and she wouldn't walk across the room to get me one. She wasn't going to tell me I couldn't smoke in her kitchen, but I'd better not. She wasn't going to tell me she wouldn't buy cigarettes for me, but she wouldn't. That's just the way it was. Without her saying so, I knew that I was not to smoke in front of her boys, or leave cigarettes around where they might get hold of them, and I tried my best never, ever to do that. It was an ugly habit, and she wasn't going to tolerate it.

We talked a bit about the boys, and how, once things were more settled, their presence on the property was going to be handled. Glory stated her concern that, since they were currently being given the run of the house, they might well like to keep it that way, but I said I was sure that once they were living in their own space, it would be a simple task to teach them what their boundaries were – especially since, for the most part, I didn't think it was going to matter much. Gram already doted on them, and I didn't think that was going to change as time went on. She'd wanted great-grandchildren, and these would do just fine. I mentioned that to Glory in terms I hoped wouldn't alarm her, and then went on to other subjects.

My bank was in a part of town Glory'd never be in, and after we'd parked and I'd opened the car door for her, she hesitated a moment before getting out. In the two minutes it took us to get from the car to the bank she was utterly silent, and every aspect of her body language said this Amazon warrior woman was scared stiff.

We went through the big glass doors into the posh interior, and every eye in the bank swiveled our direction. Glory caught her breath, and I could feel her shying to a stop beside me. I slid my arm through hers to get her going again, gave her a wink and said, "Now this, is what guys live for. Being seen in public with a beautiful girl."

She told me later it was the nicest thing anybody had ever said to her, and I was inordinately pleased. I'd said it to be kind and put her at her ease, but it had put me neck and neck in the gallant department with Rafael the romantic who waltzed on the deck in the dark, and I figured maybe there was hope for me. I could be trained...given the right trainer, of course.

I'd told the manager we were coming, so there was no standing around waiting to be noticed and helped. He came toward us with his hand outstretched, saying, "Bud, welcome! And you must be Mrs. Ruiz?"

"I am," Glory smiled.

Iggy pumped my hand, then took hers and said, "I'm Ignatius Cordoba. Please, come and sit. We'll get the paperwork started. Bud, I assume you're dropping Edythe Gustavson from the accounts formally at this point?" I nodded, watching Glory. I wondered how she would comport herself in this situation. What her speech patterns would be. Was she someone who could represent our household without needing to explain at some point where she was from and why she sounded like she did? I stopped dead in my thoughts for a moment and wondered why that would even cross my mind. Then I wondered for another split second if Gram had explained me and my accent to a few inquiring minds. Probably, and more than a few. Iggy's voice brought me back. "Mrs. Ruiz, welcome to Los Angeles. Have you been here long?"

"About two and a half months," she said.

"And how do you like our fair city compared to...where did you come from?"

"Texas," she smiled. "My husband and I worked on a large hacienda there, until the owner died and it was sold. It is...beautiful here. Very fast-paced, though. I am grateful for our hilltop retreat." The barest hint of an accent, no more. The Gullah dialect had vanished from her speech. I felt some annoyance that she made me decipher it when it really wasn't necessary, and then I looked at her hands where they lay in her lap. The knuckles were white. It was taking every ounce of concentration and energy she had to speak as she was this minute, a balancing act over moss covered stones, bless her heart. I don't remember ever worrying after that moment that the Aarons household was less than properly represented by Glory Ruiz in any situation.

I asked her afterward if she wanted to go for coffee, or something cold to drink, and she just shook her head and leaned back against the seat. It was fifteen minutes before she seemed to have enough energy to talk again, and then it was just scattered words. I finally reached across the seat and gave her a tentative pat on the hand. "You okay, Lady?"

She nodded, and after a bit she said, "I was just so scared he'd laugh at the way I talked, and you'd be 'shamed of me. When I was workin' in Texas I was in that kitchen cookin'. I watched, and I learned how to run a big household, but I never had to be a representative of that household, speakin' on its behalf and all. Here, I surely am on foreign soil."

"Now you listen to me," I said, checking my mirrors and easing right to get off the freeway, "I didn't hire you for how you sound or how you look, or the fact that you can reach the top cupboard, though that's a real plus. I hired you for who you are and what you can do. And as for being on foreign soil...Glory, when I first set foot in that house up there, I literally *was* on foreign soil. I didn't speak a word of English, I was scrawny and sick, I was scared half to death of everything and everybody, and that house, and the people in it, were like a fortress for me. My grandmother would take me out on the balcony in the sunshine, and hold me in her arms and rock me in that big old rocker of hers, and we'd listen to the birds sing and she'd tell me what kind they were, and what colors they were. I didn't understand a word she was saying, and it didn't matter a bit. She'd tell me that when she first came to this country her English was terrible, too. Now, her accent is barely noticeable – unless she gets mad – then she gets Italian. My accent's barely noticeable anymore. Give yourself time. The birdhouse will fix you wherever you're broken, I guarantee it."

She just smiled and looked out the window at buildings and passing cars, but I saw her shoulders drop slightly in either exhaustion or relaxation. "Do you need to stop for anything?" I asked, "and when are you going to want to be stocking and refurbishing that upstairs apartment?"

She turned to look at me. "What do you mean?"

"You know, putting in your own groceries. New linens, definitely new carpet and curtains. The carpet store is right on the way home, and they have curtains, or drapes or whatever. We can stop. Or we can have them come to us."

"The curtains is fine. They just need a good cleanin'." There was both weariness and dismissal in her voice.

"They're not fine," I said. "I don't want to sound like Baron VonTrapp, and you can make little clothes for the children out of those suckers if you want, but they are ugly, they're dark and out of date, and they need to be gone. The carpet needs to be replaced, too."

She was giving me what I came to regard as her voodoo woman's eyeball, but I just eyeballed her right back. "What?" I said, "You think I'll settle for having you live in squalor?"

"I have lived in squalor," she said quietly. "That ain't it."

"Well, it's too close for my taste. Now, you can pick out the carpet and the drapes and shop for the things you rightly deserve in order to get your new household going, or you can let me do it, but it's going to get done, and don't complain about the colors I choose. I ask you again, do you want coffee?"

"Fine!" she snapped. "Let's you and me just go waltzin' into some uppity coffee shop and get turned down for service why don't we? Then we can go to that fancy carpet store and get glared at. I would surely love that, wouldn't you?" She put her face in her hands and burst into tears, leaving little doubt in my mind that my approach needed work.

I shot off the street and whipped the car into the little coffee house where Kit and Tommy and I often stopped, shut off the engine, and dropped a hand onto her gently heaving shoulder. "I...you don't get nearly enough sleep, do you? Look, I didn't mean to upset you. Just...there's tissue in the glove compartment. I'll be right back with some coffee, hm?"

I jumped from the car like it was on fire, and strode into the shop. God, was she right? I'd never been denied access to anyplace my whole life, and she was a black woman from the Deep South. The gulf yawned.

Gordy hailed me from behind the counter, and I gave him a smile, looking around as I crossed the small room. No suits, though they came in from time to time. A pretty oriental girl smiled at me from the table where she was sitting...with an Anglo. There was a black couple – fairly young, casually dressed – sitting at another table. A whitish couple, a table of college kids. "Bud," Gordy said, eternally wiping the counter, "what's up? I never see you in here alone. Where are Kit and Tommy?"

"I'm not alone," I said, hitching up onto a stool at the bar. "My new housekeeper is with me. Heck of a nice girl."

He rolled the toothpick he was chewing over his tongue to the other side of his mouth and smiled at me. "And she's in the car because you don't drink with the hired help? Somehow I doubt that."

I just shook my head. How much worse could this get? What exactly should I say? "She...aw, hell, Gordy, she's African American, or Black, or whatever I'm supposed to say these days, and she's from the south, and when I asked her if she wanted to stop for a cup of coffee, she just...well, I made her cry, is what I did. She's afraid of what people will say, I guess. I know she's afraid of being refused service. She's really new here, and I don't think as a friend I'm being much of a success. We're fine at home, but out here.... Anyway, I need two cups of Espresso, black...to go."

"I have two parrots, a dog, and a horse who come here for my coffee. Actually, I think the dog and the horse are dating. Did you tell her I serve absolutely anybody who loves good coffee?"

"No," I chuckled. "I'd already made her cry. I wasn't going to hound her, no pun intended. Besides, she probably wouldn't have believed me."

"I'll be right back," he said, came around the counter, and headed for the door, motioning to the black couple at the closest table. "Reuben, Jennifer, they say a picture's worth a thousand words, and there's a lady outside who's worried she won't be served here because of her color."

As if raised by invisible hands, all ten people in the coffee shop stood up, grabbed their coffee cups, and went outside with Gordy. I just sat there, chuckling softly to myself and waiting to see what happened. Three minutes later they were back with Glory in tow, laughing as a group. The black man was saying his name was Reuben Teufert. He was the pastor of the local Baptist church, and would Glory please come on Sunday, and would we sit and join him and his wife, Jennifer, for coffee?

He stuck his hand out to me, and I said, "Pastor Teufert, I'm Bud Aarons. Glory takes care of me and mine." Glory looked at me, and I gave her a slight nod and a slow wink as I went to pull out her chair for her. "Welcome to Los Angeles," I said in her ear as I seated her. "Oh, and you know, I've been thinking, I love lamb chops with mint, and *bleeny* with caviar, hot oatmeal with brown sugar and almonds, and warm apple cobbler with vanilla ice cream."

CHAPTER FIVE

The phone next to my bed was ringing. Loudly, incessantly. It was my private line. Only a handful of people had the number, so it was probably important. I pried one eye open and looked at the clock. Five A.M. "Gawd," I groaned, trying to moisten my mouth. I'd been in bed a grand total of two hours after a raucous night of playing drums in a band with some college buddies in a trendy little dive over at the beach. I'd smoked too much and had a little too much to drink, and come home in a taxi because I knew I was polluted, and now...the phone was ringing. Maybe they'd impounded my car. No, I'd left my car at Walter's...hadn't I? I fumbled for the receiver, and grunted something unintelligible to indicate that I was there.

"Good morning," my father said. "I need your help down at the studio. How soon can you be here?"

"Dad?" I managed, clearing my throat, "It's...five O'clock in the morning."

"And we have a full day's shooting to get underway. George lost a man, and I volunteered you because I knew you weren't shooting or rehearsing today and you're the type he needs. Bring your jump rope, and your guitar...oh, and some gym shoes because I know we can't fit you. And shake a leg. You can eat breakfast while you're getting into makeup. Don't shave." He added, "Thanks," as an afterthought, and hung up.

I spent about fifteen seconds hoping fervently that this was one of those frenetic dreams you have when you've abused your body. When that hope fizzled, I crawled out of bed, into the shower, put on jeans and a tee shirt, grabbed my guitar, went downstairs and got my jump rope, scrawled a cacographic note on the message board for Glory, and went out to my...I had no car. Shit. I had no car. Glory needed the Volvo every day, it seemed. Rafael would kill me if I touched his new truck. My Grandmother...was out of town, *sans* car. I went back in and got her keys, backed her Benz out of the garage, and headed for the studio.

When I thought about it, which was most of the way there, I realized I didn't have a clue where I was going. The studio was not one building, but a complex of many, and it was a darned big place, especially just at dawn on a morning I'd planned to sleep in. I didn't usually get to sleep in, and last night's activities had been an exception to my usual routine. I'd been on the set of *Apache Pass*, every day for nearly three weeks, putting in long hours, then coming home and pounding my Steinway in preparation for autumn's concerts. I'd given myself a night out as a reward. I needed a break. I'd worked harder before, and I have since, but never under more unpleasant circumstances.

We had children on the set – several children – difficult children, and with them came their difficult mothers, who spoke comfortingly to their little darlings during filming, which meant we had to re-shoot, and imperiously demanded that the director change his blocking to put their children in a better light, and generally made nuisances of themselves. To upset one of those children, was to invite the wrath of some earth mother goddess, and all of us in the cast were pretty well on our way to being nuts – not just those of us noble red men who were supposed to be manhandling these hapless captives, but the white folks who had to stand around while we shot the same scenes over and over. Next week we left for the location filming, and all of us were dreading it; stuck in the middle of nowhere with those kids and their parents.

I was especially uncomfortable. One of the girls, Amber Kestrel, who was fourteen, looked twenty, acted ten, had decided I was worthy of conquest. She flirted mercilessly and inelegantly, and reminded me of Racheal, who, as luck would have it, turned out to be a friend and schoolmate of hers. When she'd finally irritated me to the point of saying something to her about professionalism on the set, she'd said condescendingly that she'd heard I was gay. Maybe this proved it. I told Reggie Clevenger, the director, that I was fed up with the whole scenario, and he was only too happy to chew her ass, which put me, not only on her short list, but her mother's and Racheal's as well. The movie was a pet project of my dad's, and he took my side.

The ensuing high drama with Racheal was enough for him and Mother to send her packing to a girls' summer camp in Vermont. Mother headed for British Columbia with some friends for a couple of weeks, Esther and Gram took off for Italy to visit Great Aunt Viveca for a bit, and Dad and I were left to bury ourselves in our work, which we happily did. Two days later on the set Amber started flirting with me again.

I pulled up to the main gate and said to the guard on duty, "Johnny, good morning, I guess. My dad called and told me to get down here, but he didn't tell me where, exactly."

"His office called a bit ago," the man smiled. "I have directions for you."

I was barely inside the sound stage when Dad grabbed me and dragged me with uncharacteristic heat in the direction of makeup and wardrobe. "I thought you were giving up this end of things," I said accusingly, and he rewarded me with a jet black glare.

"Oh, believe you me, I am, just as soon as I can. But some little pissant of an actor decided to give us a ration of shit at the last minute – wanted changes made to his contract – wanted more lines, more money. Where do these people get off? This is a major motion picture, not Talent Search. Anyway, here's your script." He thrust it at me like he was passing a football. "Your parts are marked in yellow. All you have to do this first scene is jump rope. It's a scene in a gymnasium and you're in the close background, so try not to miss too many beats. Oh, and you're not supposed to have a shirt on."

I obligingly pulled mine over my head as we walked, and he literally jumped. "Your...they shaved your chest?"

"Waxed it. And my arms, and my legs. Native Americans have very little body hair," I said, trying not to chuckle at his expression. "Want I should wear a tee shirt or something?"

He studied me a bit. "No. I like the look. Here." We turned right into a small, brightly lit room, and Dad gave me a gentle push into a chair that was presided over by a heavyset, middle-aged lady with flaming orange striped hair and a radiant smile. "Anita, this is Bud. You have fifteen minutes," he said, spun on his heel, and left.

"I don't suppose you can tell me what's going on, can you?" I sighed, realizing Dad had forgotten about breakfast for me – not that I'd want it before jumping rope. I should have taken the two minutes I needed to stop for coffee.

"Lazlo Guidrot crossed your father, is what happened. Mister Aarons refused to negotiate, and when Lazlo said he wouldn't shoot, he was fired...and here you are."

"Scab labor," I muttered. "No wonder he didn't tell me over the phone what was up." I contemplated her in the mirror as she began to apply my makeup, wondering whose side she was on. Her expression told me nothing. "So tell me," I said at last, "who all is going to spit at me when I walk out on that set?"

"Probably...nobody. Lazlo is an arrogant pain in the ass who thinks he's far better as an actor and an athlete than he really is. Of course your father is also an arrogant pain in the ass. But he's every bit as good as he thinks he is and then some. People are going to assume you're just like him, so while you don't have to worry about flying saliva, you shouldn't expect any handshakes, either."

My next stop was wardrobe, which was simple. Boxer shorts. I added my own gym shoes, athletic supporter and jump rope, they taped my knuckles, and sent me out the door to my right onto the sound stage.

"Peter, good morning. Thanks for coming on such short notice," George Deaton said, and in the next breath shouted, "Places! We have one hell of a lot of film to put in the can today." A stagehand grabbed my elbow and put me on my mark while I asked George if there was anything in particular he wanted me to do. He shook his head, said, "Skip rope," and inside two minutes we were rolling.

I just...skipped rope – faster, slower, pausing from time to time to shake out my arms and legs a little, since I hadn't had time to do warm-ups, and stopping whenever George hollered "Cut!" Lazlo...whomever he was, had walked off the set, and this was his part? Why had Dad told me to bring my guitar, anyway? By the time we were through shooting the scene, I was thoroughly exercised for the day, verging on pooped, and very thirsty.

When I told George I needed a drink of water before we went on, he told me I was through for the moment. I could go get a drink, and then I needed to report back to makeup and wardrobe for my scene changes. I decided at that point I'd best take a peek at the script.

To my dismay, the character had lines. Not a great many, but he had lines. Besides which, he sat on the stoop of this old gymnasium and played his guitar and...sang. He sang? Not even for my father was I willing to do that. We'd have words over lunch. Of course after we had words I'd do it anyway. Unlike Lazlo, Peter Aloysha Aarons the third, wasn't crazy enough to cross Peter Aloysha Aarons, Junior. But willingly, no. Fortunately for me, the character, whose delightful moniker was Pansy and should have given me a clue, sang something I was familiar with.

I stuck my nose in the script, and by sheer force of will and fear of my father, I kept just ahead of the lines I needed to know. I was supposed to sound Italian, which was no trick. I did my imitation of my grandmother when she was angry, throwing in some Italian words from time to time for effect, and George was happy. When I wasn't on camera I stayed out of the way and kept my mouth shut. I made no suggestions, passed no criticisms, and at lunch I was beckoned over to join the other actors and the crew at table.

I accepted, figuring my father had better things to do, and when, after a tentative silence, one of the boom operators asked me what it was like to be the son of Peter Aarons, I swallowed what I was chewing and said, "It can be pretty scary, let me tell you." There was laughter, and I added, "Don't get me wrong, I love my father with all my heart, and he's very good to me. He has a reputation as a hard man, but at home...he's very different."

"Nevertheless...." the pretty girl next to me said with a wink, and I nodded.

"Nevertheless, I try very hard never to cross him, and I'm sure most of you know why."

"He is a hard man," someone said, "but he's fair, and damn, he does know what he's doing. I've made five films with him, and I've never had to be ashamed of the work I did, or the overall quality of the finished product."

"I hear," someone else said, "he's going to make that big film about the Indian wars, and then he's going to go strictly upstairs. Do you know anything about that...what do they call you, Bud? Is that what I heard?"

"Bud is fine," I said, even as I shook my head. "Like any guy with a dozen irons in the fire at all times, he says one thing one day, and another thing the next. I know it would please my mother if he got off the set and into the boardroom."

"He's still married to your mother?" the girl next to me asked. She sounded incredulous.

I smiled down at her and nodded. "Oh, you betcha. It's the kind of love match I'd give my eye teeth for."

The guy across from me looked a little incredulous himself, and oddly disappointed. "I thought you were..." he stopped abruptly.

"I was what? Gay?"

He nodded. "Not that there's anything wrong with being gay these days, Bud." His tone spoke volumes.

"Except that it'll get you fired, evicted, hated, and maybe killed, which I think is wrong. But the fact is, I'm not gay." I said it quietly but with emphasis. "Where the rumor got started I don't know, but please spread this one. I'm not a homosexual, I'm a pianist. I love my dad, but I'm not like him. I love horseback riding and waltzing through the moonbeams on the beach, and I'd like to find a female of the species who enjoys those things, too. Now, if you'll excuse me, I need to study my script."

I studied my script for fifteen minutes and the inside of my eyelids for another fifteen. Later, when I had time, I'd brood about the fact that the rumor of my being homosexual seemed to have a broad base in the film community. Right now, I had to apply myself to my work or be yelled at. I knew I was a ringer, and I didn't want to be the weak spot in the movie.

The costumer spray painted me into tight jeans and a tight tee shirt, and it was time for me to sit on the gym steps with the neighborhood girls and a couple boxing buddies and play my guitar while I sang. Junior Keiger's words came back to haunt me. Bullfrog in heat. *Hey, Aarons, you sound like a big old horny bullfrog.*

"You've had voice lessons," my father snapped. "You can carry a tune." He looked at my clammy little face and shook his leonine head in disgust. "Oh, for Godssake, *Peter.* We'll dub over it if we have to. Just get on with the rehearsal, will you, so we can shoot this thing?"

George leaned around a camera and said, "JR, he looks damned silly as a flat broke Wop kid with that six thousand dollar concert twelve string in his hands. Is he supposed to have stolen that, or what?"

Dad hadn't noticed, which didn't improve his mood any. "You had to bring that one?" he demanded of me, and I tried not to cringe. I was really tired, and just a tad pissed off. The jeans were tight enough that I figured I was probably a baritone by now, and parts of me were beginning to go numb.

"Dad, you said to bring my guitar. I did. This is the only one I have that's strung."

"Get him another guitar," George and my father bellowed together, and the rest of the cast groaned. Stalled again.

"I can rehearse with this one," I said quickly, and began to play, *Santa Lucia.* "By the way, to add to your communal annoyance, I only know this in Italian. If you want it in English you'll have to give me time to make the tune fit the words."

"Just sing," George commanded, "and lighten up a bit. You're supposed to be gay, you know?"

I felt like I'd stuck my finger in a live socket, and for the space of about five minutes I could cheerfully have murdered my father with my bare hands. When I had time to think it through, I realized that nobody would be crazy enough to repeat to his face that people thought his only son was a queer, and he'd probably given Racheal's comments so little credence that it had never entered his mind to be sensitive on my behalf. I felt a little better, and the urge to throttle him began to recede.

I played, and I sang, using the upper end of my register, and it wasn't at all bad – in a bullfroggy sort of a way. They brought me a beat-up old six string from the prop room, and I hastily tuned it, aware of all the eyes on me, and on the clock. I played and sang again with the cameras rolling. I didn't get it in one take, but I did get it in two, and the starlet who'd sat next to me at lunch told me I had a very nice singing voice, which made me feel better.

Along about six O'clock in the evening I got myself beaten to death by a gang of intolerant thugs and lay, comfortably snoozing in a pool of panchromatic blood while the leading man stood over me and swore vengeance. When I was on my feet again, George stopped things for a minute and actually said, "Bud, thank you so much. You did a damned good job, and you saved our butts."

"You're welcome," I smiled. "I'm done?"

"You're done," he grinned. "Go home."

I was only too happy to oblige. I took a shower to wash off the blood and the bruises, found my guitar, and was heading out the door into the deepening twilight when my father's voice stopped me. "I owe you one," he said. "I'll cut you a check."

"No," I said, turning to face him, "I'd rather you owed me one – a big one."

"Any particular reason, Son?" He was mellow. The crisis was over for the moment. He was at his best, and I wasn't above taking advantage of it.

"Yes, Sir. I have a friend coming into town in a couple of days, and I want you to put her on the payroll and send her out on that shoot in Monument Valley with me."

"Bud..."

"Dad, she's not useless. She's a registered nurse, and that can be her main job on the set. But...she wants to be an actress, and I want a part for her. It doesn't have to be a big one, by any means. Just a line or two added in somewhere. Make her one of the passengers in one of the stagecoach scenes or something."

"You don't want much, do you?" he growled.

"For the woman who saved my life in Southeast Asia so I could be here for you today? No, I don't think I do...do you?"

He looked at me, then advanced on me until he was within arm's length. Suddenly, he began to chuckle, and reached out to pull me to him and kiss me, Russian-style on each cheek. "No," he said, "I don't. Go home. Get some sleep. I'll find something for your lady-friend to do. What's her name?"

"Bobbi Bates," I grinned. "Thanks, Dad. You'll like her." I returned the kisses, picked up my twelve string again, and went home.

I still had my grandmother's Benz. How hard would it have been to call Rafael and ask him to take Glory along and go get my car? Not very, I supposed, but I hated to take him away from his work. He was determined that Gram should come home to a largely restored meadow, and to that end he labored tirelessly and skillfully.

He had three men working with him. He'd not even tried to recruit anybody locally. He'd gone to...who knows where...where the Mexican laborers stood on the corner and hoped to be chosen to work, and brought back three men who worked like ten, dawn to dusk, as long as there was light. Apparently they slept and ate with the Ruizes, and how Glory managed it, I haven't a clue, but she seemed perfectly comfortable with the arrangement, and so I was, also. I was glad Gram wasn't home and Dad wasn't much for coming around, mind you, but...other than that, I was comfortable.

When I got home my beloved old Benz was parked in its accustomed spot, and I nosed Gram's bigger car in beside it. Amazing. I walked over to the house, expecting to find a sandwich, a salad, and a note, and found Glory setting the kitchen table with a blessedly fragrant and substantial supper.

"You are so kind," I smiled. "You really don't have to go to all this work just for me. When Gram's home, that's different, but..."

I collapsed into the chair without really meaning to, and Glory gave me a tender pat. "No trouble," she smiled. "This here is just regular food, nothin' fancy. I cook for all of us at once when Mrs. Aarons not home. I figure you just got outta the Army, you got no taste buds for fancy food just yet. Where you been all these hours?"

I told her, and then asked how my car had found its way home. "Walter telephoned here to ask if you'd forgotten, so I called Max and asked could he spare me a couple hours and we went and got it."

"Glory, thank you. That was a lot of trouble to go to."

"Not really," she said, and I swear I could see her blush. "Max, he brought Britt along, and I took the boys, and we all went to the beach, just for a little bit, but it was real nice. Royal and Titus? It was their first trip to the

Pacific ocean." She put a steaming hot bowl down in front of me, and hastily added, "I don't want you thinkin' I sneak away from my duties to indulge my family thataway very often..."

"Good God, I should hope not," I scowled. "Life should never be fun, and you must never do anything impetuous, or anything to indicate you have a mind or spirit of your own, if you want to stay in my employ. Heaven knows, I never do anything precipitant, like play drums in a band all night and then have to leave my car with a friend because I'm too drunk to drive."

"You had the brains to leave the car," she smiled. "Can I get you anything else? You shakin' like a leaf."

"I'm just tired," I smiled. "This is delicious, and it'll go a long way toward perking me up. So, how's the work going on the meadow? It looks great, from what I could see."

"Most of the plants watered in at this point. They gonna set some perennials and some grasses, and Rafael, he found some native sod to be cut somewhere not too far from here. Another couple 'a days, they be done, I think."

"And you'll have your little place to yourselves again. How are you managing the crowd?"

"It was right kind of you to let them stay here, Bud. It save Rafael a lotta time every day goin' to fetch 'em, and they got a good roof for a week or so."

I wondered if she thought she'd answered me. I ate for a bit in silence – fresh corn bread, a green salad, a stew that was rich and slightly sweet with chunks of carrot, celery, winter squash, potato, yam, turnip... something I couldn't identify that Glory said was kohlrabi...plenty of lean beef, and a hint of good California Burgundy. "Should I try to find them a place to stay?" I asked at last.

"Who?"

"Rafael's crew."

"No. They fine." She went back to preparing a cut of lamb to marinate.

"You know," I said, "We should get a house started for you guys. I thought out there where the old conservatory is. We could use that footprint, more or less, and the location is nice and private. What do you think?"

She was quiet for a full minute, maybe more, and I had time to wonder if I'd said the wrong thing again. Maybe they didn't like it here and weren't planning to stay. Rafael was polite to me, but he also avoided me whenever possible, and subtlety wasn't one of his strong points. He was tolerating me, no more. I wasn't sure why, and I wasn't sure how to ask, and so I just let it dangle and annoy me. Glory seemed happy enough. The boys were doing well, though I didn't see them often since their move to the chauffeur's quarters. I rarely heard them. I was gone a lot, and when I was home I was either busy in my study, pounding my Steinway, or pounding my ear.

I'd had time to forget what I'd asked her before she said, "Powerful big investment to make in a couple of newcomers, don't you think?"

"I'd like to think I'm investing in the future, and that you'll be part of it, which is why I'd like your input. If you're uncomfortable with that for some reason..." I made myself say it, and casually, "...for instance if you're not planning to stay on, I'll drop the subject. Otherwise, I do think we should get started before the weather turns. Getting plans and permits and that sort of stuff out of the way can take weeks."

She had stopped what she was doing and was just looking at me. It scared me and I said, "You know what, let's just drop this whole thing. I'm tired, I have a lot on my mind, and if you told me you and Rafael and the boys weren't planning to stay on, I might just cry. I do that you know. I'm not particularly proud of it, and I don't have any idea from whom I inherited it, but...I cry about things."

I stuck my face in my plate so I didn't have to meet her gaze, and didn't look over until she sat down close beside me and her hand came to rest on my forearm. "Bud, what on earth would give you the notion we was wantin' to leave you? I thought we was family."

"God, I don't know," I sighed. "I'm tired, and I get weird when I get tired. My dad put me through the wringer today at work – learning lines, acting, lots of pressure and very little rehearsal. I hadn't even read the damned script and the character turned out to be homosexual, which really bothered me. Anyway...I just...I guess I'm afraid you two will disappear in a puff of smoke. I don't think Rafael is happy here..."

"He love this place, and you gram."

"Me, he can do without."

"That's exactly right," she said firmly. "He got absolutely everything he can deal with right now. He don't need to deal with you, and he not gonna. That meadow...he eats and sleeps that meadow. Fixin' that, is his ticket to salvation – his gift to you gram for snakin' us in outta the cold. He don't hate you, Boy. He was so tickled when you took him down and let him choose a pickup – no requirements 'tall – didn't make him get a new one, or a used one, nor a Chevy nor a Ford, let him choose which one'd serve his needs best."

"I told him up front I didn't know boo about trucks except the ones I drove in the Army, and they were undependable one and all."

"And then you let him alone to choose. Bud, you doin' okay with all this. Don't go second guessin' youself and then wishin' it off on us, you hear me? We fine. That apartment is fine. They no need to be spendin' money to build us a fancy house. You got other things to do with you money."

"Glory, Gram and I...we have plenty of money to see that you are comfortable. The boys are growing up. Soon Royal will be in school and he'll need some privacy. He'll need a place to study, and practice his piano. He did ask me to give him lessons, you know, and he or Titus may decide to play a band instrument. Another twenty-five or thirty years we'll be old, you and me and Rafael. I'll probably need tons of help, and you'll be too tired and stoved up from chasing our grandkids to be running up and down those stairs and these stairs, too. Where are you going to have Thanksgiving and Christmas when all the kids and the grandkids come home? Where are you going to host church socials and Easter egg hunts and Sunday dinners with the Teuferts? Have you thought about that?"

Her laughter rang in the kitchen, and she planted a kiss on top of my head as she stood up. "Never gave it a thought, but now that you mention it, you right. We better get crackin'. I would like to wait until Rafael get that meadow done up to his satisfaction."

"Sure. Look at some plans on your own. Make some sketches. Get some idea what you'd like that's a one story around fifteen hundred square feet. That's roughly the size of the space the conservatory occupies. Think about interior colors, I guess. I'm assuming we'll go with the early California motif on the outside so it blends with the rest of the place."

I heard myself beginning to babble, my mind and my mouth going off in different directions. Glory asked me if I wanted anything else, I shook my head, and she took my plate away. Then she poured me a cup of coffee, and one for herself, and sat down with me at the table in what was to become a blessed ritual. "Tell me about you day," she said gently. "Playin' somebody who ain't straight sexually really spooked you, didn't it?"

My elbows thudded dully onto the worn oak table top, and I didn't even try to hide the misery in my eyes. "God...Glory...why does half the film community think I'm gay? Do I send out some kind of signal? When you met me, did you think I was a homosexual?"

I learned, in the hour that followed, that I could speak of absolutely anything that was worrying me, or angering me, or intriguing me, and Glory Ruiz would listen in confidence. Her presence was soothing, her input loving and insightful and I'd not meet her like again until a beautiful woman author with electric blue eyes breezed into my life a quarter of a century later, and stole my heart in the course of a day.

When Glory excused herself to go to bed, I sat at my piano and played for a little while, knowing that I'd far rather be thought of as gay than give up my music. Then I went for a swim, and went upstairs, feeling a little lonely and wishing either the house wasn't so darned big, or that I had someone in it with me. When I was smoking a cigarette out on the balcony I could hear laughter from the chauffeur's quarters, and for the inkling of a moment I had the brash thought of inviting myself over. Even as I thought it I knew it wouldn't work. For all my homely ways, I was different. I'd show up and they'd shut up like clams. I'd spoil their evening and embarrass myself in the process.

I was blowing the last of the smoke skyward when my private line rang, and I went muttering to pick it up. If it was Dad, or Kit, wanting to go get in trouble...maybe it was Walter, making sure the car had gotten home safe. I said hello, and the voice at the other end of the line said in a soft Texas drawl, "Hello, Bud. This is Bobbi."

"Well hello there!" I said. "Are you all packed and ready to head west to the Promised Land?"

"I guess so," she said, and I heard some hesitancy in her voice. "I wanted to touch base with you. I know we talked last week, but I just...are you sure I can find work out there? I don't want to flop at your place and be a sponge. Do you have roommates or anything?"

"I think I have a job lined up for you, as a matter of fact," I said, and avoided the question about roommates. I'd told Bobbi where I lived, as in, which town, but not how I lived. I'd told her what I did for a living, but I hadn't mentioned that at twenty-six I was already wealthy and considered one of Hollywood's more eligible bachelors. I was pretty sure she wouldn't find out before she got here unless I wanted her to.

You see, there were two distinctly different Hollywoods. There was the glitzy, new money, lots-of-publicity Hollywood, and there was the real power, old money, behind the scenes Hollywood that rarely made the gossip columns because not many people wanted to hear about a bunch of stuffy old producers, largely Jewish, and their daughters and their nose jobs and their sons who occasionally bolted over the line into acting or music making and thence into the glitzy, new money, lots-of-publicity Hollywood. Because I was a character actor, and because I did quite a bit of legitimate theater, I wasn't followed closely, not like Kit, who was a leading man. I was one of Hollywood's most eligible in the old money lots of power sector, but not in the sector that made the gossip columns and the supermarket rags. I was counting on that to keep me anonymous as far as Abilene, Texas in general and Bobbi in particular were concerned. She hadn't reacted to me being named Peter Aarons. With any luck at all she'd never even heard of Dad.

Don't ask me why I didn't want her to know my family had money, and whose kid I was, I don't know. Well, I do know. I was so darned sensitive, and so desperate to have people like me for who I was, and I'd been stung a few times, most especially by girls. They went out with me because I had money, or because my father was a powerful presence in Hollywood and he might just get them a job, or because I was an actor and was therefore glamorous to go out with, or for my...well, for Nina Goldman's reason, and you'll never convince me that any girl who goes out with a guy because of the rumored length of the handle on the pump, can possibly be interested in the quality of the water in the well.

I just had too much superficial stuff going for me to be comfortable with people's motives. If some girl had been attracted to me because I was highly educated, or because I played the piano like a young Rachmaninoff, it would have been fine, but I didn't think, so far at least, any of them had. Not that I was planning on dating Bobbi, or any of that kind of thing, I wasn't. She was just a friend, but still, she was one I wanted to keep, and I figured if I already had her out here and up the hill, she wouldn't be quite so inclined to bolt on me.

I tried couching that to my housekeeper the day Bobbi was to arrive. Glory'd already gotten in the habit of bringing me coffee and saying good morning while I was wrapping up my workout. She'd flip me a towel and we'd visit a bit, then she'd go back to the kitchen and fix my breakfast while I showered.

Now as I caught the towel and began wiping down she snickered and said, "I think you lyin' to somebody, Mister Aarons. Maybe me, maybe you, but when you talk about Miss Bobbi, you do light up some."

"Nonsense," I sniffed. "She's a delightful woman, and a lot of fun to be around, and I owe her a great deal, certainly, but she and I as a duo? I think not."

"Why not?" she persisted. "She got somethin' wrong with her?"

"No," I scowled. "Of course not. What do you mean, *wrong* with her?"

"Don't be askin' me. You the one who won't date the woman. What she look like? Is she pretty?"

"Very. She's about five foot seven or so, nicely curved and ever so slightly plump, lots of red hair and freckles, and brown eyes. She has a wonderful sense of humor, great laugh, and a dazzling smile. You'll like her."

"How old?"

"Ah...thirty-four, I think?"

"That's a right good age," Glory nodded solemnly. "Not real harum-scarum no more, but fresh enough to be a lot of fun, and to be teachin' you plenty, young man. Where you goin' to be keepin' this prize? Which bedroom?"

"Not mine, if that's what you're implying. I think the room in the northwest corner...no, the one next to it. More convenient."

"To what?" Glory twinkled.

"Will you just stop it!" I laughed. "If I don't scare her off you will! Get thee hence and fix me some breakfast while I go take a shower. Then I need to get down to the studio."

Not that I didn't trust Glory, I most certainly did, but I did have a wee chat with her, just to make sure there wasn't going to be a red rose on the pillow or some such nonsense. It was a long haul from West Texas to Los Angeles on a bus – two days and then some. Bobbi would be tired, and in need of good food, a hot shower and a soft bed. A joke played now could be disastrous. Anything with sexual overtones, undertones...any tone at all, could make her ill at ease, and I'd feel terrible. She'd traveled so many miles, counting on me. I was flattered, and I felt the weight of responsibility for her well-being.

"You go on to work," Glory said comfortingly. "If Miss Bobbi call, or that bus schedule changes, I let you know."

"Thanks," I smiled. I didn't tell her that Bobbi didn't have the number for the main house phone system. That was because I didn't want someone answering the phone who identified herself as my housekeeper, or himself as the gardener. My grandmother...that would have been all right, but Gram was still whooping it up in Italy, or maybe it was Greece by now. She and her little namesake were having a high old time. Mother was enjoying her holiday. Nary a peep from Racheal. I'd have to hope Bobbi didn't really need to reach me.

Kristoffer Miller and I sat hip to hip listening to Florian Swift, the assistant director, talk about the location shooting and what was expected of each of us. It would be hot during the day, and bitterly cold at night. It could be dangerous if we weren't careful every minute. There were snakes, to be sure. All the water had to be trucked in so we were to be conservative. No boozing, no bickering. We would be heat stressed, the horses and livestock would be heat stressed. It was not to be assumed that the people indigenous to the area particularly relished our presence. We were to be respectful, and give them a wide berth whenever possible. The area where we were to be shooting had no hotels or motels so we would be in tents, with portable showers and portable toilets. There were no restaurants, no caterers. We would be taking a kitchen with us and eating as a group. There were two things on the menu, take it, and leave it, period. Anybody with allergies or a medical need to be fed differently, needed to see him ASAP. There would be no doctor, but we were taking a registered nurse. We were responsible for our own supplies, whatever they might be, and for taking enough clothes to last us. There were no laundry facilities close by, and clothes would be sent out for washing a grand total of twice in the eighteen days we'd be there. Clothes needed to be washable, and properly labeled. Sleeping bags and cots would be provided, along with pillows and towels. Sounded very much like the Army, and I found myself tuning in and out. Kit gave me a pinch on the butt, and I realized I'd dozed off just for a second.

"Sorry," I whispered.

Flo was saying, "Child actors, you're all paid for, of course. Parents, if your child is more than ten years old and you insist on coming, it's going to cost you to eat, and you're going to have to provide your own lodging." He was trying to make it harder on them – probably hoping to keep a few of them home. Most of the kids fit into the over ten category, and we'd have a truckload of clucking mothers and whining fathers if all of them decided to go. The little ones weren't a problem. There were only three of them; a set of eight-year-old twin girls, and Flo's son, David, who was six. The others were in their early teens. "And you, Bud Aarons, can you make it two and a half weeks without your dad and your Steinway?"

"I'll do my very best, Sir," I winked, and Flo laughed as he turned to the others.

"Questions, comments, thoughts, ideas? Now's the time."

The floodgates opened, and the room was awash with questions and complaints. We'd already been shooting all day, it was hot, many of us were still in costume – at least mine was cool, buckskin leggings and a loin cloth – and the noise and confusion wasn't helping anybody's mood, including Flo's. I found myself glancing at the spot on my right wrist where my watch should be. "Where's she coming in?" Kit asked.

"Downtown LA. It was the straightest shot, least number of bus changes for her."

"Are you going to be late?"

"Not yet," I muttered. I heard my name, and looked up as Flo said it a second time.

"Do you still want to ride your own horses?" he asked. "If you do, you'll need to see that they're here no later than Sunday evening at six O'clock. We want to haul them in the cool of the evening. No studs, no mares in heat."

"I was going to bring Buck for Kit to ride, and Cochise for me." Cochise was Racheal's big black and white paint. She'd wanted to show horses, so Dad had spent the requisite fortune, after which, wanting being better than having, she'd quickly lost interest and gone on to other things. She was too anal and selfish to sell him to somebody who would use and enjoy him, so he stood. I liked the horse, and when Kit and I rode, he took my buckskin gelding, and I took Cochise. Not that he was too much horse for Kit. Kit was an excellent rider. But if something happened to Cochise, I wanted it to be me who got an ass chewing from little Miss Racheal.

"How appropriate," Florian chuckled. "Are you going to be able to figure out which Cochise we're hollering at?"

"Hopefully I'll be the one on top," I said.

"Sounds scrumptious," a female voice said in my ear, and Amber brushed by me. I felt myself flush with annoyance. I was hoping her whining, aggravating mother chose to come along, otherwise I'd be kicking that child out of my bed at night. The very thought of what she could do to my reputation gave me the willies.

Apparently, my reputation was already in question, as I discovered very quickly. "We're not bunking alone, are we?" I asked, raising my voice to be heard, and Flo shook his white-blond curls.

"No," he said. "We'll be two or three or four to a tent. Why, do you need your privacy for some reason? You're not planning on sneaking in any of those guys you were messing around with all night a few nights ago, are you? Because we don't need the bad publicity."

It was suddenly quiet, and I was shocked to the point of blushing. I could feel the prickle. "What...the guys in the band, is that who you mean?"

"That's exactly who I mean, young man." He made me feel ten years old. "You didn't even see the papers, did you?"

"What...in the hell are you talking about?" I murmured. "You're embarrassing me to death for no reason. Why is that?"

"Because this film doesn't need bad publicity, Peter, and having one of the co-stars flitting around an iffy bar with a gay band, is bad publicity. It's a political hot potato..."

"Are you accusing Walter and Kevin and Jack...and Bonner, of being homosexuals?" I asked sharply, and Kit's right arm came across my midsection before I could stand up.

"They *are* homosexuals, you goober," he hissed. "They've always been homosexuals. I thought you knew that, Buddy. My God, you speak Russian, you speak Italian, you speak Spanish, and five or six other languages. Don't you speak body language?"

"No," I said quietly into the silence of the room, "I guess I don't. We just...we've played together for years...off and on. When we were undergrads at UCLA I played drums for them...I never thought about anything but the music, you know?"

"I know," Kit said comfortingly. "Flo's only teasing you, and you're letting him get your goat."

But he wasn't teasing. His ramrod stiff back, the discomfort on his face said he wasn't. The people in the room slowly picked up the threads of their various conversations and the volume came back to something like normal, but I was mortified. I wanted to run – cry – throw up. I wanted to tell my daddy and have Flo fired. Mostly, I wanted to be out of there. When Flo cut us loose I couldn't hit the locker room fast enough.

I showered in silence, and Kit told me sharply that if I was going to sulk like a baby he'd go get Bobbi, because I sure as hell wouldn't be a very welcoming sight. He softened immediately and added, "That...the way he said what he did to you...that's just not like Florian. Wash my back," he said, handing me the soap.

"You sure you want to turn your back on me," I said, trying to tease and lighten up, but it came out flat and ominous.

"There's nobody I'd rather have watching my back," Kit chuckled, "or washing it, for that matter. You know, it does seem odd, doesn't it, that Racheal makes one of her usual shitty comments in front of your dad, you play with the band as you have for years, and then suddenly you find yourself thrust into a homosexual role – no warning – and now Florian, who is directing one of your dad's movies, steps completely out of character and kicks your balls in front of God and his public?"

"In English."

"Okay. I'll be blunt, not that it's my bailiwick, mind you. I think this little dip in liquid shit is about as coincidental as me getting a big, fat scholarship to UCLA when my grades weren't all that stellar, or you and me finding ourselves in the same movie every so often."

I slid the soap over his shoulder and just stood there, massaging the suds into his back so I didn't have to look him in the face. Kit was like a big dog – as long as I rubbed him, he'd stand there and let me. I mulled over what he'd said, and finally sighed and nodded to myself. "Dad," I said, and rinsed the soap off my hands.

"I don't think he's trying to be mean, Buddy. I just think he wants you to realize..."

"Realize what? That he can make my life a living hell in the blink of an eye? Kit, I've known that for a long time."

"That *you* can make your life a living hell in the blink of an eye," Kit said firmly. "All of a sudden you're out in left field and all over the place. You hire a black woman who's married to a Mexican to run your household. Don't get your back up, just listen to me. Glory's the greatest. She's been lovely to me, and more importantly, she's lovely to you, which Mrs. Gustavson never was. Rafael is a wonder worker in the yard. There is nothing in the world wrong with those people except their color – and that's enough this day and age. It's not just the fact that she's black and half the blacks in the country are in full uprising. He's brown, and half the brown people in LA are getting ready to revolt. They're starting to call themselves Chicanos, and they want equal rights and an equal education, and they quite probably deserve it, but....*but*, it's scaring people, and it's pissing them off, and your gallantly obtained and mismatched staff could be the poster couple for civil unrest. Your dad knows that, and you know how he loathes negative publicity on the mundane level. Now you decide to start romping again with the Backdoor Four..."

All of a sudden I found myself laughing. "Nice mouth, Kristoffer! I swear to you, I didn't know they were fey..."

"And that, right there, is the problem," he said, shutting off the shower and grabbing a towel. I followed suit, and as we began drying off he continued. "You're twenty-six years old, and you don't have a clue what's going on. You are without a doubt the most naive person I know, at least among males. I know a few females with less moxie, but not many. You're incapable of telling a fairly flamboyant fag from a straight, and yet you've passed on some really nice girls because you suspect them of ulterior motives they quite probably don't have. You're warped, Aloysha." He finished drying my back, and I was drying his when I became aware that we were not alone. Flo was leaning against the end of the last bank of lockers, arms folded in silence, listening to the conversation.

I shot him a look, and he dropped his eyes. "Is there something I can do for you?" I asked, trying to sound like I wasn't carrying a grudge the size of a small European country.

"Peter," he said, "This town is going to hear from you. You're a brilliant musician and a fine young actor. You have a good head on your shoulders. You are kind and accepting of people...too much sometimes. You keep a civil tongue in your head and behave like a professional on the set, and as far as I can tell, off the set. You are also the only son of a relentlessly power-hungry strategist who would be euphoric if you were just like him. You aren't, but he adores you anyway. He dotes on you. He's going to try everything he can to bring you around to his way of doing things, and he's going to do what he thinks he needs to do to give you a real-world education and protect you from the world at the same time. If that entails making you feel foolish in front of a couple dozen people, or a hundred, or a million, then so be it. I don't envy you...and yet, I do. Listen to Kit, will you?"

"I'll...thanks...yeah, whatever," I said. "If we want an RN this trip, I have a bus to meet."

As I drove into the deepening evening I thought about how lame that had sounded. How ungracious I'd been in accepting his apology, for that's what it had been. I'd ducked my head, given him a half-smile, thrown on my clothes, and exited, stage left, with my tail still firmly tucked between my legs. The fact that I was naive I could deal with, the fact that I was my father's puppet, I couldn't.

I parked in the lot next to the bus station. It was one of those totally grey places that left me wishing mightily that I had locks on my wheel covers, lock-nuts on my wheels, and a tire iron in my hand for the walk to the terminal. I figured Bobbi, who was big, athletic, and all-Texan, could defend me on the way back. The bus station reminded me a little of the market district. It was a confusion of noises and colors, but it didn't smell nearly as nice, and there was a kind of underlying restless desperation. People seemed so rushed, or unsure, or uncommunicative. Their eyes were veiled to intrusion, yet they studied me as I walked past, and I tried to seem nonchalant about keeping one hand on the pocket my wallet was in. It was smoky in the stalest sense of the word, and the distortion on the public address system made it utterly impossible to understand what was coming from where, and what was leaving. It made me think of the comedian who joked about them using winos to announce where the buses were going, and I laughed softly to myself. I figured I'd look for a buxom redhead in a mini skirt and go-go boots, and hope it was Bobbi.

I was there an hour and fifteen minutes. Apparently there is a rule that buses and trains may never arrive on time, and it was in full force. I watched legs and suitcases and tired faces, and every once in a while another bus would pull in and I'd stand up long enough to watch it disgorge its passengers through the main doors, and then flop down again into one of those rows of suspiciously sticky seats. I was going to put these jeans in the dirty clothes the second I got home.

I was on something like my fifth cigarette, my seventh bum, when the passengers getting off a westbound bus included one Bobbi Jean Bates. The second I stood up she spotted me, and pushed through the crowd and into my arms. "God, Bud, you look wonderful! I'm so glad to see you!" she laughed, gave me a kiss on the lips and took the cigarette from my fingers.

"Oh, oh, oh, my God...I haven't had a cigarette in hours. I thought I was going to die and be buried in the garbage on the floor of that damned bus. Have you been waiting long?"

"Not long," I smiled, enjoying the look and the feel of her. "Where's your luggage?"

"Still in the belly of that cross-country slug," she grimaced. "I suppose we should stand around in hopes of claiming it, or some that looks like it."

"Would you like your own cigarette, or are you keeping mine?" I chuckled, and she pulled it slightly away from me.

"I'm keeping yours," she said with an arching brow, and turned to walk ahead of me back to the bus. "When's the last time you had to ride one of these things?"

"When I mustered out, and I hope never to do so again, believe me," I said. "How was the trip?"

"About like one of Sergeant Krantz's pep talks – long and boring. You do look wonderful. Much better than the last time I saw you. I hardly recognized you standing up with clothes on."

A few heads turned, and she burst out laughing at the look on my face. "*Pobrecito*. I forget you're just a baby yet. I didn't mean to embarrass you."

"The first comment didn't embarrass me as much as the second one," I chuckled. "See any luggage you recognize?"

"That one," she said pointing at a wildly floral suitcase that was just coming off, "and..." she looked around a bit. "I don't see the other one. I hope to hell it didn't go to Seattle, or Denver or some other place." The baggage handler pulled the last of the suitcases out from under the bus, and the other bag appeared – a substantially bigger version of the first.

I grabbed them both and jerked my chin toward the exit. "Vamoose," I said. "And you'd better be rich enough when you leave here to go by plane, because I'm not coming back to this place."

"I'm never leaving," she sighed. "But I am going to be rich. Which way?"

"Out onto the street. To your right and then right again." I followed her, and soon my car appeared in the pooling glow from a parking lot lamp post. "The red one just to your left. The old Mercedes."

"Classy," she said with a whistle. "Yours?"

"Yup. My..." I started to say, *my Gram gave it to me for my sixteenth birthday*, but since it was obviously about ten years old, it would also be obvious that she'd given me a brand new Mercedes sports sedan when I was but a puling infant. "My pride and joy." I put the huge, heavy suitcases in the trunk, glad I'd removed my golf clubs to make more room, and opened the door for Bobbi. She was wearing what she said she'd be wearing, a yellow tank top, a flowered mini skirt that more or less matched the luggage, high white boots...and she looked and sounded disturbingly unlike the woman I remembered. Along with the uniform, she had put away her nurse persona. She was less soothing, more stimulating, full of bright talk and ribald humor, and her smile had become laughter.

"It's a good distance home," I said. "Do you need anything before we get out on the freeway?"

"I should have peed before we left the bus station, but to tell the truth, I've seen, and smelled enough bus station toilets in the last two days to gross me out for a lifetime."

"Not a problem. I need to fuel up before we head home. How does twenty minutes sound on the scale of do-ables?"

"I give it about an eighty-five percent," she grinned. "I'll buy the gas."

"Not necessary, Bobbi."

"I didn't think it was," she replied. "I'll buy the gas."

I let her, though the attendant at the station where we had our accounts gave me a puzzled look. I returned it with a brief shake of my head, and he took the cash. He thanked me by name, just as he had greeted me, and Bobbi lifted an eyebrow my direction as she got back in the car. "That's much, much better. No longer looking through a yellow film. You do a lot of business here, I assume?"

"Yup. My whole family does. This station is in a major flight pattern – my house, my parents' house, groceries, the studios, the gym, and the stables."

"Wow," she sighed, "you're really an actor? Well, I know you are. Once I met you I checked out some of your roles."

"I don't do any more acting than I actually have to," I admitted, heading briefly up onto the freeway. "I'd prefer to be a musician."

"You sing? I'm not surprised with that beautiful speaking voice. Oh, wow, this is the Hollywood freeway, isn't it? I'm really in Hollywood!"

She gave herself a squeeze, and I laughed, "No, I don't sing I play the piano, and technically, you're in Los Angeles proper, heading north kind of toward Burbank, more toward the San Fernando Valley, but this is indeed the Hollywood freeway. We'll be getting off of it soon and over onto Mulholland Drive heading west."

"You don't live in the city?" She sounded disappointed.

"No. But trust me, you'll get all the city you want, and you'll be glad to head for more pastoral surroundings."

"I've seen enough pastures to last me a lifetime," she snorted, and gave me a wink. "Tell me about this job you think you have lined up."

"No think. It's a done deal. I...well, I took it on your behalf. I hope you don't mind. There's a big cast and crew headed for Utah in four days to work on the movie, *Apache Pass*, and they needed a nurse. I'm sure the thought of traveling doesn't exactly make you jump for joy, but it is a job, and it is an in with the studios...and, it does involve being an extra in some of the scenes. You may even get a line or two out of it, which will put you on your way to getting into SAG, the Screen Actors Guild."

"You doll!" she exclaimed, leaning across the seat to hug me and kiss my cheek, "How in God's name did you pull this off?"

"Just happened to be in the right place at the right time to hear the conversation. In other words, dumb luck."

She sat back a little and studied my profile. Then she said, "I doubt that, somehow. I doubt much of what you do has anything to do with dumb luck."

"Trust me," I chuckled. "I can do dumb with the best of them. Actually, somebody owed me a favor and I cashed it in."

"Which means...I owe you a favor."

There was something in her tone of voice that made me tingle just a little, but I didn't let myself react to it. Could have been coincidence. "Delightful prospect," I smiled, and said nothing more on the subject. "Griffith Park to your right as we turn left, ladies and gentlemen. Well, ultimately we'll turn left. Nothing is ever that simple in LA."

We got squared away and I said, "I probably could have saved us some miles and some time by going south a bit, and taking Santa Monica Boulevard over to the San Diego freeway, but it can be really crowded sometimes. It's starting to get really crowded, period, around here."

"Not out here it's not," she frowned, squinting into the darkness. "Do you live out here in these hills all by yourself?"

"Oh, mercy no. Tons of people live out here."

Her head came slowly my direction. "Do you need to be slapped? I can arrange that."

"I'd rather be spanked," I chuckled. "My mother says slapping a child is demeaning."

"Okay, do you need to be spanked? Never mind, I don't want to know. Do you live alone in your house, trailer, tent, burrow, whatever?"

"No. I live with my grandmother, though you'd never know it. It seems like if I'm not gone, she is."

"Is she home right now?"

"No. She called last night from the fair isle of Crete. She says to tell you hello and welcome, and she'll see you in about three weeks."

"And you have room."

"Yes," I nodded. "We have room."

We chatted about things in general for a bit. She had two parents just like I did. Her dad was fairly well off, partnered in a couple of used car lots and a dealership. Her mom had been Homecoming Queen in high school and just couldn't seem to get over it. Nice lady, but too much mascara and not enough ingenuity. She was trying to get by on giggles and cute when she was way past the stage when either was really effective, and couldn't seem to figure out why people were increasingly unresponsive. Dad was a bit of a blowhard, but a nice guy. Pot belly, smoked a cigar and was pretty much, coupled with his frothy blonde wife, a living, breathing cartoon about life in the south. There were two brothers, the football player and the village idiot. The football player, who had knocked up one of the cheerleaders and married young, worked with Dad selling 'caw-wers'. Two syllables.

The idiot thought the future of the planet was in computers, and was hell-bent on seeing a little bitty one in every living room in America. It would turn your lights on for you, call the cat, cook breakfast, and let you work from home with people miles away. It would have a screen like a television set, and would talk to you, and play music when you needed soothing. He was perpetually in college, though Daddy would have preferred an institution with bars on the windows and pads on the walls. Both nice guys, though. Nice family when all was said and done. Church every Sunday, then fried chicken and football, or baseball, or basketball or boating – but always fried chicken. A Sweetwater Sunday, she called it. "Sweetwater Texas, home of the...holy shit! I guess you have room, don't you?"

We had arrived. The lights were on to greet us, and I parked in the middle of the herringbone brick drive, not too far from the kitchen door. "I said we had room, O' Doubting One. Are you hungry? I can smell dinner clear out here."

"Me? I've had a big bag of potato chips, about a pound of peanuts, and six candy bars in the last two days. I'm a walking zit. Yes, I'm hungry!"

"Well then, allow me to welcome you to my home," I said, and went around the car to open the door for her. Of course by the time I got there she was already out and swinging herself a little to loosen the kinks in her back. "Right this way," I said with a gesture, then dropped an arm around her shoulder and walked her into the house. The air was warm, and I could smell the chlorine in the pool over the fragrance of the pines. "We can swim later if you'd like." I opened the kitchen door, and Glory turned smiling from the kitchen sink.

"Bus late, of course?"

"Of course," I replied. "Glory Ruiz, this is my friend, Bobbi Bates. Bobbi, Glory."

They gave each other a tentative, smiling nod, and about that time I heard the trunk close on the Benz and in a few moments Rafael came through the door with Bobbi's suitcases. "Thanks," I said. "I can take those up, along with Bobbi, so she can freshen up. Rafael Ruiz, my friend, Bobbi Bates."

"*Senorita*," he said with a gracious nod.

"*Senor*," she replied, and there might have been just a tinge of hostility, or incredulity. She looked from him to Glory, then at me, and I could see her eyebrows working just a little bit under the heavy copper bangs.

I have no clue what came over me, I swear I don't, but I hung my head and said, "These are my parents. That's why we live way out here in the middle of nowhere. They're ashamed of me." Bobbi jumped about a foot straight up.

"He lies!" Rafael said hotly. "We are his brother and sister. We two just have the same last name because we are also married." He shrugged nonchalantly and turned away. "It was so much cheaper than dating a stranger."

"Honey, don't let them two mess your head around," Glory said sympathetically. "You know how men can be, and there's times I'm right sorry I married either one of 'em. But there was the children to think of, and you know how people can talk – so cruel. None of that goes on in our little refuge, here, and none of it *gonna* go on."

Bobbi just stood there, rooted in bemusement. The door opened yet again and in popped Royal with Titus in tow. "Excuse me," he said quickly. "I didn't know you had company." He extended his hand and said, "I'm Royal Rafael Ruiz, and I was four years old in July."

Bobbi kind of shook herself, took his hand and said, "I'm Bobbi Bates. I'm a friend of...the tallest one. Is he your daddy?" I could tell by the tone of her voice that she was teasing, and so could Royal. He giggled obligingly.

"Him? Neh, I like him though. This here one's my daddy." He sidled up to Rafael, who dropped an arm around his shoulder and gave him a wink.

"And you," Bobbi said, turning to Titus, "Which one is your daddy?"

Titus just blinked at her and shoved his thumb in his mouth, and Royal laughed, "That's Titus. We both belong to this daddy."

"Oh, I see. Then Bud is your uncle?"

"I wish he was," Royal sighed, smiling at me. "He is my angel, though. He's all our angel. This is our home now, and it's nice and safe and there's plenty of soap. Are you going to live here, too?"

Bobbi studied me for a long, long few seconds in silence, and Kit's words came back to me with reverberating clarity. I was one naive sucker. I'd brought a southern white woman into this living arrangement and never thought one thing about it. "According to your Uncle Angel I am, but he hasn't offered me any supper, or any soap, so I'm not real sure he wants me."

"I know where the soap is!" Royal exclaimed, and went tearing off down the hall before Rafael could grab him. The four of us looked at each other, and burst into gales of laughter. She had passed the test with good grace. We had all passed the test. It was good practice for all the tests that were yet to come.

"Bud, get this poor woman up to her room while I put supper on the table," Glory said, wiping her eyes on her apron, and about that time Royal came skidding up with a bar of soap.

"There's lots more where this came from," he said.

"Good, because I was on that bus a long time, and I really need a scrubbing," Bobbi said. "Thank you so much for the soap, Royal."

"You're welcome," he said graciously. He grinned at me, added, "Good night, Uncle Angel," and turned to ask his parents whatever it was he'd come in for in the first place.

I picked up Bobbi's suitcases and proceeded through the house. "I'm sorry. I truly don't know what possessed me," I said after a bit.

"Uncle Angel," she chuckled softly. "What rock did you find them under?"

"I love those people..." I began in a warning tone, and her hand came down on my shoulder as she walked behind me.

"Of course you do, and they love you. You're their angel. I'm just amazed they're not dead."

"They're from Texas."

"*From* being the operative word."

"You're offended?"

"You assume too much. I'm amazed. I said I was amazed, and that's what I meant. How did they escape being lynched, and what preacher would have married those two?"

"I never asked. I'm a Californian, Bobbi. We can be weird out here, but compared to everyplace else, we're pretty accepting, I think. Because I've always been a member of the film community, which is more open-minded yet...here, this is your room...I've never even thought about the kinds of questions you're asking, much less sought to have them answered." I set down her suitcases, noting with pleasure that the French doors were already open to the evening breeze. There were fresh flowers in a vase on the dresser, fresh linens just outside the bathroom door, and a plush terrycloth robe at the foot of the bed. "Have I put you in an awkward position? Are you going to be uncomfortable here?"

"I," she said turning to put her arms around my neck, "am going to be very comfortable here. Thank you for having me."

CHAPTER SIX

I slept that night with the French doors open and just a sheet over me. It could be hot here during the day, but it usually cooled off at night. Not so this particular Thursday. I tossed a little, achy and uncomfortable with the heat, and wondered if Bobbi was sleeping well. She'd gone up shortly after supper, saying her internal clock was still on Texas time. Of course, coming from the hellish heat of a Texas summer, she was probably wrapped up in her blankets, sleeping like a baby.

I was spread-eagle on the bed when the first fly of dawn tickled my nose. I batted at it, and it obligingly let me alone for thirty seconds or so, and then came back. I swung a little harder, and again it departed. The third time it came back I swatted and cursed, and it giggled.

"Wench," I muttered, prying my eyes open and rubbing at my face. "I'll get you. Damn, it's barely light out."

"Your doors were open. I assumed I was invited." She was sitting on the edge of the bed holding one of the daisies from the bouquet on her dresser. She was barefooted, wearing the green robe from the foot of her bed, and it was a perfect color with her red hair. "I want to go for a swim," she said, and tickled me again with the flower.

"The pool's not in here," I muttered, trying to stay annoyed. It was no use. I was amused, and I was awake. "You know, when we start location shooting, we're going to be dug out of bed every morning at the crack of dawn or before, we're going to work our asses off all day, sweating like a team of horses, and we're going to be sleeping in sleeping bags on cots! And *you*..." I sat up, seized her shoulders, and shook her gently, "...are throwing away our last few mornings of sleeping in!"

"Go swimming with me and then you can go back to bed," she smiled, pushing my hair back off my forehead. I'd been letting it grow all summer so that it would be easier to weave my apache hair into it, and it was nearing the completely unmanageable stage. "You look like a little boy with all these curls," she said tenderly. "Makes me want to cuddle you...except for the beard and...Bud, they shaved your chest?"

"Which you wouldn't know if you weren't in my *boudoir* at the crack of dawn, young lady. Do you have your suit on?"

"I certainly do," she said as she stood up, and let the robe slide off to reveal a lovely tan body with bikini lines – unusually good tan for a redhead – but no bikini. "My birthday suit." It was my turn to jump, and she laughed aloud. "I shocked you. *Pobrecito*, I keep forgetting, you're..."

"Just a baby, I know," I muttered, chuckling a little and hoping to God I had enough of a tan of my own to hide the fact that I was blushing furiously.

"Here we are on this gorgeous morning way out in the mountains, nobody else is up yet. Why do we need suits?"

"You don't," I smiled. "If you're comfortable, I'm cool with it. I do need one, though, so excuse me a minute, Flower Child."

She folded onto the floor in the standard yoga position and began chanting, "Beads, flowers, freedom, happiness...beads, flowers, freedom..."

I just shook my head and grabbed a pair of trunks from my dresser before disappearing into the bathroom. God, I was a prude! I was a naive little guy! I stood in front of the mirror and tried to look myself in the eye and I couldn't. Why in God's name had I kidded myself into thinking I'd had a normal childhood? I was the most sheltered kid on the planet. While the other guys were out playing baseball and breaking windows and going to the movies all summer, I was in Europe playing the piano. I'd had sex, and pretended I'd had relationships. Not so. I was cornered in this damned bathroom with a real live woman outside. A real live woman with no clothes on who wanted me to go swimming with her. God...what was my next line? Not a stage manager in sight. God...oh, God....

When I opened the bathroom door Bobbi was sitting on my bed in an emerald green bikini, the robe draped loosely around her shoulders. "It's about time," she grinned, "I was about to come in there with a rope and fish you out."

"Aw, Bobbi, You didn't have to go and..."

"Yes I did," she smiled quickly. "It was either put this on, or put you off, and you are more important. Come on, let's go swim. It's beautiful out there." She turned away from me and headed out the French doors into the widening dawn.

It had been a test. She'd had that bikini in the pocket of her robe. It had been a test. A payback for last night? Perhaps. If so, it had been paid in spades. I followed her down the wide, outside stairs onto the patio and out to the pool. When she'd dropped her robe and was stretching to greet the morning, I snatched her roughly into my arms, and unceremoniously chucked her ass in the pool. She surfaced, choking a little and blowing the water out of her nose, and I pointed a finger at her and growled, "Don't ever test me again. And don't cross me."

She looked at me for a few seconds, and then laughed in my face. "I'm sorry!" she gasped. "You are a dear, sweet man, Peter, but don't try that approach when it matters, because you have all the predatory male swagger of a puddy tat. Less, as a matter of fact. Better make that a teddy bear. It's just not your style."

"And appearing naked in men's bedrooms is yours?" I retorted, trying to find all the places I'd been stabbed.

"I did not appear naked, I became naked. And, no...not guys in general. You asked me to stay with you. I wasn't sure just what that meant."

"But you were willing to find out. Why is that?"

"When is the last time you looked in a mirror, Bud?"

"Why?" I muttered, "do I have spinach in my teeth?"

"God, you're hopeless," she sighed, and began swimming laps. I allowed myself a moment to smirk and feel good about myself, and then dove in beside her.

I told her I had a morning routine that was pretty well carved in stone, and that she was free to establish one of her own. Since I was already in the pool I worked out on the springboard and the platform, which usually followed jumping rope, weightlifting, and or jogging. I didn't spend hours at it, but I did concentrate when I was working out. I still do, as a matter of fact, and my family knows, that is my time. Bobbi watched me diving for a bit, and then went in the house, which is where I found her an hour later when I got back from what had turned out to be more a crawl than a run up the mountain – drinking coffee and talking to Glory. They both clammed up when I walked in, and I knew I'd been the topic of conversation. I just shook my head, said, "I promised I'd have you at the studios at ten O'clock this morning for your interview," and kept going.

"You feelin' all right?" Glory called after me. "You lookin' a mite red in the face, Darlin'. I think you need you temperature took."

"Holy Toledo, they've cloned my grandmother!" I snapped by way of reply, and dragged myself upstairs, thoroughly annoyed.

I was at the piano – scales run, hands warm – working on Schumann's *Allegro affettuoso*, from his *Piano Concerto in A minor Op. 54*, when I became aware that Bobbi was sitting partway up the floating staircase, watching. How long she'd been there I couldn't say, but I felt her big brown eyes on me, and it spoke volumes that I was aware of her at all. Fact is, she disturbed me.

I'd wanted her to come stay with me and be my little friend, so we could have fun together and talk in the evenings and I wouldn't be lonely. And now when I thought about having fun together I was definitely thinking in terms of grown-up games. But I kept on playing the piano, looking nonchalant, and I told myself it was just sex...with a flower child...who probably would cheerfully have had sex with anybody. Why that mattered, I didn't know for sure, but it did. I was ready to be in love, though I didn't recognize the symptoms.

I crashed to a stop, pulled my hands off the keyboard, and as I reached for a cigarette Bobbi said, "I was wrong about you."

I lit up, inhaled sharply, and eyed her through a blue haze. "How so?"

"You are no teddy bear, and you're no puddy tat, either. You're... different, but you are full of passion. Wonderful, deep, mature passion, which is probably why I missed it. I'm used to the high school, hard dick kind of machismo that we call passion. But it isn't, is it? That's lust. That's a stalking mentality. This...what you're doing...that's passion."

I felt a flush of pleasure at her words, but I smiled and said, "That's kind of you to say, but I think you're comparing two different kinds of nuts, here. One is sexual, one is artistic. I doubt that my kind of passion is particularly deep or mature, but I am glad you think it's wonderful. I think sometimes I'm a little staid and boring for a guy my age." I looked away from her and flipped the ash off my cigarette.

"You're steady, Bud. I think that's why I forget how much older I am than you are." It was her turn to look away and uncomfortable, and I felt like we were going have awkward moment after awkward moment for as long as she was here. This wasn't easy, and it wasn't particularly fun.

"Well, I've spent about all the time I can at this piano," I said abruptly. "We'd best be getting down off this mountain."

We judiciously avoided the issue of passion during our drive into town. Of course the precipitous serpentine of road kept Bobbi pretty much riveted on my driving skills, and the second time she cringed I said, "Am I making you nervous?"

"We just..." she gulped, "we don't have roads like this in west Texas. This is so steep and winding I just...."

She was squeaking, and I took my foot off the gas. "I'm sorry," I soothed. "I've been riding and driving this same road my whole life. I know every twist, every turn and pothole. I can tell you to the tenth of a mile how fast I can go on these curves."

"So, you really are an actor?" she said yet again, abruptly changing the subject. She looked a little green, she was still swallowing hard, and I slowed down even more. We would be late, maybe, but we would be unsoiled. "Did you take any classes for that?"

I arched an eyebrow her direction without taking my eyes off the road. "For what, my driving, or my acting?"

"You obviously haven't had any driving lessons, Peter. I meant the acting."

"I have a degree in Acting from UCLA," I chuckled. "It's more or less right here at the bottom of the hill and off over that direction." I jerked my chin southeast. "Have you taken any classes?"

"At the college where I did my nursing degree, but they didn't have anything serious to offer."

"We'll get you into some classes here," I said, easing us into the heavier, flatland traffic, and picking up a little speed.

"They'll cost money, won't they?" she asked. She sighed and sat back in the seat to light a cigarette.

"They can be spendy," I nodded, "but Daddy has kept the village idiot in college for ten years, why not you?"

"He's not done yet. I am. I'm a nurse. If I want to go to school, I'm going to have to pay for it, which means I need a steady job."

I looked over at her for a moment. "Do you mind working as a nurse until you get your break?"

"Noooo, I don't think so. Why?"

"Good nurses are in demand at the studios. Actors and crews get banged up a lot making movies, as you'll see when we go on location. You do well on this shoot, they may just want you to stay on as a soundstage Med Tech. I'll try to talk a couple of people into falling off their horses so you can show 'em your stuff."

"Thanks," she laughed. "Just be sure you're not one of them."

"Wouldn't think of it," I said, took her cigarette from her, and began pointing out things I thought she'd be interested in.

She was like a jack-in-the-box, up and down in the seat, head revolving as she tried to see everything at once, and I laughed and asked her how she could get carsick on a simple country road, and then swivel herself around like that and stay well. She had no real answer – she was too giddy. I may have acted older than I was, but she definitely acted younger in a good sort of way. She was so excited I couldn't help but get caught up in it.

Hollywood! I'd been raised here. It was all too familiar to hold much glamor for me. I'd seen these people without their makeup and their good manners on. But still, seeing it through Bobbi's fresh eyes, it was a pretty wonderful business to be in. I still think so – maybe even more than I used to.

The guard at the main studio gate gave me a friendly salute and said, "Good morning, Bud. I thought you had today off."

"I do," I grinned. "Bobbi has an interview. Bobbi Bates, Johnny Georges." She smiled and said hello, Johnny gave her the same jaunty salute, and waved us on in the direction of the studio business offices.

"All right, beautiful lady," I chuckled, "you need to seem more like a nurse and less like a kid in a toy store. I told these people you were capable, and steady, and calm. Calm." I put my hand over hers and gave her a long, penetrating gaze over my sunglasses. "Calm, Miss Bates. Do you know the meaning of the word?"

She just shook her head, laughing, and took a deep drag of cigarette smoke to steady herself. "Seems to me I used to. It really does. But that was long, long ago, and far away in Texas. Bud, this is Hollywood! I just came through the gates of a motion picture studio in a Mercedes Benz with a real, honest-to-God, handsome as all get-out actor, who is a personal friend...and you expect me to be calm? Are you *crazy*?"

"Contrary to popular belief...yes. Come on, let's get you in there before your head explodes." I went around and let her out of the car, and when she was standing in front of me I smoothed her hair and brushed imaginary lint off her shoulders, just to keep my hands on her for a bit in hopes of having a soothing effect on her. It was pretty much a lost cause. She was so wired I nearly got a shock off her. I just sighed, and shook my head, which was beginning to ache, and offered her my arm.

She took my hand instead, and swung it back and forth as we walked. She had a delightful laugh, and a sweet, twinkling smile that was to be the downfall of more than one poor boy in Hollywood, though I had the honor of being the first. Glory had been right, as she inevitably was in cases like this. She could see Bobbi in my eyes, and Philippa...but not Meg – never Megan. And I did not love Bobbi Bates at first sight, nor ever with even remotely the intensity with which I love my wife, but that day as I walked with her hand in mine, I did want her, very much.

It was Friday, and the studio was alive with the bustle and noise of any huge enterprise. Flats were on the move on forklifts, materials poured out of the sign shop, people scurried on foot, by bicycle, on roller skates, in golf carts, and Bobbi tried to see it all. When I went inside the offices and firmly closed the outside door, her face just fell. "Sorry," I said, shaking a warning finger, "business before pleasure."

She tightened her grip on my hand, and I opened the door to Reggie Clevenger's suite. His secretary was sitting there – a sweet woman in her early fifties who put up with Reggie's endless creative snarl of information and kept smiling all the time she was organizing him. I gave her a nod and a smile of my own.

"Mrs. Norris, this is Bobbi Bates. We have an appointment to see Mister Clevenger."

"So you do," she twinkled. I could tell by the way she looked at us she thought we were a cute couple, and that we were just that...a couple. Could be worse, I thought to myself. I wouldn't mind being seen around with Bobbi Bates. She reached for the intercom and said, "Mister Clevenger, *Mister* Aarons is here." She deliberately held down the speaker button, and there was a hearty curse of dismay from inside the room. She waited a pregnant moment, winked at me, then added, "Bud is here with Miss Bates."

"Not funny," came Reggie's voice. "Send them in."

I nodded to Mrs. Norris and opened the door to Reggie's office. He was sitting there with Florian Swift, and both of them rose as we walked in. I introduced them to Bobbi, and the change that came over her was phenomenal. She was everything I'd teased her about. She was calm. She was professional, she was cool as a cucumber. I gave the interview about three minutes, then quietly excused myself, and went back outside. I needed to take some aspirin, and be making arrangements to move Buck and Cochise. Maybe I'd do it myself. It would be quiet Sunday morning, not so dangerous to be hauling a horse trailer through the streets to the studio corrals. I borrowed the phone from Mrs. Norris and called the stables.

I had time to get transportation arranged for the horses, call Glory and ask her to put my name in my underwear, stride nervously around the sound stages, and pounce the length of Mrs. Norris's office a few hundred times before the double doors to Clevenger's office opened, and Bobbi came strolling out, arm in arm with Reggie. He gave me a nod and a wink, but said nothing. That had been our agreement. If he really liked her, would have hired her himself anyway, he said he'd give me the nod. "I'm going to show Miss Bates around the studio," he said. "Maybe let her see what it's like to be in front of a camera. Do you want to tag along, Bud, or would you like me to bring her home later?"

Tag along? It made me feel like the unwelcome little brother, and I could feel my hackles rising up just a bit. I resisted the urge to snap my reply, and as my mouth was coming open to say a gracious farewell, Bobbi said, "Please come, Bud. I'd be more comfortable."

Reggie flashed her one of his Hollywood smiles and said, "Do I strike you as the dangerous type, Bobbi? I can assure you, I'm not."

"I'm sure that's true," she drawled, patting his arm, "but you must remember I'm just a little old gal from way out in Texas, and I don't have any experience with slick, handsome, big city types like you. I know Bud. He's my friend, I trust him, and I'm not ready to be here without him just yet, even with someone as charming as you."

Her smile told me she meant it, and Clevenger sensed it as well. There was a moment's hesitation that said he wasn't particularly pleased, but he acquiesced. "Of course," he said with a gracious nod. "Let us be off, then."

Actually, I would have preferred to go home. I was much too hot, a little agitated, and the throb which had taken up residence in my head and my aching joints told me that damned fever had kindled another fire in me, just as Glory had suspected. But I nodded, and fell into step behind the two of them until we were outside, then I walked up on the other side of Bobbi. She linked her arm through mine, and we went down the sidewalk three abreast.

It wasn't long before I was glad of Clevenger's company. The stress and the pace of the last few days had caught up with me. When was the last time I'd had a cup of what Glory and I referred to as 'nas-tea'? Everyone else looked comfortable in their shirtsleeves – some people were sweating a little as they walked, and I was suddenly cold. I wished for the jacket in the trunk of my car. Bobbi's grip tightened on my arm, and I realized she was studying my face with a scowl of concern. "I'm fine," I whispered. Clevenger was talking and pointing and didn't notice, but Bobbi nodded slightly before giving him her full attention again.

A long, silver limo glided up to keep pace with us, and I turned to give Max a smile and a wink. "Are you out cruising all by yourself?" I asked, and Clevenger and Bobbi became aware of the car.

"No, Master Bud. If you would be kind enough to leave your companions for a moment?"

"Certainly," I smiled, and turned to Bobbi and Reggie. "I'll catch up with you?"

"Soundstage three," Reggie said. "You haven't done anything else to annoy the big boss, have you?"

"I certainly hope not," I sighed, and got in the car, which had pulled to the curb just ahead of us.

When we were moving again my father said, "Is that the girl?"

"Um hm. Dad, thanks for getting her the..."

"If she's such a fine nurse, how come you're out walking around with feverish eyes and a flushed face?"

"I'm also a fine actor," I smiled.

"Not that good, you're not," Dad snorted. "I've got a good mind to slap you in the hospital and have some serious tests run."

I tried not to laugh as I looked at him, hunched and cranky in the seat across from me. "What you need, is to have your wife and babies home," I said. "You're just not happy unless you're fussing over somebody's well-being."

"That's not true," he snapped. Then he chuckled softly and shrugged with the effort of sitting up straighter. "At least I don't want to think it is. How are things at your house?"

"Good. Dad, you should see that meadow. It's just amazing. Rafael brought in big rolls of native sod from someplace close, I'm not sure where, and...poof! There's the meadow, much the same as it always was. A few things are different, of course, but by and large the man's a miracle worker. Even the birds are coming back. I'm so glad I found him. Gram's heart would have broken for sure."

My father just nodded. "She must think a great deal of his abilities, or she wouldn't have gone off and left him alone with a project like that." He was quiet for a bit, and then said, "You need to reward him in some manner for his efforts."

"I don't think he expects that," I said, surprised at my father's benevolence, "and his pride would probably keep him from accepting anything overt. He keeps saying it's his job, though Glory told me it was his...how did she put it...his thanks for salvation, or something like that, only she said it much better. I just can't remember."

"Because you're sick. You should be home in bed."

"Dad, I'd love to be," I admitted, "but Bobbi wasn't comfortable with having me leave. She'd already committed to spending some time with Reggie and we were on our way before she realized I wasn't feeling all that well."

"She doesn't want to be alone with Reginald Clevenger?"

"Apparently not," I shrugged.

"Smart woman. He's a lecherous bastard."

"Dad, I thought you liked Reggie."

"I think the world and all of him just like I do Kit Miller. That doesn't mean I can't see right through him."

The image made me shiver a little, and I realized the air conditioner was on. Dad tapped on the glass and said, "Max, what's the temperature in here?"

"An even seventy," came the reply.

"Well, turn off the AC. Bud's cold."

"That's because Bud needs to be in bed resting," Max growled, mostly to himself, and the fan exhaled gently to silence.

"Where were Reggie and Bobbi going?" Dad asked.

"Ah, soundstage three, I think. No need to drop me off. I can walk back." Truth be told, I wanted out of that cool car and into the sunshine. I was trembling slightly, and my teeth wanted to chatter with cold.

Dad gave the glass another tap and said, "Max, park us and go find Mister Clevenger and Miss Bates in soundstage three, will you? We're going to have lunch together. Oh, and roll these windows down."

The windows came down, the warmth poured in, and the car swung around the corner and back around the lot until we came to the spot I'd gotten in. Then Max parked us, hopped out, and trotted off toward the soundstages. I put my head back against the seat and closed my eyes. I wasn't going to have to spend the afternoon following Reggie and Bobbi, and eating in the studio commissary and freezing and cooking by turns. Dad was taking us out for a two martini lunch somewhere on a quiet rooftop back in the direction of my house, after which he'd casually say he'd just drop us off at home and he'd send my car up with a driver later. "Thanks," I said softly, and Dad just patted my knee and said nothing.

Shortly, I could hear Reggie and Bobbi coming down the sidewalk, and Reggie was saying that they could always see the soundstages, but it wasn't every day that a newcomer, or even a director of some standing got invited out to lunch with one of the most powerful men in Hollywood. This could be a break for her, since she'd be working on the set of one of his movies. By then Max was opening the door, and Bobbi slid in, a look of awe on her pretty face, to sit beside me, while Reggie sat down next to my father. "Good morning, J.R.," Reggie said. "What's up?"

"Boeing, Richfield, and Standardex," my father replied, and Reggie chuckled a little.

"Bobbi Bates, I'd like you to meet someone," I said, but by that time she was looking at me, her hand on my wrist.

"You need to go home, or to an emergency room, and I do mean now," she said quietly. "Sir, I don't mean to be rude, but..."

"Of course not," my father said quickly. "Should he be in a hospital?"

"Shit, there goes the location shooting," Reggie muttered, and gave my dad a quick glance out of the corner of one eye. "I know Bud's health is more important, of course."

"I, am not in need of a hospital bed," I said firmly, "and we are not going to miss our shoot. I do feel a little rocky at the moment, and I would deeply appreciate being able to go home and sleep it off. Bobbi, I'm sorry. I know you were looking forward to today."

"I would be more than happy to take over for you, and show Miss Bates around the studio," my father said.

I felt Bobbi shrink, almost imperceptibly against me, and said, "Bobbi, it's okay. This is my dad, the real Peter Aarons."

There was only a moment's hesitation. "It's a pleasure to meet you, Sir," she smiled, extending her hand. "And I would be honored to have you show me around the studio, but...I know Glory is capable of taking care of him, I do...but..." she made a small gesture of capitulation, "I think I'll just go home with Bud. If something were to go really wrong, which I'm sure it won't...."

My father nodded. There was that lightening of his countenance that was not quite a smile, but approval, nonetheless, and I knew Bobbi had said exactly what she was supposed to. "Reggie, I have things I want to discuss with you, but not now," Dad said. "Max, let Mister Clevenger out, and then take us to the Birdhouse, post haste."

Reggie slapped my knee as he got out, and though his mouth was smiling, his eyes were not. I'd robbed him twice today – an afternoon with Bobbi, and lunch with my dad. "Rest up, Kid," he said, and strode off down the sidewalk.

Dad walked me into the house, up to my room, watched while Bobbi took my temperature, then waited while I took a long, hot shower, and saw me safely propped up in bed, which was most unusual. I wondered if having all of his family gone at once was making him nervous. The thought of Dad being nervous was almost comical. I thanked him, patted his hand, and assured him that I was fine – I just needed to sleep a little. I was fine now that I was lying down.

There was a tap on the door and Glory walked in with a tray. She had my usual, foul tasting herbal tea, and lunch for my dad, who looked surprised, then nodded and said thank you. "Max said youall hadn't got to eat lunch," she said shyly. "It's no good bein' hungry. Bud, you want anything to eat?"

I shook my head. "No. Thanks. Just this divine tea is more than enough."

"You go on bein' a smart alec if you want to," she grinned, "just you drink that down. It'll break that fever, you know it, and Miss Bobbi agrees." She turned to my father and gave him a diffident smile. "May I bring you anything else, Sir?"

"No...thank you," he said. "Mrs. Ruiz, how are your boys by now?"

"They doin' well," she smiled. "Gettin' lots of exercise and growin' big and strong."

"And Rafael, how is he?"

"Now that meadow's done to his satisfaction, he settlin' right in. Even noticed what I fed him this mornin'."

"Good news," I grinned. "Does this mean you've cancelled the exorcist?"

"I ain't gone that far yet," Glory chuckled, "but I am gainin' hope."

"Do you people have family someplace?" my father asked casually. It amused me. Of all the things Dad wasn't, it was casual. He took a sip of coffee, and nodded his approval. "Very good."

"Thank you, Sir. It be my...it is my specialty. My people's on the sea islands off the Carolinas. Rafael, his folks all in Texas, scattered 'round north and east of Laredo."

"And that's where you recently came from?"

She shook her head and looked a little sad. "No. We worked over toward El Paso on a big hacienda. We ain't neither of us...we have not been home since the boys was born. Rafael, he misses his people somethin' fierce."

"I'm sure he does," my father said, then added, "Don't let me keep you from your work, Mrs. Ruiz. And ask Rafael if he will take me on a guided tour of his project before I leave, will you?" He paused a heartbeat or two. "Oh, Glory...thanks for calling Max this morning."

She didn't even look at me when I gasped, she just nodded and left, turning at the door to fix me in her gaze. "Next time I ask you if you sick...."

"I will answer you," I muttered.

She nodded once more. "You drink that all down, and then you get some sleep."

"Yes, Ma'am," I said, and she quietly closed the door.

My father just shook his head and looked after her. "You're really going to let her talk to you like that, aren't you? The perfect shepherdess for you and that crazy old woman you live with. You do as she says and get some sleep." He put his hand on my face, and his eyes clouded with concern. "Aloysha, you're really hot and dry. That can't be good."

"I swear, all I ever have to do is sleep it off," I said, patting his hand. "I'll be good as new in a day or so."

"And ready to fly out Monday morning?"

"Absolutely, positively," I muttered, and I could feel my eyes closing on me. If I screwed up the schedule on this movie – the last major motion picture my father planned to actively take a hand in....

I awoke a bit later, gasping with heat, and flung off the covers. There was a nice breeze coming from outside, and on it traveled men's voices, my father's, and Rafael's, and a piping voice that could only belong to the precocious Master Royal Ruiz. I got up and walked to the edge of the balcony, and I could see them walking in the meadow – Rafael with Titus on his shoulders, Royal scampering ahead through the greening grass. Amazing. I realized I was cold, and went back to bed.

Bobbi joined me and took my temperature and sat with me a bit. She didn't look as worried as she had earlier, and I wondered if I'd been a handy excuse to get away from Reggie. I rather hoped so. She told me I looked better, and that I should try to eat something, at least some soup, and drink plenty of water and tea.

I slept all afternoon, and obediently drank my soup at suppertime, though it didn't sit particularly well. I was sitting up in bed reading when there was a knock on the door and Rafael let himself in. "How are you feeling?" he asked in his softly accented voice. "Your father is very worried."

"I'm fine," I smiled. "No worse than a touch of the flu. How did Dad like the meadow?"

"He didn't say too much. Asked a lot of questions. And..." he paused, and if he'd been carrying a hat, he'd have been twisting it in his hands at that juncture, "...and, when he found out I was from around Laredo, and that my family has worked the land there for three generations...he took sudden interest, and told me he wanted me to fly down there next week and take a look at a ranch he's thinking of investing in. What do you think?"

That old sweetie. People could say all they wanted to about my dad being ruthless, and maybe on some fronts he was, but he had more insight into the human psyche, and the human heart, than anyone I'd ever known. I looked at Rafael, and tried not to burst out laughing. For one thing my head ached, and it would have hurt like hell. "I find it prudent to do what my father tells me to. If I were you, I'd be flattered that he valued my opinion, and I'd go where he wanted me to go. I, personally, would appreciate it if

you could take Royal and maybe Titus along for company, though. That way
Glory wouldn't be stuck with the boys plus the house with Gram and me
both gone. Your folks live there, don't they? Couldn't you arrange for one
or both boys to stay with them while you tended to business?"

"I suppose I could figure something out," Rafael said. He didn't
smile too much, but his eyes were dancing. "Since you think I should go.
Anyway, I should get out of here and let you rest."

"Thanks," I said, and he vanished on his cat feet through the French
doors and across the balcony. I leaned back and chuckled silently to myself.
I did so love my old man – still do, as a matter of fact. I truly don't think
Rafael was ever the wiser, and if Glory figured it out, she stayed mum on the
subject.

I awoke in the dark, burning up, stomach churning, and when I
vaulted out of bed to go to the bathroom, I made it about four long steps and
went flat on my face – my head connecting solidly with the corner of the
chest of drawers. I don't know how long I lay there before I realized that I'd
bloodied my nose, whacked my already throbbing head, and thrown up on
my precious teakwood floor. I wondered groggily if I was going to be able to
get up, because if I couldn't, I was going to do worse things yet to that floor.
I got to my knees, steadying myself against the dresser, and wondered if I
could manage the vast space left to traverse to get to the bathroom.

I had one knee still on the floor, one foot under me, when the door
opened quietly, and then Bobbi was beside me. Was I happy to see her?
No. Was I grateful she was a nurse and could help me? No. I'd rather have
crawled to the bathroom on my hands and knees and slept on the bath mat
than have her see me like that – see that mess. How undignified. How...
unlovable.

"Coming, or going?" she asked, and her voice sounded like it was
reverberating through a long, metal tube. It hurt my ears, and gave me a
panicky, other-worldly feeling. "Peter, can you hear me?"

"Mmmmm," I groaned, and managed to nod. "Bathroom." She
came up on the side of me that was without benefit of a dresser to hang on to,
and eased me through the doorway. "Thanks," I whispered, hating the sound
of my own voice, "I can manage."

"Bud..."

"I can manage," I said through my teeth.

She pulled a towel from the rack and departed, leaving the door partway ajar. "Not too bad," she said from the bedroom, "Just a little liquid... enough acid in it to eat the finish off the floor, but nothing disgusting." She knew what I was thinking. Was that because she was a nurse and was used to dealing with sick people? And was she beginning to think I was perpetually sick?

After she heard the toilet flush, she opened the door the rest of the way, and, having tossed the soiled towel into the tub, she came to stand beside me at the wash basin. She didn't say anything, she just stood rubbing my back and watching me wash the blood off my face with one hand while propping myself up with the other. "Would you like some help?" she asked after a bit, and I winced in spite of myself. "The sound of my voice hurts your ears? Bud, Sweetheart, you're borderline delirious, and that could be dangerous. Maybe we should call a doctor."

I shook my head a little – too much and it would fall off in the sink. "Please, no. Just...more of Glory's tea. I..." things were spinning, and I caught the side of the counter with both hands, not wanting to fall against anything porcelain, like the toilet, or cast iron, like the bathtub. I already had a visible knot above my left eye.

Both Bobbi's arms came around to steady me and she asked, "Need the toilet? Are you going to be sick?"

"Just dizzy," I whispered. "I'm so sorry..."

"Oh, for heaven's sake, shut up," she chuckled, and half-carried me back to bed. She brought me some 'nas-tea', and helped me drink it, then turned the bedroom light off, turned the bathroom light on, set the door open a crack, and slid into bed beside me. "I hope you don't mind. I don't want to leave you, and I don't want to sleep on the floor."

"No," I murmured, "I just wish...I was in a position to make you happy you'd done it."

"You may get your chance," she said softly. "Try to go back to sleep."

My dreams were full of sharp faced people with bulging eyes who made quick movements and startled me, and said things that hurt my ears and made me queasy. I tried to answer them – to tell them things that would satisfy them and make them go away, but they lingered. I could feel Bobbi's hands on me from time to time, and once, a washcloth cool on my face. I was so hot...the room was so close...and I was on something higher than a bed... what was that? Where were my clothes? I was embarrassed, and scared...so scared. What had they done with Mother? I pulled the thin blanket around my shoulders and looked fearfully around in the grey dimness of the place. Then I heard his voice, the man who said he'd take care of me – the man in the red uniform – only the uniform...was gone. He was naked, and smiling as he approached me. "Turn around," he said softly. "Get on your hands and knees. That's a good boy. You'll like this." He was stroking my buttocks with something soft, rubbing it up and down between my cheeks. It didn't hurt, but I didn't like it, and then he was making strange noises like he was hurt, and there was something wet on my backside. "Turn around," he said again, and when I did, there was this evil, evil face leering at me. "Put this in your mouth," he said, but don't touch it with your teeth, or I'll knock the rest of them out, and then I'll kill your mother, and I'll make you watch, little Peterkin. Put this in your mouth," he said again, with a voice like silk, and I did as he asked, and he pushed himself against the back of my throat, making me gag and sob, and that made him frantic, and there was something thick and slightly sweet in my mouth, and he was making those noises again, and pushing, and pushing, and I was choking and trying to spit, trying to swallow, but he didn't stop, and his fingers were pinching my testicles, and his other hand was pushing my head into his crotch, harder and harder....

By the time I realized what was happening to me I was sitting bolt upright, sobbing, ejaculating, vomiting tea onto the blankets. I just pulled my knees up, buried my face in my hands and wept, and Bobbi rubbed my back, and gently kissed my bare shoulders, and said nothing for a long time. At some point she stripped the blanket off the bed, took the comforter from its rack to put over us, and slid back under the covers. "The fever's broken. You'll sleep better now," she said, very softly, and took my trembling, sweating, miserable body in her arms.

I did sleep, and when I awoke, I felt much improved in the stomach and the head. Parts of me were mortifyingly sticky and damp, and I was exhausted, so I knew my night visitor had come upon me. Bobbi was not with me, though the comforter was over me rather than the blanket, so I knew it hadn't been entirely a dream.

God, did she know what I'd done? I really didn't think I could face finding out, and how would I ask, anyway, and what would she say to me? I tried to remember the dream from last night, but all I could remember was the terror and the indignity, not the details. Like always. How could I face it and fight it if I couldn't remember it? I wondered if I could get myself out of bed without falling on my face. I eased myself over the edge one leg at a time, and then sat up...slowly. The room stayed where it was. My back ached, my legs felt like lead, my knees like jelly, but the fever was gone, or seemed to be.

The way my legs felt, I had no desire to try stepping up into that tall, footed tub to take a shower in my own bathroom, so I got to my feet, put on my robe, got some clean underwear out of the drawer, and went through my Grandmother's room into the master bath. It had a big, glass shower in it, four feet wide, six feet long – two shower heads – and I felt like I needed both of them. I scrubbed myself, and scrubbed myself again, feeling the anger, and the guilt, and the helplessness of being trapped in a past I couldn't understand and a present I couldn't control. What was the future going to be like? Would I dream this terrible dream the rest of my life? Other young men dreamed about women to get these results. I was...different. I got off on fear, and men...or little boys. God help me, what was that damned dream? Why was...wait, what had Dad said? My head was clearing a little by then. There was some evidence that I'd been abused while I was in the prison camp. Was I the little boy? I closed my eyes and tried with all my might to recall the dream. Was it always the same? Did the same thing always happen? Could this man-thing be red because of...his German uniform? There was an icy tingle up my spine. That was it! Or was it?

"Bud, Sweetheart, are you feeling a little better?" Bobbi's voice, clear and distinct – no reverberation.

"Much, thank you," I said. "I'm very sorry to have caused you such a rough night."

"It just means you'll owe me a night somewhere along the line," she said, and I could hear the smile in her voice. "Your bed is all changed, and I think you should get back in it. Are you hungry?"

"No," I said, "but I am thirsty."

"I'll be back," she said, and when I was sure she was gone I turned off the shower and got out. As I was drying off I wondered...if I could confide in Bobbi Bates. What if I'd said something that would help me unlock this dream? If she didn't know what I was going through, she couldn't very well help me. But to admit to having been sexually abused as a child...could I do that? It made me feel so nasty. I shuddered, and quickly dressed myself to hide my shame.

I was back in bed when Bobbi came in with cool apple juice for me to drink. What a relief. The thought of that herbal concoction on my tender stomach, was more than I could bear. She took my temperature, and said it was just under a hundred degrees. A day of bedrest, a good night's sleep, and I'd be ready to fly tomorrow.

"Bobbi," I ventured, looking past her and out the French doors, "did I say anything last night? I have this recurring nightmare, and I can never remember the damned thing, and maybe if I had some verbal clue..." Her eyes were on my face, and I looked away, stammering to a halt. What was I doing? What was I thinking? I took a sip of apple juice to swallow the lump in my throat and sat staring into my glass. "Never mind, really. It's a silly, kid thing that I need to shake on my own." I felt her hand on my forearm, and I looked up at her, then quickly back into my glass. "I appreciate the drink," I said.

"Bud, look at me," she said. I had to take a deep breath first, but I managed. "You are one of the most self-assured people I know. Why is this so hard for you to talk about?"

I shrugged with my eyebrows. "Because my self-assurance is an act?"

"No," she said quietly, "it's not." She became business-like, and sat back in her chair. "Fever's going to make a nightmare worse yet. Things will be much more vivid."

"It was worse than usual," I admitted. I didn't tell her how much worse.

"You did say some things last night, but..."

"But what?" Suddenly I was scared. Why had I dragged her into this? "What did I say?"

She just shook her fiery head and sighed, "I don't know. You were speaking a foreign language, just like when you were sick overseas."

"Damn," I said under my breath. "Damn."

"English...isn't your second language by any chance, is it?" she ventured. She was wearing dark blue flowered shorts and the bright yellow tank top that set off her tan and her coppery bob, and I realized I'd slept with her last night. She'd spent the night in my bed. That body had spent the night with this body, and not one positive thing had happened. She probably thought I was a complete idiot. "Bud?"

"Hm? Uh, why do you ask?"

"It's just that when people are really ill or disoriented they often fall back into the language they first learned to think in. But you have no accent. Your dad has no accent..."

"My mother has an accent you can cut with a fork. What did these words sound like?"

"If I had to guess? Russian, maybe?"

"But the words themselves," I scowled. "The words?"

"I honestly don't know," she said with an apologetic smile.

"Would you recognize them if you heard them again?" Now that, was a stupid question, wasn't it? Where would I start, with the thousand most common words in the Russian language?

"I might," she said, and sat forward again, stroking my hair back off my face. "But this is not the time to be worrying about it. You need to sleep now. Your eyes look like two holes burnt in a blanket. I'll see if I can remember sounds, and you see if you can remember how to be well enough to travel."

I just nodded, and when I let myself relax, I went almost immediately to sleep. I stayed that way except for bathroom breaks, and drinking water, or cool apple juice. The fragrance of frying chicken wafted upstairs, and I smiled. A Sweetwater Sunday. Glory came in and packed for me, and visited just a bit in quiet tones, and Royal came and climbed up to snuggle beside me and whispered, "I'm sorry you're sick, Uncle Angel. Please get better." I held him close and promised I would.

The next morning, except for a tender stomach, I was pretty much feeling like my old self, and the fever and the nightmares faded into the background of my life. Dad's limo rolled up our driveway at eight O'clock to take us to the airport, and when the big jet roared out of LA International, I was on it, laughing with Kristoffer and Bobbi.

CHAPTER SEVEN

It was a short trip, but because it was a chartered jet, there was a special meal in-flight. The brass, probably including Dad, didn't want us disembarking hungry in Flagstaff, which, as it turned out, was a stroke of genius for all involved. There was precious little between us and Monument Valley, and time was of the essence in getting there. My spirits had improved faster than my stomach, and even the smell of food was unwelcome. I ate some mashed potatoes with no gravy, and outside that, I stuck with lots of water to rehydrate myself.

Early afternoon we were loaded onto chartered buses and whisked away with assurances that our luggage would be shortly behind us. It was a breathtaking ride, but the area added new dimensions to the term, the middle of nowhere. By the time we turned off highway eighty-nine onto one-sixty, still heading north and east across the Navajo Reservation, most of the children and a few of the adults were beginning to whimper.

We saw the Painted Desert, and the occasional Navajo hogan, some sheep, a few goats, a horse or two – a pickup going past about every half-hour, and that was pretty much it. But the scenery...was like looking upon the face of God – vast, unknowable, terrifyingly beautiful. I didn't visit. I just looked, and wrote music in my head, and occasionally dozed for a few minutes.

We turned off onto highway one sixty-three, then again onto something I missed. The road went from pavement to gravel and then to dirt somewhere around the Utah state line, and still we kept going, more or less toward Goosenecks State Park and Medicine Hat...but not quite. We followed something for a while on roads so twisting it turned out to be our own tail lights, and the whimpering turned to moaning – either fear or bus sickness. When we finally stopped there were these vistas right out of a John Wayne movie.

They shot so many westerns here. It seemed to me kind of a shame to be using such familiar surroundings for such a serious subject. I thought about that another minute or so, and began to chuckle. This was the kind of country where our story *had* taken place. The factual, historical part of our story had started it all. The other stories? Those were the stereotypical ones. I gazed around and took a deep, deep breath. What a setting! It was evening, and the breeze had a slightly cool edge to it, and the huge monolithic plateaus were purple against an orange sky, and I just...stood, rooted...and watched the whole world slowly, slowly going out like a dying ember. What a perfect spot, I thought.

The tents were all set up in a double horseshoe with their backs to the prevailing wind. There were portable toilets and a shower tent behind each side, and the dining tent at the open end of the horseshoe. The cast had the front loop of tents, the crew had the back. The makeup and costume trailers were off to one side along with the auxiliary vehicles and camera trucks. The air was fragrant with the mingling spices of supper, and at first I thought I was hungry, but when I actually got into the tent, the smell of food was too strong, and I excused myself and went back outside.

"Bud," someone said, and I turned to see Florian Swift walking toward me in the deepening twilight. "How are you feeling?"

"Great," I said. "And this...." I just gestured in a sweeping arc, and Florian nodded.

"Beautiful, isn't it? If you've had supper I'll show you to your temporary domicile. Arabian Nights meets the Boy Scouts," he chuckled. "I have you bunking with Kit, of course."

"Of course. How else could it be?"

We walked a bit in silence and he said, "Bud, do I need to tell you how sorry I am for what I said the other day? I was just tired, and...well, I didn't mean to get down on your friends. I sure as hell didn't mean to ruin your friendship with them."

I dropped a hand on his shoulder to stop him. "Flo, it's okay. Holy Toledo, look at those stars popping out. This is the most incredible place I've ever been. It's so...is the word, virile? Inhospitable? Enchanting? I just can't put my finger on the right one somehow."

"You better watch where you're putting your feet, young'un," he chuckled, "You'll go off in a chuckhole and break your leg, and then we'll have to shoot you."

"Did the horses get here in good shape?"

"Listen," he said, and we stopped walking. We were pretty well beyond the light and the sound of the mess tent, and when we'd stood a moment I could hear them – champing softly and blowing in the stillness. They were somewhere slightly below us, and off to my left. I could see their dim outlines by starlight.

"I feel a hundred years old," I whispered, and a chill went up my spine. "I feel like I've fallen into a history book."

"Keep that feeling," Florien said, patting me gently on the back, "It will enhance your already excellent performance. Here we are, tent number nine, as far away from the mess tent as it gets. The bathrooms and the showers are right behind this back row of tents." He flipped up the tent flap and stepped inside to light a propane lantern that was sitting on a camp table. There were two canvas chairs, one on each side of the table, and two double air mattresses with pillows and blankets on them, and there was still plenty of room to spare. "I know I said there would be cots," he said apologetically, "but we got a few that were broken, which we didn't know, and I figured since you're so tall, and so broad shouldered, you wouldn't mind a little extra room."

"I'm ecstatic," I chuckled. "I was dreading that cot."

"Well, these bigger tents have bathtub floors in them, so that should help keep out the tarantulas and the scorpions and the occasional sidewinder. Sleeping on the ground should be relatively safe."

"Oh," I said, wide-eyed, "*that's* why you wanted to use cots."

"Like I said, you should be fine. Do I hear a truck?"

I cocked my head. "I think so, yes."

"Probably the luggage. I'll go flag him in."

I went along, and watched the big van roll in next to the mess tent. People were finishing up their meals by then, and the crew cranked up a generator and set up some flood lights so everybody could find his or her luggage. There was the usual milling and grumbling and cursing as everybody got their stuff and spread out to find their tents. Bobbi was three tents down from us, housed with Amber Kestrel and her mother. I said nothing to her about Amber's propensity for unpleasantness, but I did roll my eyes meaningfully in Kit's direction, and he gave me a slight nod of agreement.

I took him to our tent, and he looked around with pleasure. "Remember," he said, "when my mom and dad took us up to the Kern River camping that first time, and we were so hot we jumped in the river with all our clothes on, and Dad jumped in with us, and Mom laughed? We had that big, eighteen foot tent almost like this one, and a propane lamp, and we sat and played cards and Battleships until all hours, and..."

"...it didn't matter because we were big kids and had a tent all to ourselves. And we went rafting on those rubber rafts and got so sunburned our shoulders and the backs of our legs blistered. Yeah, I remember." I dropped my arm around his shoulder, his around mine, and we went and stood staring up at the stars. "We laid on our backs and looked up through the trees at night, finding shapes in the branches, remember?"

"Yeah," he sighed. "Oh, hey, remember when we went to camp that time and we had those cabins with a crawl space under 'em, and we crawled in there and thumped and moaned and scared Keiger so bad he peed his pants? That was one of the high points of my life."

"Bought a pickup from him a while back...or from his dealership, anyway. Didn't see him, though, I'm sorry to say."

"Oh, yeah, I'll bet." Kit dropped his voice, became nasal, and chanted, "'you sound like a bullfrog in heat, Aarons. Like a big, old horny bullfrog.' Why'd you buy a truck from that asshole?"

"Just to prove I'm the bigger man, I guess," I chuckled, and Kit gave me a knowing look.

"Now that, was never any contest. You have always been the bigger man...if you get my drift."

"That must have been it, all right. He was always jealous of me," I said loftily.

We laid in our beds that night, talking softly and laughing like a couple of kids, and when makeup complained the next morning that our eyes looked puffy and tired, we laughed some more, even as we mouthed apologies.

Actually, I'd been up at daybreak with all my camera equipment set up, photographing the long fingers of dawn as they spread themselves slowly to grasp the desert and hold it in their heated grip. By eight O'clock it was warm. By ten O'clock it was hot, and I could feel Cochise sweating between my legs as we cantered easily along the desert floor. We were shooting about a quarter of a mile from camp, where they'd set up a settler's cabin in a little protected draw. With a few modifications, a different camera angle, it would become the stage station, and the Butterfield stage would come rumbling through to its appointment with destiny. There was also a wagon train, or the skeleton of one, two wagons that actually moved, and parts of several others to give the illusion of a bigger train. At the moment, it was under attack from me and my ilk.

At a long lope I hooked my moccasined heel into my horse's side and leaned around under his neck – something I'd done often and easily, but this morning my leggings were wet with sweat, and so were my moccasin heels, and I found myself studying the desert floor close-up. Cochise realized he'd lost me about the time Reggie hollered, "Cut!" and both of them contemplated me with some amusement as I got up, trying in vain to brush the sand off my sweaty arms. "Problems, Bud? Are you hurt?"

"Only my ego," I chuckled. "Do we have any rosin?"

"I think we do," said the prop man, and he trotted off toward one of the jeeps while somebody else went after me with a soft brush.

"You look really good out there," Clevenger said, "except for the part where you fell off your horse. All right, everybody, let's try this again. Amber, more drama, fewer theatrics, please." She responded with something snippy.

We shot the rest of the morning, and then went back to camp for lunch, leaving the horses in the shadowed draw with plenty of water and a couple wranglers to keep them company. I was leaning against the shaded side of one of the trucks, visiting with Bobbi about how her first morning on a real movie set had gone and waiting for the chow line to go down when little Miss Amber sashayed by in her pioneer finery and said, "Don't bother flirting with Peter. He's gay, unfortunately."

I cringed, and expected Bobbi to do the same, but she slid her arm through mine, leaned seductively into me and purred, "Oh, I can tell you with absolute assurance, little girl, he's not."

Amber halted, and slued her eyes around at Bobbi, who by that time had her arm around my neck and was giving me a lingering kiss on the mouth. "Not in front of the child," I chuckled, pulling slightly away, and Amber snapped her nose into the air and hurried away in a ruffle of petticoats and feathers.

"That should shut her nasty little trap," I said, looking down at Bobbi.

"Now shut yours," she said softly, and kissed me again.

I'm sure a few people saw us. I, for one, didn't care, and I know Bobbi didn't. If she was doing it for effect, she was well on her way to becoming an accomplished actress. Amber was convinced, and so was I. I pulled gently away from her and murmured, "One more like that and I won't be able to concentrate at all this afternoon, Miss Bates."

"Glad to hear it," she purred, running her finger down the middle of my bare chest, "With that pouty bottom lip, I knew you were kissable, Peter Aarons. What have you done to Missy Amber?"

"Nothing," I chuckled, "which is the problem. She's a friend of my little sister's, and I have a feeling they talk, like girls will do, you know?"

"Your sister thinks you're gay?" Bobbi was astonished.

"I honestly don't know what she thinks. I do know not all sisters adore their brothers, Bobbi. Esther and I are like two peas in a pod, but Racheal and I are like oil and water." I was uncomfortable with the subject, so I put my arm around her waist and spun her lightly away from the shadow of the truck. "Come on, let's grab some lunch."

All afternoon and into the evening we worked on the introductory scene between Cochise and Thomas Jeffords, the intrepid New Yorker who was to become his friend. Jeffords was a superintendent of U.S. mails, and having lost fourteen of his drivers to Cochise and his warriors, he decided to go see the great chief in person. He did this by riding alone into Chiricahua territory, lighting signal fires as he went, while Cochise watched him come every step of the way through the valleys and across the ridge-lines. I got to sit on my horse and look impassively upon his progress, forbidding my warriors to kill him, while Kit got to get on and off his horse and light fires in the blazing heat. By nightfall, Kit was nearly dead of heatstroke, and my back was pretty well cooked even through sunscreen and makeup. We got a quick, tepid shower – there was no such thing as cold water – and a late supper, and worked on our lines for a bit before falling into bed. "Night shooting tomorrow," I said comfortingly.

"After shooting all day," Kit groused, blowing out the lamp. "Why exactly did your father want me in this part?"

"I didn't ask him," I yawned, stretching out on the bed. The covers were momentarily cool, and it felt so good. "But I can, if you'd like." Kit mumbled something...something, and I was out.

I was awakened from a sound sleep by the tent flap being thrown open, and an armful of stuff came flying in. I said something incoherent, and Bobbi's huffy voice said, "I'm moving in." There was silence for a bit – I probably went right back to sleep – and then an armload of bedding came flying in, followed by Bobbi. "That little...*female*...I'm supposedly bunking with...I swear to God, if she asks me another question about our sex life...."

Kit was suddenly awake and interested. "You two have a sex life? Bud, congratulations. I had no idea."

"Neither did I," I mumbled, still trying to wake up.

"It wasn't his doing, it was mine," Bobbi snarled. "I thought if I fell all over Bud, Amber would back off. Well, it backfired. The slutlet thinks we're bedmates, and she wants all the details. I'm going to get my cot."

"I'll go," I began, and she just snarled again and stomped out. If I'd been more awake I'd have been howling with laughter, but as it was I was completely bemused. "I could help you..." I quavered into the darkness. The flap came open one last time, and the outstretched legs of a cot were outlined in black against the starry sky.

"It came...from out of the desert night," Kit began in his most somber tones.

Bobbi snapped, "Shut the fuck up, Miller," and he did. He huddled over against me to make room for the cot, and neither of us made another sound the whole night for fear of being devoured.

I surveyed our tent in the first light of dawn, and it looked like Macy's after Christmas, with stuff flung willy-nilly over and under surfaces. Bobby was sound asleep with her hair askew and her face to the wall, and Kit's even breathing told me he was asleep, also. I finished tying my shoes, adjusted my headband, and stepped out to greet the desert morning. I had the strangest urge to stretch forth my arms and say, "Good morning, God," and on a whim, I did. I wasn't a religious person, and I hadn't been taught at that point that one could be spiritual without being religious, so I felt a little silly, and glanced around, but nobody seemed to be near me. The voices I could hear were in tents, or down with the horses, and I walked for a bit before kicking myself into a slow run down the hard-packed, sandy track that served for a road.

This was the lightest, driest air I'd ever experienced. I felt ten pounds lighter. It was cold before sun-up, and in shorts and a tank top I was well aware of the need to keep moving. I crested just a bit of a hill and swung in a switchback up along the edge of a butte, where I could look back on the big encampment below, and further away yet, the dot that was the trading post and a couple stores off across the valley south and west of us.

The light was spreading, thick and rich like yellow paint from an overturned bucket, onto the brown floor of the desert. I looked away toward the buttes and monoliths, changing from purple to orange, to gold, to brown, and felt the thump of my heart in my chest like a tom-tom, and let the old west and the fate of a great nation take me. I was Cochise – greatest of all the Apache chiefs – not a bloodthirsty, murderous savage like Geronimo, but a statesman, a shrewd businessman, a man described by Captain John Bourke as: *a fine looking Indian, straight as a rush - six feet in stature, deep-chested and roman-nosed. A kindly and even somewhat melancholy expression tempers the determined look of his countenance. There was neither in speech or action any of the bluster characteristic of his race.* Melancholy for good reason. There was no stopping the tide of whites. Already in 1870 there were ten thousand of them – ranchers, gold miners, farmers, entrepreneurs – overwhelming the native population.

"We kill ten, a hundred come in their place," Cochise told his council. He could see the end of their way of life...perhaps life itself. Maybe that's why he chose to speak to Jeffords, and to become friends with him. In a little more than a year, Cochise would negotiate peace with the white man, and see the Chiricahua and Dragoon mountains become a reservation, with Jeffords as the reservation agent who had absolute authority in all dealings with the Chiricahua, and the whites, whom he kept at bay. Two years later, Cochise would be dead.

I closed my eyes as I ran, and I could feel the grief well up in me for the people who were lost to greed, to jingoism cloaked as Manifest Destiny – for all the people who had ever been prisoners in their own houses in their own land – including me and my family. What beastly thing rose up in man to make him kill and conquer and take more than he needed? How well the Aboriginal people knew land was the ultimate gift from God. How carefully they preserved it and all within it. How quickly they lost it to those who knew only the steel plow, the gold pan, and the iron heel of what they chose to call civilization. When I died as Cochise, here in a week or so, part of me would die – part of Peter Aarons – as penance for the sins of all those who shod their ponies with metal and rode over the land to take it at any price.

I stood at the top of the world – the center of all things – and looked out over the pathetic thread of roads that sought to lessen this vastness. Part of me wanted to laugh, and part of me wanted to cry, and for a few seconds I thought I understood...but...the feeling went away, and I turned and ran back down the mountain, my sneakers leaving tiny puffs of dust as Jeffords had left puffs of smoke with his signal fires.

The camp was awake when I got back. I was sweating heavily and blowing hard, trying to outrun the haunting scenes of death and privation I could see in my mind's eye. No part of this land spoke of mercy, and I had been running from it, albeit subconsciously, for the last five or six miles. I stopped, stripped off my sweat-soaked tank top, stretched out, and then put my hands on my knees, rolling forward to ease my labored breathing. The heavy hair woven into my own and clinging damply to my neck and shoulders wasn't helping any. I stood like that for a few minutes, and then became aware that about fifty people in the dining tent were watching me. I straightened up, glared at them and hollered, "What? Am I the only one who thinks regular exercise is important?" They just waved and laughed, and I went off to take a shower and shave before breakfast.

There is nothing quite so magical as a well-made movie, and nothing to tell of the making of one. When we were not on camera we sat in chairs under shades made of heavy net, and watched, and prayed for a breeze. Bobbi got her chance to be one of the passengers on the Butterfield stage, and she had three lines to say – Clevenger had added one. When she came later to sit by me she was flushed with warmth, trembling with excitement, and she was truly beautiful to behold. "Thank you, thank you," she whispered, and turned my face to give me a lingering kiss. Just then, just for a bit, I regretted having my best friend for a tent mate. I knew if I wanted Bobbi I could have her, and I definitely wanted her. The really nice thing about it was that I didn't feel like she was coming on to me out of gratitude. I truly felt like she found me attractive. She'd told me so earlier, after my shower, when I was sitting in the dining tent having breakfast.

"Do you know why everybody was looking at you this morning?" she'd asked, sitting across from me with a cup of coffee and folding her arms on the checkered tablecloth.

"My fly was open?" I'd chuckled. "If it was, please don't tell me, okay?"

"Bud, they were staring at your gorgeous body. You don't have any idea, do you, how good looking you are."

I'd just shaken my head and willed myself not to blush and say something like, "Aw, shucks, Ma'am." I sipped my coffee and said, "I'm the ugly duckling in a phenomenally good looking and talented family. I guess I've always concentrated on trying to be as talented as everybody else, and let the physical aspects of it go by...but thanks. I'm glad you think I'm..." I just shrugged and focused on my hash browns. I could feel another folksy comment coming on, and I swallowed it with a forkful of food.

Her hand had come to rest on my forearm. "You're glad I think you're...what, Bud? Can you even say it?"

"Probably not with a straight face."

"Try."

"I'm glad you think I'm...decent to look at."

"Not good enough. I want you to use the word, handsome, and I want you to look at me when you say it."

"Bobbi..."

"Try."

"Oh all right," I'd groused. I pulled my eyes out of my plate and focused on a spot just a tad below her eyebrows, glad my irises were black enough to hide my pupils from her. "I'm glad you think I'm handsome. There, how's that?"

"Good job!" she'd chuckled, kissed the top of my head in passing, and trotted off to who knows where, leaving me wondering what it felt like to be struck by lightning, or run over by a steam roller.

I turned now in my chair, and cupped her face in my palms, for once not thinking about how huge my hands were, and I kissed her, gently and lingeringly. "You're welcome, you're welcome," I whispered, and rubbed noses with her for a moment before responding to Flo's call to get on camera.

We broke early for dinner, since we were going back out to shoot some night scenes. We just left our makeup on, and our costumes, and I'm sure we made a rare sight in that dining tent. Grownups playing at cowboys and Indians. Bobbi sat beside me, and leaned very close to ask if I'd like to go for a walk after the night's shooting – the stars were so beautiful. "You're reading my mind," I murmured, trying to sound romantic over the dull roar of the fans laboring to keep us cool. I gave her bare thigh a pat under the table, and she put her hand over mine and gave it a squeeze.

"Stomach not feeling good this evening, Bud?"

I gave her a puzzled look. "What makes you think that?"

"You're not eating much."

"He hates cooked tomatoes," Kit said helpfully, then realized he was eavesdropping, and busied himself visiting with Marlin Kinkus, who was sitting next to him.

I shook my head and smiled at her. "He's right. Besides which, Italian grandmother or not, spaghetti and meatballs is one of the few things I won't eat. We used to have it in the army sometimes..." I shivered graphically and not altogether voluntarily. "I tried it once. There's bread and salad and vegetables, and the pasta itself. I won't starve."

"See that you don't," she said, arching a carefully plucked eyebrow. "You'll need your strength."

Boy, was I making plans! How could I walk casually out of camp with a blanket in one hand and Bobbi in the other? Had I brought...shit, probably not. Why would I need condoms out here in the middle of nowhere? Maybe there was one in my wallet. Besides, I consoled myself, there were all manner of delightful things to do that didn't involve sexual intercourse... exactly. We were young and inventive. We'd make do. I could feel myself beginning to smirk, and I forced myself to think about my script. This scene was Kit and me, and precious few others. We had a big line load. I was here to make a movie. I was here to make a movie. I was here to make a movie....I completely lost interest in dinner, forbad Bobbi and Kit to follow me, and wandered off to sit alone on a rock overlooking the desert and try to regain my composure and my focus.

I thought perhaps an evening canter would help my professional frame of mind, so I cut Cochise out of the remuda, put a rope over his nose, and loped down the road toward what we loosely referred to as "town". The cool air felt good on my burned shoulders and back, the motion of the horse was soothing, and I finally got my mind in gear and my male urges under control.

Headlights were coming toward me on the sandy track, and I kneed Cochise off to one side to let the battered old pickup go by. The driver, a Navajo in a big, sweat stained Stetson, gave me a protracted look as he passed, and did not smile, despite my greeting. The children in the back of the pickup didn't smile, either, though they ogled, and I remembered Flo's words about the native population not being particularly glad to have us here. I also remembered that I was wearing a breechcloth and face paint. I wondered if he thought I was mocking him in some manner – if all of us were. It was an uncomfortable thought. I watched the lights get smaller, inching up and out of sight along the mesa, and when the dust had cleared, I turned my horse and rode slowly back to camp.

Night closed in around us like a black velvet glove, spangled with starry sequins – soft and warm. A couple members of the crew kindled a fire in the midst of the wickiups, and Kit and I sat under the lights and had our makeup touched up while we waited for the fire to reach just the right ambience. He was rubbing his stomach from time to time, and the fracture between his eyes told me he wasn't comfortable. "Kit," I said finally, "are you feeling okay? You look a little green."

"I must have eaten too fast," he said, and brushed it aside.

If I'd been a little older, or wiser, or more observant, I'd have looked around and realized we had a problem, but being none of the above, I didn't. I was pretty well fixated on that late evening walk with Miss Bates. We were perhaps a half-hour into shooting when Kit began to miss lines. The first couple times I just chuckled. The fire was between us, and I couldn't see his face. He got partway through repeating the third line he'd muffed, when his arms wrapped tight around his stomach and he began to vomit – hard. "Kristoffer!" I said with alarm, and sprang to his side. It took me a few moments to realize that there was no reaction from the crew.

I eased Kit onto the ground, then stood up and squinted past the lights into the black desert night. "Florian? Reggie? What the hell's going on?" I asked, and got a groan for an answer.

I sprinted over to where I thought they should be, and found them both collapsed in their chairs, the cameraman on the ground beside them. All of them were moaning and heaving uncontrollably. "Oh, God," I said quietly. "Oh, God. I'll go get Bobbi."

It hadn't occurred to me yet that it could be food poisoning, because I wasn't sick, and I'd eaten dinner. At the moment I was scared and feeling incredibly helpless. I had people dropping like flies around me, and I didn't know what to do. I bent over Kit, told him I'd be right back, and for the second time that day I kicked my long legs into a run and headed back to camp, which was just a few hundred yards away.

I was partway there when I pretty literally ran into David Swift, who was running the other way, up toward the shoot. "Everybody's sick!" he cried, and I caught him up in my arms – partly to soothe him, partly to soothe me.

"I know," I said. "Up there, too. But you're not sick."

"You're not sick either. Why aren't we sick?" I could see him studying my face, wide-eyed in the dim light, and I had to shake my head in dismay.

"David, I just don't know," I said softly, "but we'll figure it out, I promise. Have you seen Bobbi Bates?"

He nodded, and pointed a finger toward the dining tent. "There," he said.

That's where I found her, crumpled on the floor, folded up in a tight ball of misery. She was sweaty and pallid, and shivering with cold and dry heaves. The cooks were down, our nurse was down, everybody was down – every single person, so far as I could tell, but six-year-old David, and me.

I started to pick her up, and she groaned and pushed me away. "Don't...move me," she whispered.

"Why not? What's wrong?"

"Sick," she managed. "Food poisoning. So sick."

"Well, Dear Lady, you cannot lie here and freeze to death, either," I said firmly. I picked her up in my arms and carried her, sobbing and gagging, back to the tent. I eased her onto her cot, covered her, and lit the lamp on the camp table before kneeling beside her and pushing her hair back away from her forehead. "Bobbi, Honey, can you hear me?" I asked.

"Ummm," she murmured. "Thanks. Feels better now. Not so cold."

"Bobbi, I'm the only one who isn't sick. Just little David and me. What do I do? Is anybody going to die?"

She gave my forearm a weak pat and swallowed hard. "Doubt it," she gasped. "Littlest ones – least body weight – oldest ones, over sixty or so, most danger there. Put everyone to bed. Covers. Water. Pepto can help. No real meds here to do anything with." She paused, panting, and turned her face from me to gag against the pillow. "Sorry," she whispered.

"You rest," I said. "David and I can handle this." I kissed her forehead and left the tent to stand in the open air, tugging my hair and wondering how in the hell to go about helping anybody. This was overwhelming! There were huge pieces of equipment running. There were fifteen or twenty people over at the shoot. There were people lying everywhere, groaning and vomiting.

The temperature was dropping like a stone toward the upper thirties or low forties. "God, what am I going to do?" I said aloud. "Help me, please."

"I'll help you," said David's calm little voice, and I could see his white hair shining in the starlight. "What do we do?"

I squatted on my haunches beside him and took his shoulders. "Bobbi says nobody is going to die, but we need to keep everybody warm and comfortable, and offer them water. So...here's what I want you to do, David, and it's a big, big chore."

"Go on," he said.

"I want you to find everybody who is lying down outside, and go into the tent nearest to them, and bring out something to cover them up with. I'm going to take one of the pickups over to the shoot and bring those guys back. Is that okay with you?"

He shrugged and nodded. "We can't stand here like boobies and do nothing," he said. "I could use a flashlight, though."

"Good idea," I nodded. I got him one from my tent, and checked on Bobbi at the same time. She seemed more asleep than awake, and still very ill. "Try not to be scared by people being so sick," I said as I handed him the light.

"I'll pretend like it's part of a scary movie I'm making. You can be the dashing leading man, and I'll be the famous director," he said, and headed away from me like a little train into the darkness.

"If you need me, holler," I called after him, "and I'll hear you." God, I was sending a six-year-old off by himself in the dark...to wade through puddles of vomit, and deal with people who were wretchedly ill, maybe unconscious or in convulsions.

I knew I had to do what I needed to as quickly as possible and get back to him. I grabbed myself a jacket from the tent, gave Bobbi an encouraging kiss on the cheek, and started to run for one of the pickups. "No good," I said aloud. "Think, buddy boy. You're going after men who are too sick to stand up, maybe even to sit. Soften the back of that truck with something." I jogged over to the moving van that the stagecoach had come in on, remembering how heavily it had been padded. When I opened the big doors, all the pads were neatly folded just inside. I grabbed as many of them as I could carry, and ran over to where the vehicles were parked.

The door to the first truck was open, and the keys were in the visor. I breathed a sigh of relief, started it up, and drove the quarter mile or so to the wickiups, trying not to speed for fear of running over somebody wandering sick in the desert. I bent over Reggie, but he was moaning and seemed unaware of my presence. I turned to Florien, put my hand against the side of his face, and said his name. "Flo, it's me, Bud. Can you hear me?"

"David..." he groaned.

"He's fine. He's not sick at all. How many men are out here with us? How many men do I need to find? Florien?"

There was silence punctuated only by groans, and the snorting and stomping of horses on the set, then Florien whispered, "Fourteen men, three women...I think. I'm...sure."

"Thanks," I said. "Let's get you into the pickup and off this cold ground."

"No. Don't want to move."

"Flo, you have to," I said firmly. "It's freezing out here. Come on."

Moving him made him gag and sob with discomfort, and I felt like a real heel, but I got him up off the ground far enough to get an arm around him, and more or less carried him from there. He was not a big man. I eased him into the back of the pickup, let go of him, and he promptly fell over. I climbed in, moved him to the back against the cab, and went to get Kit. I got the same response from him I'd gotten from Flo, so I just picked him up in my arms and carried him, in return for which he threw up on me. Not much though. I rubbed a little sand on it and pretended it wasn't there. I kissed Kit's clammy face, and placed him next to Florien.

I had to carry Clevenger, and both the Geneseo brothers, who were running the cameras. I found Lea Page, and carried her over to the truck, then Elden Button, Thomas Rice, Forrest Peacock, David Daffin....by now I was staggering, and the truck was full. I got in and drove very carefully back to camp, my mind going like crazy. By the time I got all these people into tents and settled, the people still at the shoot would be suffering from exposure. I parked the truck as close to the tents as I could get, and ran to get a couple more furniture pads. These, I used as a tent over the bed of the pickup, keeping the worst of the cold and dampness off the guys in the back.

As I was pulling the padding tight I called, "David, are you doing okay?" There was no answer. God, what if he'd gotten sick out here someplace? I ran to the tent he occupied with his dad, and found him sprawled on his cot – no covers – sound asleep. I covered him up, and ran back through the tents, noting that everybody who was outside, was covered with something, bless his stalwart little heart.

I grabbed the last of the pads, and ran to the next Ford in line. By the time I got back to the bright lights of the set, the temperature had dropped dramatically – alarmingly. I could see my breath as I trotted from place to place, calling for people, finding them, helping them, carrying them back to the truck. It took me half an hour going as hard as I could, to find everybody, get them into the pickup, and get back to camp. I parked the truck I was driving, covered the people in the back, and began picking people up off the cold desert floor.

Amber was lying outside near one of the blue rooms, and when I picked her up, she woke up, and immediately became hysterical with fear. "I'm going to die!" she sobbed. "Oh, Jesus, I'm going to die!"

"You're not," I soothed, carrying her back to her tent. "You just need to rest for a while."

"I'm so thirsty," she whimpered, and as I covered her, I told her I'd be back soon with some water.

It was over an hour before I got back to her, and by then I was running strictly on adrenalin, arms shaking with muscle fatigue, back in spasms from lifting people, dozens of people, at odd angles, carrying them, placing them in bed...any bed would do. The little twin girls were resting fairly comfortably, and we had nobody over fifty-five on the set this time around. I helped Amber sit up, and gave her a few sips of water. "Not too much," I cautioned, "You don't want to get sick again."

"Oh, God no," she whispered, and I lowered her back down.

I took paper cups and water jugs, and looked in every single tent, checked every single person, including the ones I'd just recently put to bed. Everyone was covered. Everyone was breathing. Everyone who needed a drink of water got one. I left water on tables for the rest.

I went back to the set and retrieved the horses that had been standing tied all night, turning them in with the others so that they, too, could have a drink. Just about then the big generator sputtered and ran out of gas, and it was blacker than black. The new moon was already down, and it was not yet dawn. I resisted the urge to lie down and ease my aching back. If I laid down, I'd be asleep in a hot second. It was so quiet. Up until last night I'd loved it. Now, I yearned for the sound of a normal human voice. I sat down on one of the benches in the dining tent, my elbows thudding onto the table. I was so tired, and so cold, and I knew if these people stayed sick any length of time, I couldn't take care of them. I was ten miles from a telephone, a million miles from help, and completely alone.

I remembered an old Army trick, and let myself doze with my chin in the palm of my hand, knowing that if I fell sound asleep my head would fall and I'd wake up. It was not the most restful thing to do. My eyes were beginning to really bother me, and I knew I'd had my contact lenses in way too long. I dragged myself up off the bench and went back to the tent to put on a clean shirt.

Both Bobbi and Kit seemed a little more comfortable than they had been. They were not moaning or writhing, or gagging. They both appeared to be sleeping, and their breathing was even and deep. I found my glasses, and then rinsed my fingertips in a cup of water so I could take out my contacts. I had to be very careful. This was back when you didn't wear contacts for a few days and chuck them. These were hard contacts, the kind that needed to be cleaned, and the kind you didn't want to lose in the middle of nowhere. I stuck my knuckles in my eyes and rubbed – put drops in and rubbed some more. Nobody else in my family was blind. Hell, my grandmother had better eyesight than I did. Why was that? For some reason it annoyed me dreadfully at that moment, even though people told me I looked suave in my wire rimmed aviator's lenses. Like that made up for being legally blind. I put on my glasses and checked all the tents again, one after the other – gently touching each person – speaking quietly, making sure they were breathing and not shivering. Apparently, I was the only one who was freezing at the moment.

As it began to crack dawn in the east I went to the kitchen tent.

There were big propane fired stoves. Maybe there was a way to make coffee for me, and I knew David would need breakfast. Then, I'd already decided, I was heading for the nearest telephone to call Dad. Maybe somebody at the trading post knew where I could find some help until people were back on their feet. There wasn't a reasonably sized coffee pot in the place. There was coffee left in the big urns from last night, and I settled for that, putting some in a saucepan on the stove to warm. I found milk and cereal, and then went to check on David.

He had dragged his cot over next to Flo, and was huddled up beside his dad when I ducked under the flap. I could see his bright blue eyes on me, and I smiled and said, "How are you this morning, super hero?"

"I'm worried about my father," he said, and his voice was heavy with unshed tears. "He won't wake up."

I felt a chill go up my spine, but I just smiled and said, "He's very tired, David. I'm sure he'll wake up here after a bit. Are you hungry?"

He thought about it for a few moments, then slowly nodded. "Yes, I guess I am."

"Let's go have some breakfast, and I'll tell you my plan," I said.

"I hope it includes washing off that paint," David said, and I suddenly wondered how many people thought they were hallucinating when I bent over them in the night.

"I'm sure it will," I chuckled. "Get your jacket and let's go eat."

"Who's going to feed the horses?" he asked as we walked, and I sighed and tapped my chest.

"I am, but then we're going to go in to the trading post and telephone for some help."

"I'd rather stay here with my dad," he said.

"I know you would, David, but I don't want to leave you here all by yourself. I'd rather we stuck together."

He gave me a look that was a lot more than six years old. "What if I refuse to go with you?" he asked.

I put cereal and milk down in front of him, and then got him a bowl and a spoon. "I'd respect your wishes," I said. "You've given me no reason to doubt you. But...if something were to go wrong and I couldn't get back, or something went really wrong here and you were all alone, I know your dad would rather you were with me."

"Possibly," he said, shoveling in a big bite of cereal.

"Besides, what if we need to make a new plan and I need your advice?"

"Now you're being condescending," he said around the mouthful of cereal. "Don't do that."

I just sat there and blinked at him for a minute, sipping stale coffee and wondering where in the world he'd picked up a word like condescending. If he knew how to use the word, he probably understood its meaning, so after a bit I said, a little edgily, "I wasn't being condescending, David. I'm feeling my way through this, you know. People around here tend to be divided into two camps – the ones who think the boss's kid should have all the answers, and the ones who think he doesn't have any. Recognize it?"

"Um hm," he said. "Oh, by the way, I will go with you. I just wanted to see what you'd say if I refused."

"Thanks," I smiled, resisting the urge to say more. "I'm going to go feed the horses real quick, and then we can go."

"You haven't eaten," he noted, pointing at my coffee cup. "That's not much breakfast."

"I'll eat when there's time," I said. "You finish up, and let's get going. I don't want to leave these people alone for any longer than we absolutely have to."

"Please, take time to wash your face," David grinned, and I grinned back. It was the start of an enduring friendship.

Fifteen minutes later, face scrubbed and quickly shaved, horses fed, I hollered for David, and he appeared from the cook tent, carrying a plate in his hands. When he got to the truck he handed the plate to me and said, "I made you a toasted cheese sandwich. I made me one, too. It's hard to think when your stomach is empty."

"Bless you, my child," I said, and as we jounced over the sandy track at a pace that was just a little faster than was wise for the conditions, I ate my sandwich and tacitly admired the little person sitting next to me. My mind was full of those people, those sick people we'd left alone back there. Soon it would be too hot in those tents, and they'd need as much or more care than they'd needed the night before. Parts of me were numb. Parts of me were shaking. I was more grateful than you can imagine for David's sturdy presence. "That, was a very good sandwich," I said. "You're a man of many talents, Master Swift."

"I have to be," he said, looking out the window, "My mother left us, and Dad and I are all alone. He has a Mexican lady who comes in three days a week to clean and cook supper, but the rest of the time it's just him and me, you know? And a guy can eat just so many Cheerios."

I chuckled softly and nodded, but my heart ached for him. So much of what I was, how I thought, was based on the love my parents had for each other and the love and respect they had for my grandmother. Who would I be and what would I be like without that influence? "You are a remarkable young man," I said. My opinion has not changed over the years.

We got to the little trading post, or village, or whatever it was, in about twenty minutes of hard driving. There was a KOA campground, a laundromat, a general store, a one-pump gas station, and the trading post itself, which was upscale, and had a restaurant as well as a gift shop of the sort that would appeal to the people in the Airstream trailers over at the campground. Upon closer examination there was a sign over the door of the general store that said, *United States Post Office*, and an arrow pointing down an alley beside the building that said, *Clinic*.

David jumped out on my side, because the doors in the big four by four were too heavy for him, and as I swung him to the ground I said, "I'm going to go call LA and tell them we're in trouble. Why don't you see what all, or who all, goes with that arrow over there?"

"Okay," he said, and trotted off, brushing crumbs of toast off his blue jean jacket as he ran.

I did the same, then walked into the general store, which was already open despite the earliness of the hour. Made sense. Who'd want to shop in the heat of the day? There was an Anglo gentleman behind the counter, and I smiled and asked for a telephone. "Over there," he said, and pointed to a pay phone on the wall. "You with the movie they're making up the road?" I just nodded, said I'd be back in a minute to chat, and went to call my dad.

The phone was dead as the proverbial doorknob. No dial tone with or without a dime. I went back and told the proprietor, and he reached under his counter and pulled out a standard phone, set it on the counter, and held the handset to his ear. "This one's dead, too. It happens a lot out here. Sorry."

I resisted the urge to throw myself on the floor and cry. "Is there a doctor in town?"

"Not today. You need one?"

"Me personally, no," I said, scanning the shelves. It was a fascinating store, and I wished for time to enjoy it. "We've got food poisoning up at the shoot, and I could use some serious reinforcements, though."

"You might try the Berrys. He's the teacher at the local school," he jerked his chin toward the back of the store, "but she's a nurse. Done a lot for the folks around here. They didn't used to like him much – called him 'Buffalo Soldier', but they think she's an angel. Go down the alley. There's a little church that the *padre* uses when he comes, and there's a one room schoolhouse, and the clinic. They live in back of the clinic."

"Thanks," I said, and turned to leave.

"I can send somebody out to tell you when the phones are working again, if you'd like."

"I would. Thanks," I said, turning and walking backwards for a few seconds. "Thank you very much for your help."

"Wish I could do more," he said. "Good luck."

I wished he could do more, too. I closed the door and jogged around the corner into the alley, aware that it was already growing warmer. I tried to calculate in my mind how long we had before too cold became too hot. Church to my left with a couple of scrubby pines in front, little red schoolhouse in front of me, looking much the worse for wear. Part of the roof was tarped over and most of the paint had long since peeled away to reveal the greying wood beneath. Attached to it by an ancient and sagging shingled walkway, was the clinic. There was a wooden bench outside, and a couple of rickety, rusted lawn chairs.

I was looking for a door that would gain me access to their residence, when the door on the side of the clinic came open, and a portly black gentleman with close-cropped hair and a kind, white smile stuck his hand out to me. "Peter?" he said.

"Peter Aarons," I replied, taking his hand. Now the term 'buffalo soldier' made sense. The black men who had formed their own cavalry units to fight the Indians after the civil war, had been killing machines of devastating capability. No wonder the Navajos didn't care much for him. "There's a little towheaded person...never mind," I smiled, "he found you, or you wouldn't know my name."

"Sounds like you've had a long night," he chuckled. "My wife is getting some stuff together to take up there. I'm Johnathan Berry, by the way. Come in. We'll be ready in a minute." He gestured me past him into the bright interior of the clinic, which was efficiently set up, and scrubbed to a uniform shine. David was sitting in the corner petting a large black and white cat, while a lady who was very much the same size and shape as her husband was bustling around putting things from shelves into a cardboard box. She looked up and gave me a smile like pearlized sunshine. "You must be Peter. I'm Marie," she said, and stopped long enough to shake hands.

"You're..." I caught my tongue just in time. I'd been about to say, white. Instead I sputtered for a second and said, "a Godsend."

"That's why we're here," Johnathan smiled. "I'm going to go try to round up a couple folks to help you out until people are back on their feet out there. Marie, are the Begays back from sheep camp yet?"

"I think so," she said, picking up the box. "If they're not, try the Tohonos. I can't think of anybody else offhand who'd go out there with us, can you?"

Johnathan shook his head and gave me another one of his smiles. "The People don't care much for outsiders. But I can find somebody to help Marie, and somebody to help you, I'm pretty sure. You guys go on ahead, and I'll be along after a bit with reinforcements." He disappeared out the door, and Marie gestured with her lips, Navajo fashion, for me to follow.

"Let me take that box for you," I said, and she handed it over as we hurried down the alley and back to the pickup. She moved with amazing swiftness for a short, plump person. I opened the truck door for her, then handed her back the box. I could see that we were being watched with something between veiled curiosity and open hostility, and I had a twinge of fear that perhaps leaving my colleagues alone and helpless hadn't been the smartest thing to do, but then, what else could I have done? I tossed David onto the seat, and stepped on the gas.

Marie asked me what we'd done for everybody, and I told her, ending with, "It wasn't much, I'm afraid."

"It was all you could do," she said comfortingly, "and with food poisoning sometimes it's all anyone can do unless it's so bad somebody needs their stomach pumped or poison control or somesuch. Otherwise it's a little like the flu. Grit your teeth and ride it out. Any idea what made them sick?"

"Either the meat or the tomato sauce," I said. "I ate everything else."

"And I had some of the meat plain," David said.

"Must have been the canned tomatoes," Maria said. "I assume they're canned?"

"Me, too," I said. "Everything tastes canned out here."

"Well," she chuckled, "aside from the obvious, how are you liking your stay in our corner of the world?"

"I don't know about David," I said. "I think it's spectacular."

"Me, too," David said. "The light in the early morning and late evenings...when the shadows are long...I see time moving in them, so slow and deliberate, but never stopping. I'd like to make a movie about time here."

Marie and I just glanced at each other over his white curls, and I let my eyes widen a little. Obviously not your run-of-the- mill first grader. Even now when I think about how David was at six, and how Royal was at six, and then how Alex was at six...so much...younger, I guess is the word. But then, Alex was a bundle of nerves when we first got him – still is from time to time – like his old man.

Like his old man was that day, for sure. The second the wheels stopped going around I was out of the truck, and when I had Marie safely on the ground I was off like a shot to open tent flaps at both ends to let any vagrant breeze through, and to check on Kit and Bobbi and offer them water. Both of them responded to my questions with a flickering of the eyelids and a wan smile, but neither of them was really awake, and neither of them had any intention of moving so much as an inch. "You guys rest, and don't start messing around with each other, okay? Kit, you're a married man. Bobbi, I have designs of my own on you, so keep it straight in here." That elicited a bit of a snort from Kit, and I considered my mission accomplished.

I headed out into the rest of the camp, and...God, what a dismal, stinking, gut-wrenching mess it was – and me with a perpetually weak stomach. How had I made it through last night, and how was I going to make it through this morning? The barf on the ground could be kicked over and avoided, but on tent floors, on clothes, blankets, people...not so easy. I swallowed hard and made myself keep going – opening tent flaps, seeing if people needed water – wondering how in the hell we were going to get this mess cleaned up and salvage the shoot. This was supposedly the last movie in which my dad was taking a personal hand. I wanted it to go so well – for him to be justifiably proud of it – and all I could see was canned tomatoes, ground beef, green beans, slicked over salad and stomach acid...suddenly I was outside, and I was sick as a dog.

"Finally hit you, did it?" said Marie's voice from behind me. "Is anything more wrong in there than anyplace else?"

"No," I managed, thumping down onto my butt in the sand. "I just...I don't..."

"Rest a bit," she said. "You look very flushed. Where's David?"

"Probably with his dad," I muttered, grimacing at the taste in my mouth. "Second tent the other side of the cook tent ... over there." There was a hollow banging sound, and I realized the horses had no water. "I need to go take care of the stock for just a minute," I said. "I'll be right back."

I jumped up and hurried that direction, slowing down only when I realized I was so dizzy I was walking like my front-end was out of alignment. I shook my head to try to clear it, and nearly landed on it instead. Some lucid inner voice advised me at that point to slow down and stay slowed, and I did. Standing there while the horses drank and the tank refilled, I could feel my heart beating in my hands, and my lips, and my legs. Singularly odd feeling. I've had it since, but never before. Now when it happens I do something middle-aged and sensible like take in some liquids and rest for a bit. That day, with the sun beating down on my bare head, I gritted my teeth, splashed some water out of the horse trough onto my face, and fought the feeling with all my might. People were sick. There was no time to curl up someplace for a nap. I did go to the dining tent and get a tall, cool glass of water that was smooth going down, and very soothing to my throat and my nerves. Juice would have been most welcome, but I didn't have time to look for any, or make any, though I knew there must be some in the big, propane fired refrigerators.

When I found Marie she'd already done what she could to make people feel better, and was busy swabbing out tents with a big rag mop. "Waking up to this won't do anybody any good," she explained, and I nodded, dreading what I was supposed to say next.

"How can I help you?"

"Rotate buckets for me. Bring me cold, soapy water with a little bleach in it, then take the bucket I've been using, throw the water over there someplace, and take that bucket and put cold, soapy water in it...and around we go."

"I can do that," I said. "Where did you find that first bucket you have there?"

"In the kitchen. There are several more. Those guys sure have some set-up to work with in there."

She sounded wistful, and I wondered what it was like to live out here, far from family and friends and grocery stores, movies and miniature golf, in a little building that wasn't much more than a shack, and try to help people who didn't want you here? What kind of a stove did she have? Did she have a refrigerator at all? How did they keep warm in the winter? It could snow here, and it did. What drove her and Johnathan, I wondered, and when I brought her the next bucket, I asked her about it.

"We're needed here. Johnathan is a teacher – a window to tomorrow and the outside world of technology – a doorway when they let him be. I'm a nurse. I patch up Today so it can get to Tomorrow. So it doesn't die of malnutrition or measles, or alcohol poisoning or blood poisoning on the way."

"How long have you been here?"

"Four years last month."

"And how long is your hitch? I don't know what it's called really."

"As long as it takes, which is longer than it's been so far."

I studied her face – so honest and open. She was obviously intelligent. "But...why?"

"Why not?"

"The man in the store said..." I had blundered, and now it was too late. I just shook my head and looked about half as contrite and foolish as I felt. "I'm so sorry. I'm prying, and I don't mean to. I guess...it just seems so inhospitable here, and I'm such a hedonist."

She patted her ample middle and laughed softly. "Given the opportunity, so am I, Peter. Johnathan is a gourmet cook. We love the theater – watching it and being in it. There are things I miss, but there are things that need to be done, and looking to someone else to do them is wrong when you are the one who sees what needs to be accomplished."

I gave her an openly admiring smile. "You're a brave lady. I don't know if I could stay where I wasn't really accepted, but only tolerated. It must be very difficult."

Her eyes twinkled and she said, "'Is there any remover of difficulties save God?'"

A light went on in my brain. "You're Baha'i," I said.

She stopped her mopping and gave me an appraising look. "And you?"

"Nominal Jew, but I have a dear friend who is Baha'i, and he chants that little mantra you just used. Terrific individual. He was my Psychologist when I was a little boy."

"What's his name?" she asked.

"Steven Effendi, from Los Angeles."

"Oh, of course," she smiled. "I know Steven."

"Are you from LA?"

"No," she said, "Milwaukee." She took the fresh bucket, and went back to her mopping.

I glanced at my watch. Nearly noon. I took her another bucket, tried not to look at what she was doing, and said, "I should be finding us some lunch. I'm sure David's hungry by now. How about you?"

"I'm always hungry," she chuckled. "You should also be thinking about what you're going to feed these people as they revive. Something easy on the stomach, like gelatin, or a mild soup. Do you know how to make Jell-O?"

"I have to admit, I don't, but I'll bet David does. I'll take him with me," I said, and took the vile-looking bucket to dump it.

David was sound asleep, curled up next to his father, and I didn't have the heart to wake him. I went to the kitchen alone. It was Jell-O, for cryin' out loud. How hard could it be? Probably not very, at least in a little bitty box with instructions on it, but the gelatin I found was in a great big can, and the instructions were for fifty servings. Okay, I thought, sitting down with the can, fifty servings. In what, exactly, did one make fifty servings of Jell-O? I began to move things around without any clear concept of what I was looking for. By this time I'd been up thirty-one hours, and not much of anything was clear anymore. I found a great big stock pot and filled it with water, then set it on the stove and turned on the gas under it. Would that be twenty-five cups? Probably not. I got out its twin, and filled it, too. A thought struck me. The generator was out of gas. When it got dark, it was going to be *really* dark unless I refueled it, and how did I do that, and did I try to start it with all those lights plugged in? Maybe I left them plugged in and just turned them off first, and how did I do that? It was all too much for me, and I sat like a toad, doing nothing but blinking and occasionally flicking my tongue.

I'd come here to make three lunches, I thought, shaking myself out of my stupor. Surely I could make three simple lunches, couldn't I? Kit and I had made sandwiches at his house, and at mine when Mrs. Gustavson wasn't looking. I forced myself to get up with the same kind of willpower that kept me working on a piece of music, over and over, hour after hour, until it was perfect. Music. I turned some Rachmaninoff on in my head, and put myself on autopilot.

I found that I could indeed make sandwiches. I knew what they looked like. Lunch meat, cheese, sliced tomatoes...no. No tomatoes. Pickles, mustard, mayo...ugh, no mayo...lettuce, a second slice of bread. A sandwich. I felt like a new man. I made several sandwiches, since I had the hang of it, and while I was making the rest of them, I ate the first, and felt better.

There was a cloud of dust, a rattle akin to several rocks in a tin can, and Johnathan Berry's ancient station wagon appeared over the crest of a small hill, an equally ancient sky blue Chevy pickup close behind it. Two women got out of the pickup, but the man driving stayed inside. Marie was walking to greet them, and I went to greet Johnathan. "Lunch is ready," I said as a general announcement, "if anybody's hungry." The women veered toward the cook tent, and I stuck out my hand and said, "Hello, Johnathan. Thank you so much for coming."

"You look terrible," he said. "Even brawny kids like you need sleep sometime."

"Come, have a sandwich," I said, and he did. He said it was good, and I was absurdly pleased. I'd come to realize in the course of all this that I was one of those highly educated, multi-talented individuals who couldn't actually *do* anything of any practical value, and I vowed that was going to change when I got home. I left him eating and went to get David. It was very hot, and the tent, even open at both ends, was stifling. I carried him outside, woke him up, and sent him off to join Johnathan for lunch before going back to my rounds of seeing if anybody needed water or help to the bathroom.

To my profound relief, people were beginning to wake up. I went and got a bucket with cool water and some washcloths, and began washing hands and faces, as well as offering drinks of water. I was sponging Kit's face when his hazel eyes opened and he smiled at me. "Bud? What time is it?" he said in quite a normal voice, and I could feel tears in my eyes.

"Time for you to get some rest and get back on your feet," I said. "Can I get you anything?"

"Jell-O would be nice," he said, and I remembered all that water, boiling like crazy on the stove. All over the stove, probably.

"Shit!" I exclaimed, jumping up, and Kit shook his head and gave me a weak grin.

"No, thanks. I'd rather have Jell-O."

"Be right back," I laughed, and about that time Bobbi sat up very slowly, very timidly, felt herself all over and asked if she was alive. "You don't look it," I said, "but looks can be deceiving. Gotta run, my water's burning."

By evening, most people were ready for some of Marie's good soup, or some Jell-O, or both, and most everybody was ambulatory, either with or without help. At six O'clock the next morning my tent flap came open and Florian Swift bellowed, "Good God, Bud! We have a movie to make and you're still on your indolent ass? Just because you're the boss's kid, doesn't mean you get preferential treatment on this set. Get out of there and get to work!"

"Yes Sir, absolutely, Sir," I mumbled, and allowed myself a slow, self-satisfied smile.

CHAPTER EIGHT

It was, admittedly, a major disaster, but it was our only disaster. The rest of the shoot went smooth as silk. I got away one morning a day or so later, and went into the trading post and tried once again to thank, and to pay the Berrys for what they'd done. They allowed me to pay for the meds we'd used. Other than that, they wouldn't take a dime.

"Let me make a donation to the school, then," I insisted.

Johnathan just shook his head, and flashed his underbite at me. "We can't let you do that, Peter. We don't accept money from sources outside the Baha'i faith. It keeps us from feeling beholden to anybody or any group. You understand."

"No," I admitted, "I don't. But I'll respect your wishes. Is there nothing I can do to compensate you?"

"You can tell Steven Effendi hello for us," said Marie, and I agreed to do that. I'd also be asking him how to make an end run around these good people. Maybe my dad could make a new station wagon drop out of the sky. What if they just nonchalantly happened to win something, like a roof, or a new stove? Hey, maybe they'd win a trip to see a Broadway show. After seeing these people in action I had decided one thing – when I got home, I was going to talk...really talk...to Steven Effendi. The next time that thing came for me in the dark, or I became that thing in the dark, I wanted to be able to point fingers and name names, even if it was my own.

A couple nights after that, I was out for an evening jog on old Buck when I came across David, carrying a guitar nearly as big as he was, scuffing down the road toward the bluff. "Whither goest thou, Minstrel?" I asked, riding up behind him, and I could tell by the hasty way he wiped at his face that he'd been crying.

"In search of a song that will tell the truth about the singer," he replied in his six-year-old voice. Amazing. Who, exactly, was this tiny blond man-child with the bright blue eyes and the perspicacious brain?

"How about a lift?"

"Sure," he sighed, so I stopped my horse, hooked a heel in his side, and reached down to catch David around the waist and haul him up. I sat him in front of me and rode on toward the sunset, not saying anything – sensing that he needed some quiet time before he tried to talk. I stopped near a big, sun-warmed rock, and stepped off onto it, taking David and his guitar with me. We sat down, and got comfortable, and watched twilight inch across the valley floor.

"I saw you with Bobbi Bates the other night," he said abruptly, and I jumped a little. Bobbi and I had finally gotten around to taking our walk, and it had turned into a lot more than a simple perambulation to bay at the moon. Her instructions to me had been straightforward and graphic, and so had most of what we'd done to each other. While it had not actually been vaginal intercourse, it was my sincere wish that nobody had observed us, especially not a child.

I swallowed, and glanced at him out of the corner of my left eye. He was still staring out across the valley. "Bobbi's a friend of mine. I'm with her a lot."

"You were kissing her at the time. That's more than friends."

"What makes you think that?" I asked, really turning to look at him. "People don't have to be in love with each other to enjoy being together."

"No," he sighed, "I suppose not. It's nice though, isn't it?"

"What?"

"Being in love."

I crimped a grin and swiveled on the rock so I could face him. "Is this about the Fortner twins?"

He put his head in his hands and swung it from side to side, for all the world like a little old man, and I chuckled in spite of myself. "It's not funny, Bud. Since I helped take care of them when everybody was sick, they call me their hero, and then they sigh all stupid. Those little girls drive me crazy. They follow me around, and they try to hold hands with me. One of them even tried to kiss me! It...gives me the creeps."

"Why is that?"

"I don't know," he grumped. "It just seems wrong, but I don't know why it does, it just does. Is kissing girls fun for you?"

"It is most pleasant now, but it wasn't when I was your age."

"Why not?"

"When I was your age, I was scared to death of everything and everybody except Kit Miller. The boys teased me all the time because I was skinny, and I had great big eyes, and great big hands, and great big feet. And the girls laughed, so I thought they didn't like me. My English was terrible. I couldn't understand a blinkin' thing that was going on, which didn't help. The only thing I really understood was my piano. When my English got better, most things got better, too. But girls...I thought they were pretty evil. I still think, as a species, girls are pretty evil. Not all of them, though."

David was momentarily distracted from the issue of girls, and was looking at me with new interest. "Where are you from?"

"Russia."

"Say something for me!" he breathed, eyes wide with excitement, so I gestured, smiled, and spoke to him for a bit in my native language. "Now tell me what you said!" he exclaimed.

"I said that it's a really beautiful evening for two friends to be sitting together on a big old rock discussing the order of things in the world."

"You have a beautiful, deep voice," he said. "It rumbles in your chest, and it has soft booming sounds in it like cannon fire from a long way off, or the big tympani drums in an orchestra. I can hear different notes in it. I'll be wanting to make a movie with you when I'm big. You can be the hero."

"Thank you," I smiled. "I'll take that as a compliment. It sounds like you have an ear for music, David. Is that why you brought the guitar along? Need to write a little music?"

He contemplated the instrument, which was lying on the rock next to him, and gave it a tentative strum. "It is in me to make music when I'm sad or confused. I want to make music, but I don't know how. I want to take music lessons..." he shrugged a dismissal of hope and added, "Dad says we don't have time for that sort of thing. My acting and my school are more important."

"Would you like me to teach you how to play this?" I asked, picking up the old guitar. It was one of the props, and had seen better days, but it had all its strings, and when I had tuned it, it had a nice sound. David just watched the process, saying nothing.

"Play for me," he said, and I nodded. I didn't insist that he try it himself. He needed music, and more than that, he needed somebody's undivided attention for a while.

"What would you like?" I asked, strumming a few chords to loosen up my fingers.

"Sing me something that suits the place," he said, and he sounded a hundred years old.

I didn't tell him I didn't sing. I did sing. I just didn't do it in front of people. I had a lot of years and a lot of money in my pipes. I sang, *Tumbling Tumbleweeds* for him, and *Santa Fe Trail*, and a couple of other things from the era of The Sons Of The Pioneers – and I did some whistling for him, and even a little yodeling, though I made him swear he'd never tell a soul I could do that. We got to laughing, and talking about what we wanted to be when we grew up, and night closed in around us, and I finally said we'd better be getting back before his dad got worried.

We were riding along in silence, enjoying the moonlight and the night air – David leaning against my chest, half asleep – when I happened to look off to my right, and there were two people in the rocks about fifty feet away. They were both facing away from us, and I could tell by the spread posture of the girl's body, leaning over the waist high boulder, and the movements of the man behind her, exactly what they were doing. I recognized Reginald Clevenger's silhouette covering most of the woman... and I caught a glimpse of a bright yellow tank top.

David was looking the other way, and I didn't change that. I just muttered, "You're right. Females are a pain," but I didn't tell him where I hurt, because I wasn't quite sure myself.

I avoided Bobbi the next day, and when she asked me if I'd like to go for an evening stroll, I raised one eyebrow and said, "Why, is Reggie too busy?"

"I don't know. I didn't ask him."

"You asked him last night," I said accusingly.

"He asked me," she said, and the pleasant and inviting look on her face hardened a little. "What's this all about, Bud?"

"Let's do go for that walk," I growled, seized her elbow, and walked her, a little roughly, I'm afraid, away from the people who were finishing up dinner and spreading themselves out in lawn chairs to enjoy the onset of coolness. "I'm not a spy, Bobbi, really I'm not, but David and I were out riding last night, and I just happened to see you and Reg...enjoying one another's company, so to speak."

She gave me a look that was genuinely puzzled. "And?"

"And?" I exclaimed. "And you and I were out there two nights before, doing the same thing, for Godssake!"

"Not exactly," she smiled. "Reggie actually..."

"Stop! I don't want to know what you were doing down to the last detail. All I know is, you made love to me one night and him the next!"

She stopped our furious walk forward, pulled away from me, and went over to sit on a convenient boulder a few hundred feet from the main camp. "I did not make love to you, I had sex with you, more or less. I for sure had sex with Reggie. It's fun. So what?"

Now that, was a stumper for me. She felt no remorse at all for the heinous crime she'd committed against me. I was beginning to think..."You don't see anything wrong with that?"

"Wrong? Define the word, wrong."

I had sense enough to pass on that one, which was amazing under the circumstances. Even as I was raving at her I was asking myself why I was doing it. I'd sat there at the piano not so many days ago with her on the stairs above me, and I'd told myself just what she was like sexually, and that this was bound to happen, and yet now that it had I couldn't seem to get a handle on it. Why was that? "I guess I'm just not the kind of guy who makes love to a girl with the idea that she's going to turn around and make love to somebody else, that's all."

"Why not?" she asked, still reasonably calm, "you men do it all the time."

"Oh, no," I said angrily – actually everything I said the whole conversation was said angrily, and with a great deal of tender-egoed frustration. "Do not lump me into that category. I do not jump into bed with one woman after another. When I'm serious about a girl, I stick with that girl. I'm loyal to a fault."

One red eyebrow arched toward her hairline. "Are you saying you're serious about me? I mean, you've used the term 'making love', you've used the term 'serious'..."

"I don't have sex with people I'm not serious about," I said through my teeth. "God, woman, didn't you pay any attention to any of those films they showed us in the army?"

"You know, you said that same thing the other night, and it wasn't one of our more romantic moments. You wouldn't take my word for the fact that I was protected enough for both of us. You had to whine about never having had sex without a condom your whole life, which made me feel like a syphilitic whore, and..."

"...then you go whoring off the next night with Reggie Clevenger, who is not only currently married..." she jumped, and her eyes got big, and I realized, she hadn't known he was married. Still, hurt to the point of being cruel, I went on. "...Who is not only married, but has had half the women in Hollywood, and proving my point."

"So tell me," she grated, by now as angry as I was, "are you jealous, or are you scared?"

"Both," I said after a moment's thought. "Both. I really do care for you, Bobbi, and I don't know how to deal with this modern woman, free love, cavalier about STD's image you're projecting. I want to be with you sexually, and have a relationship with you intellectually, and I don't know how to do that on a time-share basis. I'm just not into casual sex with people I care about. Hookers, maybe. You, no."

"And how much of how you feel about this have you bothered to share with me?" she snapped. "None of it. None at all. I'm supposed to read your mind. Either you don't have the guts to speak up, or your ego is so huge you assume that once a woman has been with you, nobody else could possibly measure up, so she'll never wander off. I like you, Bud, I really do. I've indicated that right from the start, but you do not own me. If you want to own me, you'd better think of a suitable down-payment."

"I didn't think you were for sale," I said quietly, and looked at her for a long moment before walking away.

Late that night when the three of us were in bed and it was totally dark in the tent, Bobbi said, "I assume this means I'm homeless."

"Of course not," I snapped. "Don't be any more stupid than you've already been, okay?"

"Gee, Buddy, you have such a way with women," Kit mumbled, half asleep, and that time *both* Bobbi and I told him to shut the fuck up.

"This is Hollywood," Bobbi said in a reasonable tone. "I thought everybody..."

"You know perfectly well that anytime you use a term like, *everybody*, it's a lie," I said. I was trying to keep my voice low. The walls were thin, but then again, so were my nerves. "Everybody doesn't, not even in Hollywood. I don't. Sex between two people is a sacred thing. It's sacred to me." I realized right away how priggish that sounded, but it was already out of my mouth.

"Damn, what century are you from, anyway?" Bobbi asked, but it wasn't really a question, and there was a mocking edge to her tone that left me no doubt I'd chosen the wrong word. I let the challenge alone, and an uncomfortable silence added itself to the dark around us.

"So, when are you marrying Carmelita from Tijuana?" Kit asked, and I felt like he'd stuck a knife in my heart.

"I thought I told you to shut up," I muttered.

"You did, but you're my best friend. You've already made a statement that I know is hypocritical, and you're about to make a fool of yourself on top of it, so I thought I'd step in and try to do some damage control."

"Just what in the hell are you talking about?" I asked, sitting up in my bed and giving the covers an angry kick. Even as I asked, I knew what he was going to say, and I felt like I was caught in some kind of a weird time-loop, where things go just so far and then repeat themselves, over and over.

"Being in love with someone, and having sex with someone for purposes of recreation, are not the same thing," he said patiently.

"Hear, hear," Bobbi said, and I could tell by the sound on her side of the tent, that she, too, was sitting up.

"Buddy, listen to me. Sex only becomes sacred when it is love making, and to be love making, there has to be love, and commitment," Kit continued, using that tone my first grade teacher used when she wanted to make sure I understood. "Love is sacred. Sex is fun. It's the sixties. Almost the seventies."

"If you start singing about flowers and free love, I promise you, I'll puke," I muttered. He was confusing me. He was making sense, and I hated it. I'd thought all along I knew what I believed, and now I wasn't sure. The whole thing with Carmelita from Tijuana was poisonous. "Maybe it's just that I'm ready to grow up and have sex mean something – have it be part of a relationship, not just an end in itself. You're married. You should understand this."

"Bud, if you want commitment, you need to find somebody who's willing to commit," Kit said reasonably, "and you're not going to find that amongst Hollywood types. Look on the aristocratic side of the money fence. What about that precious little button of a Melanie Rosallini, or Nina Goldman, who is stacked like a brick shitter and has the brain of a rocket scientist?"

"Oh, sure. Melanie's an adorable, old fashioned girl. Really old fashioned. She thinks anybody who's black is a slave. And she's smart as a whip – says things like, 'Musicals are so hard to follow with all that singing going on.'" Bobbi let out a snort, and I found a smile tugging at my own lips. I fought it back, even though nobody else could see it. I was pissed, and I planned to stay that way. "Nina Goldman made it very clear that she was out with me for only one reason. She'd heard the legend of Old One Eye, and wanted to see if it was true."

"But you did let her in on the legend. You said so. How was it?"

"It was quick, and hot, and over. She carried on a civil conversation just long enough to get where she wanted to be, and then spent the next two hours moaning and groaning like she didn't know her own name. If she ever snapped out of it, I wasn't around to see it. Frankly, I was embarrassed by the whole thing – including my behavior. I should have told her to take a flying leap."

"Well, what about Isabelle? You never even gave Isabelle Schwartz a chance, Aloysha. She's...attractive. I remember even in high school she sewed beautifully. Made a lot of her own clothes, and she loved to cook. She indicated very broadly that she was interested in a commitment – in marriage."

"She also indicated she had the hots for you. I didn't follow up on that, either, Kristoffer. She's a flipping snob, just like she was in high school. She laughs like Woody Woodpecker, and her idea of stimulating conversation is nasaling about how hard it is to find good mascarpone cheese for filling chocolate roulades. If we tried to discuss ideas, or ideals, instead of things and people, she'd blow like an overheated radiator...and don't go anywhere sexual with that. I realized it was a mistake to say it, even as it was coming out my mouth."

"A lot of what you've said is probably a mistake, if you ever want to have sex with Miss Bates again," Kit replied, and I could hear unuttered laughter in his tone. "But I don't think you want sex. I think you want love, and that I cannot help you with, despite gossip to the contrary. Love, you have to find on your own. I offered you my sister-in-law, and you spurned her."

"I did not!" I laughed. "I thought she was very nice, and very pretty, and you know that there was not a single spark between us. We could have spent all night in a sleeping bag together and never felt a thing."

"There, see? You do feel better, don't you?" Kit said quietly. "All I have to do is bring up all the options you've already dismissed, all the girls you've had recreational sex with, and your perspective becomes twenty-twenty again. Go ahead, go steady for a while. You've never done it. Maybe it's for you, and then again, maybe you'll find out you're married to a forty-eight inch Steinway and that's all the love life you need." I heard him flip the covers aside and stand up. I could even see his outline very dimly against the blacker black of the tent wall as he put on jeans and a tee shirt. "Giving good advice just makes me starved. I am eating for two, you know. Anyway, I'll be gone for a while looking for food if you two want to talk. Bobbi, are you still here and awake?"

"Um hm," she said.

"Well, be nice to Buddy. He's as tender as meringue, but you know, he's brilliant, and he's talented, and he's passionate, and some day all that's going to belong to some lucky woman along with the cow eyes and the pouty mouth and the legendary spectre of Old One Eye."

"Kit," I said, "Please leave."

There was a chuckle, the tent flap opened, letting in a blaze of starlight, then closed again, and it was dark. "Well," I said after a minute, "I'm sure you know more than you wanted to about me and my romantic exploits. I think Kit may have forgotten you were even here. Preacher's kid, you know."

"I doubt very much that he forgot I was here," Bobbi said gently. "He adores you, Bud, but he wasn't necessarily talking to you. He wanted me to know about Melanie, and Nina, and...what was her name...that laughs like Woody Woodpecker?"

"Isabelle."

"For reals? She laughs like Woody?"

"Frighteningly real," I chuckled.

"But she isn't for you, not just because of the hideous laugh, but because she's phony. Nor is the one who was after your cock. Which is, by the way, spectacular, and I can see how the legend got started. Also, I think, the one who has hateful attitudes toward other human beings is not to your liking. Did she meet Glory? I'll bet she didn't, but you should have her over, just so she can. And...if she doesn't work out...there's always me to fall back on."

I got out of bed and flipped open the tent flap to let in a little light, and then went over and got Bobbi by the hand. "Come here," I said, and led her over to the big air mattress. "Sit," I said, and did likewise. She was beautiful – little more than an outline against the stars, but artfully made, and fragrant. "You, Bobbi Bates, are not just someone to fall back on. From the first time I met you I thought you were lovely and kind and funny, and now, since I know you a little better, I know you to be passionate, intelligent, and talented. You outshine Melanie, and Nina, and even dear Isabelle, though I doubt your bittersweet chocolate roulades can compare."

"Does that mean I'm out of the running? I make a mean chocolate chip cookie." I could hear her beautiful, even smile in the tone of her voice.

"You're definitely not out of the running," I murmured, putting my forehead against hers. "I just don't know which way to run."

"Not away," she whispered. "Please, Bud. Not away." She kissed me, long and deep, and I was already shaking when I reached for her.

It occurred to me...about half an hour later as I was having a cigarette... that Kit was right once more. I was capable of being a real hypocrite. I could cluck in fine Jewish fashion about what a pig Reggie Clevenger was, but if he had clap, so did I. She'd done things to me that made my mind go right out the damned window, and I was more than ready to believe she was protected enough for both of us. And what if she was pregnant? Whose was it? Mine, or Reggie's or whose? The cooler I got in the late night air, the dumber I felt. If Dad knew what I'd done, he'd skin me alive, or send Bobbi off on a shoot in Kenya, or the Philippines. I didn't even bother to ask myself at what point I'd lost control. I knew. I'd lost control the second I let jealousy get in the way of common sense.

I knew better than to try discussing it with Bobbi, or with Kit, or with anybody else. I'd sound like either a whiner or a fool, and though I felt like both, I wasn't anxious to spread the sentiment. I did sit and wonder why, though. Why now? I was not a new arrival on the sexual front. I'd been having sex for nearly a decade, and until tonight I'd never lost control of the situation – myself, yes, a time or two, but that was to be expected – never the situation. Now, when I was old enough to know better, I had. I didn't consider myself a fuddy-duddy, but this was a source of great concern to me. Was there just more magic in this woman, or in this place? Had surviving our food-poisoning ordeal made me think I was invincible, or that the gods owed me something for my bravery and fortitude? What the hell had happened in that tent, and just how sorry was I going to be?

I tried to seem casual when I went back to bed, but Bobbi was already asleep, so the act was wasted. I lay there, staring out the open tent flap, watching the stars go by. Kit came in, quiet as a mouse, and slipped onto the air mattress next to mine. He felt around a little first, and I think he was surprised not to find Bobbi in the spot where he'd been sleeping. I feigned sleep, and in doing so, ultimately accomplished it.

I was tired the next day. Stress and lack of sleep coupled with the oppressive heat, I supposed. A wind kicked up that blew sand and grit in our eyes while we filmed, our food while we ate, and threatened to scour the coating off the camera lenses. It made wearing contacts a torture, I couldn't see without them, and the great Cochise, I'm pretty sure, did not wear wire-rimmed glasses. Every few minutes I'd stop, and wash out my eyes, and apologize to the rest of the cast and crew. Reggie grumbled, but Flo said to leave me alone; the people trying to work without their contacts weren't doing so hot, either. My head pounded mercilessly, and I just wanted to start snarling and hitting things.

But we were nearly done. Nearly done. Wouldn't do to lose it at this point. I was the boss's kid. I had to set an example for every other person on this set. I think the only one who really understood that, was David. Between takes he came over and just sat with me, saying nothing. He, too, looked tired, and the little twin girls were giggling and pointing at him, and he was twitching with annoyance. "I hate girls," he said under his breath. "I really hate girls." I just nodded, and rubbed his back for a bit.

The noise of the wind grew, and we looked out from under the awning to see a big, corporate helicopter skimming the mesa tops, heading our direction. "Oh, shit!" Reggie exclaimed, "It's Mister Aarons, or I miss my guess. For Godssake, everybody, look alive!"

We all did our best, but the storm created by the landing of the helicopter pretty much brought things to a halt. Oddly enough, the blades didn't stop completely. The chopper crouched uneasily where it had touched down, and someone who looked vaguely familiar sprinted towards us. "Where's Bud?" he was yelling, and I recognized the voice as belonging to Max Oxenford.

I stood up and ran toward him, fear gripping my heart. What in God's name had happened? Who in my family was dead? He skidded up next to Clevenger and Florien and hollered, "I'm here to take Peter home. I'm sorry if it causes you any problems, but it's an emergency." By that time

I was beside him in war paint and buckskins, and he said, "Grab some street clothes and get in the chopper, Bud. We have to go home."

"What?" I gasped. "Max, what's wrong?"

"Bud, do as I say," he replied. "I'll tell you when we're in the air." He gave me a reassuring, one-armed hug ending with a shove, and said, "Get going."

I looked at Flo, and he nodded and made the same, quick gesture. "Go," he said. "Go!"

In less than three minutes I was ducking under the rotating blades, and even as I was buckling in, we were airborne.

Max handed me a soft towel and a jar of cold cream, and sat contemplating me while I removed my makeup. I didn't say a single word – didn't pump him for information – I just did what was expected of me like a good little Aarons.

When most of my makeup was off, Max gently took the towel from me, and as he touched up around my hairline he said, "It's Esther...she's had a heart attack."

I swallowed hard and forced the words to come. "Is she dead?"

"No, but she's not good, she wants you, and your father wants you with her."

"Thanks," I whispered, having lost my voice, and sat staring out the window. I could feel the tears running down my face, but I just left them alone. They made my eyes feel better.

She'd been so happy...off to Italy with her grandmother...she'd seemed so well. Why was it things were never what they seemed? "There's room enough in here to lie down," Max suggested. "You could close your eyes for a few minutes."

I just shook my head and patted his thigh where he sat next to me. He loved Esther, too, and I could see the grief in his eyes. "Are we catching a flight?"

"There's a plane waiting," he replied.

"How are the folks holding up, and Gram?"

He shook his head back at me. "Your Dad's pretty well devastated. But you know him. He doesn't do grief, he does rage. Your mother's distraught, and your grandmother's holding things together, as usual."

"Racheal?"

Max shrugged. "I haven't seen her. I assume she's playing her part." He paused and shot me an apologetic look. "Sorry. I just meant..."

"Yeah, I know," I said, and we lapsed into silence.

We made some tries at conversation without any real success. I should have tried to sleep, I suppose, but I couldn't. Couldn't make my eyes stay shut. Possibly it was irritation from the sandblasting, possibly it was the fear I'd wake to something worse than what was already happening.

The big corporate jet was well appointed, and I was able to do a little more thorough job of bathing and cleaning up. I took a quick shower, and while I was in there I shaved, and got the straight, shoulder length Apache hair unwoven from my own. Mine was halfway to my shoulders as it was, but slicked back with the curls plastered down it didn't look too bad. Max nodded his approval as I sat back down. "Just in time," he said. "We're about to land."

The car was right where Max had left it, and in a few split seconds we were on the freeway. Max hadn't brought the limo; he'd brought the Maserati. I sat there nonchalantly watching him peg the sucker while weaving in and out of pre-rush hour traffic. If he'd taken his eyes off the road for a nanosecond, made one tiny misjudgment, they'd have picked us up with a teaspoon, or simply buried us car and all, but I remember being horrifyingly unconcerned. I just stared at the blur of lugnuts going by my right eye, and wondered what I was going to say to my father, my mother, my beloved sister. What if she were dead already? What if the last words I'd ever have the chance to speak to her had been stupid or inane or cruel? What had I said as she'd left for Italy? Had I told her how much I loved her, how glad I was she was my baby sis?

I crept through Intensive Care and into her room, dreading what I'd find. My mother rose like an old woman when she saw me, and collapsed heavily into my arms. "I'm so very glad you're here," she said in Russian. "I have needed your presence...so much to temper the situation. Your father is just beside himself, Peterkin. He is just beside himself. You must do something or I will lose my mind."

"I'm here," I said and rocked her gently in my arms, realizing that she, too, was fragile. As usual when she was upset, her English had abandoned her, so I automatically switched to Russian, saying small things to try to comfort her. She put her palms against my cheeks and raised her head to smile at me, and instantly she was in a panic.

"Oh no!" she sobbed. "Peter, you're...J.R., Peterkin is burning up with fever! Oh, please no! You should..."

My father never even looked my way, but I caught mother's hands in mine and held them against my chest. "Mother, I'm fine," I soothed. "The wind was terrible out there, and I'm probably wind-burned. That's all, I promise. I promise. Tell me, how is Esther? Look at me. How is my sister?"

Mother just shrugged, sighed, and moved out of my line of vision. There was my poor little sister, pale as death, tubes everywhere, her hair startlingly dark against the white sheets. I gave my mother's hands a squeeze and let them slide to her sides before walking over to the bed. My father sat beside her, eyes riveted on her motionless form.

I wondered momentarily if he even knew I was there, then his head turned slowly and he looked up at me. "You could have worn something nicer," he said, and went back to staring at my sister.

"Sorry," I whispered. "I haven't been home yet." I sat on the opposite side of the bed and took Esther's hand in both of mine. It was warm, at least, which renewed my hope. "Hey, Sis," I said, leaning toward her, and couldn't think of one other thing to say. I took a deep breath to steady myself a little, and wracked my brain, and then launched into the tale of everybody getting food poisoning, and how I'd tried to figure out how to keep all the machinery fueled and running, and tried to make Jell-O, and how smart and brave David had been through all of it, what a mess snobby little Amber Kestrel had made of herself, and how vastly relieved I'd been when Kit had smiled at me and made some smart remark.

Esther's hand tightened a little within mine, her eyes fluttered open, and she managed, "Amber puked on herself? I can die happy."

"You can't die," I chuckled, "Who'll spread the rumor?"

"Ohhhh, I love you," she whispered, and reached for me with both her arms. "Thank you for coming."

"Thanks for waiting around," I said, and folded her in my arms. I didn't know if sitting up was the best thing for her, so I leaned over the bed, lowered her down, and left my arms around her. "You should sleep."

"I've been asleep. How is Titus?"

I released her and sat back down, keeping her hand in mine. "I don't know, I haven't been home yet, have you?"

"No. I got sick on the plane."

"This is your definition of sick?" I grimaced. "If this is sick, what happened to Amber?"

"Justice," she giggled, and from the corner of my eye, I saw Dad catch his breath and sit back in his chair. "I do so want to see Titus, though. I told the doctor, but he says Titus can't come in."

"Why didn't you tell me you wanted to see Titus?" my father rumbled.

She turned her head his way and gave him a smile. "I tried," she said patiently. "Every time I opened my mouth you told me to be quiet and rest."

"I'll say it again," Dad said tenderly. "Be quiet now, and rest."

"Okay," she whispered. "Peter, go see Titus and Royal for me, please?"

"Will do," I promised, and in a few seconds she was asleep.

I was still rubbing her forearm when my father's iron hand closed over my shoulder. I looked up and he jerked his head toward the door. His expression was not encouraging. I walked ahead of him, and when we were clear of the room he spun me around and hissed, "What were you thinking in there? She's supposed to have complete rest, and you're stimulating her with all this wild shit? I brought you home to help the situation, not make it worse!"

I just blinked at him, not comprehending at all. "I...I'm sorry, Sir," I managed. "I thought Max came to get me because Esther wanted to see me. I just wanted her to know I was here. I didn't know what else to talk to her about that would lift her spirits. I am sorry."

Dad looked at me for a long, long minute. His eyes welled with tears, and he stood in silence until they again receded, then he put both hands on my elbows and slowly ran them up my arms until they were resting on my shoulders. "Bud..." he began, and then stopped. He looked at my mother, who was huddled in a white ermine coat, in a white arm chair within the shadows of the room, and at Esther, who lay like death in the light. Then, he looked back at me, but he didn't say anything, and I knew...he couldn't.

I did something I hadn't done in a few years. I held my arms out to him, and he accepted my embrace. "Take Mother home," I said gently. "She desperately needs rest, and she won't go without you. I'll stay with Esther. I won't talk to her...I'll just sit with her, I promise."

Dad tightened his grip on me for a moment, held me at arm's length, and said, "You do what you think is best, Aloysha. I just...aren't you awfully tired after working all day and then flying back here?"

"I slept most of the way," I said, "and I can sleep in one of those easy chairs if I need to. You go on home. Would you like me to call Max for you?" He said yes, and with a glance over my shoulder toward my sister's bed, I excused myself to go use the phone and the bathroom.

I spent most of the night sitting beside my sister, drinking the thermos of coffee Max had brought, watching her sleep, listening to the steady beep of the heart monitor, and wishing I had more on than just a pair of jeans and a cotton tee shirt. With first light the door opened and three people in white coats with stethoscopes around their necks, walked in.

"Now there's a family resemblance if I ever saw one," said the first, a woman.

"Her vitals seem a little more promising this morning," said the second, looking at Esther's chart.

"Peter, how are you?" asked the third, and laid his hand on my shoulder.

I smiled at him without standing up. "Worried."

"This is Esther's brother, the younger Peter Aarons," our family doctor explained, and I stood up as he introduced me. "Bud, this is Doctor Linda King, and this gentleman is her husband, Glen. Glen is a heart specialist, and Linda is one of the best young Anesthesiologists in the business."

"As opposed to one of the best old Anesthesiologists in the business," she grinned, and took my hand. "You're freezing," she said, laying her other hand over mine. "Go run some hot water over your hands and forearms, while we take a look at your sister. It'll help."

"Help me warm up, or help get me out of the way?" I grinned, knowing it was probably the latter, but I went anyway, and did as she asked.

It did help, and I realized that despite the temperature in the room, I'd been genuinely chilly. I then looked in the mirror, which was a mistake. I was bleary and bearded, and my tongue was an ominous brown which underscored the taste in my mouth. I looked like some of those guys at the bus station. That set me thinking about Bobbi, and how good her arms would feel about now...her bare skin against mine...and how she was and what she was doing...and what I might have caught from her...and I found myself leaning heavily against the wash basin, nearly overwhelmed with everything in general.

I knew. I knew I had to have a talk with my family doctor. He was here, right now, in with my sister who was probably dying. How was I going to phrase this, exactly, and when, and where? God in heaven, how could I have been so damned stupid? How could I be stupid enough to be standing here thinking about how good it would feel to be having sex with the same woman who I feared had infected me with a venereal disease? The exact term I wanted, was...fucking stupid...literally.

I was most of the way back to Esther's room when a thought struck me that set me chuckling and shaking my head. I really was stupid. I didn't have to go to Jack Boyd. He was not the only physician on the planet. I could go to a clinic halfway to San Francisco. Relief washed over me and lasted a full minute before I was struck by the sobering thought that I was quite possibly more disturbed by what Jack would think of me, than by what I had done. I stopped in my tracks, gave myself a good shaking, and vowed to focus more on Esther and less on Peterkin for the next little while.

There was a small waiting room just for Intensive Care. I sat down outside Esther's room near the nurse's station, on a vinyl couch with metal arms, and felt life, or death, or adulthood or some damned thing, settle over me like a wet, wool blanket – heavy, cold, unpleasant, and ultimately stifling. My time in the Army hadn't been this stressful, and I'd been a spy. Why were there no windows in here, and how could I feel so awful and still be so hungry? The door opened and the same three doctors who had walked in, walked out, and came to stand in a semi-circle which I closed when I rose to greet them. "How is she?" I asked.

The male Doctor King nodded slowly and smiled. "She's made of sterner stuff than one might suppose to look at her. We should be able to go ahead with the surgery within the next two weeks."

"Surgery?" I winced. They were going to cut on the poor girl, again?

"If you want to see her graduate from high school and become a Kindergarten teacher like she wants to? Yes," Jack said. "The best thing you can do is keep her spirits up, which means you'll have to keep yours up, as well. And she'll need a lot of blood, so start right now donating some. It'll make you feel better. I'll ask the nurse to tap you before you leave," he chuckled.

I sucked in for air and stood staring at my shoes, feeling that wet blanket becoming a noose around my aristocratic young neck. "What?" Jack queried. "Afraid of needles? Since when?"

"I...Jack, I need to talk to you for a minute, privately. Please."

"Oh, crap," he muttered, excused himself from his colleagues, and steered me to a discreet distance. "You're red as a beet. What have you done?"

I stood there, trying to gather words and phrases into a coherent and unemotional sentence that would inform him, without making him into my father confessor. "I'm not sure what-all can be carried in the bloodstream and transmitted, so I guess...though I hate to bring it up..."

"Spit it out."

"I've had unprotected sex with a woman. One I'm fond of, mind you, but who thinks of sex as a...team sport...and...oh, shit..." He just stood there and let me splutter and blush, and his eyes were looking right through me into my most private places and I felt keenly that I'd not only done something to myself, I'd done something to him, and to my father, and to all the people in my life who'd taught me better. "I feel like an idiot," I squeaked, "but if I did catch something, I can't risk making Esther sick."

"Have you been tested?" he asked, still inscrutable and disapproving. I thought doctors were supposed to be supportive, and I nearly said so, but it occurred to me that I just might get my face slapped for insolence – and I'd have it coming.

"No," I said, "not yet."

"And how long were you going to let this eat at you, either physically or emotionally, whichever the case may be?"

"It just happened a day or two ago. I just..."

"Spare me. Your guilty conscience may be all that's standing between you and reproductive disaster in more ways than one. Do you think you got her pregnant?"

"No. I'm sure I didn't."

"How can you be sure?"

"She said she was protected..."

"You stupid sonofabitch!" Jack snapped, and the doctors King both looked over their shoulders to where we were standing. "Just how much stress do you think your father can take?"

"In all fairness, Jack, this isn't about Dad, it's about me," I said, carefully modulating the decibel level. "I admit I was stupid. I'm more than willing to do whatever penance is appropriate, but I have no intention of involving my parents or my family, which is why I told you in the first place."

He just nodded and looked pointedly away from my gaze. "Get into my office as soon as you can," he said. "Right now, get out of my sight."

I turned on my heel and went back into Esther's room, smarting more from his rebuke than my admission, and feeling just a tad sorry for myself. Was I destined to forever remain in some distant orbit around the brilliant star that was my father? Was all my light to be reflective only? Was I ever, ever going to matter as much as my sibs, my grandmother, my parents?

My sister's eyelids began to flutter in waking, and again I shook myself and forced my thoughts outward, not in. I had always been Esther's knight in shining armor. It wouldn't do either of us a bit of good for her to know how tarnished I felt at the moment. "Hi," I whispered, taking her hand. She smiled, and the rest of it went away.

An hour later my mother slipped in, as beautiful and welcome as the sun outside, and she held me in her arms a bit and told me how foolish she felt for being panicky the night before. I noted that her English had yet to re-establish itself, so I assumed the cheerfulness was in part, an act, though I didn't say so. I squeezed her, instead, and rubbed her with my whiskers to make her giggle, and she told me under no uncertain terms to go home and get cleaned up. "Max is waiting for you!" she laughed, and shooed me away.

I blew Esther a kiss and promised once again that I'd check on the boys and report back to her. As I walked out through the little waiting room, I realized I hadn't seen Dad, and wondered where he was. Might have had to go down to the studio on business, I supposed, though it seemed highly unlikely given the circumstances. More likely he was here someplace, maybe meeting with those same three doctors I'd seen earlier. That would be something he'd choose to conceal from my mother. She was dazzling, but she was also mentally fragile and extremely high strung. Nobody knew that better than her doting husband. He'd have made some kind of an excuse and sent her on ahead to be with Esther while he conferenced. I nodded to myself. That was it.

I was allowing myself to sleepwalk – letting my mind go blank for a bit – when I heard a voice that could only belong to one person. Actually, it was a vocalization, not a voice; something between a bellow and a roar – filled with intense anger and frustration. I looked quickly to my left into the conference room, expecting to see the offender already airborne.

"Calm down!" the male Doctor King was saying, "You're going to have a heart attack of your own, Mister Aarons! The fact is, rules are rules, and you may not, *may not*, bring those little boys into this hospital."

"I think you'd better change that policy for this occasion," Jack Boyd squeaked. "If Mister Aarons wants his daughter to have those specific visitors..."

"For Godssake, Doctor Boyd, stop groveling," King snapped, glaring first at Jack, then at my father. "You think you're doing what's best for Esther, and you're not. You're doing what she wants, and there's a big difference. What if those kids are carrying cold germs, or the flu, or something worse, and she catches it? It could kill her."

"And not getting to see them could break her heart," my father said through his teeth.

King just shook his head. "You do have a flair for the dramatic, and it serves you very, very well out there. In here, it won't do you a bit of good. Esther seems much perkier with her big brother here. Now that, was smart, having him come home." He shook his finger a little at Dad and gave him a ghost of a smile to diffuse the situation, "She's weak, but nothing you can do to please her is going to keep her alive, or make her dead, I guarantee it. Sitting there like a dog on guard all day every day is making you crazy and you need to go back to work."

My father began to twitch a little, and I knew...I did...that I should get the hell out of Dodge, but I'd never seen my father lose an argument before. This was a whole new world for me, and part of me wanted to chortle madly and rub my hands together. "How dare you," my father snarled – not loudly, but with an anger that was shaking him like a leaf. "Doctor Boyd, find a hospital that will let the boys in to see Esther, and then get Esther ready for transfer. As for you two, I don't want you near my daughter."

"J.R.," Boyd said in a tone that was a slavish caress, "the Kings are the best in the business..."

"I don't care," Dad replied in that same, stalking growl.

Then I heard some idiot say, "I do," and realized it was me. "Sorry," I hastened to add. "I didn't mean to eavesdrop, but this conversation is being broadcast locally, and I do think..."

"Go home," Dad said flatly. "This is none of your concern."

"Begging your pardon, Sir, but it is my concern. These people are supposedly the best in the business, and if Esther dies, Racheal will be my only sister and your only daughter. Now how damned scary is that? We can take home movies of the boys and bring in a projector. Hell, we can bring in a whole crew and shoot a documentary about them, or maybe Glory will bring them to the window. There's an outside window, isn't there, and if there isn't, where can we move her so there is one? We could make it into a giant TV screen for her...uh...are we even on the ground floor?" He was going to kill me now. I could see it in his eyes. I'd never make love to another Steinway.

There was a moment of utter silence, then Dad took a deep, steadying breath and said, "Did you really have a food-poisoning scare on the set?"

"Oh, yes sir."

"And Reggie didn't bother to tell me?"

I just shrugged. "Aside from the fact that the phones don't work out there a lot of the time, I personally think there's quite a bit he's not telling you. When I saw the chopper coming yesterday I was hoping it was you and he was hoping it wasn't, which should tell you something."

He studied me for a minute. He was still in the room. I was still in the hall. He'd stopped shaking, and I'd started. "Are you done out there?"

I looked around myself and puzzled momentarily. "Oh. You mean out on the set? Me, personally?"

"Yes."

"Pretty much. What didn't get done could quite probably be shot on a soundstage without any degradation of quality."

"Reggie's fucking things up out there?"

I just shrugged and looked apologetic. "That's really not my bailiwick."

"You couldn't have called me?" he demanded, voice rising again. "Do you know how much money I have tied up in that production?"

"You never said anything about wanting me to birddog..."

"I thought you'd have enough sense just to do it!" he exploded. "Now, on top of everything else, I need to go to the back of badass nowhere and fix whatever mess Clevenger has gotten himself into. Damn, Bud, where is your head? Are you never, ever going to get the hang of the movie making business? It sure as hell feeds you well enough. Here! You seem to have an opinion about what's going on, and since you opened your big mouth, you straighten this mess out while I go fix the one you left behind!" He never even looked back. He just brushed by me none too gently and stormed off down the hall toward my sister's room. He'd say goodbye to his girls, and then he'd be off...along with Max and my ride home.

I watched him until he disappeared through a door, and then turned back to the three people still standing in the room. I wanted to sag against the wall, and I was having trouble meeting their eyes for some reason. Jack's mouth came open and I said, "He's my dad, and I love him, so be careful what you say."

"I've seen Reginald Clevenger's movies," mused Linda King, "I've never seen one that wasn't well done."

I just shook my head. "Things are fine out there. He'll find that out, and chalk it up to my lack of expertise. Was there some kind of meeting going on here? What do I need to know?"

By the time a taxi got me to my doorstep three hours later, I felt more dead than alive, and I was hungrier than I'd ever been in my life. I stumbled like a drunk up the back step and smack into my housekeeper, who was holding open the screen door for me. "Lordy, Lordy, look what the cat dragged in," she clucked softly, and plopped me into a chair at the kitchen table. "When you eat last, Boy, before or after your last bath? Been some time back for both I'd say."

"Must be," I muttered, "I can't remember either one."

"You got the energy to crawl upstairs and into the shower? I make you a nice lunch in the meantime."

"Thanks," I said, trying to keep my head up and my eyes open. "Where's...Gram? Where's Rafael?"

"Mrs. Aarons over in Bel Air at the big house, tendin' to Racheal. She just got in from back east here a bit ago. Rafael, he around here someplace workin' on somethin'. When Mrs. Aarons got home, even with all the grief and the confusion, she found the time to walk in that meadow with Rafael, and she hugged him and thanked him. What a lovely woman she is."

I just nodded. I wanted to share her joy, and Rafael's victory, but I felt like if I pulled my palms from under my chin, my head would fall right off onto the table. At the very least, my neck would break. "Please," I said quietly, "Just feed me...nothing fancy, but I feel a little funny all of a sudden, and if I don't eat, I'm going...to be sick." I looked up to smile at her, and realized the room wasn't where I thought it was. I squeezed my eyes shut to keep it from spinning, and when I opened them a few seconds later, I was on my back on the floor with Glory's face just above mine, her hand on my cheek.

I blinked, and my mouth opened, though nothing came out, and for the life of me, I couldn't figure out what had happened. "You passed out cold," Glory said gently. "I ask you 'gain, when you eat last? More important, when'd you last have somethin' to drink?"

I just laid there. That hard teakwood floor, felt so good. "I...breakfast yesterday? Or did I have lunch? I did have two or three cups of coffee last night. I guess I really don't know. Glory, I'm sorry if I scared you. It's probably just my blood sugar bottoming out. Esther desperately wants to see the boys, has Dad told you?"

"Let's worry 'bout you right now, shall we?" she said, and straightened up. "I'm gonna heat you some soup, just to get somethin' warm inside you, and I'd suggest meantime that either you stay right there, or that we walk you to your recliner."

"I'm happy here," I mumbled. I was embarrassed, realizing how silly I must look. "But...I suppose if you wanted a big dog underfoot you'd have gotten a Newfoundland or a Shetland Sheep Dog."

"Not without askin' you, first," she grinned, and came back to ease me into a sitting position.

I managed to hold that for a minute or so while I drank a glass of water, which remains to this day Glory's cure for nearly any malady, and then got to my feet with Glory close beside me, telling me to slow it down a little. "Your folks got enough on their minds right now without you crackin' you skull," she admonished, and walked me to my big leather recliner in the living room. Sinking into that old chair...was better than sex. I sighed with contentment, opened my eyes to thank Glory for the escort, and she was offering me a mug of thick, homemade split pea soup and a spoon.

"It ain't real hot," she smiled.

It wasn't. It was just right, and having that warmth spread through me, was like being wrapped in the arms of Morpheus. I felt her put something light over me, and when I awoke, the slant of the sun through the windows told me we were far into the afternoon.

I came out of the chair with a guilty start. Here I was, sleeping the day away when I was supposed to be taking care of the Aarons women. The house smelled wonderful, and I sincerely hoped whatever Glory was cooking would be ready when I finished with my shower, because I was way beyond politely interested in food. I went upstairs and let the hot water beat on me until my blood started circulating. It really wasn't cold outside, or even very cool. It was a typical, beautiful late summer's day. I ignored my stomach, took my time, and got really clean – making up for the weeks of short water rations in the desert, and the abbreviated shower on the plane coming home. I also gave my mouth a thorough scrubbing, and felt much better for having done so. I spent some time getting my hair to fall into a respectable style, took a deep breath and contemplated myself in the big mirror in my room. Much better. I put on slacks and a polo shirt rather than jeans and a tee shirt, and went back downstairs.

Glory was already putting a meal on the table for me, and I took a moment to marvel at the treasure I'd found in her. I could only hope Gram was as happy with her as I was. And where was Gram? "At the hospital," Glory said before it ever came out my mouth. "You sit here and eat somethin', now, and we figure out how we gonna keep all of you rested and still keep somebody with little old Esther, bless her."

Her tone was wistful, and after I'd thanked her for the nice dinner I said, "You should go see her, too. I know she'd love it."

"Really?"

"Absolutely. This is excellent. What kind of meat is this?"

"Possum. Trapped it myself just up the hill. What would the hospital say 'bout me comin' in there?"

"What do you mean, what would they say?" I chuckled, then pointed my fork at her, "and Gram had better not catch you poaching the wildlife...so to speak. Possums do get hit a lot on that big curve down by the McKenna's place, you might keep an eye out for a fresh one."

"I thought that was strictly a southern concept," Glory laughed. "It's marinated pork loin, and you know 'zactly what I meant about the hospital."

"It's delicious, and I honestly don't. Is this a racial thing like the coffee shop a few weeks back? Sit down. Talk to me." I took her hand and guided her into the chair beside me, and we talked as old friends do – as family does – as my mother and father did – quietly and comfortably, while I ate. I asked her how Rafael's trip to Texas had gone, and she produced pictures from the morning room and showed me Royal and Rafael with his parents, brothers, sisters, cousins, aunties, uncles, grandparents. I wanted to ask her if Dad had actually purchased whatever piece of property Rafael had been sent to check out, but I refrained, afraid my amusement would be obvious in either speech or demeanor.

She asked me about how the shoot had gone, and I gave her a few of the highlights, pointedly leaving out the part about getting to know Bobbi a little better, but she was not deceived. "How does Miss Bobbi do?" she asked, and though her face was innocent, there was a devil's twinkle in her eye that set me laughing.

"She does well," I managed, laughed again, and just shook my head in capitulation. "She does exceptionally well." I just...went ahead and told her everything that had happened, and how I felt about it, and what doubts I had, and that they were pretty well balanced out by Bobbi's level of expertise, her tenderness and gentleness.

Glory patted my hand and drawled, "Well, if it's the dumbest thing you ever do, you gonna be one lucky man, Bud Aarons. Just be sure you get wiser from it, not tighter. Ain't nothin' gonna fall off, I'm pretty sure," which tells you it was in those blessed days before we'd even heard of AIDS. "I just hope Doctor Boyd don't tell your daddy." Her mouth set itself in a firm line of disapproval, and I was surprised. "He was by here a day or so ago to check on you gram, Doctor Boyd was, his nose all in the air when he looked at me and the babies. I don't trust that man."

"You know, I can't say I care much for him, myself," I admitted. "He's our doctor because he bought Doctor McKenna's practice – the McKennas down on Flat Possum Corner – when Paul retired. That was about six or seven, maybe eight years ago. I haven't needed him for much, so I haven't had to face the fact that I don't trust him very much. He's just..." I shook my head. "Glory, I watched him this morning trying so hard to please my father that he was willing to jeopardize my sister to do it. That doesn't inspire much confidence in me."

"Couldn't be you just smartin' because of what he said to you 'bout you...presence of mind, could it?"

I chose to study the food on my plate rather than looking her in the eye. "I'm really not sure," I said at last. "I do know I'm glad the Doctors King are there as backup. I should stop eating and talking, and get to the hospital so Mother and Gram can come home. Is Racheal there, too, do you know?"

"I imagine if she is, she bein' real subdued about now," Glory said soothingly. "I don't 'spect she'll give you any trouble."

"It's not that," I said hastily. I paused and thought about it, and realized...that *was* it. I had just about all I could handle at the moment – my sister's illness, decisions regarding her, the care and feeding of my high strung mother...the spectre of STD's and the indelible imprint of Bobbi's body against mine. It would feel so good right now to be tangled up and sweaty. What had we been talking about? I just shook my head and finished my dinner without further conversation. It was too much effort – at least the thinking part, and I hated to do the talking part without it. Glory seemed to understand. She just sat there with me for a bit, then she got up and began putting some things together for me to take along; a thermos of coffee and various snacks from plates and trays sitting on the counters. It was at that point I noticed all the food staged around the kitchen – beautifully prepared, carefully covered – waiting. "What's up with the petit fours and the canapes?" I asked. "What's the occasion?"

"Garden club comin' tomorrow, along with the Audubon Society to look at that meadow," Glory said. Her expression, even her posture changed, enhanced itself somehow, and she added, "Mrs. Aarons gonna have my Rafael speak to all of 'em 'bout how he done it."

"And then you're going to wow all of them with your cooking," I said. "Gram is really going to rub their noses in it, isn't she?"

"In what?" Glory said warily, knowing full well what I meant. "I don't see it thataway 'tall. Rafael gonna do what he does, I'm gonna do what I do, that's all."

"That's all it has to be!" I laughed. "Glory, you're an angel. Thank you so much for dinner. I'm heading out. Do you want me to try sending Mother and Gram here for dinner, or should I encourage them to go toward Bel Air?" The look Glory gave me that time truly was uncomprehending. "Do you have too much to do this evening to want to deal with them?" I asked, rephrasing. "The Bel Air house is fully staffed, you know, and closer to the hospital by several miles."

"But this be home," Glory said. "You don't do no steerin' one way or another. You let them decide."

"As you wish," I smiled, and went to brush my teeth.

When I got to the little waiting room at the hospital, the first thing I saw was Racheal, sitting as tight to one corner of the couch as she could get – feet drawn up, arms around her long legs – staring at the floor in front of her. "Rach?" I said quietly, and her head snapped around in my direction. "Hi, Baby."

She didn't say a word, she just unfolded off the couch and ran into my arms, sobbing, clinging to me like she was drowning. "I'm so scared," she sobbed. "Bud, I'm so scared."

I petted her and soothed her for a bit without saying anything, then I kissed the top of her head and murmured, "We've always known Esther was frail. There's nothing to be scared of."

"You don't understand," she choked. "I've been so mean to her. I've said so many hateful things to her. Just before she left for Italy we had this...fight about her going and me staying home, and I said some terrible things to her! I love her so much. I love you so much. I don't know what I'll do if she dies!"

"I love you, too," I said softly, and buried my face in her hair.

CHAPTER NINE

Sit down," my father said, jerking his chin toward a seat across the desk from him. He leaned back in his leather office chair, smoothed the lapels of his jacket with expert, immaculately groomed hands, and studied me with his disturbingly inscrutable eyes. There was little I could do but sit for it, and study him back. I'd been summoned. It was not my place to speak. I did wonder why I was there. I assumed it was for a tongue lashing, though for what I wasn't sure. There had been so many trespasses of late. "You don't own a suit?"

Geez, he wanted me in a suit? Now *that* was alarming. "Sorry. I didn't know I was supposed to dress. You just said you wanted to see me."

"Which is something I haven't done much of, lately. Shooting all wrapped?"

He knew it was, but I nodded anyway. "Um hm."

"Happy with it?"

"I think so. I haven't actually seen it put together, yet."

"You know," he drawled with studied indifference, "that trip to the desert was pretty much unwarranted." I knew which trip he meant. There was no use in being flip and pretending I didn't. I just looked at him and said nothing. "Why?" he asked.

Again, I knew what he meant. I thought a moment while I watched him light a cigarette. "Remember that day I was at the studio with Bobbi, and I was feeling really sick? I felt like I needed a way out so I could go home and relax, but nothing graceful was coming to mind because I was too uncomfortable and duty-bound to think straight. And then up you rode on your silver steed with your trusty sidekick, and you immediately recognized that I was in trouble, and you offered me a way out. You took possession of the situation – not just control – you owned the situation. You do that so well. I thought...maybe I'd practice the art on you."

He exhaled, and smoke came out his nose and his mouth, and his eyes studied me, and I felt like I was facing old Smaug, Tolkien's famous dragon. What a time to forget my magic ring. "Your sister tells me you've been playing your guitar and singing for her and for some of the children at the hospital these past weeks."

"Um hm."

"You'll sing for her, but you won't sing for me in a movie?"

"It's the old thing about love or money, I suppose," I chuckled. "She asked me to sing *The Teddy Bears' Picnic*, for her one day just before her surgery, and I couldn't very well refuse, and one of the nurses walked in and said there were some kids who could sure use some cheering up, and I couldn't very well refuse, and that's how it got started. When Bobbi got home from the shoot she joined me one afternoon, and we became an act. And I did sing for you in a movie, if you'll remember."

"Because you couldn't very well refuse," he added, and I thought I caught a bit of a twinkle in the fathomless black depths of his eyes. "I understand this has led to you being asked to sing and play the guitar for the children's concert tour you're working on? And you're also going to do some drumming, play the piano, and sing some folk songs with Miss Bates? Are they even bothering to take anybody else along, or are you going to do a one man show?"

Where the hell was he going with this, I wondered. Was he amused? Was he annoyed? Did he want me in a suit because he was going to kill me and wanted me to look my best when the police got there? What? "For the concerts here, we'll have the full orchestra and all the trimmings. For the touring part, we'll take a smaller contingent – more an ensemble, I suppose, and we'll take Bobbi, who is technically our EMT though she has an absolutely stunning voice. We do want to do a variety of things, Dad. Trying to introduce kids to classical music can be a pretty daunting task unless you have a little froth on top of the elixir to make it attractive."

"And I hear through the grapevine that you were offered a television series last week, and that you turned it down flat."

"I did. It was too big a part, and I do have prior commitments and... promises to keep, as Mister Frost would say."

"Such as?"

"I want to see Bellwether off the ground, and I have this concert tour, which is of tremendous importance to me. I need to have some time free to spend with Esther while she recovers, I want to be working on a repertoire that will get me into Juilliard for my Doctorate, and I do want to spend some quality time focusing on my stock portfolio and learning more about what it is that you do."

"You don't want to be an actor, do you?" he asked flatly, casually, but there was a thin edge of disappointment in his voice.

"What makes you ask that?"

"I didn't hear it mentioned anywhere in that long list you just rattled off. You did turn down a co-starring role in a new series. One makes certain assumptions at that point."

"Well, please don't assume I don't want to act. I enjoy acting, Dad. But it's not the be all and end all for me. Music, could fall into that category, but not acting. For one thing, I don't like the part. I felt like the producers were bent on perpetrating a stereotype, and that the part was being offered because I'd just finished playing Cochise, whom I would be playing again. *Apache Pass* was a quality production. The writing was great. I have a feeling *Ironwood* is going to be a mile wide and an inch deep. I have a lot of things I want to learn right now, and locking myself into a series, and the exhausting schedule that comes with a series, would preclude most other activities for however long the series runs."

"But...even though she is playing nurse to your concert tour, Miss Bates is taking a part in the series?"

"Um hm. It's not a big part, but is recurring, and she's delighted with it. It won't interfere with the concerts, and I do think she's ready for a break from taking care of Esther."

"She gets along well with your grandmother?"

"Seems to. I don't think they spend a lot of time together, but the time they do spend seems amicable enough."

"She's a nice young lady," my father nodded. "She has potential. She'll make some young man a fine wife." The look said it all. Some young man, but not me. It was not to cross my mind, much less come out my mouth. I knew all the reasons why without being told. I dropped my eyes to the desktop for a few seconds to regain my composure.

When I think back on it from the vantage point of advancing middle-age – twenty-twenty hindsight, as the old saw goes – that was the moment I should have had it out with my father about the women in my life. His father had not arranged his marriage, but I knew, he was planning to arrange mine. Matter of fact, he did, more or less. He picked out Megan for me, which to this day makes my blood run cold, and I might have headed it off with just a little bit more intestinal fortitude than I was possessed of at the time. But that day, in that office, I sat there and let it happen. I gave him *carte blanche* that would last for the next quarter of a damned century. I nodded like a good little Aarons and agreed with him, even though Bobbi was living under my roof and sleeping in my bed...or, to be more precise, I was sleeping in hers most nights.

I loved her very much. We fought like cats and dogs, and in many ways we were not suited to one another, but damn, we had so much fun together. We went on picnics to the beach. We went dancing. We sang together, and we weren't half bad, but more than that, she made me want to sing. We played cards, board games, and partied with an ever-expanding group of friends. We had quiet chats by the fire on cool autumn evenings and spoke of hopes and dreams, and then went up to bed together.

I had stood my ground on the issue of STD's, and after some grousing and pooh-poohing, she'd gone with me to get tested. The fact that we'd both turned up positive was a real wake-up call for her. She was embarrassed, and she was profoundly apologetic. When the doctor told her she absolutely had to inform her other sex partners that they might be infected, it turned out to be a blessedly short list. Needless to say, Reggie Clevenger was not pleased, nor was his wife, who tended to turn a blind eye to most of his shenanigans. This, was a bit much even for her, and Reggie spent some lonely nights in his office at the studio while I snuggled up with Bobbi and snickered wickedly to myself.

I was learning so much in our sexual classroom – not just techniques, but timing. I learned some of the mental and spiritual aspects of lovemaking – how women differ in their thinking from men – the importance of gentleness and thoughtfulness before and after. It sounds so trite to say she made a man of me, but in many ways, she did. I began to relax with my manhood, and the fear that I might be homosexual began to recede.

"Lose something?" my father queried, and I came back to the moment.

"No," I said, and it was one of the biggest lies of my life.

"How is the most famous gardener in all of *Alta California*?"

"Good," I chuckled, forcing myself to focus on the moment.

"You two any closer to seeing eye to eye?"

I just shook my head. "I really don't know, Dad. He's always polite, and some days he's even friendly, but overall...there's this distance between us. Maybe it's just because he's so devoted to Gram. Glory has gone out to church and into the community and made new friends, and Rafael hasn't. I think that's part of the problem. I think he's lonely. We are working together on the housebuilding project, and I have hopes that we'll find common ground."

"Don't count on it," my father chuckled. He had the oddest sense of humor back then. I'm pretty sure he'd figured out part of what was wrong between Rafael and me, but he wasn't about to let me in on it and spoil the fun, and I didn't have a clue. "Racheal tells me you and she are going to be showing horses together here soon?"

Was he deliberately trying to get me off balance and keep me there with this rapid-fire interrogation? "Uh...yes. She suggested it, actually. It's just the show out at the Club, but they're having a special class for sibs, and she thought it would be fun."

"I appreciate your effort," Dad said, and his face changed with his tone. "You do love your baby sister, don't you, Bud?"

"What a silly question. Of course I do."

"It was rhetorical. And you really do want to know more about my end of the movie making business...and about international business dealings in general?"

"Absolutely," I nodded.

"Good, because I'm putting you on the board of Aarador LA, effective at ten O'clock this morning." I began to splutter like all that water I'd found, boiling over on the stove that day in the desert – except that day Marie had come to my rescue. He held up a placating hand. "Adolf Katz is retiring. The board thinks it's time you started taking some responsibility, and so do I. Now that I know you don't particularly want to act, you can devote some serious time to the financial end of the business." He did everything but add, *that'll learn yuh!* And I sat there...stunned. I felt like I'd been hit by a truck.

Why couldn't he take anything casually? How did me wanting to learn a bit more about what he did, translate into a seat on the board of directors for Aarador LA? Was this a reward, or a punishment? Was this because he was learning to trust my judgment, or because he thought I didn't have the brains God gave a goose? I did understand one thing. I understood why I should have been wearing a suit.

What to say next? Glib? Grateful? Funny? Sincere? Slavish? Nothing? That seemed the most likely choice. "I'm...flattered, and I'm honored," I said at last.

"Don't you want to know if there's a salary that goes with this?" he snapped.

I blinked a couple times, like a lizard on a hot rock, and wished I was far away in the desert someplace where things were slow moving and uncomplicated. I could hear the rumbling sounds growing louder beneath my feet. I could still refuse. I could jump up and run. I didn't want to be an actor, but I didn't want to be a movie mogul, either. I did want to learn about international finance, but I didn't want to be an international financier. I wanted to be a pianist. Why couldn't everybody leave me alone and let me be a pianist, for Godssake? To this day I chuckle when I think of how gracefully Wenonah entered her grandfather's world, when I had been so terrified. All I could think about was the fact that maybe there would be no going back – no reverse on the juggernaut shifting into motion and taking me with it.

"Bud?" my father said, and I looked up at him from the depths of the alpaca carpet. "What on earth is going through your mind?"

"I'm scared," I said quietly, and he gave me one of his rare, gentle smiles.

"Now that, is the most sensible thing you've said so far this morning," he said. "The day my father put me on the board of Aarador LA, I was so nervous I nearly peed myself. Of course I was better off, because I was wearing a dark suit, not tan slacks and a polo shirt." He stood up abruptly and came around his desk. "You're the fourth generation Aarons son to take this leap, and you're not going to do it in that Ivy League look you're wearing. Come on, we have an hour to get you into a three piece suit."

"Dad, all you had to do was say something," I protested, but he yanked me out of my chair and propelled me through the outer office into the elevator, bellowing over his shoulder as we went.

"Mrs. Killingsworth, call the tailor and tell him I need a navy blue three piece suit for Bud. White shirt, burgundy tie, small print! We'll be there in ten minutes!"

"Right away, Sir," she replied, and there was laughter in her voice that I didn't appreciate one damned bit.

Here I was, going for a walk with my daddy – toddling along on my little legs, waving and smiling – Daddy's little man. What a cutie pie. Why on earth did he have that effect on me? Waving and smiling – saying cute baby words of greeting. Waving and smiling....

I was escorted down the street and double time through a set of heavy glass doors with mahogany jambs, into the sanctum of the brothers Weiss. One of them jerked my shirt off over my head while the other one got my pants off me with as much dexterity as any hooker. In five seconds flat I was in my briefs, standing in front of an astonishing array of mirrors, while the Weiss brothers asked me what I wanted, and my father told them.

This was it. The suit of legend. The one Glory and I laugh about so often. I've never had a suit that fit me so well, and I had it in thirty minutes flat. I wore it for the next four years, until I came home to find Gram chucking the boys in the pool to hone their survival skills, and I ended up in there...in my beautiful suit...pulling one of them out. It was never the same after that, despite the best efforts of the Weiss brothers.

"Now," my father said, "you look like a businessman." We were standing in front of the doors to the boardroom of Aarador LA, and he was looking me up and down with a great deal of satisfaction. The suit was a phenomenal fit. It made me look broad shouldered, slim waisted, and long legged. Too bad this wasn't a beauty contest. I was far more worried about what idiocy might come out of my mouth, than I was about the cut of my clothes. Polonius might have said, *Rich, not gaudy, for clothes oft proclaim the man*...or somesuch, but I was not convinced. I could have been dressed like Roy Rogers or Liberace, or both, and not felt any more conspicuous. Well, at least I had the consolation of looking like an idiot with impeccable taste, and that was something. I gave him a slight nod. He gave the lackey at the door the same nod, and those doors swung open on a venture, an adventure, which would make me forever financially secure in my own right before I was thirty.

The only thing missing from that perfect room with its glass window wall, its table of Gabonese Ebony, and its one painting, a Renoir, was a nice Steinway. There was space for one over by the potted palms. Ten pairs of eyes turned our way, and my father quipped, "I had quite a tussle getting the little guy dressed, but here we are." Either he knew what I'd been thinking and feeling, or I'd been thinking and feeling that way for very good reason. Actually, I was bemused in the presence of my father until I was...somewhere in my early fifties. This was just the point where I began to get used to it.

"Good afternoon," I smiled, taking the chair my father indicated, and Adolf Katz jumped, literally. "What? Adolf, what?"

He smiled and reached over to pat my big hand with his small, wizened one. "I just didn't expect a grown man with a deep voice and a wise smile, Aloysha. I expected J.R.'s boy."

"He's here," I twinkled, "cleverly disguised as someone who knows what he's doing."

Adolf leaned closer and said, *sotto voce*, "Your father has been looking forward to this day for many, many years, Aloysha. He keeps us up to date on what you're doing and how you fare. He wants us to be comfortable with our future CEO. That doesn't apply to me, of course, as I shall have been for some time, dead, but...."

He went on, and I smiled and nodded, but the words which penetrated and stuck like fish hooks in my soul were, future CEO. Oh God, oh, God, I was a tycoonlet. Was this what had happened to Dad at some point in his life? Had someone...namely my grandfather, whose portrait scowled at me from the upstairs landing...usurped my father's hopes and dreams in just such a precipitous manner? Had he gone into his father's office one bright autumn day with the idea of having a pleasant chat, and ended up being stuffed into a suit and presented to the barbarians like a suckling pig with an apple in its mouth? Probably not. My father had been born wearing a suit. My father was a hopeless snob. Whatever it was, if it trumpeted power in a tasteful sort of way, Dad was into it. When his father had died tragically in the crash of a small plane, my dad, a young man of twenty-eight, had stepped in to run his father's empire, and nobody – not one single person, had questioned it. He was that good. He was ready. I was not, nor did I want to be. I wanted to play the piano. Suddenly, that sounded trite and spoiled in my own head, and I was rather ashamed. Unrepentant, mind you, but ashamed. I gave Adolf's little old hand a pat, and my attention to my father.

"Adolf," my dad was saying, "you were here the day I walked into this boardroom and began my training. You were here the day I walked in after my father's funeral and took up the reins he'd let drop with his death. You're here to see my son begin to train to take your place so you can retire. What say you?"

Adolf eyed me up and down for a few moments in silence, then his face folded upward into a hundred humorous wrinkles. "I know Bud is a very busy young man with a career of his own to think about. I'm touched that he would make time for a bunch of old fuddy-duddies like us. I know he'll never be the businessman you are, and I don't suppose he aspires to be...preferring, rather, to be the next Sergei Rachmaninoff...but his eyes are young and his legs are strong, and when on occasion he steps forward to represent our concerns, he'll make a powerful impression. I know you have other, pressing concerns, J.R., and I know having a surrogate will be helpful to you. Bud has seemed ever to have a sensible head on his shoulders, and I know that however much time he chooses to give us, will be of excellent quality."

Chooses? I had a choice of how much time I gave them? That was encouraging. I gave Adolf a gracious nod, and smiled at the others sitting around the table. When I really opened my eyes and looked and stopped thinking like an adolescent, I knew these good individuals. My father was ruthless, perhaps, but he was not dishonest, nor would he surround himself with men who were. Aarador LA had been around in its present form for fifty years – since before people were even calling Los Angeles, LA. Grandfather had revamped the company along with Cecil Radnovich and Dorian Wraithwaite, two of his chums from UCLA. Cecil's nephew, Andy, gave me a wink from down the table to my left. Dorian's son, who was also Dorian, was staring out the window at the moment, watching the clouds scud along the skyline. He wasn't much older than I was, eight or ten years, maybe. He'd joked once that he was evidence of his dad's midlife crisis. He was crisis. I was indiscretion. But...neither of us was a prisoner. I was here to please my father, and because I'd pretty much indicated that I wanted to be. Dad wasn't trying to take anything away from me. He was trying to give me something. This was no different than any other kid being given the opportunity to learn the family business.

I took a deep breath and smiled at my father. "Thank you," I said. "I have no plans to take over from my father, nor does he want me to, I'm sure, but I will do my best to make myself an asset to the company rather than a liability."

Dad gave me a curt, unsmiling nod. "He does humility so much better than I do. Let's get down to business, shall we? My daughter's coming home this afternoon, and I want to be there for her."

He was. We both were. He personally lifted Esther from the wheelchair as though she were made of cut crystal, settled her between my mother and my grandmother in the car, glared at the press, snapping away at a discreet distance, and said, "Home James, and don't spare the horses," before plopping on the seat next to Racheal and me.

"Yes, Sir," Max replied, the door shut, and in moments we were skimming out of the parking lot.

Esther smiled at me in silence for a bit and then said, "You look so... grown up. You haven't really done anything that silly, have you?"

"What," I grinned, "grown up? You know me better than that. It's just the suit."

"Well, it looks very distinguished," Esther smiled, and I reached over to give her a pat.

"Bud and I are having outfits made just alike," said Racheal, abruptly and matter-of-factly. "We have big plans for week after next, don't we, Big Brother?"

"We do," I nodded. "Racheal and I are..."

"Bud and I are showing horses together at the club," Racheal said, and there was an edge in her voice that made me cringe a little with premonition. "We look just mega-awesome together, and everyone says we should win."

"Which doesn't mean we will," I chuckled, searching Esther's drawn features. I knew how much she loved being out with the horses, and I wished...rodent, reptile, rotter that I was...that Esther and I were showing together, instead of Racheal and me.

"But our outfits will match, and we're riding Mother and Daddy's horses, so our horses will match, and Mocha and Java are both champions..."

"And Custer had the snappiest horse at the Little Big Horn," Mother cautioned. She was a superb rider, and had advised us, in her gentle way, to ride our own horses – the ones we were familiar with – and I heartily agreed. But Racheal could not be dissuaded, and I had gone along with it to save a family row that nobody was up for. I'd promised my mother I'd ride her horse, Mocha, who was high strung and sensitive. Java, could take care of himself, and I feared he might do so at Racheal's expense – not that getting tossed on her uppity butt would hurt her any in the long run. When I realized I might actually enjoy seeing such a spectacle, I tried my best to feel immediately contrite.

"Well, if we get out there and practice enough, we just might come home with a little satin," I said quickly. "Whatever the outcome, it'll be fun." What a fervent prayer and vain hope that was. "You better feel well enough to come see us compete, Sis."

"Of course I'll be there," Esther said, and turned to stare dreamily out the window. She looked a little sad, and my father reached over and took her hand.

"Do you feel all right, Baby?"

I saw Racheal give him a slew-eyed glare. That was her pet name, not Esther's.

She nodded and smiled at him, her eyes flickering across his face without meeting his gaze. "It's such a beautiful day to be outside playing."

"It is, isn't it?" Dad smiled. "I bet you're thinking about Titus and Royal, playing under the big oak trees at Gram's house, aren't you?" She looked a little startled, then smiled and nodded. Dad gave a couple of sharp raps against the glass with his knuckles and the car changed directions.

"Now where are we going?" Racheal asked with some exasperation. "Daddy, I have school tomorrow. I have homework."

"And your sister has waited patiently for over a month to see her little..." the word eluded him. "Glory and Rafael's boys. An hour's visit won't make any difference in your grades, Missy. If you truly need to go home, I'll have Max take you after he drops us off."

"Fine. I love being by myself," Racheal muttered.

How worried she had been, and genuinely so. How much she loved her sister when she didn't have to be around her, I thought. Racheal was not without love, but she had virtually no tolerance at all, which just would not work in this situation. Esther had had open heart surgery, and whatever Esther wanted, Esther was going to get, including the lion's share of affection. I settled back against the seat and braced myself for the tantrums I knew were coming.

I'd told Glory that I wouldn't be at all surprised to see us head that way after getting Esther, and she was prepared for us. We pulled into the drive and stopped near the kitchen door, and two seconds later the screen flew open and out ran Titus on his stubby baby legs – scrubbed until he shone – a bouquet of meadow daisies and marigolds clutched in one hand.

As Max opened the door to let us out, Titus was in like a shot. "I miss you!" he exclaimed, hugging Esther's knees. "I miss you, Esser!" He extended the flowers as an afterthought, and Gram set him in her lap so he could have better access to my sister, who was tearful and flushed with delight. Titus reached out his little arms to her with all the gentleness of an angel. "Careful wiss my Esser," he said, and kissed her cheek.

Esther folded him to her. "I missed you, too," she laughed. "Thank you for all the pictures you colored for me, and the nice letters you wrote." He had just turned two in July, so the letters were just that, letters. Some T's and a very nice E or two.

"There you all are!" Glory laughed, coming up beside the limo. "Miss Esther, welcome home. Come in here and have something to eat, all of you. Titus, I don't believe that is where, exactly, you was supposed to end up, young man."

"Esser's home!" he laughed, and Glory just shook her head.

"Ain't no breakin' up a match made in heaven," she said. "Here, Miss Esther, give me you hand."

Esther slid out of the car into Glory's arms, and I was laughing softly to myself, until I saw the look on Racheal's face. "Racheal, Baby," I said softly, "would you like me to take you home so you can study?"

"Not until you get out of that stupid suit," she said, still glaring at her sister, who was blessedly oblivious. "Daddy said an hour. We'll see if he keeps his word to me."

"Well, don't expect too much," I cautioned gently. "The world is revolving around Esther right now...because she needs it to, not because she wants it to. Try to be patient with everybody, including yourself."

She sighed, and flexed her slim shoulders as though shaking off some demon I couldn't see. Then she stood on her tiptoes and kissed my cheek. "Don't mind me, Bud. I'm just jealous. The suit looks great, and if Dad isn't ready to go in an hour, I'll take that ride home. How good are you at Algebra?"

"I'm a whiz," I chuckled, returning the kiss, and as my father had carried Esther into the kitchen, so I carried Racheal, laughing, with her arms around my neck. It's one of the few truly tender memories I have of my sister.

I did my level best that afternoon to focus on Racheal rather than Esther, and the fact that Esther's attentions were riveted on the little boys, helped considerably. All the adults realized she was exactly where she'd wanted to be for the last month, and they pretty much sat back and practiced the lost art of relaxation. It was only when we attempted to have normal conversations and couldn't, that we felt the true weight of Esther's illness. We'd all been totally preoccupied for a month, with Esther. Would she live? Would she die? What could we do to make her happier, more relaxed, to take her mind off things, to reassure her?

She turned from where she was snuggling in my big leather recliner with the boys on either side of her, and gave me a smile. "Have you sung, *The Teddy Bear's Picnic* for these guys?" she asked, and I shrank about two sizes inside. "Has Uncle Angel sung for you?"

Both Titus and Royal shook their heads vigorously and looked expectantly my direction. Damn, where was Bobbi when I needed her? Why did she have to stay late at the studio today of all days? She should have been home...I glanced at my wristwatch...nearly an hour ago. It wasn't that I minded singing for them, but I really didn't want to sing wearing a three piece business suit. No, that wasn't it, exactly. That wasn't it at all, when I thought about it. I was sitting on the floor in the thing, for Pete's sake. I guess I didn't want to seem frivolous in front of my dad, who had just this morning put me on the board of directors for Aarador LA. He'd made that crack earlier about me being a one man minstrel show, or words to that effect, and I knew, or thought I knew, where on my list of priorities he thought my music should be, most especially the singing of children's songs to guitar accompaniment. Plus, I knew Racheal would be annoyed because I'd taken my focus off her, and God only knew where that would lead. We were already well past the one hour cut-off time to take her home, and so far she'd remained content to play chess with me. From the look on her face, that was about to change.

"You promised you'd take me home and help me with my math," she said, almost immediately, and Esther's face fell.

It was more than I could stand. "Tell you what," I said, chucking her under the chin. "I'll run upstairs and change my clothes and grab my guitar, sing one song for the boys, and we'll be off, how's that? We can stop someplace and have dinner on the way, just you and me."

"Whatever," she said, dropped her eyes to the chessboard, and swept the pieces away with her hand.

"Give me five minutes," I said to the audience in the armchair, nodded to the rest of the family, and hurried upstairs. I took off my suit, put it on the bed, and, resisting the urge to take a shower, changed into jeans, and went back downstairs, still pulling my UCLA sweatshirt over my head. I grabbed my guitar from its stand by the piano, and went back into the main part of the living room. "Good as my word," I smiled, and the boys clapped their hands with delight. "This is a song about bears," I said soberly. "This isn't going to scare you, is it?"

They both shook their heads and laughed, so I strummed a couple chords to get the key in my head, and began. The look of them, cuddling there with Esther, was so enchanting that I forgot my hesitancy, and concentrated on delighting them. When I got to the part about...*for every bear that ever there was, will gather there for certain because*...my father joined me on harmony, and made me the happiest person alive. I was singing with my dad!

We got a round of applause and rave reviews, and about that time Bobbi walked in and was hailed over, and she and I sang a couple of the folksongs we were going to sing on the concert tour, and when I thought to look around again, Racheal was gone.

"Max took her home," Mother said, and I felt like a heel.

Later that evening after supper when things had quieted down, I called her on the private line in her room, but she shrieked something about me being a lying, egocentric fucker, and hung up on me.

I went to my piano, and sat there playing and thinking about things, and when Bobbi came to sit beside me, I told her I'd really screwed things up with my sister.

"You couldn't have won," Bobbi said gently. "There would have been something wrong with the food at the restaurant, or with the way you construct an algebra problem. She'd have gotten you one way or another."

"What makes you say that?" I scowled, and Bobbi stuck a cigarette between my lips while I played.

"Because it's true," she replied, kissing my cheek and laying her head over on my shoulder. "I've been around her pretty steady for the last month, you know. She's in competition with everything, and everybody. She's the most frustrated person I've ever met."

Bobbi remained of that opinion until after she'd dealt with my first wife a time or two. After that, Racheal had competition of her own. Racheal also had an intimate friend in Megan, and one of the few who ever truly understood her, I think.

Nevertheless, I did try my best to apologize to Racheal. I arranged to be through with rehearsals by the time she got out of school in the afternoon, and we'd go together and ride under the tutelage of the hunt master at the club, and by the time the horse show came around, we were riding well together. That is not to say we were trophy quality – we weren't, though Racheal stubbornly held onto the fantasy that we were going to win because we looked like we ought to. I was just happy that we didn't look like idiots, and that she'd actually gone through with preparations for the show, and stuck to our riding schedule, which was a big step for her.

I was content to ride for fun. I showed Buck in a couple of the western classes in the morning, and picked up a ribbon in each – a blue and a red. I tried to convince Racheal to do likewise, but she spent the morning primping within an inch of her life. She washed her face two or three times because she couldn't get her makeup just right, or so Mother told me, and when I showed up to get dressed for our event, she snapped at me for not taking the thing seriously enough.

"I've been out heaping glory on the family name," I said, tossing my Stetson into a chair and forcing a chuckle I didn't feel. "Besides, I don't need to put on makeup or get my hair all fancied up. I just have to change clothes, and I'm ready."

"Well, you look like some stupid ranch hand, you need to shave more closely, and if things don't go right, it'll be your fault," she said through her teeth, and my mother and I exchanged glances.

"We're going to have fun," I chanted, and went to change into English garb. I was kind of wishing for a shot of good, smooth bourbon about then, and if it hadn't been for Bobbi's cajoling as she helped me change, and Esther's cheerful thumbs up from the family box, I might have despaired even earlier than I did.

As it was, we made it through the first cut in fine style. Racheal was paying attention to her riding, and we made it over the jumps with no faults anywhere in the course. As we were waiting for the jump-off, Java started getting restless, and Racheal immediately began reining him around in tight circles and kicking him, which just made him worse.

"Walk him out a little," I said, trying to sound soothing, hoping she'd listen to me. "Take him over there in the grass by the stables and just talk to him a little. He'll calm down."

"He needs his ass kicked, is what he needs," Racheal grated. "If he makes a fool of me, I'll knock his damned block off."

A couple heads turned our way, and I resisted the urge to groan. "You work him up, and he's going to lose his concentration and falter on the course," I warned quietly. "We've worked hard for this. Don't throw it away now."

Andy Ashbrook, who had groomed and trained the Aarons' horses for eight or nine years, came and stood at Racheal's stirrup. "You have a few minutes before your round," he said. "Why don't you let me have this bad boy and you go touch up your makeup."

"Why don't you mind your own damned business?" Racheal sneered, and before Andy could turn away I said,

"Racheal, you mind your tongue. Mister Ashbrook is responsible for Java, and you know it. He's trying to help you."

"I didn't ask for his help," she snapped.

"That's beside the point," I snapped back. "You do not speak to anybody in that tone of voice." I caught my breath and forced myself to calm down. Heads were beginning to turn in earnest. "Racheal, Baby, listen to me. You're going to lose your focus, and you're not nearly as pretty when you're not smiling. Come on, give Java, and Mister Ashbrook, and me a break, hm? Take a couple of deep breaths. We're going to be up in a minute."

"Trade me horses," she said abruptly. "I don't want to ride this one. He doesn't like me, and I don't like him."

"Baby, we're riding the horses we practiced on," I replied. I wasn't about to tell her my mother didn't want her riding Mocha. "Check your girth now, and let's get cued up."

"Check my girth," she said to Andy, and swung her leg out of the way.

"Please," I said firmly.

"Please," she said sarcastically, "since it is what you do for a living."

"I apologize for my sister," I said to Andy, and the look Racheal gave me was murderous. "You're prettier when you don't have blood in your eye," I teased, but I knew, it was all over, and I was really wishing I'd had that drink. Java had been standing still only because Andy was beside him. The second we moved into position to begin our round, he was all over the place, and Racheal was heavily into his mouth, which made him bow his neck and fight the bit all the more.

By the time the clock started for us, Java was lathered under his reins and had sweat running out from under his saddle pad. He started out at a lunge with his head too high, hopping rather than cantering toward the first jump. "Calmly, calmly," I murmured to Racheal, reaching my hand toward Java's neck to steady him.

We cleared the first jump, but Java's back foot caught one of the rails. I heard a hollow *thonk*, but it didn't fall. The second jump was easy, and we both cleared it. Java's gait smoothed out, and I relaxed just a little. I leaned over Mocha's neck to speak to him, and lost track of Racheal, just for a second, just before the water jump. The next thing I knew, Java was bouncing off Mocha's hindquarters, refusing the jump. Racheal was still with us, but Java wasn't. She somersaulted at the end of her reins and landed in the water with Java still on the other side of the jump. He crow hopped over it just as I was swinging Mocha in an arc to go back, and splashed Racheal with a little more muddy water, to the delight of the onlookers.

I resisted the urge to laugh, myself, then lost all desire to do so as Racheal yanked down on Java's reins with all her body weight, and went for his beautiful face with her riding crop. I couldn't stop the first blow, but I caught her arm on the backswing of the second. "Stop that, you imbecile!" I hissed, and jerked her by one arm across my saddle before sitting her up in front of me. I caught Java's reins in one hand as they trailed away from me, and shook my head at the judge, indicating that we weren't going to finish the ride.

I stopped both horses momentarily, and said something quiet and encouraging to Java to get him to come with me. It was at that point I realized I could hear myself plainly. It was utterly silent in the stands. The only sound was Racheal, sobbing hysterically. "Come on, Java, it's okay," I said. He still pulled back, so I slid off Mocha, and Racheal immediately kneed him and galloped away. I could see Andy and my father over by the gate, and I knew she wouldn't get far. One of Java's eyes was bleeding and swelling shut, and I just stood there, patting him gently and talking to him until he dropped his head and let me rub his face, then I swung up onto his back and rode him slowly off the course.

Racheal was still sitting on Mocha when I got to her. Andy was holding the horse, and my father was lecturing Racheal. His voice was quiet, but I could see from the expression on his face that she was catching particular hell. I dismounted, and Andy handed Mocha's reins to my dad before coming to get the big gelding. "Thanks," he said through his teeth, gave the horse a gentle pat, and led him away through the growing semi-circle of curious onlookers. I took off my helmet, stuck it under one arm and walked over to Racheal and my dad.

As I got to her left stirrup I asked, "Racheal, are you okay?" Instead of answering, she twisted around with the jumping bat and struck me full in the face – all the force of her hysteria and frustration behind it.

I staggered back and dropped to one knee, and she shrieked, "You made a fool of me! You wanted that to happen! You wanted everybody to laugh at me! You planned this all along and that's why you made me ride Java! I hate you!"

I was aware that my father jerked her off the horse and threw her down none too gently on the lawn, and that he was bending over me, saying my name. Mostly, I was aware that I had blood running through my fingers where my hand was pressed to my face, and I wondered if she'd broken my nose. I had a concert tour starting in nine days. I couldn't sing with a broken nose.

"Bud, look at me," my dad said again, and that time I responded. He grasped my wrist and pulled my hand away from my face. "Son of a bitch," he said softly. "I'll bet that hurts."

"Please, tell me she didn't break my nose," I managed, and in doing so, figured out what she had broken. My lips felt ten times their normal size and would barely articulate for me. I could feel the inside of my mouth swelling.

"She didn't break your nose," Dad said. "I don't think."

Someone handed me a clean, wet towel and pushed me gently onto my butt on the grass. "Hold that against your mouth and cheek...like that, nice and firm," Bobbi said. "Damn, your ear is bleeding, too. Doesn't she have any self-control at all, for Christ's sake?" I saw her glance at my father and then quickly away. "I'm sorry. I didn't mean to...you know. Racheal took off, by the way. I can take care of Bud if you want to go after her."

"I do not," Dad muttered. "I have servants for such things. I want to get the rest of the family together and get the hell out of here. I've never been so embarrassed in all my life. Bud...I swear to God, I've got half a mind to quirt you myself. I can't believe that you made a scene in front of the whole damned club over a horse. A stupid horse, for Godssake! Get up off your ass and get someplace less public to do your bleeding, please. My God, my children are barbarians, except for the one who's dying." He grabbed me by one arm, jerked me to my feet, and walked abruptly away from us through the crowd toward the private boxes.

"Well, I guess we can forget about him carrying you in his arms," Bobbi muttered, and I chuckled in spite of the pain in my face, and in my heart.

"That's just Dad for you," I mumbled. "Please tell me she didn't break my nose. I can't sing with a broken nose."

"She didn't break your nose," Bobbi said, putting an arm around me and steering me toward the parking lot. "I think we'll forget the valet and just find the car ourselves, don't you agree?"

"Excellent idea," I said, nodding as best I could with the towel still pressed to my face.

"Your contacts are okay, aren't they? It doesn't look like she hit you in the eye. Caught you a good one right underneath it, though."

"I'm fine," I replied, though I could tell I wasn't.

We were most of the way to the parking lot when Bobbi said, "You know, it pisses me off that there were probably half a dozen doctors standing in that crowd of lookee-loos, and not one of them offered to help. Is this what being a wealthy pillar of society is like? Because if it is, I think it sucks."

"Dad walked away from me. That meant, 'He's pissed me off, so don't help him.' You just have to know the code." I leaned heavily against the front fender and bent forward a little to ease the throb in my head and face. Even my neck hurt, and I wondered what it felt like to be a chicken, getting its head wrung from its body. "Bobbi, the keys to the car are in my jeans, and my jeans are in my dressing room."

"Stay," she said firmly. "I'll be right back."

I closed my eyes and let the late autumn sun beat down on me. Such warmth as it had, felt good on my shoulders. My shirt was totaled. My breeches were totaled. And, I was afraid, my relationship with my father might be, also. Tires crunched on the gravel beside me, and my grandmother said, "Aloysha, are you all right? Get in here and let me take you to the doctor."

I just took the towel away from my face and looked at her, too tired and discouraged even to lie. "What do you think?" I said, trying for no inflection whatsoever. "Where's...the rest of the family?" I looked closer. "Oh, that's right. You brought your own car today. Hello, Rafael. And I see you have little Racheal with you. So nice to see you again, Sunshine."

She wouldn't even look at me. She just held up her middle index finger and continued staring the opposite direction. Gram ignored her, which was all she could do, really, short of belting her one, which never seemed to do any good.

"Your father didn't think it would be wise to put the two girls in the same car together," Rafael said. "Can we..."

"I want to go home!" Racheal shrieked, and Rafael just shook his head. "Damn You! I don't want that fucker in the car with me!"

Rafael turned ever so slowly and looked at my sister over his shoulder. "You, *Senorita*, are right on the edge of a very unpleasant experience," he said quietly, "now shut up and let me talk to your brother." Amazingly, she did shut up, and promptly. Maybe those stereotypical movies about vicious, knife-wielding Mexicans weren't completely useless, after all. "Bud, can Mrs. Aarons and I take you home?"

"Thanks, no," I said. "Bobbi's coming with my keys. She'll drive me home."

She didn't drive me home. She took me to the emergency room at UCLA Medical Center. I sat, hunched up in a chair, hurting all over. My father...thought I was responsible for what had happened. That just blew me away. He actually thought letting Racheal beat a horse in the face with a quirt, was better for our family image than having me stop her? I sat there trying to figure that out. The times Bobbi spoke to me, I could barely reply, and I knew I had but nine days to remedy the situation. This was my fault? I'd brought this on myself? I wanted to discuss it with Bobbi, but I knew I couldn't – physically. Besides, I already knew where she stood, firmly on my side, which was gratifying, but it didn't help me sort things out.

When the doctor asked me what had happened, I simply said I'd been hit in the face with a jumping bat. She didn't pursue it, and I was grateful. My stomach was upset from churning for a couple hours with what felt like a pint or so of blood in it. My head ached. I could see my lips without looking down – at least out of one eye. The other had a cut under it that had pretty well swollen into my line of vision. And where was my family? Where were the people who told me I should do more with my little sister? Where were they? Where was my grandmother, who loved animals, and should have been on my side? The only sympathy I'd felt at all, was from Rafael. And just how upset was Esther by all of this? I'd invited her to come and see us ride. What if she got so upset that she had another heart attack? Who would be held responsible? Me. What's worse, who would actually be responsible? Me. Oh, what to do. Should I cry? Should I puke? Both sounded like real possibilities at that point.

The doctor laid me down, numbed me up, and began taking stitches in various places, all the while telling me more than I wanted to know about the damage I'd suffered. As soon as the swelling had gone down inside my mouth and the stitches were out, I needed to get to the dentist. I had three broken teeth on the upper left – badly cracked, actually – they could probably be saved, probably just need root canals or something. I shouldn't try chewing for two or three days. My mouth was so swollen inside I'd undoubtedly be chewing on myself as well as my food. And no smoking, either.

"This little bloody nick right here on the outside? It goes clear through. One of your teeth got driven through your cheek. Not to worry, though. This happens a lot. We see it in surfers all the time. They go running into the surf with their boards in front of them, and *Whammo*! Front teeth right out through their lips." I thanked her for sharing that with me.

She opted not to stitch the cut under my eye, and put a butterfly on it instead, saying that with time it would fade into the natural lines of my face. She was right. Twenty years later, it did.

Dear Bobbi, was so patient, and so upbeat. She sat and held my hand and chatted about medical stuff with the doctor, saving me the trouble of trying to make conversation, which is hard to do with someone working inside your mouth and taking stitches in your lips. All I wanted to do, was get home, get out of my English riding boots, and into a hot shower. I had rehearsal tomorrow, and I was dreading it. What if they decided I might not heal up in time and had someone else take my place singing with Bobbi? I'd have the drumming and the piano playing, which was the main thing, but still...I was looking forward to launching my vocal career with Missy Bates.

I was fine until we pulled into the driveway, and then I was scared. I just wasn't sure what would face me when I walked into the house. I was so damned tired, and I knew that if anybody started in on me, I'd cry like a baby. Luck seemed to be with me. Dad's limo was not in the drive. What if Racheal was here with Gram? No problem. I'd just...kill her. "Bud, honey, you're stiff as a board all of a sudden," Bobbi said, reaching across the seat to squeeze my hand, "is anything the matter?"

I just shook my head. "No." I said, very carefully articulating around the swollen spots, "I'm just really worn out, and I'm worried about Esther. You can't understand a word I'm saying, can you?"

"Good," she smiled. "Come on, I'm starved, aren't you?"

"Right," I muttered.

We walked into the kitchen, my favorite haven, and the fragrances of supper filled my nostrils rather than the smell of antiseptic, and whatever else it is that gives hospitals that scary, sterile odor they have. Only Glory was there, and she turned from the stove to study me. She was shocked. I could see it in her eyes, though it did no more than flicker across the rest of her face. "How can I help?" was all she said.

"I need to get out of these boots and take a shower," I said, and she nodded.

"I'll get you some supper ready. I assume you ain't chewin' anything for a day or two?"

I shook my head, gave her what I had for a smile, and trudged on upstairs, telling Bobbi to stay behind and eat something. Bending over to get the boot jack was not pleasant, but other than that, I really didn't feel too bad. I stripped my clothes off, wondering where Gram was, and went into the bathroom to bathe. My first look in the mirror, made me wonder why Glory hadn't screamed. Actually, it's a wonder I didn't scream. I looked almost as bad as the evening I'd laid in that pool of panchromatic blood and played dead. This didn't wash off, nor did I try. I scrubbed myself from the neck down, did a gingerly job of washing my hair, and called it good.

"You Grandmother spendin' the night at the main house, helping ride herd on the girls," Glory said as I entered the kitchen. "Miss Bobbi gone to take a shower. You set right down there and let's get some food in you."

"Too bad everything can't be fixed with food," I sighed. "Can you understand what I'm saying?"

"Physically, or philosophically?"

"That answers my question. Rafael give you all the gory details?"

"Java? He may lose an eye, Bud. Nothin' deserves to be treated like that. You done the right thing, Darlin', and Rafael, he says you was real gentlemanly 'bout it, too – real gallant. You drink some of this here soup I pureed, and I made you some tapioca. Miss Esther, she's mad as hops, but she feelin' fine, so don't you fret none 'bout her. Don't nobody blame you, though your daddy said to you he did. He feels so bad 'bout sayin' it. He don't handle bein' embarrassed real well, and havin' Racheal turn into a demon in public like that, it shook him up some. He was here for a bit with Esther, and he was frettin' 'bout you and how you was. Didn't say much, but I could tell. Oh, Honey, that too hot for your poor mouth?"

I just shook my head and blinked at the tears watering in my eyes. "Jabbed my cheek with the straw. Some places are still numb, and some definitely are not. What did Gram have to say?"

Glory just shook her head and sat down beside me, lowering her voice as she spoke. "She was real quiet. Somethin' worryin' that one way deep down. I wouldn't be surprised but maybe she be thinkin' Miss Racheal... needin' help, you know? Look at the damage she done to you. What could she do to Esther if the mood come on her?"

"God, I don't even want to think about it," I groaned, and I could feel the hair standing up on my arms.

"She don't want to bring it up to you folks. They got so much on their minds, and you Mama, she's high strung, you know. Mister Aarons, he's so concerned with how things is lookin' to others...I just don't think she got anyplace to turn with her worries."

"Well," I sighed, "I'll have to say I think her worries are well founded. Maybe I'll bring up the subject when we have some quiet moments together."

"She does count on you," Glory smiled. "You the man who listens in her life, Aloysha. Let me get you some tapioca, then you get yourself some rest. Sit at that Steinway and play youself to sleep or somethin'."

"That's a very good idea," I chuckled. "I have a rehearsal tomorrow morning, and my Sunday has been less than productive."

A couple of hours at the piano did relax me. I worked on the next day's music, and when I went to bed, I slept well. My spirits improved with a good night's rest, but not my face. I really wanted to put a bag over my head to go into rehearsal, but I knew sooner or later I'd have to face everybody, so I toughed it out and pretended that I looked just fine. Bobbi linked her arm through mine as we walked in, and it made me feel better.

Albert Saucedo was waiting for us. "Bud," he said, "I need to speak to you privately. Bobbi, would you excuse us, please?"

She gave him a blithe nod, gave me a kiss on the undamaged cheek, and strode off to join the others who were tuning up on stage. "I do apologize for this face," I began, and Saucedo gestured toward his office. Something in the way he made that motion...chilled my heart.

"Sit down," he said, and I did. He sat across from me, and we looked at each other for the space of ten seconds or so. "There's no easy way to say this," he said at last. "Bud, your services are being terminated."

I felt like he'd butted me in the stomach. "What?" I gasped. "I know I look like a prize fighter right now, but my hands..."

"...are some of the most skillful I've ever heard at the keyboard of a piano. You're a brilliant musician, Bud, and we're going to miss you during this series more than you can possibly imagine, but you don't match the profile of the young person we want to project, and we just can't take you along."

"Why? What have I done, besides get in the way of my sister's riding crop?" There was no point trying to gloss over it. The story had made the society page of the papers. I hadn't spoken to my father, but I knew he was livid.

"That isn't enough? Bud, you were involved in a brawl with your sister during a horseshow. This is a young peoples' concert. How would it look to be featuring somebody who abuses his little sister?"

"Mister Saucedo," I said with some heat, "I have never raised a hand to my sister. Racheal was beating her horse in the face with a whip. I stopped her...forget it," I sighed, "I can see by the look on your face that nothing I can say is going to change your mind, is it?"

He just shook his head and looked genuinely sad. "It is the whole spectre of impropriety, Bud, and not just that you might be abusive. There has always been the possibility that you were homosexual, an issue that seems to have been momentarily dispelled by the fact that you have a live-in girlfriend, which is only marginally better than the original charge. But I defended your right to privacy, and I still do. People were incensed over certain...racial improprieties regarding your staff that they feared might lead to community upheaval, and I thought that was downright funny. I defended you there, too. But all put together, they're just too much. A couple of our most influential patrons – ones who have been concerned all along about things – were at that horse show, and you came across as the bully. They want you pulled from the tour, and I have no choice but to honor their wishes. I'm sorry."

"Me, too," I said, choking back my tears. I took the hand he held out to me, then turned on my heel and hurried out of his office before he could see me cry. I bolted for the car, slammed the door, and began pounding on everything in sight, just to hit something. "Son of a bitch!" I cried, "Son of a bitch!" My chance to sing, to play the guitar, to play the drums and the piano, to share my love of music with young people all over the United States and Canada, was gone. For the first and only time in my life, I had been fired.

CHAPTER TEN

I sat in the car, numbed with disbelief and despair. I felt like the whole word, everything I'd worked for, had collapsed in a single shout of derisive laughter around my shoulders. I knew, somewhere in the back of my mind, that I should go back in there and let Bobbi know that I wouldn't be around today...or any other day, and that she did need to buy that car we'd talked about but never gotten around to finding.

There was this overwhelming urge to start pointing fingers and yelling. *Who the hell are these patrons, anyway? They're dead when I find out! And you, Rafael, you're barely civil to me, and this is what I go through for you? See, Racheal, what your temper has done to me? See, Dad, what happens when you choose to walk away from a situation or a person? See how much power you have? And while we're on the subject, what, exactly, is it that I've done to you, God, that you should allow this to happen to me? I'm innocent in all of this - every bit of it - and yet I've been visited with this terrible punishment. Why is that? Why?*

It was a hard, hard lesson for a young man to learn, and I got most of it out of the way sitting right there in my car in the symphony parking lot. I half hoped Bobbi would come storming out and get into the car with me, saying she'd told them to flat go to hell. I'd have sent her right back in there, but the gesture would have been gratifying. She didn't appear.

I could hear bits of music escaping the building through their open windows and mine, and I couldn't stand it. I started the car and just drove... anywhere...crying and raging until I saw the red lights behind me and looked down at my speedometer. By then of course it was too late. I took a deep, shuddering breath, and with one last heartfelt curse, pulled over and reached for my registration.

The officer walked up beside me, and I handed him my paperwork. "Good morning, Sir," he said. There was no need for that question about seeing license and registration. "How are you today, Mister...Aarons?"

"It has definitely not been my day," I said, and for the first time in what seemed hours, I heard more than just my inner voice. I sounded like a drunk. I saw his ears come up, and hastened to add, "My mouth is full of stitches, I just got fired, now I've probably been speeding, and I'm a pathetic mess. How has your day been so far?"

"Better than yours," the officer replied, which surprised me. I didn't think they actually had conversations that weren't written down in a book someplace. "What happened to your face?"

"I got hit with a riding crop at a horse show yesterday. Sorry if I'm hard to understand."

"Are you taking pain pills?"

"No, but I wish I was," I muttered. "No. I'm not."

He studied my face for a few heartbeats, then closed his pad and said, "I'm giving you a warning this time, but you need to slow down just a bit. Don't take your frustrations out on the highways of Los Angeles. Have a good day, Sir." He handed me back my license and registration, gave me a curt nod, and went back to his vehicle before I could even say, thank-you.

He was sitting behind me, waiting for me to pull back into traffic, or I'd probably have been sitting there yet, not having a clue where to go next. As it was, I had to move or risk having him get out of that cruiser a second time. I flipped on my signal and eased back onto the roadway, headed south. Where was I, anyway? I spotted a landmark that told me I was traveling in a huge, imperfect circle, and that home was behind me, Dad's house to my left in the haze. Kit was off visiting his in-laws, so it was no good trying to find him. I could go check on Esther. I should go check on Esther. But...I looked in the mirror...I was positively terrifying. No good going to see Esther in this condition. Besides, what if Mother was home, or Dad, or Racheal? I just was not ready to tell them I had failed at something I'd wanted more than food or drink. All those weeks and months of planning and practicing... gone. What would make it worse, walking in and telling my father what had happened, or having him go and pick up the phone and fix it? I wasn't sure I could keep it from him for very long, but I wasn't going to hunt him up and blurt it out, either.

I had...to go home. Much as I was dreading it – didn't have a clue what I was going to say when I got there – I had to go home. I had to pick a starting point for facing up to this, and home was the best place. I got off the freeway, made a turn, and got going back in the opposite direction. As I drove up out of the valley I left the fog behind, and found that even the clarity of the air was intimidating. Everyone could see me. There was no place to hide. I had failed without anonymity. I was my father's only son, and somehow, in some manner I couldn't sort out, I had failed, and it was only a matter of time until everybody who knew me or my family, would know...I had failed at the very thing I wanted to do more than anything in the world. I was numb. My head was splitting just from the effort of trying to think this through. My eyes burned from crying. My contacts were probably halfway to my brain by now. I blinked. Nope. They were still in place. Amazing. When I thought about it, they had to be where they were supposed to or I'd be blind as a bat, wouldn't I? See, I'd thought that out. How tough could the rest of this be?

I parked the car in the driveway, not wanting to know which of the other cars was home. I could hear Royal and Titus laughing out back somewhere, probably enjoying their new tire swing. I'd watched Bobbi playing on it, her long, full skirt blowing about her thighs as she pumped skyward. I'd never played on a tire swing.

The kitchen door opened, and Glory was standing there, looking puzzled. "Bud, are you...what..."

I just shook my head. "Don't ask," I muttered. "Is Gram home?"

"No. What you doin' here?"

"I live here."

"Where's Miss Bobbi?"

"At work," I said, brushing past her into the kitchen.

"Why ain't you at work?"

"Because I don't work there anymore. Is there anything in here to eat that doesn't have to be chewed?" I'd traded grief for hostility, and so far it was working.

"Bud, look here at me."

"Can't do that," I replied, busily rummaging in the refrigerator.

"Why not?" Her hand closed over mine where it rested on the refrigerator door. "Bud, look here at me. You done somethin' you ashamed of?"

I thought about that while I sorted through bottles. "No. Well...yes. Hell, I don't know."

"Why ain't you at work?"

"Because I got fired," I said, drawing a deep breath which, to my delight, remained steady. "I think I said that once already. Where's my grandmother?"

"Went to Catalina Island to look at some matin' ritual, I believe. Hopefully it's birds." She put her hands firmly on my waist and motored me out of the way of the open refrigerator. "You lookin' for somethin' hot, or somethin' cold?"

"I assume it's all cold in here."

"Peter Aloysha Aarons, for the love of heaven, sit down and tell me what happened," she demanded, pushing me on over to the chair I usually occupied at the kitchen table. She pulled a small pan off its burner, shut the stove off, and sat down beside me. "You been chewin' on this long enough. Now spit it out," she said.

"I told you. I got fired...from the tour, the symphony. I got fired. I really want something to eat."

"No, you don't. Bud, you have yet to look me in the eye. Now tell me what happened."

I pushed my hands down on the table to force my chin up, and met her even, chocolate brown gaze. After a moment of trying to swallow, I said, "They fired me because I am not a good influence on children. I am abusive toward my sister, I am a homosexual, I have a live-in girlfriend, and I'm involved in racial rabble-rousing. Or that's what I gathered from what Mister Saucedo said to me as he was giving me the boot."

Glory bristled all over like a big, black cat. "I never heard such a passel of damn nonsense in all my life, Aloysha! Does your...." She trailed off, dropped her eyes, and patted my hand.

"Does my...what?" I said quietly.

"No. Never mind."

"I already know what you're going to say, so you might as well out with it. Does my father know?"

She looked momentarily uncomfortable. "Well, does he?"

"How old are you?"

"I'm...twenty -five. Why you askin'?"

"You're not twenty-five. You won't be twenty-five for another week. When your truck caught fire, did you call your dad?"

"Just tell me where you goin' with this," she sighed, "I got church come Sunday."

"Did you call your dad?" I persisted.

"No," she said, "I did not. But that be an altogether different thing, Bud. My daddy got no way of helpin' me..."

"But my father does, is that it? You're younger than I am, but you have the right to stand on your own two feet because your father is not a powerful man. When I hired you...well, you had me going, I guess."

"Meanin'?"

"You treated me just like a grown-up. And that lasted until just about the time Esther fell in love with your boys and you really figured out who my father is and what he can do. Now, I'm not your employer, with a career of my own, I'm Peter Aarons the lesser, always needing Daddy to give me an in or bail me out. Why is that?"

"It ain't," she said with just a hint of annoyance. "Your imagination gone and got the best of you. What I meant, and all I meant, was that you daddy, if he took a mind, could give you a real public forum to fight these ugly, untrue things that's been said. You leave 'em lay, people gonna think they true, Aloysha. That ain't gonna solve a thing."

"Neither is making it public," I muttered. "This is nobody's business but mine."

The press, did not see it that way. My dear Bobbi, in a moment of righteous, redheaded outrage, said something during a coffee break in front of...as I got the story, somebody who worked for the UCLA school paper who was going with somebody in the orchestra...anyway, he recognized a story somebody would pay for, and by the next morning the whole pile had hit the fan.

I came downstairs prepared to be stoical about the whole thing - to check the help wanted, musicians, section of the Melbourne Gazette while sucking my breakfast through a tube, and there was my grandmother in a fine Italian temper. Her opening salvo consisted of, "Thank God your father is in Seattle!" First in English, then in Italian, for emphasis. "Just wait until your father gets home!"

There was no point in playing dumb. She was waving the newspaper like it was Old Glory at the Battle of Bunker Hill, and all I could do was shake my head. "Leave it be," I said. Glory was making chest-clutching motions behind my grandmother's back, and I knew what she meant. Do something calming. Immediately, would be good. "It's quite probably just people playing power games and using me for bait, and I'm not going to dignify the fracas by getting up on a soap box and pleading my innocence."

"You and Bobbi Bates are...?" she stuck the newspaper under her arm and made a subtle gesture with both hands.

"Yes, Grandmother," I sighed. "Bobbi and I have been..." I returned the gesture, "for some time. Good morning, *Senora* Ruiz."

"Good mornin' Mister Aarons," she said, and despite the situation, her eyes were twinkling like crazy. "You sleep good?" I nodded, and she went on. "You gonna try exercisin' before breakfast?"

"Sure. May not do too much to jar myself, but..."

"Why didn't you tell your father immediately?" My grandmother exclaimed. "You can call him in Seattle. I'm going to go call our lawyers!"

"It's six O'clock in the morning," I reminded her. "Please let it go. I just want to...." What did I want to do? Did I want to hop a jet for Australia? That really sounded good. Did I want to sue their collective asses? And whom, exactly did that involve suing and what would be accomplished? The opportunity would still be gone, and the symphony itself would suffer. Then there was Dad, the instant solution. Whom had he crossed? Hell, he'd crossed everybody in Hollywood at one time or another, and there were other men...just as powerful...more powerful than he. And finding out who they were, those nameless, faceless serpents at the horse show, and adding them to the lawsuit, would accomplish...what, exactly? I was screwed. "I just want to forget this as quickly as possible." Fat chance. Thirty-some years have gone by, and I can still feel the pain, the weight, the length of those days.

I fought a terrible battle within myself, and at times, when neither side was winning, I was completely immobilized. I could only pray for forgetfulness, and hope for survival. What I dreamed of...was the man in the red uniform, or the red man in the uniform...doing unspeakable things to me until I was exhausted, like a lab rat in ice water, with no hope left. Gram and Glory and my mother and Esther and Bobbi, even Andy, when I went to visit Java, all told me what I should do. I didn't want to hurt them by telling them to leave me alone, so I hid, coming out only to find food, and crawling into bed at night. Even making love to Bobbi didn't have much appeal for me, and she took it to mean that I was upset, either because she was going on the tour and I wasn't, or because she'd opened her mouth when she shouldn't have. I tried to explain to her that neither of those had anything to do with my lack of passion, but I did a lousy, garbled job of it, and ended up in bed alone.

The fourth morning when I crawled downstairs to exercise, my father was sitting in the living room, drinking coffee with my grandmother, waiting for me. I almost groaned aloud – caught myself at the last second and turned it into a yawn. Twice now the demon had come for me in my dreams, and my ability to cope was rapidly eroding from lack of sleep and ability to control the situation. "Good morning, Sir," I said, trying to look pleased. "How was Seattle?"

"Beautiful little city. We have a meeting with our lawyers at eight O'clock this morning."

I just clapped my hands to my forehead and spun around on one foot, gnashing my teeth. That brought me to my senses pretty quickly. Those broken teeth on the top left...damn! "Dad," I said, "No. If this is about that thing with the symphony..."

"What the hell else would it be about?" he snapped. His face was set heavily against me, and I knew he was angry.

"Please listen to me," I pleaded. "This is something I have to work through on my own. I'm a grown man..."

"With a very prestigious family name, and you're not going to let it be dragged through the dirt with your indecision! If Bill Skorks thinks he can pull this shit on me..."

"Dad," I said sharply, "I'm the one who got fired."

"And you're also the one who's been sitting on your ass for four days like some goddamned weeping Buddah, instead of standing up for yourself. You make me sick!"

"Now, now, J.R.," my grandmother said, patting his knee, and he turned his smoldering black gaze on her.

"Stay out of this, Mother. This doesn't concern you," he said, not unkindly, and she smiled at him like he'd offered her flowers.

"Which is what I asked of you four days ago," I said quietly. "There is nothing this can do now but get worse. Please, I'm begging you, both of you, let me handle this my own way."

"And what way would that be?" my father asked, taking his mother's hand and pressing it to his lips. He was like some big jungle cat, caressing his family with one paw, holding his bloody prey in the other. For purposes of the analogy, I was definitely not family.

"I just want to let this go," I sighed. "The more I kick and scream, the more I'm going to look like I'm guilty as charged. I have Bellwether to work on. I have my seat at Aarador LA to learn about..."

"If you're going to turn out to be some gutless wonder who turns tail at the first sign of conflict, you can forget that seat on the board. We don't need people who are afraid of a fight! Mother, it's time you left." She nodded to him and scurried out. It was the only time I can ever remember being disappointed in my grandmother.

Another shock. I just took a deep breath, too hurt and exhausted even to grunt or duck anymore. Lucky for me, I realized later, that I was so exhausted. It kept me from losing my temper, which kept me from losing a few more teeth. "Dad, there is no fight. There were comments made by patrons. You know as well as I do that half the film community thinks I'm gay. There's the thing with Bobbi..."

"I'm glad to see she's earning her room and board, at least," Dad said, and I resisted the urge to reach out and pop him one.

"Bobbi is my friend – whatever else she may be – she is my friend. The biggest issue, is that I came across at the horse show as being abusive toward my sister. With all due respect, I think you could have done a lot for my case if you'd just sided with me at the time instead of walking away from me like it was my fault."

"It *was* your fault!" he exclaimed, rising from the couch. "You should have gotten off your horse, given your sister a hug and a leg up, and led her off the course instead of heaving her across your saddle like the Hun master of the rape and pillage detail! It may have made female hearts go pitty-pat, but I thought it was beastly. I still do."

"Java has lost part of the vision in his left eye. He'll never jump again," I said, hoping at least for sympathy for the horse.

"Beside the point. He's a dumb animal."

"So..." I lit a cigarette and eyed Dad through the smoke, "You think I got what I deserved."

He went up like a rocket. "If I thought you'd gotten what you deserved I wouldn't be mounting a cadre of lawyers in your defense, now, would I?" he bellowed. "Oy fucking vey, I don't know what I'm going to do with you! I'd love nothing better than to leave you alone to wiggle your way out of this mess."

Oh, please do! I thought. As it was I stood there as dumb and impaired as poor Java, who'd likely be sold for dogfood. I wanted to fall face forward onto the Persian carpet and sleep and sleep until this whole thing went away.

"Don't just stand there like an idiot, go get dressed!" he demanded, and I went, tacitly vowing that one of these times I was going to stand on my hind legs and tell him off.

I'd just gotten out of the shower when there was a knock at my door, so I pulled on my robe and went to answer it. No point pretending like I wasn't here, which was my first choice. It was Glory. "Brought you some breakfast," she said, walking in with a tray. She glanced at the clothes I had tossed on my comforter and shook her head. "Not the blue suit. Wear the grey one."

"Thanks for the food," I said, taking the tray from her. "Why not the blue suit?"

"He picked it out. He dressed you up in it like a toy he was takin' for show and tell. You go see you lawyers wearin' it, he gonna be able to say, 'See, I even pick out his clothes for him.' You gonna need all the autonomy you can get, Boy, and that suit ain't gonna help any at all."

I studied her face for a few moments. She was angry. For me, or with me, but probably not at me. "I should have told him flat out I won't go," I sighed.

"Sit down and eat while I find you somethin' to wear." she commanded, and picked the blue suit back up off the bed.

She was rummaging in my closet when I said, "I'm surprised you're not pleased about this. I mean, you thought I'd been wronged, and Dad's going to set about righting that."

"Is he?" Glory muttered. "Fancy that. Here I thought he was just gonna push you 'round on his personal chessboard." She pulled my grey suit and a pink shirt from the closet, tossed a burgundy and grey tie on top, and dropped them on the bed. "If you was pleased, Aloysha, I'd be pleased. You ain't pleased. Why is that? You don't think you been wronged?"

I snorted softly, shook my head, and lapped at my Cream of Wheat. "I don't know," I said at last. "No. I take that back. I do know. Yes, I was wrongly accused...or my actions have been wrongly interpreted...but, I don't think this is going to solve anything, and the fact that my father is initiating it, makes me feel exactly like you think I do – like a pawn – or like a single item on a much larger agenda."

"What you gonna do 'bout it?"

"I don't know yet," I muttered, "but I'm damned sure not going to roll over and play dead. I can't imagine this could get much worse, anyway. I've already lost my chance to travel with the orchestra...God, I still can't believe that when I hear myself say it. I can always go ahead and cross Dad and then move to Turkey, or Patagonia, or Morocco for a few years until things cool off. I know you'll take good care of Gram."

"And I'll say goodbye to Esther for you," Glory added soberly, and bent to kiss my forehead as the tears welled up in my eyes. "Stop runnin'. You already bloody. Might as well put up your dukes and defend yourself."

"Go away," I said softly, and she went, turning briefly at the door.

"Rafael, he say he gonna need some help from you this afternoon, so don't be dilly-dallyin' in town."

I thought about what she'd told me as I stood looking in the mirror, combing the errant curls out of my thick black hair, tying a perfect full Windsor, studying my face. Most of the swelling was gone, and I no longer looked like a chipmunk with nuts in one cheek. I was going to have a scar under the corner of my left eye. The welt along my cheekbone had turned to an ugly, yellowing bruise. My lips were no longer terribly misshapen, though there were two deep cuts, one in the bottom lip, and one in the top, just under my left nostril. That one had three tiny stitches in it. Overall, I could conceivably have looked worse. The pink shirt helped brighten my face a little. I looked like I'd been hit, but I did not look pathetic. It was the best I could hope for.

As I walked back out into my bedroom I was seized with the sudden need to call Albert Saucedo and tell him what was about to come down on his head. Almost, almost, I reached for the phone. I was sitting beside it when it occurred to me that telling him, apologizing to him, would only make things worse. He would think I was tipping him off to curry favor, I would be further compromised, and nothing would be helped. I stood back up, shrugged into my suit coat, and went downstairs.

It was an hour's drive in traffic to the law offices of Penn, Petty, Goldberg and Sutton, and in that time my father said not one single word to me. For my part, I didn't even try to have a conversation. I sat looking out the window and wishing I wanted to play the piano, or make love to Bobbi, or play with Royal and Titus, or any of the things which usually brought me pleasure. I didn't. I didn't want to talk, didn't want to think...didn't want to even acknowledge what was happening to me. For some reason it filled me with unspeakable dread, and for that hour in the car, I could almost remember my nightmare – could almost touch it – get in touch with it. Everything I had wanted, everything I had worked so hard for, practiced hour after hour, day after day, year after year for, was gone, and I felt, with the heightened emotion of youth, that I would never get it back. I would spend the rest of my life as a walking shadow of the artist I wanted to be. Rachmaninoff would be ashamed.

When Max said my name I jumped, realized the door was open, and wondered if I'd dozed off. As I stepped out I noticed people on the street; tourists, possibly, whispering and pointing, looking enviously at the car and the fantasy it represented. *If only you knew*, I thought. I gave Max a slight nod and a thank-you, and for the briefest of seconds his hand touched my forearm before I followed my father.

I did not hurry to speak. I sat listening to my father explain things as he saw them. I had been fired from the orchestra, not because of actual, provable transgressions, but for political reasons. William Skorks and Malachi Kendeski, of Glenhaven Industries, had been trying for six months to purchase a controlling share in JetAce Corporation. My father had outbid them. Glenhaven Industries, because it was a major supplier of school cafeteria equipment, was a heavy contributor to the children's programming associated with the symphony. It was not a message to me about my behavior, it was a message to my father to back off. Simple.

Solomon Goldberg sat listening to my father, but watching me, stroking his beard idly with one hand, making some notes with the other, nodding from time to time. Dad wrapped up the particulars, sat back, and lit a cigarette. He was watching Sol, and Robin Sutton, who was sitting off a little to one side, smoking a Meerschaum pipe, listening, saying nothing. I was trying to watch all of them – trying to get some sense of the mood in the room. I liked Sol and Robin, both. They were loyal to my father, but they were honest with him. I wanted to hear what they had to say.

"Bud," said Solomon, "what have you to say about this?"

I cleared my throat to give myself a second to think. "I just heard about the possibility of a lawsuit this morning," I said, "so I'm not really in a position to have an opinion."

Robin pricked up his ears, took his pipe from his mouth and said, "You're the one who's suing these people, Bud."

I just shook my head. "No. My father is suing...whomever it is... Skorks and Kendeski, or the Greater Los Angeles Symphony, or both. I am acquiescing to my father's wishes."

"You sound reluctant," Robin said.

"Frankly, I am. I fail to see what greater good is being served by this. I..."

"That about sums it up," my father said mildly. "He fails to see. I'd like you to proceed with this at once."

Robin ignored him, for which I gave him boundless credit. "Go on, Bud," he said.

"I just...don't see how I am going to be helped by this. No lawsuit is going to prove that I don't abuse my sister, or that I'm not a closet homosexual, and the press is bound to get wind of this and get all over the fact that Bobbi Bates is living under my roof and sleeping with me on a regular basis, which could bring embarrassment to her. I didn't even understand the part about being a racial rabble rouser because of whom I've chosen to hire as staff. I don't think Mister Saucedo got it, either, truth be told. He's just the messenger and I don't think he bears me any ill will. I'm already embarrassed to death over having been...fired from a job that was my... that meant a lot to me, and I just want this to go away and die a natural death."

"You're afraid," Sol said flatly.

"A little, yes. I'm also embarrassed and ashamed and I feel helpless and used. I don't even know who's being sued, and I can't say I'm happy to think it's Saucedo and the GLAS. They struggle with money for their programs as it is. How does it look that I get fired and then retaliate?"

"You were fired for no good reason," Robin said. "And you're wrong. We can prove, as publicly as you want, that you do not abuse your sister. Bud, I was there. I wanted to stand up and applaud when you tossed her over your saddle like a dirty little sack of laundry, and the way you handled that injured horse...it brought tears to my eyes. I think..."

"My daughter is not going on trial here," Dad said flatly. "She has a problem with her temper. Her mother and I acknowledge that. But she's just a little girl, and little girls do rash things."

"Like injure beautiful, expensive horses, and physically abuse and injure their siblings? Maybe Peter today and Esther tomorrow? If they do, they figure prominently in any lawsuit that comes along," Robin said, and I could tell by the way he said it, that he was enjoying himself. "If we're going to prove he didn't abuse her, we will have to prove that she abused him, J.R. That's the way it works."

"I want this to be about Skorks and Kendeski, and about them applying undue pressure on a third party for financial gain, not about my children."

"Then you can't involve Bud and the symphony in the lawsuit," Sol said reasonably. "Either this is about Bud, or it isn't. J.R., I know you've been under a lot of strain lately, and this may seem like a good way to blow off a little steam, but I don't believe you've thought this through with anywhere near the clarity you usually bring to such a process. You can't just accuse Skorks and Kendeski of applying undue pressure. You'd never be able to prove it. They'd laugh at you. Who is your main witness going to be? Albert Saucedo. Enter the symphony. Now, that is not to say I don't think we can win this one – I most assuredly do. But the case I'm talking about is Bud versus the GLAS, not Aarador LA versus Glenhaven industries. You have two separate cases here, one very weak, one very strong. Choose one."

It was one of those few blessed moments when I realized, and had actual proof, that my father was not omnipotent. He sat there, eyes blazing, chewing on the side of his cheek by pushing against it with the knuckle of his left index finger. The huge, perfect diamond in his wedding ring glinted coldly from the light of the lamp beside his leather easy chair.

I was glad I'd worn the grey suit. It was nicely tailored, but it was plain, like me. I had no rings on my fingers; no jewelry of any kind. The watch on my right wrist was a Rolex, but it was not ornamented. I was happy that my car was ten years old, that I had no valet to trim my hair and shine my shoes. Why I was so keenly aware of those things I'm not sure, but I did know I was deeply grateful not to be my father at that moment, nor his spitting image, nor anything close to it. The only resemblance was the bottomless black eyes. I resisted the urge to issue a tacit challenge, and kept mine respectfully averted while he thought.

I realized, sitting there watching his forceful and studied gesticulations – the way his jaw muscles rippled under his tanned skin – that I didn't want to be a prominent member on the board of Aarador LA. I was excellent with finances and investments, but I just did not have a nose for blood and political maneuvering. I was more than happy to get ahead financially, but not at the expense of others. Money was not a game for me. I'd always taken that term for granted...the money game, the real estate game, the stock market game. Dad was a player. Now, I understood a little better. In any game of consequence there is a winner and a loser. The game Dad played was a high-stakes, cerebral wrestling match over the slippery slope of financial destruction. He could very literally plunge to his death, or send another plunging. This was about triumph...about ruin...about not caring what happened to the other guy. I was just a piano player. No. I was a pianist, with the hope of greatness still lingering on the far horizon of present despair.

"Bud," Robin said very softly, "come here and let me have a look at you."

I did as he requested, moving across the room to the comfortable leather chair immediately opposing him next to the window. I sat down, and he leaned forward with his hands on his thighs to contemplate me. "I'm very uncomfortable with this," I said, mostly for the sake of inane conversation, and he just nodded.

"I know you are," he said, "but you can't let people defame you and lie about you and get away with it. Nobody should have to tolerate that, and you are going to be very high profile someday. You, especially, can't afford it."

"You mean my father can't afford it, and won't tolerate it," I muttered.

"Bud, Bud, Bud," Robin chuckled, patting my knee, "Your father adores you, don't you know that? This is the only way he knows to express it. You should have seen him when he found out you weren't going on that concert tour. He was absolutely beside himself. Now, I know you doubt his motives and at times so do I, but the outcome of this will be honorable, I promise you. He is our client, but then again, so are you. When we represent you, we represent you against anybody we have to, even your dad." He paused to study me. "Does your face hurt?"

"Not much," I said truthfully. "My teeth hurt."

"Your teeth?"

"Yes. Racheal broke three of my teeth, and..."

"She broke your teeth?" he asked, incredulous, "with that jumping bat?"

"Badly cracked, actually. The oral surgeon couldn't repair them until the swelling went down. I have an appointment tomorrow morning for whatever it takes to fix them."

"J.R.," Robin said evenly, and in a slightly louder voice than he'd been using with me, "Why didn't you tell me that Bud has stitches in his face, and that he has three broken teeth from the assault?"

My father's head turned slowly our way. "You have broken teeth? I didn't know that. And it wasn't an assault, Robin. It was a family spat."

I just nodded, resisting the urge to say what was really on my mind at that moment. "She hit me pretty hard, Dad."

"Are you going to lose them?"

"I don't think so."

"Well, that's all that matters," he said, and turned back to Sol. I did notice his gaze didn't meet mine. He was ashamed of what Racheal had done, and I knew it. It told me, too, that despite his hard words, he loved me, and that was nearly as good as a warm hug in this time of trouble. Nearly. Actually, I could have used a hug, but I shrugged off the need as the weakness I thought it was.

I just gave Robin a look and hiked an eyebrow his way. Surely he knew this man by now. For his part, Robin sat shaking his head and staring out the window for an uncomfortable space of time. I could hear Dad and Sol speaking softly together across the room. "For something so intangible," Robin said abruptly, without turning his gaze from the skyline, "a reputation is such a fragile thing. Easily damaged, easily lost. It can be exquisitely hard to retrieve or repair." His head came around and his green eyes fixed themselves on me. "Bud, I'm sorry, but I agree one hundred percent with your father. This organization, needs its ass sued. If Skorks and Kendeski get caught in the backdraft, so much the better, but you need to force GLAS to retract its statements defaming you. Can you understand why?"

"Because my father wants it done," I said irritably.

"Because your father loves you and knows what's best for you, at least in this case. True, he has a personal agenda. That's just J.R. for you. He always has a personal agenda. But if you look at his reputation...don't give me that stare, Buddy Boy...if you look at your father's reputation, as far as honesty, it is flawless. As far as judgment, it is flawless. That does not come without a strong defense. This is the time for you to take a stand in your own defense."

"Apparently, I can't," I said, and I could hear my own, pettish tone. My teeth ached, my jaw ached, my face ached. My ego was tarnished and dented. "My reputation is all well and good, but my sister's is more important. We can't make a little girl into a monster."

"Yes, you can," Robin said, and there was the hint of a challenge in his slightly British accent. "The burden of proof is on GLAS to show that you did abuse your sister, that you are gay, and so on and so forth. All we have to do is provide reasonable doubt."

"I don't want money," I said. "I want vindication, not money."

"As you wish," Robin nodded. "Any monies sued for, will be returned at the close of hostilities."

"I do this, not my father," I said, slightly louder.

Robin just nodded. "I'll call you when the papers are ready," he said.

We drank coffee, spoke of the latest Hispanic student uprising in our fair city, and after a civil amount of time, we said our goodbyes and went back to the car.

My father was quiet, but if he was gloating, it didn't show. We were a few blocks down the road when he said, "Have you been to see Esther since the horse show?"

"Of course I have," I said, staring out the window. I was so angry, angrier than I'd ever been with my father. I wanted to bellow at Max to pull the car over and let me out. I wanted to bellow at my father. I wanted to take out all my frustration on somebody or something, because keeping it bottled up, was eating me alive. "Given half a chance I'm not a bad brother."

"You're angry," he said.

"You got that right," I muttered, and about that time something snapped and my fist hit the glass two or three times in rapid succession. "Max," I snarled, "Let me out of this...thing. Now! Please."

"No," my father said mildly, "Max, drop me at the office and take Bud on home."

"Goddamn it, leave me something!" I cried. "I'm tangled up in all the strings you're trying to pull and I'm choking to death on them! Let me out!"

The car swung over to the curb, and if Max and my father had words about it later, I wasn't aware of it. I got out, thanked Max, and shut the door quietly, like a little gentleman should. And now where was I, exactly? A long way from home, for one thing. Whom should I call? Too far to walk, too early to get drunk, too nicely dressed to go sleep on a park bench someplace, or even to be anonymous.

After a brisk walk and some good, deep breaths of autumn air, I got myself calmed down, called a cab, and got home in time for lunch. Glory caught my face in her hands, kissed me, and asked me how things had gone. I tried to tell her without bringing any particular tone to the telling. I was still fighting that floating, half-sick feeling in my stomach and head that comes with confrontation and anger, and I was still wishing I could just disappear somewhere, though just where a tall, hundred and ninety pound man could vanish to escaped me. I did know I was tired unto death of trying to pretend like I was handling things I wasn't handling at all, and I was wishing mightily that I'd gotten together with Steven Effendi, as I'd promised myself I would. I had meant to. I really had. But having Esther get sick had shifted my focus so abruptly and so thoroughly I'd not even thought about my past and my nightmares until a few nights ago.

Rafael walked through the kitchen while Glory and I were talking, and he threw over his shoulder, "Remember, I'll be needing your help this afternoon."

I knew he didn't actually need my help so much as he was tolerating my presence on the jobsite. It was one of the things I'd promised myself out there in the desert – to learn how to do practical, useful things, and carpentry had presented itself as one avenue of self-improvement. I went upstairs, changed into jeans and a long sleeved Henley, and presented myself to him out at the building site. I couldn't help the bitter thought that I sure didn't need to worry about the state of my hands and fingers anymore, and stood there morosely contemplating them.

The little house was going up fast, and it appeared to be blending in well with its surroundings. A couple of guys were changing a spot in the living room, framing in a fireplace. I'd heard Glory sigh and say she'd love to have one for sitting beside with Rafael on cool evenings, toasting marshmallows and wieners with the boys...and because I'd had absolutely nothing in mind to give her for her birthday, that's what I'd settled on, to Rafael's tacit displeasure. I'd sensed it, and asked him if he objected. He'd said he didn't. But he did. He was watching those two workmen when I got there, and he still looked displeased. "Have you told Glory about this yet?" he asked me, glancing at my hands. I shook my head. "What's the matter with your hands?"

"Nothing," I said.

"Why are you looking at them like that?"

"Like what?"

"Never mind," Rafael sighed. "Do you feel like working this afternoon?"

"Sure," I said, trying to sound convincing.

"I thought you might be too...what is the English word for it? Overwrought." He turned and began walking toward a pair of carpenter's belts which hung from sixteen penny nails to one side of the jobsite.

He took the one that was his, and as he was turning to hand me the other, I said, "What do you mean, too overwrought?"

"Perhaps that's the wrong word," he said, concentrating on his belt. "I want the word that means extremely emotionally upset so that you cannot function physically."

"That's the right word," I said, feeling my hackles rise. "Do I strike you as too emotional to function?"

"Not at the moment," he said, "but it wouldn't do to have you get up on a ladder and pass out now, would it?"

"I assure you," I snapped, "I'm not going to faint and fall off any ladders."

"I did not mean it as a disparaging comment," he said, and he looked disturbingly inclined to smirk. "I know what you have been through these last few days, and if you wanted to spend some time in the house resting...or with my wife...I would understand."

I dropped the tool belt and came squarely to face him. "I don't think you would," I said quietly. "We've danced around this for months. Just say what's on your mind, Rafael."

"I don't know what you mean," he replied, and his eyes were cool.

"Yes, you do. This is about me, and your family. You're jealous of the boys, and I understand that. You're jealous of Glory, and I can understand that even better, but..." I stopped to listen to myself, and the light which had eluded me, began to dawn. "Aw, Rafael, you don't think...aw, hell, you do, don't you? You think I'm in love with your wife." He just looked at me and said nothing, which was more than enough. "Well, you can just forget that nonsense. I could never, ever be in love with Glory."

Then, he bristled. His shoulders hunched up, and though his hands stayed at his sides, they made fists as he said, "Are you implying that she is beneath you, *Amigo*?"

"God, no! She's kind, she's beautiful, she's wise...and she's your wife. She adores you. I'm not sure I'd have the guts to marry a black woman, no matter her mettle, but if I did I'd look for someone exactly like Glory." I could see by the shape of his eyes, that I was getting nowhere with this line of reasoning. "I don't want to get married at all, truth be told. I'm married to my Steinway, even though the honeymoon is apparently over before it began...."

"Only postponed," Rafael said, and a bit of a smile flicked momentarily across his dark features as his fists relaxed. "I watched you the other day...patiently teaching Royal to play some notes on the piano. You allow him to call you Uncle Angel, though it makes your father cringe." We both laughed a little. "You are a kind and gentle man, Senor Aarons. Perhaps a bit too much into the sympathy of the females...but," he shrugged, "to each his own. I think you have yet to come into yours."

"As opposed to you?"

"Because I have had to. I grew up helping to support my family. I knew early what I wanted, because I knew how hard I was going to have to work to get it. That is not to say you have not worked very, very hard to become such an artist as you are. I have watched you drive yourself, hour after hour at the piano, striving for perfection – the imperfection perceptible only to you. In all of this travail, remember the words of Thoreau: *'Public opinion is a weak tyrant compared with our own private opinion. What a man thinks of himself, that it is which determines his fate.'"*

I stood gawping at him like the idiot rich kid I was. My Mexican gardener was quoting Henry David Thoreau to me in his softly accented voice. I knew he was intelligent – very – but I was totally unprepared for Thoreau. What's more, it was a quote that made sense. I was the one eating myself up. I shook my head and turned away so he couldn't see the tears welling up in my eyes. He thought I was too much into being coddled by the ladies. It wouldn't do to have him see me cry.

"Tell me something, Aloysha," he said, walking past me toward a ladder that was leaning against the garage, "Do you regret having become a pianist?"

I was amazed he would ask me such a thing. "No, of course not. What makes you ask?"

"It is obvious you regret something. I just want to know what it is. Those friends of yours in Malibu – with the band – do you regret your friendship with them?"

"No. I like them. Regardless, they are my friends, and they have always been kind to me."

"As you have been with your sisters?"

"Tried to be."

"Esther, she adores you. She lives for you, and now for my sons. Titus calls her his little mother."

I stood where I could again see his face, at least in profile. "That bothers you?"

"Not at all. Does it bother you?"

"Why would it?"

"I only ask," he said gently. "You must have played the events of the horse show over many times in your mind. What could you have done differently?"

"I honestly do not know," I sighed. "I've conjured up a hundred different scenarios. Should I have let her beat on the horse and just ridden away? Should I have walked up to her expecting she'd swing on me? Should I have refused to get involved in the damned thing in the first place, knowing from experience it was bound to end badly? No. Probably. Definitely. Did I solve anything? Probably not, but given the time and the brain I had to work with, I did the best I could."

"I think you showed great restraint," Rafael said, "in the emotion of the moment. And *Senorita* Bobbi...you are so deeply involved with her, and so different from her. So much younger in so many ways, so much older in many others. What is the bond that keeps you together?"

"I don't know," I said. "At least for her part, I think quite probably I'm a convenience more than anything. That is not to say I don't think she likes me. I do. And I, in turn, am very fond of her. I guess...she makes me laugh. She makes me want to try things I've never done before, like singing in public and enjoying it. She was the one who talked me into singing with her for the tour, you know. She was the one who told Mister Saucedo I could sing. Funny thing is, I didn't strangle her for saying so." I stood kicking the sawdust and chuckling humorlessly to myself...at myself. "I honest to God did not invite her to stay with me with the idea of sleeping with her. It just happened, and I sure don't regret it. I know a lot more than I did when she got here."

"Yet she will go on tour. She will go off and leave you, who got her the job singing with the symphony."

"Well, of course she will. What kind of a friend would I be if I asked her to stay home because I had to stay home?"

"What kind of a friend would you be if you denied those fellows in Malibu because they are homosexuals? What kind of friend would you be if you allowed someone helpless to be beaten in anger by another? And as for today, what kind of friend would you be to yourself if you did nothing to defend yourself against those who would do you harm? What good does it do to defend others against and protect them from injustice, then not defend yourself? Stand there and tell me all the things you could have done differently, given the circumstances, to alter the outcome."

I looked at him – really searched his face while I searched my mind, and then shook my head. "Nothing," I said flatly. "Not a single thing."

"Then let it go," he said gently. "Give it to God to sort out, and help me build this house. We have much to accomplish if Mamacita is to have her new home for Christmas."

I stood there about one more minute, then I nodded and said, "You're right. Show me what to do."

CHAPTER ELEVEN

Glory got her house by Christmas, and I got a kiss for my gift of the fireplace. I took a picture of Rafael carrying her over the threshold, though she was the taller and heavier of the two. Then I took a picture of Glory carrying him over the threshold, and kept a copy of it to remind myself that it doesn't really matter who carries whom, only that things are accomplished.

There was joy in that winter, despite my loss. Esther quickly gained her strength back and began to frequent our home again. We sat playing the piano together, or reading beside the fire, often in the company of the boys. If my grandmother objected to our familiarity with them she never said so, and over the months which followed, she began spending as much time with them as Esther and I did. We took them, along with their parents, to the Christmas parade at Disneyland, then out for an evening, and I was comfortable. If people stared at us, I was unaware, and that was the real beginning of acceptance for me.

Kit and Billie welcomed a beautiful baby girl into their family, and I held her cupped in my hands and marveled that she could be so tiny, and so perfect. The stress which had arisen between the two of them seemed to have dissipated with Krista's arrival, and the holidays were full of laughter and good cheer – Hanukkah, and Christmas, and New Year's.

Bobbi spent Christmas in Texas with her parents, and I spent Hanukkah in Tahiti with mine. Racheal and I were not close, but we did not fight. She went one way and I went the other whenever possible. We were civil to one another, but we no longer made any attempt to do things together, nor were we encouraged to. I spent time with Esther, and Racheal spent time with Amber Kestrel, who had come along on vacation with us. She, too, left me alone, and I was profoundly grateful.

I spent time with my Steinway, but I also spent time with my father, learning the family business as best I could through his eyes. We did not have the same personality, and therein lay the difference, of course. Nevertheless, I made progress, and he was pleased with me. I, in turn, was pleased with the choice I had made in Rafael and Glory. Gram and I went off as we pleased with never a backward glance, never a moment's wondering, and the place had never looked better inside or out.

When the holidays were over, and the concert tour was over, Bobbi and I found ourselves closer than ever, and I began considering asking her to marry me. I was twenty-seven, and Bobbi was the only woman in my life. More than once it was on my lips – during romantic walks in the moonlight, after making love, when I saw her laughing with Glory's boys or holding Kit's new baby – but the words never formed themselves. I suppose partly it was the knowledge of my father's displeasure, but it was more than that, though exactly what, I had no idea. I forced it out of my mind and focused on enjoying the time we had together.

The lawsuit dragged on. They were casting Shakespeare's, *Henry the Fifth*, in London. I sent a tape, won an audition, and being thoroughly tired of wearing a suit to work every day, I flew to London and read for the lead. To my amazement, I was offered the part. I asked for a day to think it over, and called home. I got no negatives from that side of the globe. Everyone said to give it a shot, so I did.

Since *Ironwood* had been a near-instant flop, Bobbi flew to London to join me, and we set up housekeeping in a small flat overlooking the Thames. We went for long walks along the river, to plays, and out to dinner. It lasted about a month. I was overwhelmed with lines and rehearsals, and she was overwhelmed with homesickness and the need for Hollywood's magic. I kissed her, and put her on a plane for California.

I worked so hard – harder than I'd ever worked in my life – to portray that young monarch to the very best of my ability. I was grateful beyond measure for the chance they were giving me to redeem myself in my own eyes, and I wanted them to know I'd been wrongly accused. I was someone who could be trusted with a large and demanding part. I was not going to bring shame upon them in any way.

I did go out from time to time with the friends I'd made among the cast and crew. Some of us went to Ireland on a riding holiday, and I met a dark haired, laughing lassie who was very tempting. I did not seduce her, nor did I allow myself to be seduced, but I did make it a point to remember her telephone number. She was the daughter of a landed Irishman, and would have made me a good match. Her name was Colleen, and there are times to this day when I think of her.

We opened to fine reviews, and among my telegrams of congratulation, was one from Albert Saucedo. My first urge was to crumple it in my hand and throw it in the grate, but...I didn't. I made myself read it, and then place it carefully with the others in my dresser drawer.

The next evening when the cheers had died down and I was back in the green room taking off my makeup, I glanced up in the mirror, and my father was standing behind me. "Well done," he smiled, and I was vindicated.

They were all there – the whole family, and Bobbi. It was so good to see them, to wine and dine them and squire them around London as if it were mine to show off. It was so good to hold Bobbi in my arms, and hear her throaty, evil laughter as we undressed each other and fell into bed. We were busy wearing one another out – she was looking down at me, my hands wound in her hair as I pulled her down and kissed her. I was pretty well a gonner at that point, and I was wondering what would happen if I were to get her pregnant. I'd catch hell from Dad, but I'd also be a married man in short order.

I was about three strokes short of yet another deeply delightful orgasm when she took her lips off mine and whispered, "Reggie Clevenger is getting a divorce."

I just...stopped...and stared up at her. "Say what?" I scowled.

"Oh, don't stop," she murmured, taking my bottom lip in her teeth, but I caught her tightly against me and rolled with her so that I was in the superior position. She blinked up at me from where I'd been a moment before. "Is something wrong, Bud?" She murmured, then smiled, moved seductively, wrapped her languid arms around my neck, and I remember distinctly resenting the ejaculation she elicited. For the first time, I felt used by her, and even as I was caught up with her in the throes of passion, I knew... our days together were numbered, not because she desired it, but because I did.

I was standing by the window having a cigarette when I felt her hands slide around my ribcage and felt her cheek pressing against my back. "I shouldn't have said anything. It just...you know, popped into my head, and I thought maybe you'd like some news from back home."

"It's okay," I said, staring into the blackness of the midnight street. "So...have you and Reg set a date yet?"

I heard her gasp. "What on earth are you talking about, Sweetheart? Reggie is somebody to have fun with, that's all. There's nothing serious between us."

"Reggie Clevenger is many things, Bobbi, but he is not 'somebody just to have fun with'. If he's getting a divorce it's because he's got his eye on somebody else. That's always the reason he gets a divorce."

The teasing voice. "You're not jealous, are you?"

"Of course I am," I sighed.

"Then come home with me. I'm lonely, and I get restless when I'm lonely."

There was my invitation. All I had to do, was say the words. Somehow, the beginnings of self-control, I guess, I didn't. "I believe, you encouraged me to make this commitment, Miss Bates, and now that it's made, you want me to break it? What would that do to my reputation?" Even as I was speaking, I was thinking that I should be trying to persuade her to stay in London with me, that I should purr seductively as she did, and try to make her see how much I wanted and needed her to stay...but I didn't, because I realized that, even though I wanted her, I didn't need her, and even though I loved her, I didn't trust her as far as I could throw her. That knowledge made me very sad, and I turned from the window and gathered her into my arms with a gasp of emotion that was painful. "God, I love you so much," I said. "I love you so much."

"I love you, too," she whispered, but her actions told me her thoughts were on sex, not love, and I wondered if she could separate the two. For that matter, I wondered if I could.

It was an odd, unexplainable feeling, like the relief that follows the death of a loved one who has been sick for a long, long time. It hurt. It was a relief. I wasn't sure how to appropriately react to it. I thought about discussing it with Dad over an early breakfast, but he had other things on his mind. He put his napkin in his lap, picked up his coffee cup and eyed me through the steam. "They settled," he said. "Along with a tidy sum, which Robin tells me you're not interested in keeping, GLAS is going to issue a public apology to you for discharging you without merit." He took a sip of coffee and waited a space for my response. "Bud, did you hear me?"

"Um hm," I replied, fiddling with my grapefruit.

"And?"

"And that's good, I guess."

"You guess?"

"Yeah, I guess," I sighed. "It doesn't change what happened, or replace that opportunity for growth and advancement. It won't heal things between GLAS and me, or between Racheal and me. I guess it makes me feel better in a way, but...it really doesn't change anything."

"Yes, it does," my father said quietly. "It makes you the winner."

I thought about that over the next weeks and months, and tried to make sense of it. I felt a little like that old political cartoon of the guy crawling out of the fallout shelter to complete devastation, who stretches out his arms and cries triumphantly, "Mine! All mine!" I had won. What had I won?

I traveled to Greece with friends and viewed the place where the first Olympic Games had been held. What had they won? A wreath of olive branches and the intense admiration of their fellow citizens – both of which faded fast – but for a brief time, it must have been glorious indeed. Then... they went back to work at whatever it was they did to survive. I was winning rave reviews as Henry the fifth, and I wanted to be a concert pianist. I wanted to be the next Sergei Rachmaninoff. I wanted to dominate the latter half of the twentieth century as one of the world's great pianists, but to survive...I was playing Henry the fifth. For whom was *that* the ultimate dream? Whose dream had I stolen along with the part, as someone had stolen my dream and gone off on tour with the symphony? I pondered these things, and got razzed for being morose on holiday.

We took *Henry* on tour to France, Italy, Australia, Canada, and America. We wowed 'em in Paris, Rome, Sydney, Toronto, New York, and most importantly for me, in Los Angeles. I was touted as one of the finest young Shakespearean actors to come along in a good while, and my biggest joy in hearing it, was knowing that Albert Saucedo was hearing it, too. I had survived. Of course I was a plumber when I wanted to be a rocket scientist, but apparently, I was on my way to being one hell of a plumber.

My success with Henry brought me offers in quick succession. I played Petruchio and Bassanio, Edgar and Iago, and I spent the next two years working steadily at something which brought me increasing fame and frustration. As I became better and better known as a serious and versatile actor in the legitimate theater, I got further and further from my dream of being a concert pianist, and there were times, as I practiced hour after hour, that I wondered, "Why am I doing this? Why am I working so hard for something that feels like a hobby, or therapy?" Still, I skimped on sleep so I could keep up on my piano as well as my acting.

The summer of my twenty-ninth year found me home from New York, a sheaf of good reviews in one hand, and an invitation to Bobbi's wedding to Reggie Clevenger burning in the other. I'd known it was coming, of course. I'd known since that night in London, though she swore it had been another fourteen months before she'd had a clue – an odd statement, given the fact they'd been living together for most of that time.

Gram sent her best to me from up near the Arctic Circle, telling me to stay put for once until she got home, and Glory just held me close and shook her head and smiled that inscrutable smile of hers. She had liked Bobbi, but she knew...we weren't a match. She fixed me all my favorite foods, put my favorite flowers on the table and my favorite old comforter on my bed and told me at least twice a day that she was glad I was home. Titus and Royal climbed in my lap, kissed me, and called me Uncle Angel. They thanked me for the presents I'd sent them from all over the world, and I thanked them for their bright, sticky letters, full of love, that had followed me on my travels. Rafael smiled, nodded curtly, and went back to his gardens.

The wedding was out at the club, which pretty much said it all for me in terms of bad vibes. It was a big, frothy affair with lots of bridesmaids and fabric that made noise, and I got the chance to meet Bobbi's mother, who was a complete ditz and hysterically funny. I was jealous, maybe, but I was also profoundly grateful that this woman was Reginald's Clevenger's mother-in-law, not mine. She was a pain in the ass and so was he. Should be a perfect relationship. Bobbi's dad was beside himself with the importance of the whole thing – his daughter marrying a big name director in Hollywood – and I was pleased mostly because I got to play piano for the thing. My first public gig in a very long time. If any of the club members remembered my riding disaster, and the larger disaster which followed, they didn't indicate it by word or deed. It was as though I'd never left; not so much because of their love for me, as their indifference, I suppose. Saucedo was there, and we exchanged nods. His smile seemed genuine enough, and I felt like a heel for avoiding the sonofabitch, but I did. Pointedly.

During the reception I took Bobbi in my arms to dance with her, and as she scowled across the room at Reggie, who was laughing with some leggy infant blonde, I said, "Don't say I didn't warn you, Lady. It's going to be a very bumpy ride."

She slid her arms around my neck and looked intently into my eyes. "Did you really love me?" she asked. I could feel her breasts against me, remembered the lovemaking and the laughter, and it made me ache inside.

"You know I did," I smiled.

"But you never asked me to marry you." I didn't say anything, and she laid her head over on my shoulder. "I would have, you know. In a heartbeat. I adored you. I still do."

Again, I didn't say anything. My father smiled at me from the other side of the dance floor. I just sighed, and held Bobbi close and danced with her, and that night I cried myself to sleep for the last time over Bobbi Jean Bates.

CHAPTER TWELVE

It was summer, and I was absolutely grim about taking some time off to enjoy myself. I'd been working so hard for so long, I'd really forgotten how to relax for more than a few hours at a stretch. I was home for more than my usual couple of days. I wanted to check on Bellwether, and Aarador LA, and that whole aspect of my life...or that whole life...I wasn't sure which it was. No plays on tour. No lines to learn. No costumes to keep track of. No blocking to remember. I was home with my family, and Glory, and Rafael and the boys.

I had Esther to play with. She looked and sounded wonderful. College was agreeing with her, and she even had a beau, so I had to share her, but I didn't mind. He was a nice, imported young Scotsman named Aengus McBride, and, like my sister, he was studying to be a teacher. They were precious and benevolent together. Esther was so soft, and Aengus looked at her with his heart in his green eyes and spoke quietly to her in his lilting brogue. He laughed often, and the first time I caught him kissing her, he blushed to the roots of his dark, curly hair, which I found charming. He spluttered an apology, and I walked away chuckling, sensing for the first time what it was going to be like to be a father with daughters.

Often, they came to my house to relax. Not so many prying eyes of sisters and parents and such. I watched them visiting quietly beside the pool in the shade, or playing with Royal and Titus, who were shooting up into beautiful, intelligent youngsters. Occasionally, I had the opportunity to watch my father watching Esther and Aengus, and seeing the tenderness in his eyes got me through a lot of the rough times with him when I felt he loved me not at all.

Racheal flashed me around a little when I first got home because I was a semi-famous actor and it brought her the attention she so desperately craved when she was with me, but privately she was cool and condescending, and the tone of even seemingly innocent statements had a wounding bite. She had just turned seventeen, and while she was lovely to look at in a too-much-makeup sort of a way, she had a manipulative manner, an acid tongue, and a small, cold heart. As soon as I could, I began avoiding her.

For good or ill, I had Kit to play with. He'd cheated on Billie one too many times, and she'd caught him. Apparently, her definition of cheating more closely resembled mine than his. Their relationship had been strained for half their married life, and now it was over. Billie had taken the kids and moved to Orlando, and Kit's dad had taken a church near there to be close to them. Kit, was alone.

He was maddeningly philosophical about the whole thing. If he missed his children it didn't show much. If he missed his wife, it showed less. He sold the house, got a luxury apartment in a trendy part of town, and took up where he'd left off – or hadn't left off – with the ladies.

We partied a lot that summer, but we also spent some serious time working together with Tommy Sinclair to bring Bellwether Productions into its own; a project put on hold by my unfortunate encounter with Racheal's riding crop, and my subsequent withdrawal from all things familiar.

I suppose it was to our credit that we realized we didn't know what we were doing, and our fourth partner, Dad, stepped in and gave us some pointers. He told us what to look for in marketable productions, how to estimate production costs, how to pay ourselves first, and how to stay solvent over the long run. So far, we had only dabbled. I had been on the run, Kit had been on the make, and only Tommy had been really serious about Bellwether. Now it was his turn, and it was mostly to him that my father talked. Dad was a patient investor and a thorough teacher, but he was also a man who expected to make money from his investments, and what he taught us, he did not teach lightly.

It was like going back to high school. No. It was more like going back to junior high, where all the teachers know exactly what's going on with you. They know you're a lost cause but they try to teach you something anyway and they do their best to keep you alive long enough to grow into yourself and out of your state of pubescent idiocy. The three of us were pushing thirty...Tommy was already thirty...and by then my father was going underground with his power – long arms, broad shoulders – into everything, still ruthless and manipulative, but from a distance, where he could view the whole board and all the players on it.

In many ways it wasn't real to me. It still isn't. He was my dad. He was increasingly distant, but I chalked that up more to my age and my lifestyle than his. I said the words to myself, though I would never, ever have told anyone else that my father was a rich and powerful man. I'd gone to school with those kids and that train of thought; fast cars, designer sweaters, and not enough common sense to come in out of the rain. I laugh when I think of how it stung when Maddy O'Halloran...she was Maddy Ovcharek, then...accused me of not wanting to get baby pee on my expensive sweater. She might have been right, but the fact she noticed the expensive sweater, embarrassed me half to death.

I was Gram's boy. Classic cars, classy clothes, *nobless oblige.* I knew I was privileged, and I was grateful. The thought of being better than anybody else honestly never occurred to me. Mrs. Gustavson had only vocalized what I had always known – if not for the graciousness and love of my grandmother, I would be dead or in a mental institution, grappling with my demons.

I sat with Tommy and Kit and focused on what my father had to tell us, and I have never regretted it. Say what you will about dear old Dad, The White Lion of Hollywood, but he has more business sense than anyone I've ever known, and I've known some sharp people. Whatever time he found for us, we found for him. For a couple months Kit stopped playing every woman's heartthrob, I put my piano and my Shakespeare aside, and we gave our workdays wholly to Tommy and Dad.

Still, that was only eight or ten hours out of those long summer days. We were young and energetic to a fault. We had plenty of time left to play guy games. We revisited old haunts, old dreams, and in doing so, Kit and I realized we'd left our beloved *Tiger Lily,* tied up alone at the dock for far too long. Neither of us could remember the last time we'd been to see her, though I feared it was the time Kit had chucked that unrecognizable part into the green water of the marina, and we'd wound up in Tijuana with our pants over a chair. That seemed like such a long time ago. Not long enough ago to be able to forget it, mind you, but a long time ago, nonetheless. I wondered what kind of shape she was in. The boat, that is.

A couple days later, while the guilt was still fresh in my mind, I was on my way with Rafael to a little nursery with great heirloom roses not too far from Malibu, and I asked him if he'd mind if we stopped for a bit at the marina so I could run down to the slip. He looked across at me from the driver's seat of the pickup and gave me a nod. "Fine," he said, and when I got out of the truck I asked him if he wanted to come along.

"I don't know what we'll find," I warned, but he just shrugged, and followed me down the fork of docks to the boat.

When I got there I stopped short and groaned. She was afloat, but that was about all. The bottom was crusted and misshapen with barnacles clear to the waterline, the zincs long gone. She was dirty, curtains faded and sagging, rents in what had once been her marine blue canvas.

Rafael gave me a look that made me feel like a child abuser, and I cringed under its weight. I knew how he felt about his children, animate and otherwise. I remembered how carefully his rusty old pickup had been cleaned for our first meeting. The Ford F-250 I'd bought him the first month he'd come to work for me looked better than it had the day he drove it off the lot in San Fernando. His tools were sharp and shiny. Everything in his care spoke of intrinsic value and meticulous attention to detail. I was scum. There was an apology sputtering at my lips when he said, "Nice boat." There was no inflection.

"Well, see, that's just it," I responded, trying not to wring my hands and look as guilty as I felt, "she could be. We just...I just..." I exhaled sharply and slapped my hands at my sides. "Damn. I screwed up. Just look at that beautiful old boat. She's a bigger mess than she was before, and that's saying plenty. I'm amazed they haven't made us take her out of the marina."

"Fortunately, ugly is not grounds for expulsion," Rafael said, and for some unfathomable reason there was laughter in his voice. "Let us take a closer look at this treasure of yours."

I looked at him out of the corner of my eye. If he was being sarcastic, I wasn't getting it. I walked instead of talking, and when I looked up and to my left toward the marina office, I could see Steven Schooler's round, bespectacled face in the window, watching us. I gave him a casual, Rose Parade sort of a wave and tried to telegraph with body language my concern over the condition of this poor boat. What idiot, I ask you, what idiot had allowed this travesty?

By now Rafael was running his right hand slowly along the side of the boat, thumping gently with his palm. "Very nice boat," he said again, and to my amazement, he meant it. "Solidly put together. She has many good times left in her."

"You...know boats?" I ventured.

He shrugged with his eyebrows more than his shoulders. "My father, he was always a man of the soil. Always he worked the big haciendas, and his father before him. But my mother's father...he was a boat builder." He reached for the zipper on the canvas and carefully worked it up, bits of deteriorating cloth making a forlorn blue fuzz in the watery, late morning sunshine. "He fished, my grandfather, but his love was for the wood and the sails and the engines, and after a while the other fishermen came to depend on him for their repairs, and so he put his nets away and spent his days repairing old boats and building new ones."

"The bad news is, he's dead," I muttered, then flushed at my insensitivity. Rafael's eyes had a faraway look in them, and their usual glittering intelligence had softened with remembrance.

He just laughed and stepped lightly on board. I noted that the engine compartment, which had been open the day of our Tijuana trip, was still open. I wondered if what I was thinking was showing on my face. I sincerely hoped it wasn't. I'd been without a sexual partner for long enough that Rosarita from Tijuana was beginning to sound pretty damned good, and, somehow, I didn't think Rafael would be quite as tractable as Kit had been. Rafael and I liked each other, I think, but we were not friends. We were most certainly not to the point of sharing intimate thoughts and manly desires.

"Big engine," he said. "I'll bet she can get up and move."

"No," I said flatly, "She can't. The engine's not all there, and, truth be told, Kit and I can't figure out which parts are missing."

Rafael gestured at the hole in the floor. "May I have a look?"

"Be my guest," I said, and tossed him the coveralls I'd left over the passenger's seat.

He stepped into them, though they were laughably too big, and eased himself down into the cramped space. "How long have you had her?" he asked, looking at the engine rather than at me.

"We bought her the summer after our senior year of high school," I said, squatting on my heels to watch him. "She belonged to a guy everybody called Old Man Bill, and when he died, his wife just wanted to get rid of the boat. She didn't want much for it. Just wanted out from under the upkeep, the slip fees...the memories, maybe. Anyway, Kit and I bought her. We had such big plans, you know? She was going to be the classiest boat in the marina. But, life started happening, and this is the result."

Rafael didn't make a direct reply. He was quiet for a bit, poking and clanking around, and then said, "My grandfather...I would go every summer and work on the boats with him. He taught me to repair boats, and to build boats, and to sail..." he chuckled, "as much as one can teach a small boy anything. But he gave me his love of the sea and of boats, and it feels good to be here." He glanced briefly up and smiled, then reached for a screwdriver and bent forward again into the engine compartment.

The hope was almost more than I could contain. "Do you think this boat can be...fixed?" I grimaced. "She looks pretty literally like the wreck of the Hesperus to me."

"All cosmetic," he chuckled. "You just don't know what you're looking at, that's all. Where is the distributor cap?"

"Distributor cap," I intoned, and made a show of looking for whatever that might be.

"Looks like a little black octopus," Rafael said, and I sat back onto my butt with a humorless grunt of remembrance.

"Oh. That, I think, is what dear Kristoffer sent flying off into the deep water," I said, pointing with my chin. "Thataway."

I heard Rafael sigh. "Why, exactly, would he do that?" he asked, and his elbows came to rest on the rim of the engine compartment as he studied my face.

"Well, he said he didn't know why a diesel would have one of those."

"Why would he think this was a diesel, Bud?"

"Uh...." That was a stumper. "I guess we thought all boats, or at least one this big, would have to be a diesel?" It came out as a question. We'd been puddling around in the guts of this thing, and we didn't even know what kind of fuel it used. That had to make a difference in the way the engine was constructed...didn't it? I swallowed what was left of my pride and asked.

"It's gas," Rafael said, and to his credit he didn't laugh, but his eyes and the determined line of his mouth said he was about to. He held something up. "Do you know what this is?"

"A sparkplug." I said. I knew that much from the motor pool in the army. I said it in a deep voice, so this bit of knowledge would make more of an impression on the chuckling Chicano in front of me.

"That's right. A gas engine uses spark plugs. A diesel uses glow plugs. A gas engine has a distributor. A diesel doesn't."

"I thought, I really did, that marine engines were different, you know? It was such a beautiful boat. Look at all this mahogany, and that nice big cabin. Full galley, vee berth up front. I just assumed we could..." I sighed and looked away. All of a sudden I was a tad melancholy. There had been so many things I'd taken for granted these last few years. So many things I'd 'just assumed'. I'd just assumed that young people's concert would launch my musical career, and instead I'd found myself stuffed in a closet. I'd just assumed Bobbi would be a fling I could forget, and I was keenly feeling her loss. I'd just assumed by this age I'd know what I wanted to be when I grew up, and so far all that was a faraway dream. I'd just assumed that if we read the manual, Kit and I could put forth a minimum of effort and have something enduring and beautiful in *Tiger Lily.* What we had, was an embarrassing, demoralizing mess. I wondered if my dad had strolled by here on one of his visits to the family yacht, which was moored in a boat house in another hub of the marina. Why he would be interested was beyond me, but the fear that he'd see how I took care of my things gave me a slight but very cold tingle down my spine, and I never forgot it.

"Don't feel so bad," Rafael said, misreading my concern. "She will forgive you. She needs lots of work, but it's summer, and you have much time. I will help you...if you'd like."

"I'd love it," I said, "if you have the time. You can be our third partner."

Rafael flushed just a little. "I would not presume..." he began, and I cut him off.

"No. You work on it, it's part yours. You cruise on it, you fish from it, period," I said.

"Her," he grinned, and we shook hands. That, I think, was where our friendship finally started, and it has endured for many years.

Each time we left to work on the boat that summer, Glory shook her head and stood with her hands on her hips, reminding us of what all needed doing on our hilltop, but we always had a good lunch with us when we went, and often we had Titus, and Royal, and Esther with us. And because we had Esther, we often had Aengus, as well. Aengus was a mechanic of some talent, and while Kit and I scrubbed and scraped and polished and sanded above the waterline, and Esther sat at a portable sewing machine in the galley, sewing new curtains and watching the little boys sand woodwork, Aengus and Rafael took the engine completely apart and proceeded to rebuild her, part by part, inch by inch, with lots of new chrome and freshly painted covers.

I put on my wetsuit and my tanks and got underneath, scraping away the barnacles and replacing the zincs. It was hard work, but *Tiger Lily* once again rode level in the water. Her railings sparkled with polish, her aging wood shone with much scrubbing, and the teak trim on her deck glowed a rich, deep brown. I was in the water cleaning one of the screws when Rafael told me to swim clear, and I heard the engine crank over and come to life with the throaty, coughing growl of a tiger in the bush.

We all cheered, and our neighbors in the boats around us came out and applauded, and that afternoon we cast off with much ceremony and eased over to the fuel dock. We never left the marina, but it was a cruise of great import, nevertheless. That week we had her hauled out and painted bright white with marine blue trim and bottom. The lettering blazed above the newly plated swim steps:

Tiger Lily
Malibu CA. USA

There she was. New ropes, new canvas, new curtains, new paint, new life. She looked loved, and somehow, it shook me free of the stagnation I'd been feeling – the aimlessness, the determination to "have fun" at... something. This was done, and would never be done. This was for life, and it was life. Each of us had done what we could, and it had been enough. We got Glory, and all of us went for a boat ride along the coast. We laughed, and ate, and fished, and on the way back to port we got written up for not having our current registration sticker displayed. It didn't matter. I was pleased that *Tiger Lily* needed a registration sticker at all. "A birth certificate," I thought to myself, "It's a girl."

We dropped Esther and Aengus off at the Bel Air house, and when we got home Glory and Rafael took the little boys straight to their house for a nice cool bath before supper. I checked myself over and headed upstairs to do likewise. I was stripping off my sweaty, salt sprayed shirt when I heard a noise in my grandmother's bedroom. Gram was in Alaska and I knew she wasn't due home, so I cracked the door without knocking, not sure what I'd find. I thought maybe it was Docker.

Gram had gotten the boys a puppy for Christmas, because after all, boys needed dogs. It said something about her age, I guess, and how mellow she was becoming. I'd never had a dog...not that I'd ever wanted one, and Dad said that even though he'd begged for years for a dog, he'd never had one, either. They chased the birds, you know. Well, squatty little *Master Widget of Waddles*, AKA Docker the cocker, though admittedly adorable, was a world class bird chaser and troublemaker, and I wondered as I cracked the door open if he'd escaped his chain link and nudged open the outside door to my grandmother's room. Serve her right if he was on her bed, chewing up her favorite house slippers.

It was not Docker. It was Racheal who was in our grandmother's beautiful big four poster, and she was not alone. She and the boy she was with were both very naked and extremely busy, and even if I'd kicked the door open they probably wouldn't have noticed for all the groaning and gasping and squeaking of bedsprings that was going on. Actually, neither of them was aware of my presence until my hand closed like a vice on the back of the young man's perspiring neck. "And you would be...besides dead?" I growled.

He jumped under my hand and struggled to roll toward me, his breath reeking of alcohol. "Shit!" he yelped, "Oh, Jesus shit!"

"Goddamn you, Bud!" my sister said at the same time, and the slur in her speech told me she was as drunk as he was. Rage and disgust boiled up in me, and I heard my own teeth grinding together – fighting the urge to shake this kid like a rag.

"You're cursing at me?" I grated, still grasping the boy by the scruff of his neck. I lifted just a little and pulled him the rest of the way off my sister, who grabbed at the sheet they'd kicked aside and sat up, hate and fear mixed about evenly in her eyes.

"Please, don't hurt me," the boy said, and his voice was ludicrously high. It went well with the pimply face and the scrawny ass. "Racheal said nobody would be home."

"You'd better have a condom on that limp little dick of yours," I growled, lifting him still higher to examine him. His hands dropped protectively across in front of him as though he feared I'd bite the thing off, but before he got himself covered up I could see...no condom. "If you've done anything to damage my sister..." I began, and Racheal snorted in disgust.

"Don't worry, Vernon, he's not going to hurt you," she said.

"Oh, please don't do him the disservice of telling him I won't hurt him, Racheal. I most assuredly will," I replied, "and I might just hurt you, too, for good measure. Now, get up, get your clothes picked up, get in the bathroom, and get dressed so I can take you home."

She glared, and she sneered, but she went, cursing me all the while. I let go my grip on Vernon's neck and he slumped back onto the bed, dragging the sheet up to cover himself and pulling his knees up in a protective posture. "Don't hurt me," he said again. His face was white, and his eyes filled with tears. "Please, don't hurt me," he groaned, and puked on my grandmother's imported tapestry bedspread.

"Oh...for Godssake," I grimaced. "I ought to rub your nose in that, you pissant. How long have you been screwing my sister?"

"Just this once, I swear to God," he managed, wiping his forearm first across his mouth, then across his sweating forehead. "She just...it was her...." He looked up at me, then quickly away, and his expression hardened just a little. "It's not like I'm the first guy who ever fucked your sister," he muttered. "I'm not even on the first team who ever fucked your sister." His eyes widened a bit as he considered the wisdom of this revelation, and dropped his eyes back to the stinking pool of vomit on the bedspread. "She's not pregnant. She's got one of those...things. A diaphragm, you know? She showed it to me."

"Oh, well...that makes it all okee dokee then, doesn't it, Vernon?" I asked. My hands were still twitching with the need to choke him until his eyes popped out.

He must have noticed that, because he bolted from the bed, gave me a sudden push, grabbed his jeans, and hit the French doors at a dead run. A minute later the squealing of tires on brick told me he'd gotten to wherever he'd stashed his car – probably still naked – and was putting the whole thing behind him as quickly as ever he could. I looked around. His shoes and socks were over by Gram's rocker, his tee shirt tossed casually across one arm. His briefs lay near the open French doors, where they'd fallen out of his jeans. Despite the gravity of the situation it struck me funny, and I was chuckling when Racheal opened the bathroom door.

"Go ahead, gloat, you sonofabitch," she muttered. "How many times have you screwed somebody in this bed?"

I raised my eyebrows and smiled at her. "Never," I said. "I have more respect than that for our grandmother."

"Oh, the great you. You screw them in the next room and let Gram listen to it instead. Does she get off on it? I'm surprised you two aren't in bed together...or are you?"

"You're drunk," I said, "and you're even uglier than when you're sober, if that's possible."

"Big deal," she tossed over her shoulder, and headed for the French doors.

"Where do you think you're going?" I asked, and she spun on me, staggering a little in the process.

"I'm going...somewhere...away from here and from you," she said. "I don't have to take this from you."

"Take what, Racheal?" I snapped. "I haven't even started with you. Get in the bathroom, get a damp towel, and clean up this mess that little Vernon left on Gram's bedspread."

"What if I don't?"

"I'll rub your nose in it," I said, and took a step toward her. Then, she began to scream.

Before the echoes had died, Glory and Rafael were both standing in the French doors. "He's going to kill me!" Racheal sobbed, pointing at me with a shaking finger. "He says he's going to kill me!"

Glory's eyes moved from my sister's face to mine, then around the room, taking in the sights and smells without changing expression. "Any particular reason?" she drawled at last, "or just a whim?"

"Just a whim," I said. "Actually, I told her to clean up the puke her boyfriend deposited on the bedspread before he left. I suppose that qualifies as a fate equal to or worse than death."

Glory's eyes turned back to Racheal. "Child," she said, "I believe we done had this conversation some time back. You remember?"

Racheal's eyes narrowed and her mouth twisted with hate. "You lying, fucking nigger," she hissed. "You promised...." Glory's hand came up in silent warning, and Racheal bit off her words and stood gasping and shaking with unspent emotion. I had gasped in turn, but Glory graciously ignored me and went on as though Racheal had said nothing at all.

"You Gram and me said we wasn't goin' to say nothin' that once, but she also told you to keep you love life outta this house. I see you ain't done that, and now big brother's involved. That complicates matters some, don't it, Missy Racheal?" Racheal just stood there, balling and unballing her fists, flaring her fingers with their blood red nails like talons, and staring at the wall between Glory and me. I opened my mouth, and Glory shut it for me with a shake of her head. "Time Mama and Daddy knew about this," Glory said gently. "You gonna get yourself hurt, and you gonna take them with you. This gotta stop."

"It's none of your business!" Racheal exploded. "You're a servant!

You're a servant!" She flung herself at Glory, eyes blazing with fury, fingers arched into claws. As she spun away from me toward Glory her long hair whipped out behind her, and I caught it in my left hand, pulling down as I did so. She landed flat on her back and lay there sobbing, screaming, and pounding her hands and feet on the floor in an apoplexy of rage.

I looked at Glory, and at Rafael, exhaled very slowly to be sure my voice wouldn't shake, and said, "Leave. Please." Rafael nodded curtly and bowed out, fists still tightly clenched at his sides. Glory remained a moment longer in the doorway. Her expression asked, then warned, then acknowledged, and she, too, was gone.

When Racheal had kicked and screamed all she could, and lay sobbing on the carpet, I jerked her up by one arm, hauled her into the bathroom and shoved her clothes and all into a cold shower. When the screams had subsided once again, I jerked her out, and tossed a towel at her. When she began to dry herself I said, "It's not for you. It's for that puke on my Grandmother's bedspread." That time, she cleaned it up, stormed outside and flung the towel off the balcony to the lawn below. I poured a cup of Glory's strong hot coffee in her, and hauled her uppity little ass home. She thanked me by puking in my car – twice.

Eight weeks later, she was out of the very private school she'd been attending and off to a very, very private boarding school in Vermont. I didn't ask why, and didn't want to know. I'd dreaded taking her home that summer's day as much as she'd dreaded going, and for good reason. My father had taken one look at her, sent her to her room and turned on me. "This is the best you could do with her?" he'd demanded, and I'd just stood there, shaking my head.

I wasn't sure what to say. Had Gram said anything to him about the previous incident? Incidents? I didn't know, and I didn't want to. I was trying to get my own act together, and being my sister's keeper didn't figure in there anywhere. He'd dismissed me with a summary wave of his hand, and, like Vernon, I'd scurried to my car and gotten the hell out of Dodge.

I never asked Gram or Glory about what had been said either before or after the incident. Glory was summoned for a conference at the Bel Air house that I was not invited to attend. When Gram got home a few days later, she and Glory put their heads together for a bit, and I made myself scarce. I did notice that about the time a pregnancy would have begun to show, Racheal was on her way to Vermont. She did not say goodbye to Gram, to Esther, or to me.

With Racheal's departure a rare kind of peace settled over the deepening autumn. I found myself working longer hours at Aarador LA, and spending less time at the keyboard. I began to think I could be happy as a businessman – a tycoonlet. My father had had so many disappointments. I could do this for him. I thought more in terms of suits than costumes, of books more than sheet music. I could sense Glory watching me, studying me, and I assured her that I knew what I was doing. "I'm just growing up, I guess," I'd smiled, thanking her for breakfast.

"Growin' old is more like it," she'd said without inflection, and turned back to her chores in the kitchen.

I was walking arm in arm with Esther in the drifting leaves on the UCLA campus, when she said more or less the same thing. "You seem...too old for your years," she said, shading her eyes with one hand as she smiled up at me. "You're not going to do anything stupid like give up your music, are you?" I was startled and it must have registered on my face, because she chuckled, catching a bright yellow leaf on the toe of her boot as it drifted near the ground. "You must promise me never, ever to do that, Bud. You were born to play the piano."

"I can still play the piano," I said, and she shook her head vigorously.

"No. You can't ever play the piano as a hobby. It's your life. You were born to play the piano. You have to promise me you'll never lose your focus."

"And what makes you think I've lost my focus?" I grinned.

"That suit you're wearing. The dull, businesslike set of your jaw. You were born to make music. You have to promise me you'll always make music." She picked up a sycamore leaf and waved it under my nose. "Weren't you going to go to Juilliard and get your doctorate? What happened to that?"

I stared up through the branches which were growing steadily more bare, and wondered what I'd tell her. Should I say I'd lost my forward momentum? That I was afraid of never being good enough to justify the time and the work? Was that the truth? Should I say I was comfortable just being home on my hilltop with my grandmother and my housekeeper's sons? That I was content to watch them grow and be a part of their lives? Should I say I was trying to make up for Racheal by being extra good for Dad? All that sounded painfully juvenile, and just admitting I didn't have a clue, sounded painfully stupid. Esther's brown eyes said she expected a reply.

I was saved by Aengus, who hailed us from the steps of Pauley Pavilion and walked to meet us. He gave my sister a kiss, and took her from me, tucking her arm securely beneath his and blowing on her hand to warm it. It gave me a little twinge of jealousy deep in my soul, but I didn't let it register on my face. Instead I said, "Well, tomorrow's Halloween, Aengus. In this country we dress up as something weird and go party, so what's your plan?"

Esther took a deep breath. "I know what I'm going as," she said, and when she looked up at me and smiled it was like looking into the sun. Aengus put his arm around her, and she slowly drew her left hand out of her coat pocket and took off her glove. "I'm going as an engaged woman," she said, and showed me the ring.

"And I'm going as her proud husband-to-be," Aengus said. They stood, waiting for a reaction.

I exhaled sharply, and wiped at the tears in my eyes, and laughed. "This...is wonderful," I said, and I could hear my voice shaking. "Aengus, welcome to the family." A thought crossed my mind and I added warily, "You have told Dad, I assume."

"Aye," the young man laughed. "I went to him and asked for Esther's hand in marriage like a proper gentleman should. To my everlastin' relief, he didn't eat me, nor even roar overmuch. We've set the summer solstice as our weddin' day, Bud, and I'd be proud of you'd be my Best Man."

"Oh, please say yes!" Esther laughed, and so of course I did.

I congratulated them both again, reminded them to be at the appointed spot at four O'clock so I could pick them up, gave Esther a kiss and a squeeze, shook Aengus's hand, and was walking back toward my car when Esther called, "Bud?"

I turned back. "What, Mrs. McBride, mother of all my nieces and nephews?"

She just laughed and shook her dark hair. "Remember what I told you!" she called. "Lose the suit!" I made a deprecating gesture and kicked my way through the leaves back to the car. I was very happy...and very sad.

Dad and I had lunch together, and his eyes were dancing like a little kid. All he could talk about was Esther's wedding. Where would it be? What time of the day? What would she wear? What sort of flowers should she carry? Where would they go on their honeymoon? He never spoke of trivial things, and it tickled me to listen to him, so I egged him on by asking for details. He had them all. I realized Esther was going to be lucky indeed if she had anything to say about her own nuptials.

We pointedly avoided the subject of Racheal and where she fit into all this. Would she be one of the bridesmaids? It was only proper and traditional, and everybody else certainly seemed to be spoken for in this. It would be a double ring ceremony, so both Titus and Royal could be ring bearers, and a job would be created for Britt, so he didn't feel left out. Of course Titus would carry Esther's ring; it was her first and dearest wish. Would Racheal deign to be in a wedding with the sons of the hired help? Quite probably not, which solved the problem of proper and traditional, not to mention my dark notion that she might appear in a maternity smock...no... silly thought. The wedding wasn't until June. She'd have had her baby by then...if she was having a baby. God in heaven, what would that little witch do to a helpless baby? She wasn't having a baby, was she? I chewed my salad and blinked my big cow eyes at my dad, and kept those thoughts and others like them, to myself.

I excused myself from the office just a tad early and headed up to UCLA. The traffic could get really heavy, even on campus, and I wanted to be on time. I had a dozen questions – a hundred! Being Best Man was a great honor, but what about the music? Who would play the piano for her? Who would play the wedding march for my beautiful sister? I began arranging it in my head, tapping out counterpoint with my left hand on the steering wheel and wondering if I should play the organ instead of the piano, and what kind of ceremony it would be, since Aengus was Christian and Esther was Jewish. I knew it would be very big, and very traditional. God, she was going to be beautiful. She was going to be so beautiful. Maybe Aengus would wear a kilt....

There was a jam of traffic in the very spot I wanted to be. I could see it from half a block away. Not just cars, but people milling around. Then...I saw the ambulance pulling out, slowly, lights but no siren...and an icy shock went from my testicles to my throat. I stumbled out of the car and ran.

Aengus was sitting on the bench where we'd arranged to meet. He was sitting up very straight, staring straight ahead. He had Esther's book bag clutched to his chest. I pushed through the loosening knot of onlookers and skidded up beside him. "Where's Esther?" I cried. But I knew.

He turned toward me in slow motion, and to this day I can tell you how many times his eyes blinked before any words came from his half opened mouth. Six times. Six. "They...they wouldn'a let me go wi' her," he whispered. "They took my Esther, and left me here. They said she was gone and there was nothin' I could do, you know, but...I could have held her hand. I could have held her wee hand so it dinna get cold. She always has cold hands. Wee, cold hands."

He began to sob, rocking the book bag. I took it from him, and took him in my arms, and we rocked together for what seemed a long, long time. Then, in a fog of grief so thick we could hardly see, we found my Benz with the door still ajar, and went back to my father's office.

CHAPTER THIRTEEN

My Esser's dead?" Titus asked again. He was sitting in my lap at the kitchen table, head tipped slightly to one side, watching the tears slide down my face. "My Esser's dead? Forever?" He was not a baby anymore, but this was beyond his ken.

I nodded, grateful for the weight of Glory's hand on my shoulder as she stood behind me. "Her heart stopped beating," I said. That was what the man at Dad's office had said – massive heart failure – not a moment's suffering.

"She has gone to heaven to live wi' Jesus," Aengus said from his seat across the table. He put down the cup of coffee he'd been struggling to drink, and forced a smile. "She won't be sick anymore, or have pains in her chest anymore. She'll be able to run, and play all the rough and tumble kinds of games."

"And we won't see her ever again, will we?" Titus asked.

"Only in our hearts," Aengus said, and two more tears rolled out of his green eyes and down his cheeks. His expression of sheer and utter exhaustion did not change. "Do you know what the last thing was that she said, Titus? She was talkin' of you, and how you were going to be carryin' her weddin' ring on a little satin pillow, and that you'd be wearin' a little blue tuxedo, and that you were goin' to be the cutest little man in the whole world. Her little friend. 'My little friend, Titus,' she said, and in the next breath she was just...gone."

"God, this is not happening," I grated. "Please tell me this isn't happening."

I heard the kitchen door close and Rafael's voice behind me.

"What?" he said, voice sharp with alarm. "What isn't happening?"

"Esther's gone," Glory said softly, and I could hear the tears in her voice.

Rafael gasped, and for a long minute or so there was no sound but him, breathing heavily into his palms. The door opened again and I heard Royal say, "Mama, there's nobody...." He trailed off and I knew he was looking from face to face, though my cheek was against Titus's head and my eyes were closed. "Uncle Angel, why are you crying? Why is everybody crying?"

I had to say it again. Through numbed lips and an icy fog that didn't lift, I told him my sister was dead...that our beautiful Esther was dead.

"Come," Rafael said suddenly, in a voice that jarred all of us. "Bud, get on your feet. You, too, Aengus. Mama, get your coat and jackets for the boys." I gave him a bleary look and he caught me by the upper arm and heaved me to my feet, taking Titus in the process. "I dropped your grandmother in Bel Air without walking her to the door," he said. "You need to be with her. At a time like this we must be *familia*. We need to go."

I nodded without comprehending. Apparently I put on a jacket, because I remember Rafael stripping it back off me again as we walked into my parents' house. I know Aengus was with us, and I remember Titus and Royal running to my grandmother and swarming into her lap, and I remember that Glory did nothing to stop them. She headed for the kitchen while Rafael collected the coats, and Max and Coco were relieved of their duties and allowed to grieve, and soon there was hot coffee, and fresh tea, and a nip of this and that for the nerves, and we sat in that unspeakably huge, cold, elegant room, looking from one to another and trying to grasp what had happened to us.

I was sitting next to my grandmother, holding her hand, and my mother was leaning against my father's chest, sobbing as though her heart would break. He'd tried everything to comfort her – all manner of soft words and stroking and gestures – to no avail.

His eyes blazed suddenly with the utter frustration of it all, and when they landed on me, I quailed inside. I tightened my grip on Gram's hand, as though she could protect me, but she'd missed the intensity of my father's gaze. She returned the squeeze for what she'd assumed it was, and excused herself to go check on Aengus, who'd gone upstairs to Esther's room. I was alone. I met his gaze by the physical effort of raising my chin, and gave him a tight knot of a smile.

"Why did you leave?" he asked.

"I..." There were no thought processes. "What do you mean?"

"You know what I mean," he said. He was replacing grief with anger. I knew him, and I knew it was going to be terrible.

"I'm sorry, Sir, I don't," I said quietly. "Just tell me what you mean."

"Why did you leave me at the office and take off?"

I blinked at him. "You told me to," I said.

"You found it necessary to drive all the way up that goddamned mountain, instead of coming here to your mother?"

"But..." I fought the stammer I could hear rising in my voice. "I needed to tell my family...I mean...."

"We're your family," he said through his teeth.

"I thought maybe Gram was home, and I wanted Glory and Rafael and the boys..."

"We're your family," he said again in a dangerous voice.

"Gram..."

"You knew where she was, and it wasn't up there on that mountain. What the hell's the matter with you, that you choose your servants, your staff, over your family, Aloysha?"

I just shook my head, and took a deep breath, swallowing at the soreness in my throat. I didn't have a clue why I'd gone home. Why do children hide under their beds? Where should I have gone? I found my tongue and articulated my last thought.

"You should have stayed with me," he grated. "You should have helped me tell your mother."

"I left because you told me to," I mumbled. I wanted to jump up off that white leather sofa and run...right to Glory's warm and comforting arms. Then, of course, I knew why I'd gone home. Glory was my dear and understanding friend. She wasn't a servant. She was my friend and I needed the comfort and stability that she and her family provided me. I needed it right then, but I didn't move from the couch to get it – suicide has never been my thing.

"I'm sorry if I disappointed you," I said, and my voice was a little firmer than it had been. "I wanted to tell Glory and her family, who loved Esther very much, and I knew deep down that you needed time to be with Mother. We're here now and we'll do anything we can to help you get through this." The sound of my own words made me want to laugh. I wasn't in any shape to help anybody, least of all my powerful, self-assured father. Hell, I couldn't even help myself.

A hand came down gently, firmly on my shoulder and Max's faintly British tenor said, "Who's going to tell Racheal?"

The look my father gave that dear man was enough to freeze water. "Did I ask for your input?" he said, and his lip curled ever so slightly at the corner and stayed that way as his eyes strafed the presence beside me. There was no reply. "Then get back to your duties," he said. The hand patted me twice, and the warmth I'd felt departed with Max.

"He's right," my mother said, moving slightly away from my father and sitting up a little straighter to dry her eyes. "Being rude to poor Max isn't going to help things, J.R."

The curl relaxed out of his lip, and my father reached over and patted my mother's hand. She pulled it back slightly, and he was nonplussed. "Cat..." he began, then sighed, and got up from the white leather sofa. "I'll be right back," he said, and headed toward the servants' part of the house.

I was amazed. Stunned as I was by events, there was yet room for amazement. Dad was going to apologize to Max, simply because my mother had implied that he should. He got about ten steps before he slowed; another ten before he faltered and stopped. I could have counted to three slowly before he turned around, when he did, his face was frozen into the icy crags I had come to dread over the years. Even my mother quailed a little, and he was far easier on her than on me.

I didn't wait for his mouth to open. "I'll go get her," I said. "I'll go get Racheal." I ran the back of my hand under my nose and realized I was long past needing a handkerchief. I sniffed and looked away from my parents into the gaping maw of the marble fireplace on the opposite wall, feeling light and detached from all sorrow and sadness. Feeling...nothing. "I mean, somebody has to go get her. We can't just call her with the bad news and tell her to get herself to the nearest airplane."

There was a long pause while Dad worked his jaw and stared after me into the fireplace. It was very black, very cold, and looked very inefficient. I thought about the flames dancing on my own hearth, and wondered which unlucky child would inherit this opulent mausoleum. I wondered how my mother, who loved the bright reds and golds of the fleeting Russian sun, could live in these unwelcoming and austere surroundings. I looked from the hearth to the hunting scene, and shuddered.

"She never loved Esther," Dad said, just above a whisper, as though it were being strangled out of him. "She..."

"Racheal adored her big sister," I said firmly, and was appropriately surprised. Apparently, so was Dad, who turned and gave me his attention. "She's going to need a shoulder to cry on, or someone to yell at. I'll go get my sister. You guys take care of each other, and the..." I made myself say it, "...funeral arrangements, and I'll be back with Racheal as quickly as I can. I'll get Rafael to take me to the airport. If I fly standby, I can probably catch a flight out tonight."

My father waved me aside over his shoulder as he turned away. "I'll see what we have at Hollywood-Burbank," he said, and proceeded up the staircase without a backward glance.

It was Max who drove me to the airport, "Because," he muttered, stuffing me into the limo, "I just might do your father bodily harm if I stay around. That wouldn't do now, would it?"

"I don't even know where I'm going, do you know that?" I sighed. "I don't even know where I'm going."

"I do," he said, and shut the door. I slumped against it, only half listening to the instructions he gave me while we drove.

My mother had been crying, and the kiss I'd given her in parting wasn't nearly enough. I'd opened the door to Esther's room, and Gram, holding Aengus in her arms, had waved me absently away. Glory had told me not to worry. Coco had told me to remember to eat. Royal had said I needed some soap and a shower. Titus had told me to be good. Rafael, had given me no advice, just a shake of his dark head. I had been dismissed. I had volunteered, and to my dismay, they'd let me go. What the hell had I been thinking? Had I meant what I'd said, or was it just one of those gallant, rhetorical sorts of gestures that nobody was supposed to take me up on?

Whatever its original intention – and I didn't know what that was – I was on my way, and at the other end of this very dark tunnel, punctuated by the smell of my own sweat and the rumbling of my empty stomach, was the spectre of Racheal. I took a deep, shuddering breath and sank lower into the seat. And which came out of the door, I wondered, the lady, or the tiger?

"Vermont, is that pretty little state just west of New York," Max was saying, "The one that forms a rectangle when put together with New Hampshire. If you get off the plane and someone with a strange accent says, 'Welcome to Concord,' you're in the wrong half of the rectangle."

"Very funny," I muttered, but I caught his smile in the rearview mirror. He was trying to make me feel better, bless his heart. "And where, exactly am I to go if they say, 'Welcome to Montpelier?'"

He looked at me again, his brows drawing together into a quizzical frown. "You really don't know where she is? You haven't been corresponding, or communicating?"

"Shit no. Do you really think she'd open the letters?"

"She might," he said quietly. "Strange things occur in life."

"And speaking of that, why do you stay with my father?" I asked, looking out the window into the gathering night. "He's arrogant, he treats you like dirt, and Racheal treats everybody like dirt."

There was an ominous silence and I looked up to see Max's eyes riveted on me. "I might ask you the same thing," he challenged.

"I'm his son," I sighed. "Besides, I do love him, and …"

He cut me off. "Your father and I were young boys together, Master Aloysha. My father served his father, as my son will serve you someday, if he so chooses."

I noted with some amusement that it wasn't my choice whether I'd have him or not. "You didn't answer my question," I said. "At least I tried to answer yours."

"I don't really have any expectation that you'd understand," he said, and there was dismissal in his tone. "Ah...here we are at last." He sounded relieved, and I wondered if I was a bigger pain than my dad.

He opened the door for me, and as I was stepping out beside the corporate jet, he popped the trunk and handed me a flight bag. "There will be toiletries on board," he said, "and a change of clothing should make you feel better. Call me when you have a return time, and I'll be here to get you."

I nodded, took the bag and a few steps up the ramp, and then turned back. "Max," I said, "Thank you."

"Of course," he smiled. "You remember which way to go when you get off the plane?"

"Yes sir," I said, and he was gone with his usual, jocular salute.

I remember taking a hot shower. The space was cramped for a man my size, but it felt good, and Max was right about the change of clothes. When I went back out into the main cabin I realized I was not alone. There were other executives flying this night, and some of them didn't look too pleased to see me. It took me a couple minutes to decide that this jet had quite probably been headed directly for New York City before being hijacked to haul the boss's kid God-only-knew-where. I tried to smile and look apologetic, but I'd glanced at myself in the bathroom mirror, and I looked drunk, or stoned, or something that definitely wasn't businesslike, and it wasn't apologetic. I settled into a seat where I could get my racehorse legs out in front of me, and fell to contemplating the absolute blackness outside the window.

A very nice young lady offered me something to eat, and I accepted. It looked appetizing; far above the usual airplane fare in the days when the usual airplane fare wasn't all that bad. But I couldn't eat much of it. Like a great wave rushing suddenly onto the beach, my grief washed over me again, and I was powerless against it. Ebb and flow, ebb and flow, leaving me more exhausted with each hour that passed. I slept a little, I think, but not much...more of an uneasy dozing, punctuated by startled awakenings – that momentary panic at not knowing where I was, then knowing all too well.

I'd been wrong about the flight being nonstop. We stopped in Denver and added a couple people, got rid of one gentleman who smiled and nodded to me in passing. A woman sat down beside me and proceeded to yap her brains out all the way to Chicago. I heard her say to someone as she walked by, "That's Peter Aarons. That's the big boss's only son." I felt momentarily like a trophy, and unpleasant memories of Nina Goldman popped into my head. She was married these days. Had a little boy...or was it a girl? No, a boy. I wasn't married. I had a Steinway. It was my baby and I loved it. But I wasn't married. At that moment I knew I never would be.

We could just as easily have gone to New York City first, and then to Montpelier, but we did not. We followed Lake Erie and Lake Ontario and the Saint Lawrence Seaway all the way to Montpelier, Vermont. I pretended to be very interested in all that water below me, because I didn't want to meet the eyes of all those people who were probably going to miss meetings and connecting flights because of me. Of course it was Dad's fault. I'd never known him to put serious money in jeopardy, so these people probably weren't going anyplace important, anyway. I sat and felt bad about having that thought.

I tried to scurry off the plane as fast as I could without looking like I was scurrying. It is not dignified for a hundred and ninety pound, athletic man to scurry. For someone who made his money acting, I didn't do a very good job of it. But here I wasn't an actor. Here I was the big boss's kid. Probably should have been wearing a sweatshirt with a varsity letter on it.

In the first light of dawn, Montpelier was a beautiful little city, and I wished for time and circumstances I didn't have in order to explore it. There were other planes coming in, and couples getting off, eager to see the high color of autumn – linking arms and chatting – smiling at one another.

Doubting that Racheal would come without...persuasion, I opted against taking a taxi, and rented a car for the drive to her school. I stopped first for breakfast. Fresh strong coffee and a bagel. The waitress was pleasant, and there was an easy sense of familiarity about the place that reminded me of our coffee shop at home. Lots of local people on their way to work. It reminded me of how alone I was here, and that picking up my sister wouldn't change that. I forced a smile, and tried to look...normal, sane, comfortable... whatever it was that I wasn't at that moment.

The scenery was absolutely breathtaking. Esther would have loved this drive in the crisp autumn air, filled with the red-gold swirl of leaves whipped up by the passing of my tires and drifting from the trees above me like a kaleidoscopic whirlwind of flame without fire. But...I'd never show Esther anything again. I'd never give her another piano lesson. I'd never link my arm through hers and scuff through the autumn leaves that were her favorites. Never play chess with her, laugh with her, swim with her...hear her voice or hold her children or see her teaching a class or cuddling with Titus and Royal. I pulled to the side of the road for a bit, sobbed, wiped my eyes, and continued the long, winding climb into the hills.

I identified myself at the gates of King Solomon Academy for Young Women, and there was not a glimmer of recognition on the face of the attendant. My father hadn't called and told them I was coming. No one had called and told them I was coming? Not even Glory, or Max? Damn. I said we had a family emergency, and I had to pick up my sister.

The attendant disappeared into his cubbyhole beside the gate, there was a muffled conversation, and I was told to proceed to the visitor's parking area. Not until my first visit to a prison, many years later, would I see security like this. The building itself was formidable and hoary; not a lot of ivy, but redolent with austere, affluent old age.

I figured it was a Jewish school, but still, I expected Catholic nuns. Great big ones in black habits. They did not appear. No one appeared. I checked myself in the rearview mirror. Did I look more like a ruffian than a solicitous big brother? Absolutely.

I sighed, and got out of the car. It wasn't a small car, but the door opening was awkward in the way of American cars, and I felt like a jack-in-the-box. I was punchy and disoriented, and I wondered if even one of these people was going to believe my story. I just shook my head in kind of a numb dismay. Nobody had called? Shame on them. Racheal wasn't going to be ready to go, and I was going to pass out on the headmistress's rug. No, it was probably a very dark hardwood floor. Damn.

A girl in a school uniform greeted me at the massive front doors – movie set doors. "This way," she said in a hushed tone, as though I were being ushered into the Holy of Holies. Should I have bells on the hem of my garment and a rope around my leg just in case?

It was a place of vaults and groins and stained glass and side passages – none of it particularly welcoming or attractive – but exceptionally impressive, and after some twisting to the left and a sharp right turn, she rapped timidly on another huge door, and at the sound of a voice from within, turned the knob and gestured for me to go in. I noted that she did not join me. Instead she dropped her head and walked hurriedly away, arms swinging stiffly at her sides, ruffling her navy plaid skirt.

"Mister Aarons," said a female voice, and I realized I'd been looking after the departing girl rather than at the person I'd been ushered in to see.

I turned back and looked into a face that was soft, pleasant, and female, framed with dark hair going grey at the temples, piled loosely atop the head, and crowned with a pair of horn rimmed spectacles, which she brought down to study me. "Here," she said after a moment, and gestured toward an upholstered chair that had wooden arms and legs. "I'm Miss Eunice Trust."

The name made me want to snicker. It sounded about as real as the rest of the place looked, but I took the hand she held out to me, nodded over it, and accepted the chair. "I'm Peter Aloysha Aarons," I said. "I've come to pick up my sister, Racheal Sophia Aarons."

A pretend conversation in a pretend place. This wasn't happening. I was looking down on it from some elevated dream-state. I was going to wake up in my own bed and start the last couple days over again. I was asleep in my car. I wasn't here to get Racheal, I was here to get Esther. I was picking up Esther and Aengus after school and I'd fallen asleep in a car warmed by the autumn sun. I blinked. Miss Eunice Trust was still there. She looked pretty solid. "I...we've had a death in our family," I heard myself say, "Racheal's older sister passed away yesterday afternoon."

"I'm very sorry," said Miss Eunice Trust. "Would you like some coffee, or juice? You look very tired."

"That's a euphemism for it," I said with a humorless snort. "But, yes, coffee would be very nice. Thank you." I was not going to be allowed to grab my sister and run. I was going to have to exchange pleasantries with this woman. Was she making sure I was who I said I was? Had she already sent for Racheal?

The latter question was answered when my sister rapped on the door and let herself in. "What do..." she began, and her eyes fell on me. "What's wrong?" she gasped. "What are you doing here?" The emphasis was heavily on, *you*, and it wasn't a pleasant tone.

I could feel my big brotherly resolve shriveling up inside me. I didn't smile, and none of the things I'd planned to say were forthcoming. I didn't stand up and embrace her. I sat there like I was carved out of mud and let her glare at me – her lip curling slightly, telegraphing contempt.

"Your brother is here to take you home for a bit," said Miss Eunice Trust, and I jumped a little at the sound of her voice. "Go pack your things."

Racheal didn't move. I tried to smile at her, but the appropriate muscles wouldn't respond. There was an intensity in her malevolence that made me want to scream and run, but I was a grown man and some rule said I couldn't do that, so I looked away and studied the parquetry in the floor as I spoke. "Racheal...Baby, listen to me..."

"Fuck you," she hissed. "I'm going back to my room."

"Your sister has passed away," Miss Trust added in the same tone of voice she'd just used. "Your presence is required at home, now go pack a bag or you'll miss your plane."

Racheal didn't even flinch. "Finally!" she said. "I hope you at least brought my make-up." That was all. She studied my face for another moment, then spun on her heel and was gone.

I sighed and pulled my eyes up, expecting a criticism that didn't come. Miss Trust was smiling at me, but not with amusement. "Has she always been so...difficult?" she asked.

I nodded. "Within my memory, yes."

"I do think she loves you," Miss Trust said. "She speaks of you often, and the roles you've played, and all the other things you've done."

I just pursed my lips and nodded. I should have said something about loving her, too, but I was just too damned tired to lie. At that moment, sitting there, I felt nothing for her at all, except a kind of dread at having to be in her presence. I didn't want to take her home for Esther's funeral any more than I'd wanted to take her home for Esther's wedding. She was a complete, self-absorbed...psychopath. Just the word – thinking of Racheal in those terms – filled me with a sorrow that threatened to bow me clear to the floor with its weight.

"She is in counseling," Miss Trust said, and I looked up, startled. Had I spoken aloud?

"I didn't mean..." I stammered.

"Body language speaks volumes," she said. "Your father...isn't very forthcoming about Racheal's history with anger. Has she ever had psycho-therapy of any kind that you know of? I mean, before this?"

I shook my head. I could form sentences, couldn't I? I decided to give it a shot. "Dad always said she was...high strung, I think was his term. I don't think he ever considered her anger more than simple growing pains."

"Far more than simple growing pains," Miss Trust muttered. "She needs serious help if she's going to get well."

I must have winced, because she immediately apologized. "I know this isn't your problem," she said, and I almost laughed out loud. I almost said, *wanna see my scars*? I didn't. "It's just that I've had so little luck trying to speak to your father," she went on. "But he did send her here, so he must recognize that there's a problem. I know he's an extremely busy man, and that your mother is...." She trailed off, looking expectantly at me to fill in the blank.

What, I thought, *under my father's thumb? Is that what she thinks? Maybe she's right.* If my strong-willed grandmother knuckled under to him, certainly my retiring, sensitive mother could do no less. Nor could I. I forced myself to sit up and straighten my shoulders. "My mother allows my father to make most of the decisions regarding the children," I said, sounding ridiculously priggish in my own ears, "but I can speak to her if you think Racheal's condition warrants it. There are times...I think my sister...forgive me for saying so, but there are times I think she belongs in a mental hospital."

Eunice Trust studied me a moment, then nodded. "Aloysha," she said, fishing absently, self-consciously around on her desk for the words, "this is a mental hospital." She laughed and hastened to add, "or as close to one as a school for young ladies of the privileged class gets."

What else we talked about, I don't remember. How long I sat there, I don't remember. It was confirmed. Racheal was mentally ill. Bad enough that Esther – my beautiful Esther – was dead. Racheal was mentally ill. I do remember thinking that if there had been anything in my stomach, I'd have puked. I'm not sure now why it bothered me so much.   I mean, my opinion of Racheal was pretty much validated, which should have made me feel better, but at the time there was this harrowing sense of loss.

Racheal put in an appearance, dressed in street clothes and carrying a small backpack. She and Miss Trust exchanged a few words I wasn't privy to, and we took our leave. All the way to the car, all the way down the mountain, she said not one word to me. I made a couple of attempts at conversation – how beautiful the leaves were, how nice Ms. Trust seemed to be – but Racheal never even looked my way, never cocked an eyebrow, never even sneered. She glued her eyes onto her right shoulder and left them there. I gave up, shut up, and drove, realizing now that the leaves weren't beautiful, they were dead. It was years before I enjoyed autumn leaves again.

It was only when we reached the airport and someone recognized me from *Apache Pass*, that Racheal responded to me at all. At the cooings of the two women who sat with their husbands across from us, she linked her arm through mine and snuggled close against my shoulder, smiling up at me with a lover's eyes. I didn't shake her off like a spider on my sleeve, because I didn't want to make a scene. I did give her a condescending little pat and say, "Well, Sis, how will it feel to be home from school for a bit?" When my admirers asked her what grade she was in, and I felt her stiffen beside me, a cold little part of my heart rejoiced. Bitch. How dare she not be grieving when our sister was lying on a slab somewhere? How dare she be alive and touching me, when I would never touch Esther again. I could feel myself starting to quiver, not from exhaustion, but from hatred of my own sister. My baby sister...my only sister. I bit down hard on my lip and willed myself not to cry.

A Standardex jet skidded onto the tarmac, and Racheal said in a rather too loud voice, "There's Daddy's jet, Bud. Let's get the hell out of this backwater and back to civilization."

I let my eyes roll briefly back into my head for the benefit of the ladies in the chairs across the way, and picked up my jacket. I'd left my satchel on the plane, and I knew it would still be there, a fact which both gratified and embarrassed me. How did I rate...we rate? Who had been diverted from his business day to save two healthy young people the trouble of catching a commercial flight back to California? How hard would that have been?

In any case, it was moot. We stepped out into the first cold raindrops of an autumn that was nearly over, and the leaves which had been crisp and vibrant just that morning, turned to slop beneath our feet.

CHAPTER FOURTEEN

We'd been planning the arrangements for what seemed like eternity – no pun intended – and hunger had finally overcome my grief. I'd left my family in the living room of my father's house, and gone to the kitchen for coffee and cookies, and one of Glory's long, loving hugs. Coco was caring for my parents' personal needs, and my father's household had fallen temporarily into Glory's capable hands. I spent a moment wondering uneasily if I'd get her back, then dismissed the thought. This was not our home. Our home was up in the blue distance to the west, and I missed it. I knew Glory did, too.

Fortified with ginger snaps and coffee, I was returning to the living room, when the lash of Racheal's voice stopped me in my tracks. I peered from the hallway into the room, not knowing exactly what to expect – except, of course, that it would be unpleasant. I wondered who her victim was this time.

It was Titus. Tears welled up in his brown eyes, and his little head bowed under the weight of Racheal's slant-eyed stare. "I wanna help carry my Esser," he said again, nearly under his breath.

"Well, you can't, so just shut up!" Racheal hissed, "and what is that?"

"Coco sent it for you to take your pills with," Titus said, extending the glass in one trembling hand. It slipped just a little – not much – and a few drops of the liquid dribbled onto Racheal's slacks.

"You stupid little mud baby bastard!" she cried, and as she swung her palm, I cleared the fifteen feet from the doorway to the couch, and caught Titus up in my arms.

He buried his little face against my neck and sobbed, not because he'd been hit, but because he'd spilled the water he'd been entrusted with. "I didn't mean to spill it," he gulped. "Poor Coco have a mess now. I didn't mean to."

"It's not your fault," I grated, and turned to leave the room with him. "It's okay, Titus."

I planned to hush his crying, take him either to his mother or my grandmother, and then return...and kill my remaining sister, who sat on the white leather sofa, cracking her knuckles, chewing bubble gum and smiling ever so slightly to herself.

I'm not sure what brought my father – Racheal's angry outburst, my castigating bellow, or the sobs of little Titus Josiah Ruiz. In any case, there he was, filling the doorway I was charging into. I slammed on my brakes and stood, shaking, in front of him. I expected him to bellow, too, but he didn't. He put his hand over mine on Titus's heaving back, and bent himself around to look into the small face on my shoulder. "What's the matter?" he asked, very quietly, obviously talking to Titus and not me.

Titus took a deep, shuddering breath and squeaked, "I wanna help carry my Esser. She was my Esser." Not a thing about being slapped, or yelled at. What a guy.

"Come here to me," my father said, and Titus went. Dad carried him across the room, sat down in his big, black leather chair and placed Titus on his lap so he could look at him. "Tell me what you want," he said.

"I wanna help carry my Esser so she won't be alone." He contemplated for a moment what he'd just said, then added, "I was gonna carry her ring. I was gonna wear a little blue suit and carry her ring. Now I carry her instead, okay?"

This was where Dad would explain to him in terms he couldn't possible understand, that it just wouldn't work to have someone so tiny help carry a casket. There was just the slightest pause. "Of course you can help carry your Esther," Dad said. "Did you think we would leave you out, Little Man?" Amazing. I could hear Racheal's intake of breath from across the cavernous, unwelcoming expanse of the living room, and resisted the urge to look at her.

Titus smiled, then a realization struck him and he hung his head. "I spill the water," he said.

Dad's brows came together a little. "What water?"

"The water Coco send Racheal. I spill it..." he pointed, "There."

"What does that have to do with carrying Esther?" Dad asked.

"I...don't want to spill her," he whispered.

Dad's eyes welled with tears, and he chuckled and pulled Titus over against his chest for a moment. "We'll see that you have a very special job just your size," he said. "No spilling Esther."

"I can help carry my Esser?" Titus breathed, eyes wide and delighted. "I can carry her?"

"Yes...I think you can," Dad said. His voice was gentle and low, but he was frowning, and one finger stroked the reddened spot on Titus's left cheek. "You run along and tell your mother that you're going to need that little blue suit, all right?"

"Okay!" Titus grinned, then, on impulse he picked up one of my father's huge hands and laid it momentarily against his cheek. "I love you," he said. "I'll do good. I promise. I go get a rag for the water, okay?"

"You do that," Dad said, and Titus was gone toward the kitchen.

Dad's eyes followed him as he disappeared down the hall, and as they slowly turned on Racheal they changed shape, going from warm to cold. "What in the name of God is the matter with you?" he asked.

Racheal gave him a look that was no less cold, and I began looking for a way to subtly slink to the nearest exit. "What do you mean?" she asked in a nonchalant tone that belied the set of her jaw. "You must be so pleased, Daddy. Having that little pickaninny love you. Doesn't that just warm the cockles of your aristocratic old heart?"

My father chewed the inside of his cheek. "Did you slap that child?" he asked.

Racheal shrugged. "What a silly question."

"Indulge me," he said pleasantly. "Did you hit Titus?"

"I may have," she yawned, "what of it? They don't feel pain the way we do, you know."

That exit was looking better by the second. Bidden or not, I was getting gone.

The voice from over my shoulder startled me with its intensity. "You hit Titus?"

The face Racheal turned to our grandmother was no less impudent and disinterested than the one she'd been wearing for Dad. "Oh, for Godssake. The little shit spilled water on me. What was I supposed to do?" She studied her nails and blew a bubble.

"You two," my grandmother said quietly, "out."

"Now, Mother..." Dad began. There was a pause while he reassessed his position, his eyes crinkling up a tad at the corners as he withered in her gaze. "Come on, Bud," he said, and the last thing I caught in my peripheral vision was Racheal's bubble gum flying across the room.

We were killing each other. Esther had been our hinge pin of civility. Gram had turned into a tyrant, Racheal to an unspeakable bitch, Dad to a confused, muttering, middle-aged man. Mother was near collapse, and had lapsed into Russian – clinging to Coco and sobbing hoarsely as the last of her strength ebbed. Aengus had lapsed into some completely incomprehensible dialect, and sat in Esther's room, still holding her backpack – not eating, not sleeping – still uncomprehending.

Glory was here in this mausoleum, and my welcoming home was cold and dark. My piano sat idle, and I'd promised my beloved sis it wouldn't. The only place I had any right to want to be, was the last place I desired to be. I wanted to stick my head in the sand and wait for this blackness to pass. I wanted to run far, far away and not have to think of civil, comforting things to say to people. The coffee and cookies churned themselves into an acidic brown gruel in my stomach and reappeared unbidden about ten minutes after Dad went to his study and slammed the door.

I wandered out of the bathroom and landed with the grace of a beanbag in one of the chairs in the kitchen. "Boy," Glory said, "You know it annoys you daddy when you spend time in the servant part of the house."

"He's in his study," I muttered. I stared at the lustrous surface of the heavy oak table for a few seconds. Lots of wear, but so beautiful and... sturdy...serviceable. "I...want to go back up the hill. Things are under control here."

"You know that just ain't so," Glory said without turning around.

"You and me both needed right here, Aloysha."

I ignored her. "I want you to go up to the birdhouse and open it up. Get it warm and bright and fix something uncomplicated for supper. Something we can eat in the kitchen, so Gram can wear her robe and slippers, and I can wear my jeans. I need that."

"You can need it all you want," Glory said, and there was no hint of sympathy in her voice, "but of all the people who don't need to be pampered 'bout now, you at the top of the list. I got arrangements to make, and dinner to fix, and havin' you under foot is more than I can deal with. Now, shoo."

"Shoo?" I echoed. "Shoo? Really?"

"Scat. Scram. Skedaddle. Pick one."

I hunkered down a little tighter in the chair, fearing that if her words dislodged me, I'd blow without control or purpose, like a leaf, or a discarded paper bag, trying to make it across a busy intersection. I felt like a dog, cowering, frightened, comprehending only the fear and uncertainty. Nobody was who they should be. How could I appropriately react to that? Glory had been my..."...last hope," I shuddered. "I....You're my last hope."

When I pulled my eyes off the table, she was sitting beside me. I could feel the warmth emanating from her, though she wasn't touching me. "You need sleep," she said gently.

"I need sanity. I..." a thought struck me. "Have you seen Titus here in the last few minutes?"

"He come got a rag to clean up some spilled water," Glory said.

Yet another cold wave sloshed its way up the back of my neck. "Did he...say anything to you?" What if this was it? What if this was the last straw? What if these good people packed up their lives and went off to serve any of the ten dozen households who now coveted their services? What if Racheal had pushed away the last of the people I truly loved?

"Bud, you shakin' like a leaf," Glory said, and her hand closed over mine. "What's happened?"

I looked into her eyes, and saw concern, but not alarm. Not yet. "Did Titus tell you..." I couldn't do it. I couldn't look her in the eye and tell her. I dropped my gaze, squeezed my eyes shut for a moment, then forced them back to Glory's open, worried face. "Did he tell you that Racheal slapped him? Not hard. I mean, I pretty much grabbed him out of the way, but still... she slapped that little boy, Glory, and called him an awful name, and I'm so sorry I just want to...I don't know what I want to do. I'm appalled, and I'm ashamed."

Not one muscle in Glory's face so much as twitched. The longest five seconds of my life ticked away, one by one while she stared at me. Then she said, "Dinner in an hour," gave my hand a little pat, and went back to the sink.

I fled. I gave up the sanctuary of the kitchen chair, and let myself blow like that ragged, discarded paper bag through the house. I heard someone – a man – crying really hard, and I wondered who it was. I wondered where I was going, and if I'd find my mind when I got there.

"Bud?" Someone said. A young woman's voice, full of laughter.

I looked around. Where had the voice come from?

"Bud, come in here where you belong," the voice said, and when I looked through the double doors to my left and into the music room...I swear to God...Esther was sitting on the piano bench, smiling at me. She patted the bench beside her and said, "Come and play for me."

How I got into the room and onto the bench, I do not know, but when I glanced to my right, she was still there, and she was still smiling. "Ohhhh, you, are such a big silly," she said. "Here you are, trying to do everything to be such a big help, and what you could do that would help most of all, is play for me. Play for me, Bud. Play all the songs I love best. When you can put yourself in focus, you can put me in focus, and then everybody else will come into focus, too, don't you know that?"

She tipped her head over onto my shoulder, as was her habit, and I could smell the dark fragrance of her hair, and she was warm, and she was solid, and I played for her. I just closed my eyes, and played...and when I opened my eyes, I wasn't crying any longer, and it was Racheal who sat next to me with her head on my shoulder. The rest of my family was sitting quietly, along with Max and Coco...conversing...and Glory stood in the doorway. Our eyes met, and she gave me a slow, smiling nod.

CHAPTER FIFTEEN

I did not question those moments with Esther, nor did I doubt them, nor did I look back after that. I carried her on my shoulder, helped by Aengus and Kit, Tommy, Max, and Rafael. And Royal and Britt walked carefully in front of us in little blue tuxedos, carrying a picture of Esther, and Titus walked behind them, carrying her wedding ring on a satin pillow, because that's what Esther had dreamed of, and we wanted to make one last dream come true. We laid her to rest with the elders of our tribe, and pretended to get back to the business of the living.

Gram and I went back to our hilltop with Glory and the boys, my father buried himself in his work, and my mother sat...staring out the window of her sitting room...west, toward the cemetery and beyond to Russia, to dead loved ones, and places none of us could go with her. Racheal did not go back to Vermont. She went back to the private school where she'd been before, and Max dutifully drove her to counseling twice a week, though he confided that it was even worse than dragging me to kindergarten all those years ago. What was accomplished in counseling I never discovered, nor was it evident in my sister's behavior.

The holidays came upon us with few festivities planned. Even Racheal, who was big on parties and presents, didn't complain. She seemed to be more settled, being an only child, and went often after school and sat with my sad, silent mother. I'd meet her there, sometimes, and we'd nod to each other and smile with our mouths for our mother's benefit, but there was...nothing. Nothing to say, nothing to do, and we began to worry that we'd be losing our mother next. Lines of worry etched themselves into my father's handsome face, and he grew ever more silent and aloof.

We went to Tahiti for Thanksgiving, and something in the tropical air, I guess, activated the fever that had been dormant in me for so long. I tried to pass it off as a case of the flu, but within two days I was down and sick as a dog. It scared my mother half to death, and infuriated my father. "You have no right to add to her burden!" he raged, and I couldn't do a thing but lie there, sweating and shaking like a leaf, trying to explain to him that there wasn't much I could do about it.

It was Gram who came and sat with me, and told me not to worry, Dad knew I was really sick. Racheal, too, came by. She didn't stay long, but she'd drop in every couple of hours just to check, and I was grateful. Dad had banished Mother from the room, so I sent her cheerful, humorous messages with Racheal.

The caretaker's wife knew much of herbs and folk medicines, and she got me on my feet enough to get my ass on a plane back to Los Angeles. It was a long, miserable trip, and a lonely one. My family was not with me. My parents, my grandmother and Racheal stayed on for Hanukkah and New Year's, and none of them remembered my birthday. But others did.

When I got up on December twelfth, there was a special breakfast waiting for me, and a big hug from Glory. I got hugs and kisses from Royal and Titus, and presents. Titus had colored me a picture of five people fishing; Kit, Rafael, me and of course himself and Royal. "We goin' soon," he promised solemnly, and crossed his heart to seal it. Royal had gotten me a bar of soap. Picked it out himself, he said, and bought it with his own money. Kit and Tommy were over for cake and ice cream in the afternoon, but we didn't go out. I was still too shaky. David Swift called and wished me a happy birthday, and I vowed we'd get together soon for some more music lessons.

In February I was offered a part in a play on Broadway – no audition needed – and I didn't even consider it. I sat, day after day at my piano, shutting out the world as best I could by becoming Sergei Rachmaninoff. I told myself I was practicing, not stagnating, but somewhere inside, I knew I was lying.

Kit introduced me to the love of his life. "This one is forever," he assured me, and asked me to be his Best Man. I agreed, but I knew it wasn't forever, or even for very long. Nevertheless, he was my best friend, so I flew to Las Vegas and made the arrangements for their wedding, and they must have been okay. Kit seemed pleased, and so did his bride. I mouthed the words and grinned like a monkey and danced the dance, and flew home to my Steinway and Glory's dark looks.

I was working on a particularly difficult passage in one of Tcherepnine's melodies, when Glory set the receiver cradle against my neck and said, "I want you to talk to this man, Bud, and I want you to be nice, you hear me?"

I squinted at her long enough to reclaim reality, then nodded and said, "Hello?"

"Bud," said an all too familiar voice, "This is Albert Saucedo." He must have heard my sharp intake of breath, because he hastily added, "Please, just hear me out."

It was the last thing I wanted to do. I wanted to give the receiver a couple of sharp thwacks against something really hard, and then fling it across the room. But the only thing really hard was my Steinway, so I ground my teeth, spun around on the bench, and reached for a cigarette. "Fine," I snarled.

He ignored my gracelessness. "There's a job I want you to take," he said. "There's a cruise ship..."

"I don't believe this!" I exclaimed. "This is what you think of my playing? I..."

"You said you'd hear me out, remember? There is a cruise ship that leaves from Long Beach, headed for the British Isles, and Italy, and Greece. Everything on board is focused on classical music, and appreciation of the masters. Every morning there is renaissance music. Every afternoon there is chamber music, every evening there is a concert or an opera or a ballet." He paused. "Are you still there?"

"I am," I said. There was just the faintest glimmer of intrigue starting in me, though I wasn't ready to admit it. Why hadn't I heard about this cruise? Maybe that's what was intriguing me most. "Go on."

"The person who is in charge of the music and the musicians, called me and asked me to recommend a pianist, and I recommended you."

"Why?" I drawled. I was no longer interested.

"Because in the course of our conversation he mentioned that Professor Lewis Rupert was going along this trip to work with the musicians, that's why."

The name rang a bell. "Lewis Rupert, from Juilliard?" I asked.

"One and the same," he said, and I could hear the smile in his voice. "It could be your invitation to the head of the class, Bud."

I blew a column of smoke ceilingward and watched it, moving first in a straight line, then slowing, wavering, breaking into aimless curls and tendrils, and vanishing against the high, white plaster above me. "Why?" I asked again, and there was a challenge in my tone that I didn't really want there but couldn't quite keep out.

There was a pause. "I owe you," he said grudgingly. "I've carried the weight of what I did to you...for a long time. I can't change what happened, but I can help you get around it and get on with the musical part of your life."

"What makes you think I'm not happy being an actor?" I asked, and nodded my thanks as Glory set a fresh cup of coffee beside me. I was not deceived. She'd told me to be nice, and she was checking up on me. I accepted that.

"You cannot possibly play as well as you do, and be happy just being an actor," he said with some impatience. "You told me you wanted to be Sergei Rachmaninoff, and Lewis Rupert can get you a giant step closer to that goal. The ball's in your court. Swing at it, or let it bounce by." He gave me a name, a phone number and an address, and hung up quite abruptly. I wrote them down in an indifferent scrawl which Glory later helped me decipher. I found out long, long after the fact, that she'd been able to piece it together for me because she'd made Albert give it to her first.

I sat for a minute, staring at the receiver, and when I turned to hang it up, I realized Glory was standing there. "Is there something I can do for you?" I asked.

"Havin' you rejoin the human race would please me," she said, and smiled a little to ease the sting of her words. "So, you goin' to see this Mister..." she peered at my scrawl, "Mister...Olander?"

I grimaced. "I dunno. I just..." I shrugged and turned back to leaf through my sheet music.

"Listen to you," Glory said. "Listen to you self."

"I don't think I said anything."

"That's right," she muttered. "You so far gone you don't even finish you sentences no more. You gotta get outta this place 'for you can't no more."

"My mother is not well, Glory. You know that."

She put her hands on her hips, and I knew I was in for a lecture, even though she didn't have a spoon to shake under my nose. That's what she usually did – shook a spoon or a spatula at me. If she shook a knife...I knew I was way over the line. To this day, when Gloriosa Daisy Ruiz shakes a kitchen implement...we snap to, and we listen.

"I also know that you ain't doin' her no good bein' here. She don't perk up just because you come around, you know. Now, think about what would perk her up, like...gettin' into Juilliard to do your Doctorate." She eyed me, and pulled a card from the bottom of the deck. "I know it meant a lot to Miss Esther that you went and got that Doctorate. You promised her you'd do that, Bud. You ain't gettin' no closer, settin' on that bench like you growed there."

"Oh, all *right*!" I snapped, which is how I found myself in Long Beach in the office of Shea Olander.

"Well," he chuckled, gesturing toward a comfortably overstuffed chair, "I guess you were enough of a gentleman to at least let Berty get his mouth open. He was afraid you wouldn't even hear him out. Coffee? Tea? Soda?"

I shook my head and smiled at him – a round, jovial, balding man with walrus moustaches that made him look like a carnival barker. He was a little rumpled. His suit was not of the latest style nor the finest material, but his eyes sparkled with good humor and intelligence, and somehow, everything about him fit my mental image of a slightly madcap musical genius, which, as it turned out, he was.

"I'm fine," I said.

He let out a little cackle and ran his hands through what was left of his hair. It stood up and waved a little, following the static, and then lowered itself gingerly back onto his freckled scalp. "Well, if you're fine, this is a hell of an act," he said, parking on the edge of his desk and knocking a small container of paper clips onto the floor. He ignored them. "Berty says you're a man of sparkling wit and amazing talent, and I'm sure that's true. I took the liberty of watching a couple of your tapes, which is how I know," he added. "You seem...less than willing to be here, though, and that concerns me. This cruise is a lot of work, lots of rehearsal time, you know. Long hours. You'll be expected to do more than just play the piano. You'll be expected to play it with fire, and with passion, and with finesse. You may also be asked to play the guitar, the flute, or the drums, or sing or dance..." He must have seen the dismay on my face, and chuckled again. "Just kidding about that last part. Mostly I wanted to see if you could actually change expressions. Are you at least interested in seeing what kinds of things we'll be playing this trip?"

"I am," I said, and took a deep breath, trying to dislodge the spectre of Albert Saucedo from my shoulder. I knew I should do more than grunt two words at a time, for my own image if nothing else, and I forced myself to look perky. It was a herculean effort. One that scared me. "Of course I am. There must be a huge repertoire required for a voyage this long," I said, wondering if I even had the vocabulary to have this conversation. Why had I come, anyway? I couldn't do this.

"Come," he said, springing off the desk. "Never mind the paper clips, we can get those later. Come, come!" He bounced ahead of me out the back door of his office, down a long, blue carpeted hall with doors on either side, and into a largish rehearsal room with risers at one end, a grand piano to one side, and a warren of cubbyholes, cupboards and shelves to the other. He opened one of the cupboards, and began dragging out folders and loose sheets of paper. "We're playing lots of Rachmaninoff this trip, which is how your name happened to come up. You being an authority and all...." His voice resolved to a mumble as he focused totally on his shufflings.

"I'm hardly an authority," I said uncomfortably. I knew it. He was going to expect more of me than I was capable of giving.

"That's not true," he said without looking up, and I wondered if he read minds. "You are an expert." He pulled a sheet of music from amongst the others and held it out to me in a backward motion. "Here. Play this, why don't you. It'll help me focus on what I'm doing."

I took the music and held it a minute, studying Olander's back before I looked at the music he'd handed me. It was Rachmaninoff's *Piano Concerto Number Two in C minor, Opus 18.*

"Rachmaninoff wrote that when he was a puling infant of twenty-four," Olander mumbled, head in a cupboard, feet planted wide apart in a comic stance. He glanced under one arm at me and continued, "He'd just recovered from a bout of depression and writer's block, and this is what he wrote – one of the most beloved of all piano concertos." He turned full around and folded his arms to study me. "Can you do this, or can't you?"

I looked at him, then at the music in my hand and took a deep breath. "I can do this," I said, and turned to the piano. I smiled at Esther, and she grinned mischievously back as she patted the bench beside her. "I can do this."

ABOUT THE AUTHOR

Showandah S. Terrill is an award winning speaker and storyteller, as well as a lifelong writer and equestrian. Steeped in Native American culture, she was raised as the only child of an itinerant cowhand on sprawling ranches in Southern California during the turbulent 1960's.

She is currently writing two extended series: the epic science-fiction Dragonhorse Chronicles and the fictional autobiographical Peter Aarons' novels.

This is her first published novel.